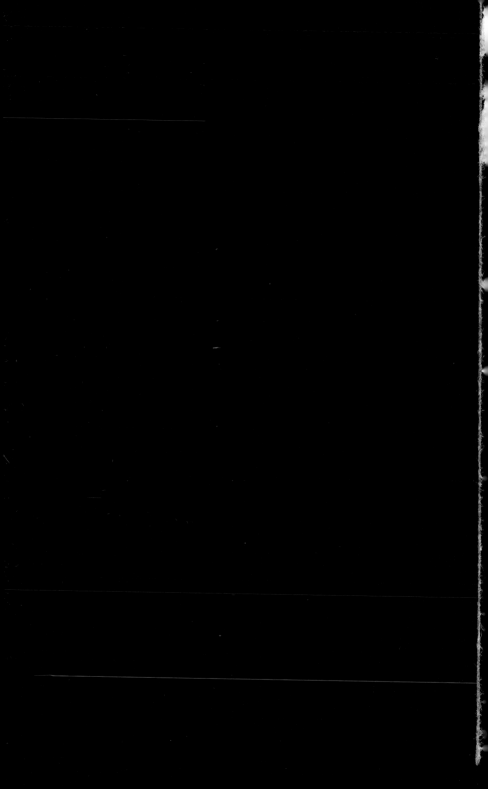

BEASTLY BEAUTY

BEASTLY BEAUTY

JENNIFER DONNELLY

Scholastic Press / New York

Library of Congress Cataloging-in-Publication Data available

ISBN 978-1-338-80944-2

10 9 8 7 6 5 4 3 2 1   24 25 26 27 28

Printed in Italy 183
First edition, May 2024

Book design by Maeve Norton

This one's for you, dear reader.

This one's for you dear reader.

PROLOGUE

Once upon a time and ever since, a key turned in a rusted lock, and a woman stepped into a small and dismal cell.

Her gown, the color of ashes, hung off her shoulders like a shroud. Her hair, styled high on her head, was as black as ebony. Her dark eyes glittered; their gaze pulled at whomever it fell upon, sucking them in like a whirlpool.

Across the room, a high window, shaped like a half-moon, was filled with midnight, yet the room was not without light. A wan glow suffused it, like that of a single candle.

It came from a child.

She was gazing up at the window, her hands clasped behind her back. "Lady Espidra, always a pleasure," she said at length, turning to face the woman.

Her pink dress, once pretty, was dirty and torn. Her hair, so blond it was almost white, was wild. Her face was open and frank. Anyone glimpsing it would guess she was nine or ten years of age, except for her eyes, which were as ancient as the stars.

Lady Espidra set her lantern down on a table. She opened the small wooden box she was carrying. "Shall we play? To pass a bit of time?" she asked, taking out a deck of cards. "How long has it been since we last chatted, you and I? A year? Two?"

"Twenty-five."

Lady Espidra laughed. It was an ugly, jangling sound, like shattered glass raining down. "Ah, it's true what mortals say—the days are long and the years are short."

She placed the deck faceup on the table, then fanned it expertly. The cards were yellowed at their edges but beautifully illustrated. The kings, queens, and jacks were framed by a thin line of black. Rich pigments colored their robes. Their golden crowns sparkled; their silver swords gleamed.

The queen of hearts blinked and stretched. Then she glimpsed the queen of spades, who was next to her, and waved excitedly. The queen of spades gasped, then laughed. She reached a hand to the frame surrounding her and pushed at it. Gently at first. Then harder. Until she was beating her fists against it.

The king of diamonds placed a hand over his heart and gazed with anguished longing at his queen. The queen of clubs, stuck between two numbered cards, stared listlessly ahead of herself.

Espidra seemed not to notice their distress. She briskly gathered the cards, shuffled them, and dealt two hands.

But the child noticed.

"Poor things," she said, picking up her cards. "Imprisoned in their boxes, just like the mortals who drew them."

"A box is the best place for mortals," Espidra retorted. "It keeps them out of trouble."

Espidra looked at her cards and smiled; she'd dealt herself an excellent hand. As she arranged them in order of rank, the queen of clubs blew a fervent kiss to the handsome jack of hearts. The king of clubs saw her do it. His smile crumpled. He gripped his sword in both hands and, with an anguished cry, plunged it into his heart. The queen turned at the sound, then screamed when she saw what he'd done. Blood flowed from the king's wound. It pattered onto the bottom of the frame, spilled out of a crack in the corner, and dripped onto Espidra's withered fingers. She slapped the cards down on the table, scowling, and wiped the blood off on her skirt.

"Such a lovely way you have about you," the child said. "Why have you come? Surely it wasn't to play cards."

"Of course it was," Espidra said. "I like a challenge when I play, and no one bluffs like you do."

"Liar."

Espidra shot the girl a baleful look. "All right, then. I wish to offer you a deal."

"Ah, now we have the truth. What kind of a deal?" the child asked.

"Leave this place. Do not come back."

"What do you offer me in return?"

"Your life."

A slow smile spread across the child's face. "Why, Lady Espidra, you are afraid."

Espidra flapped a hand at her. "*Me*, afraid? Of *you*? Don't be absurd."

"You would not offer me this deal otherwise."

"Yes, I would. Because I wish to be rid of you, and you would be wise to accept my offer. The girl is beaten. She has given up. She merely bides her time now, waiting for the end."

Pain sliced across the child's features at the mention of the girl. Espidra saw it. She leaned forward. "You cannot win. The clock winds down. The story is over."

The child lifted her chin. "Almost, but not quite."

Her words were like a torch to straw. Espidra smacked the cards off the table. She shot up out of her chair; the legs screeched over the stone floor.

"You are nothing but a trickster," she hissed, jabbing a bony finger at the child. "You come and go, as careless as the wind, leaving a trail of broken mortals in your wake. But I stay. I am here for them after you abandon them, with my arms wide open, my embrace as deep—"

"As a freshly dug grave."

Lady Espidra looked as if she would like to wrap her hands around the child's thin neck and snap it. "You will be sorry you did not take my offer," she said.

"This cell will not hold me forever."

"Big words from a small girl. I hope you enjoy the darkness."

The door clanged shut. The key turned in the lock.

Espidra's footsteps receded, and silence descended once more, suffocating and cruel.

The child sat, motionless and alone, her head bent, her fists clenched.

Trying to remember the light.

"I'm freezing my balls off," grumbled Rodrigo. "Hungry as hell, too. What about you, boy?"

Beau didn't reply. He couldn't; his teeth were chattering too hard. Icy rain needled his face. It plastered his hair to his skull and dripped from his earlobes.

The storm had swept down upon the thieves as they'd ridden out of the merchant's lands. It howled ferociously now, scouring the rocky hills around them, tangling itself in the branches of the bare black trees.

It seemed to Beau as if the thrashing limbs were warning them, waving them back. But back to what? They were lost. Riding with their heads bent against the driving rain, they'd missed the trail to the mountains. To the border. To safety.

Raphael was certain that if they just kept heading south, they'd find their way. *A few more miles . . . a little bit farther . . .* he kept saying. They'd passed ruined cottages, a deserted village. They'd ridden through dense woods and crossed a river, but still could not find the path.

Beau hunched down in his wet coat now, seeking comfort and warmth, but found neither.

"What's the matter, Romeo? Missing Her Ladyship's pretty smile?" Rodrigo asked. He was riding on Beau's left.

"Look at him, melting in the rain like he was made of sugar!" taunted Miguel from Beau's right. He leaned in close and grinned, revealing a mouthful of rotten teeth. "That pretty face is your fortune, but what happens if I carve it up, eh?" He pulled out his dagger.

"What happens is that Raphael carves *you* up, you fool, since my face is also his fortune," Beau replied.

"Poodle," Miguel grumbled, sheathing his blade. "All you do is beg rich women for treats and kisses while we do the hard work."

"Begging for treats and kisses *is* hard work," Beau said.

He pictured his mistress now. *Former* mistress. She was older than he was, but not by much. Married to a man who only loved his money. She hadn't given Beau this information; he was a thief—he'd stolen it. He'd taken the sorrow in her smile, the hunger in her eyes, the ache in her voice, and he'd used them. Just as she'd used him.

"Oh, you beautiful thing," she'd whispered to him last night, tracing the line of his jaw with her finger.

He'd been standing in her bedchamber, looking at the books on her night table. His eyes had lit up when he'd seen *Candide*.

"I've read everything Voltaire's written," he said, turning to her excitedly, thinking he'd found a kindred spirit, someone—the only one—in his life he could talk to about a book. "Could I borrow this? Just for a day or two? I'm a fast reader."

But his mistress had only laughed at him. "You're just a *servant*, boy. I don't pay you to read. Or talk," she'd said, pulling the book from his hands. Then she'd tugged at the ribbon that bound his dark hair and caught her breath as it tumbled around his shoulders. A moment later, her lips were on his, and the things he'd wanted to say, the thoughts he'd wanted to share about books and ideas, turned to ashes on his tongue.

Beau pictured her face as she'd learned that her servant was gone, and her fine emerald ring with him, and remorse pinched him like a pair of borrowed boots. He fought it, telling himself that her husband was wealthy; he'd buy her another ring. He almost believed it.

The ring was nestled safely inside a slit he'd made behind a button on his jacket—a place where its contours couldn't be felt. Raphael often patted them down after a job, all of them, and Beau had seen him beat a man bloody for keeping back a single coin. The ring would buy him the thing he wanted most: a way out. For himself, for Matteo.

6

The boy had been unwell the last time Beau had seen him, listless and pale, with a rackety cough. *A fever. It will pass*, Sister Maria-Theresa had said. Beau had written to her two weeks ago, to ask if his little brother was better, and just that afternoon he'd received a reply, but he'd tucked the letter inside his jacket unopened. There had been no time to read it. Not with the robbery planned for that very night.

"It's not fair. *I* could be the inside man. Why not?" said Miguel, breaking into Beau's thoughts, jutting his chin at him. "What does *he* have that I don't have?"

"Teeth," said Rodrigo.

"Hair," said Antonio.

"A bar of soap," said Beau.

Miguel threw him a venomous look. "I'll get you, boy. When you least expect it. Then we'll see who's laughing. Then we'll—"

"Shut up. *Now*."

Raphael's words fell across the men like the crack of a whip. He was several strides ahead of them, but Beau could still see him through the lashing rain—with his felted black hat, water dripping from its brim, and his sodden gray ponytail trailing down his back. His shoulders were tensed; his head was cocked.

An instant later, Beau heard it—the baying of hounds. Amar, his horse, danced nervously under him. The pack likely numbered a dozen or so, but the hills amplified their cries, making it sound as if there were a thousand.

"The sheriff's men," Rodrigo said tersely.

Raphael gave a grim nod and galloped off. Beau and the others followed. The wet ground made for treacherous footing and they had to work to keep their seats. The rain had let up, but a heavy mist was moving through the trees now. One minute, Beau could see the thief lord up ahead of him; the next minute he vanished.

7

Faster and faster the men rode, but the hounds still pursued them, their cries savage and bloodthirsty. Beau's heart slammed against his ribs. *Not now,* he thought desperately. *Not here.* This was supposed to be his last job. Just a few more miles, and he'd be beyond the reach of sheriffs and jails and gallows. Beyond Raphael's reach. Him and Matti both.

The baying grew louder. Amar's nostrils flared. He surged ahead, trying to catch up to Raphael's horse. Every second, Beau expected him to stumble over a fallen limb or break his leg in a ditch. He could see lather on the animal's neck; he could hear him panting. They would have to surrender. The horses couldn't keep going.

And then came a shriek that severed the night like a saber.

"Hold up!" Raphael shouted. "Nobody move!" It was his horse that had made the awful sound. He was rearing, his hooves slashing at the air. Beau, right behind him, only had a split second to halt Amar.

"Whoa! *Whoa,* boy!" he shouted, yanking on the reins. The bit caught; the horse stopped short, snapping Beau forward like a rag doll. He jammed his weight into his stirrups to keep from falling.

The others halted behind him, jostling, swearing, their hands on their weapons. Eyes searched for movement, but the mist blinded them. Ears strained for sounds, but the baying had stopped. All they could hear was the panting of their played out animals. They waited, hearts thumping, blood surging, bodies tensed for an attack, but none came.

Instead, the mist receded like a treacherous sea falling back from jagged rocks, and the men saw a cliff, high and sheer, sweeping down into nothingness. Raphael, perched at the very edge of it, had come within inches of an ugly death. Yet fear, if he'd felt any, had not lingered on his hard, scarred face. Instead, his features were fixed in a look of astonishment—a look that only deepened as the ebbing mist revealed what lay on the far side of the abyss.

Beau squeezed his eyes shut, then opened them again, but they were not playing tricks. He clearly saw the things around him—the mist, the men, their stamping horses. These things had all been there a moment ago.

But the castle had not.

- TWO -

It was a gray Gothic fever dream.

Soaring spires pierced the night sky. Towers brooded darkly. Pointed arches framed shadowed windows. A high granite wall, blackened by time and weather, encircled the castle. Along its crenellated edge, an army of gargoyles gibbered and leered.

The mist had disappeared. Moonlight shone down now, illuminating a long wooden bridge that spanned a deep moat and led to the castle's gatehouse. Beau could see that the massive iron portcullis was raised. Spikes ran along its bottom edge.

"Who leaves a gatehouse open at this hour?" he asked quietly. "Where are the guards?"

Raphael nudged his horse forward. His men followed. Their shrewd thieves' eyes darted up walls, over archways, to the tops of turrets. They noticed things they'd missed in the first flush of surprise—a crumbling parapet, empty watchtowers, a tattered flag.

"There are no guards. The place is deserted," said Antonio.

Beau's gaze settled on the bridge. As it did, a shudder ran through him that had nothing to do with the cold. The bridge seemed to him like a long ogre's tongue and the shadowed arch of the gatehouse like the ogre's mouth, and he felt, deep down in his bones, that if he entered it, it would eat him alive.

The others felt it, too. "Something's not right. We should ride on," said Rodrigo.

Raphael spat on the ground. "You sound like an old woman. The hounds have lost our scent. You want to help them find it again?" He touched his heels to his horse's sides and started over the bridge. One by one, his men fell in line behind him.

The old wooden boards creaked and groaned under the weight of the horses. One, soft with rot, crumbled under Amar's hind hoof and made him stumble. The falling chunks of wood hit the moat in a staccato of splashes.

Wary of the bridge's poor condition, the men kept their horses at a walk. Beau entered the gatehouse with the first riders, and though it was dark inside, he could make out the shape of a winch, chains, coils of rope, weights.

Raphael saw them, too. "Tell the last ones to lower the portcullis," he said to Rodrigo.

Beau felt for his dagger. They were taking a risk. There was no way the men hunting them could follow them if the portcullis was down, but what if the castle wasn't deserted? What if they needed to get out fast?

An instant later, Raphael rode out of the gatehouse and entered a wide, cobbled courtyard. Beau was close behind him, eyes scanning for threats. He expected an ambush. He expected men to be waiting for them, men with pistols and swords.

He didn't expect to see two iron torches blazing brightly on either side of the castle's towering doors or to see those doors swing open now, as if unlocked by an invisible hand. He didn't expect to see candlelight dancing in mullioned windows or to hear music playing. And the scents wafting through the air—of roasted meat, fresh bread, nutmeg, and cinnamon—made his empty stomach twist so hard, it brought tears to his eyes.

"It's not real. It *can't* be," he whispered.

Raphael paused for a moment, allowing the men who'd lowered the portcullis to catch up. And then, as if in a trance, he slid out of his saddle, looped his reins over his horse's neck, and moved toward the doors. The rest of the thieves did the same. One by one, they stepped out of the damp night and into the welcoming warmth, the dancing light.

Beau was among them, and as he crossed the castle's threshold and peered inside, his eyes widened and his heart filled with something strange, something long forgotten, a feeling he could no longer name—*wonder*.

- THREE -

Beau turned in a slow circle, arms out at his sides as if to steady himself. He'd forgotten his fears. He'd forgotten he was cold and wet. He'd forgotten his own name.

The room he'd just entered, the castle's great hall, was so magnificent it made him dizzy.

Its vaulted ceiling rose three stories high. Crystal chandeliers, each as tall as a man, blazed with candles. A gilt mirror hung above the fireplace. Adorning three of the four walls were tapestries, each as big as a ship's sail, and dozens of portraits. The fourth wall, coffered in mahogany, was bare. In one corner, a large silver music box played.

But the most wondrous thing the room contained was a long ebony table, standing in its center. Set with fine porcelain, snow-white linen, and gleaming silver, it looked like something out of a fairy tale. The thieves barely noticed the table's beautiful settings, though; their eyes were on the mountain of food that covered it.

It was a feast fit for royalty. An enormous roast beef, carved into slabs, lay on a platter. Game birds, their skins so crisp they looked as if they would shatter at a touch, were nestled on a serving tray. Golden-crusted pies of venison and pheasant stood tall. Grilled fish glistened under melting herb butters. Wine sparkled in crystal decanters.

Miguel licked his lips. "Just *look* at it all!" he said. His goatish eyes darted warily around the room. He cupped his hands around his mouth. "Hello! Is anybody here?" he shouted.

"Idiot. Of course somebody's here," Antonio said. "You think that platter of beef walked itself to the table?"

"Who's this for?" asked Beau.

"Us," Raphael said.

Antonio glanced at the thief lord. "Who says?"

Raphael patted the pistol at his hip. "I do."

That was all the men needed to hear. They fell upon the feast like wolves upon a lamb. Some didn't even wait to sit down before tearing legs off ducks or spearing slices of beef with their daggers. Ravenous after their long, harrowing ride, they ate ferociously.

Beau, used to the greasy stews and charred chops Rodrigo cooked for them, relished every bite—the gamy richness of pheasant, the bright tang of the red-currant sauce he spooned over it, the fat-crisped crackle of roasted potatoes. He finished one plateful, then helped himself to another, washing it all down with glass after glass of fine Bordeaux that tasted of earth and rain, time and secrets.

After he'd polished off three helpings, Beau leaned back in his chair and closed his weary eyes. The food, the wine, the roaring fire—they'd warmed him inside and out. For the first time that day, he took a deep breath.

It wasn't his fault everything had gone so wrong. He'd done his part and done it well. Getting himself hired as a servant at a wealthy merchant's home. Catching his mistress's eye. Smiling as he set her dinner plate down. Brushing her hand as he picked it up again.

It was just this past morning, when his mistress had brushed *his* hand and lifted it to her lips, that he'd sent word to Raphael. *Tonight.*

He'd left the kitchen door unlocked, and some hours later—when the servants were asleep, and he and his mistress were not—the thieves entered the house. The strongbox quickly surrendered to Raphael's skilled hands, but before the thieves could empty it, the lady's husband had come home. No one expected him. He'd been away for months on business, but suddenly there he was—standing in the kitchen with his men, bellowing for food and drink.

The servants tumbled out of their beds and the thieves were discovered. Swords were drawn, pistols loaded. The merchant scrambled upstairs to his wife's chambers. Beau scrambled for the window. Horses were waiting for them, hidden in the woods. The merchant's men were fast, but the thieves were faster. They leapt into their saddles and rode off, moving like smoke through the trees.

They were lucky to have made it out of the merchant's manor alive and were grateful for that luck, but gratitude wouldn't get them out of France where they were wanted men. It wouldn't get them across the rugged borderlands to Spain, then to the coast and Barcelona. From there, Raphael hoped to find a ship bound for Istanbul, Tangier, or Mombasa—some teeming port town where nobody cared who they were or what they'd done.

That was the plan, but sea passage costs money and they'd only been able to grab a small bag of silver coins from the merchant's strongbox before they were discovered.

Now Rodrigo cursed the time they'd wasted. "Before we get to Barcelona, we have to cross over the mountains and it's nearly winter," he said. "We'll need warm coats. Blankets. Food for ourselves and our horses. How are we going to pay for it all? These things aren't bought with words and wishes."

"Neither are pretty women," said a drunken Miguel. "And Barcelona's full of them!"

Beau opened his eyes. He played along. His plans involved his little brother, not a ship, but no one else could find that out. "Well, that's one expense we won't have to worry about," he said, lobbing a piece of bread at Miguel. "Even if we robbed fifty merchants, we wouldn't have enough gold to get a woman to smile at *you*."

"Bastard!" Miguel shouted. He threw the bread back but missed. Beau laughed; he gave Miguel the finger. Miguel jumped to his feet and reached for his dagger, but Antonio, who was sitting next to him, pulled him back down. "Enough," he warned.

Raphael, gnawing a bone, glanced between Beau and Miguel but said nothing. He just sat in his chair at the head of the table, his hooded eyes unknowable. His silence made Beau wary. Like a wolf, Raphael always went quiet just before a kill.

The men continued to gorge themselves until finally they could hold no more. Some loosened their belts; others leaned back in their chairs and belched. Beau unbuttoned his jacket. Miguel stood up unsteadily and pissed in a corner. The music box had wound down, and a ticking, muffled and low, as if coming from a clock in another room, could now be heard. The prickling sense of uneasiness Beau had felt, banished for a bit by the feast, returned. He pushed his plate away and sat up. His eyes flickered to the room's shadowed doorways. *How did all this food get here? Who cooked it? Where are they?* he wondered.

"There aren't many of them," Raphael said, reading his mind. "An old man, maybe. Or a widow. A handful of servants." He tossed his gnawed bone onto his plate and wiped his greasy hands on the tablecloth. "They were about to have dinner but heard us coming and hid. They won't trouble us." A cold smile curved his lips. "But we'll trouble them. I want

14

everything we can carry. Take the silver. Rip the tapestries down. Then spread out and find the strongbox."

Miguel had staggered back to the table to pour himself more wine. At Raphael's words, he drained his glass and threw it on the floor. "We'll be the kings of Barcelona!" he crowed as it shattered.

The thieves burst into cheers. They guzzled more wine. Ate dainty cakes and sucked the icing off their fingers. And then they got busy. Miguel gathered knives and forks in his hands like a sheaf of wheat. Antonio stuffed a silver ladle down his shirt. Beau slipped a pair of jeweled napkin rings into his pocket.

Raphael plucked a red rose from a vase and threaded the stem through a buttonhole in his jacket. Then he stood and struck a pose, his hand inside his jacket, an arrogant tilt to his chin, just like the grand aristocrats in the portraits. His men laughed, smacking one another with the backs of their hands. Boisterous and tipsy, they boasted loudly of the fancy pistols and fine britches, the soft boots and gold earrings they'd buy in Barcelona.

Beau was about to grab a silver pepper pot when he felt it.

It started as a soft shudder, as if the castle itself was stretching and waking, then deepened to a low rumble. He could sense the vibrations under his feet; they moved up into his body, rattling his bones. Prisms dangling from chandeliers swayed and collided, their crystalline clinking like a dark fairy's laughter.

He glanced at the others; they were frozen in place. Only their eyes moved, warily trying to pinpoint the source of the noise. A metallic whirring started. It was followed by a grinding clunk. Invisible wheels turned. Gears engaged. And then a crack, as sharp as a gunshot, sent the thieves ducking for cover. But it wasn't a firearm that had made the noise.

"Look!" Rodrigo said, pointing at the far wall, one bare of tapestries or paintings.

A thin crevice, running from floor to ceiling, split the coffering down its center. As the men watched, transfixed, the two sides of the wall began to slide apart and a honeyed gleam streamed from the space between them. Wider and wider the opening grew, and what it revealed snatched Beau's breath away. He set his dagger down and took a few steps forward, spellbound by the sheer impossibility of the object before him.

It was a golden clock that spanned the entire width of the wall and rose in three columned tiers to the ceiling. The topmost tier housed a large silver bell. The middle held the clock's shimmering dial, fashioned from mother-of-pearl. Its hands were cast from silver; inlaid gemstones formed its numerals. In the recesses of the bottom tier, a silver pendulum swung back and forth. Behind it, brass weights dangled from heavy chains.

"*Damn*," Beau breathed, his eyes as round as pie plates.

The clock had to be twenty feet high by thirty wide. At either end of it stood a set of tall double doors. A track ran between them, curving in a semicircle. Beau moved closer. He couldn't tear his gaze from it. All that silver, those gemstones, that *gold*.

The clock had been faced with thin sheets of the precious metal, ingeniously seamed with tiny nails, and there was enough of it to buy every man here his own towering castle. The thieves stood in silence, their awestruck faces warmed by the clock's golden glow. Raphael was the first one to break it.

"How does it feel, boys," he asked, "to be as rich as God?"

Beau walked closer to the clock. He tilted his head back, wondering how quickly he could scale those gilded columns.

It was then that he saw him. Standing on the platform of the topmost tier.

A man, tall and pale, thin as a whisper, gazing down.

– FOUR –

He wore a suit the color of midnight.

A gray cravat, fastened with a jet stickpin, closed the neck of his shirt. His long white hair was gathered with a length of black ribbon. A pair of spectacles was perched at the end of his nose. Behind them, his eyes glittered like two dark stars.

Looking into them, Beau had the strange, unsettling feeling that he'd met the man before, but he couldn't remember where or when.

Miguel, too drunk to be afraid, swaggered up to the clock and pointed at the man. "Hey! Mister, hey!" He snapped his fingers. "What are you doing up there, eh?"

The man did not reply; instead, he raised his arm in a stiff, jerky movement, then swiveled his torso toward the bell. Beau saw that he held a silver hammer in his hand, and that his pockets contained pliers, a pair of tin snips, a screwdriver.

"*Ha!* He's a dummy!" Miguel exclaimed.

Rodrigo snorted. "Takes one to know one."

Beau had stolen enough valuable objects to know that an artisan would often sign his work in clever ways—adding his initials to a filigree on a necklace, or carving his own face on a figure of a saint—but the man who'd made this clock had taken the conceit further: He'd signed his work by adding a life-sized figure of himself to it. Beau felt drawn toward the mysterious clockmaker. He wanted to touch his pale porcelain cheek, to take hold of his arm and feel cold metal under the cloth. He wanted, *needed*, to reassure himself that the man wasn't real.

Just then, the clock's weights ratcheted up their chains, startling Miguel, who staggered backward, tripped, and fell on his backside. The others laughed at him, but Beau didn't join in. *Who pulled the weights?* he wondered.

17

The minute hand clicked into place next to the hour hand at twelve and the clockmaker struck the bell with his hammer. The chimes sounded like a warning to Beau, and as the last one faded, music began to play—a jangling, discordant fairground tune that filled every corner of the room. The arched track in front of the clock began to move. The doors on the clock's left side swung open with a creak and a grinning jester in patched nightclothes and a jingling cap emerged from the clock, capering wildly. The bloom of color in his cheeks, the glimmer in his glass eyes, made him seem so alive. But then Beau saw that he, too, was just a clockwork figure repeating the same movements.

Behind the jester came a groom and a milkmaid, leaning in to share a kiss, then pulling apart. There was a scullery maid reaching for a sweet, and a kitchen boy cradling a big, tawny ham. A stiff-backed guard walked to and fro, rifle over his shoulder; another dozed in an alcove. Cats prowled. Dogs snored. A rat nibbled at a wheel of cheese. A lady-in-waiting mended a gown, her needle going in and out, in and out. A regally beautiful woman read by candlelight, her hands covered in rings, her silk dressing gown flowing around her legs. A handsome man dressed in a fur-lined robe played chess with his valet, moving his king into check and out again. As the figures proceeded along the track, the doors on the clock's right side opened. The jester led the court through them, and when the last one—a little page boy holding a chamber pot—had disappeared into the darkness, the music stopped and the doors swung shut with a rush of air so soft and sad, it sounded like a sigh.

Beau stood staring at the closed doors, surprised to feel an ache in his heart, sudden and deep. The other thieves, ardent with greed, hooted and whistled.

"Did you see that fur robe? It's mine, boys!"

"Keep it! I'm taking m'lady's rings!"

"We'll take it all. Break down the doors!" Raphael commanded.

Two of the men grabbed a heavy chair and dragged it toward one pair of doors, ready to batter them open.

They were all making so much noise, they didn't hear the throaty growling. Not at first.

It seeped into the room like blood through water, moving sinuously beneath the raucous laughter, but then it grew deeper, winding itself around the thieves like a riptide. By the time they realized they were in danger, it was too late. Their laughter fell away. Their shouts died.

"What *is* that?" Ramon asked, his voice barely a whisper.

"It's coming from there," Beau said tersely, nodding at the entry hall.

The thieves had walked through it on their way to the great hall. Only moments ago, the room had been ablaze with light; now it was shrouded in darkness.

"Arm yourselves," Raphael commanded.

The men scrambled for their weapons. There was a great sucking *whoosh* and the fire went out. One by one, the candle flames died. Only the moon's pale rays, slanting in through high windows, illuminated the great hall now.

"What the devil is going on?" Rodrigo shouted.

The growling rose. Whatever was making the sound was coming closer. Terror tightened Beau's grip on his dagger. Visions appeared in his head of ripping teeth and slashing claws, of deep, spurting wounds.

Cold air rushed in, carrying the smell of evergreens with it, and then the darkness in the doorway parted like a pair of velvet curtains.

"Mother of God," Raphael whispered.

He managed to fire one shot before the creature was on him.

- FIVE -

After the crack of gunshot came the crack of bone.

A scream of agony rose, mingling with an animal shriek of rage.

19

The thing in the room with them was as tall as a man. Its silver predator's eyes glinted like a knife's edge. White fangs flashed in the moonlight. Beau glimpsed a nose hilled up into a snout, dark lips edging a cruel mouth. Powerful muscles rippled under thick fur. Slashing claws curved from long fingers.

"My God . . . what *is* it?"

"It's a wolf!"

"A monster!"

"It's the devil himself!"

Raphael's pistol lay on the floor. He was on his knees beside it, cradling his right arm. His hand was bent at a sickening angle from his wrist. He raised his head; his eyes were bright with pain.

"*Shoot*, you bastards!" he bellowed.

Antonio aimed his gun, but before he could fire it, the creature swooped down on Raphael and yanked him to his feet. It stood behind him, shielding itself, a strong arm across Raphael's chest, a clawed hand squeezing his neck.

Hands raised, his gun held high, Antonio took a few steps forward. "Let him go. We mean you no harm."

The creature snarled; it curled its claws into Raphael's chest. Crimson flowers bloomed across his shirt.

"*Shoot*, Tonio!" Raphael shrieked.

Quick as lightning, Antonio lowered his pistol and aimed, but before he could fire, the creature stepped out of the moonlight into the darkness, dragging Raphael with it.

"Let him go," Rodrigo pleaded. "Spare his life and we'll never trouble you again, I swear."

A sound came from the darkness. Guttural. Mocking. A demon's laughter.

"*Help me,*" Raphael rasped.

As he choked the words out, Beau felt a rough hand close on the back of his jacket. The next thing he knew, he was being propelled through the darkness, too stunned to feel afraid.

"Take *him*! He's young and tender. He'll taste better!" someone shouted from behind him.

Beau understood then; fear had shattered his confusion. He tried to dig his heels into the floor, but they skidded over the smooth stone. He twisted around, trying to break free, and dropped his dagger. "Let me go! What are you—"

The tip of a blade pressed into his back, silenced him. "Play along," a voice hissed in his ear. "We'll come back for you." It was Miguel, sober now.

The creature stepped back into the light. With a sweep of its arm, it sent Raphael stumbling toward his men. Ramon caught him. At the same time, Miguel gave Beau a vicious shove forward. He lost his balance and fell to his knees.

The thieves scattered like rats. Beau wrenched his head around and watched them swerve past chairs, skirt the dining table, and disappear through the doorway. *Miguel said they'd come back for me,* his mind yammered. *But when?* He forced himself to look up at the beast. A cold, argentine fury glinted in its eyes. Saliva dripped from its fangs.

Beau's fear spiraled into terror. He scrambled to his feet and tried to run past the table, but the beast saw the move coming and blocked him. He whirled away and sprinted for the other end of the table, but before he made it even halfway, the beast was there. It was circling him, tormenting him. He had no weapon. His dagger was somewhere on the floor. He had to break free and run while there was still a chance of escape. But how? *How?*

Breathe, jackass, he told himself. *Think.* He sucked in a lungful of air and slowly exhaled it. His heart slowed, his head cleared, and he realized that he'd been cornered like this many times before. Stalked by town bullies. Chased by the sheriff. Hunted by his drunken, raging father.

He knew what he had to do.

He backed away from the beast slowly, never taking his eyes off it, until he bumped into the table. The chairs that had stood next to it had been shoved aside or knocked over. He moved along the table's edge, his hands behind him, fingers grazing plates, spoons, a tipped-over goblet, feeling for the one thing he needed but not finding it.

"Come on, come *on* . . . I know you're there," he said under his breath.

Napkins, a gnawed bone, a crust of bread, walnut shells . . . and all the time, the beast was moving closer. Beau could smell its musky, rain-soaked fur; he could feel its eyes boring into him. And he knew he had only seconds before it sprang and sank its teeth into his throat.

And then his fingers found it. The thing he needed. A thing that was heavy and cold and sharp. They closed on its handle, and with a roar, Beau threw the carving knife.

The blade missed its mark, but the heavy hilt hit the creature in its face. It backed away from him—just a few steps, but a few steps were all Beau needed. He leapt onto the table, clambered across it, and jumped down on the other side.

Then he ran.

For his life.

– SIX –

No one, not even God, can teach a man to pray like fear can.

As Beau shot out of the great hall, he prayed to Saint Nicholas, the patron saint of thieves. He prayed to Saint Anthony, the patron saint of lost things.

He prayed for speed. He prayed that the outer doors would still be open. He prayed that he would get to them before the beast got to him. But the saints weren't listening. He was running so fast, he didn't see the carpet in

22

the entry hall, bunched up by scuffling feet. His toe caught against it. He tripped and hit the floor hard. Pain lit up every nerve in his body. As he lay there, his eyes closed, his breath coming in short, hot gasps, two words thrummed like a drumbeat in his head . . . *get up, get up, get up, get up* . . .

With a wrenching groan, Beau forced himself to his knees. The sound of the beast pounding across the floor behind him got him to his feet.

"Please don't be locked, please, please, please don't be locked . . ." he panted as he stumbled through the dark hall. He nearly melted with relief as he reached the doors and saw that one was ajar. He heaved himself across the threshold and slammed the door shut, hoping to stop the beast or at least slow it, but as he turned away from the castle his stomach dropped. The courtyard was empty; the thieves were gone, the horses, too.

Then a movement caught his eye. A dozen or so men, mounted on their stamping, anxious animals, were bottlenecked at the gatehouse. They were shouting and shoving, each trying to get ahead of the other. Beau didn't understand why. The archway was wide. They'd ridden through it two abreast on their way into the courtyard. Had they not been able to raise the portcullis?

"Wait!" he shouted. "Wait for me!" But no one heard him; he was too far away.

I can make it to them, he thought, breaking into a stiff, shambling trot. His eyes scanned the crowd for a riderless horse, for Amar, but he couldn't see him. And then he did—the animal was tethered to Miguel's horse.

Miguel's threat echoed back to him. *I'll get you, boy. When you least expect it. Then we'll see who's laughing . . .*

Dread drove a spike through Beau's heart. Miguel had seen his chance to make good on his threat and he'd taken it. He never planned to come back. Not tonight. Not tomorrow. Not ever.

Beau ran now, ignoring his pain, arms knifing through the air, legs pistoning. He had to get to the thieves before they crossed the bridge.

Once they were on the other side, they'd gallop off into the woods and he'd never catch up to them. He was halfway across the courtyard when Miguel disappeared through the archway. Only two men remained outside the gatehouse now.

"Wait!" Beau bellowed at them. "Carlos . . . Tonio, *wait!*"

Antonio nudged his horse forward. Carlos turned around in his saddle. His eyes found Beau; he motioned at him to hurry, but then his gaze abruptly shifted to something behind Beau and the blood drained from his face. "Run, boy! *Run!*" he shouted, kicking his horse. The animal charged through the arch.

Beau risked a look back and his guts turned to water. The monster was in the courtyard. It was running, too. And it was faster. As they locked eyes, it let out an earsplitting roar. The high stone walls caught the sound and amplified it.

Beau knew he had only seconds left in which to live or die. He reached the gatehouse, only to discover what had caused the bottleneck—not the portcullis, that was up, but the old bridge. It was crumbling under the thundering weight of the horses. Huge chunks of it were already gone, swallowed up by the moat. The frightened animals were charging over the remains, their ears flat to their heads, their eyes wild.

Beau knew he had to get across. *Now.* He took a deep breath, then took a careful step onto the teetering structure, his arms outstretched like a tightrope walker's.

Up ahead, Carlos and his horse neared the far bank; they were only a few yards away from it when what was left of the bridge lurched sickeningly. The boards in front of the animal heaved up, then tumbled end over end into the moat. The terrified horse let out a shrill whinny, tensed his back legs, and jumped. His front hooves found the grassy bank; his back hooves scrabbled at loose rock, then miraculously found purchase. As he reached flat ground, Carlos turned in his saddle.

"Run, Beau! Run, you bastard, *run!*" he shouted.

Groans from the ancient bridge crescendoed to a death cry as what was left of the deck trembled and swayed. Beau grabbed for the railing, but it fell away under his hand, spiraling down into the black water. The boards under his feet bucked and splintered, throwing him off-balance. Windmilling frantically, he toppled onto his rear end, then scrabbled backward. He managed to heave himself onto the gatehouse's threshold just as the bridge crumbled completely.

There, he watched in stunned horror as the last boards fell into the moat, raising geysers of water, then he lifted his eyes to the far bank, telling himself that the men there—men he'd lived with for years, men he'd called family—would help him. He told himself that they'd push a downed tree across the moat. Or somehow throw him a rope. And for a long, desperate moment, he believed it. Until Antonio made the sign of the cross. Until Miguel gave him the finger. Until Raphael said, "Get up, boy. Die on your feet like a man." He watched, feeling sick, as they slowly turned their horses away. As the trees closed around them. Then he stood and walked back through the gatehouse.

The beast was waiting for him in the courtyard. Torchlight danced in its cruel eyes. Did it want him to run? To make the hunt more exciting? He would not. He took a few steps in its direction, then stopped.

Die on your feet like a man . . .

But he wasn't going to die. He couldn't die. Because if he did, Matti died, too. He was all the boy had.

Beau knew what to do. He would draw the creature near, then go for its throat with his bare hands. He needed courage and a little luck. He would only get one chance.

"Come on . . ." he whispered.

The creature started toward him. Beau caught its killer's gaze and held it. Nearer and nearer it came, until it was only a few feet away.

Closer, he silently urged. *Closer* . . .

The creature leaned toward him, drawing in his scent. Beau refused to give it the thrill of his fear. He didn't flinch; he didn't blink. He knew where it would strike. Somewhere soft and unprotected. His neck. His belly. He had to strike first, before his blood sprayed across the cobblestones and his guts hit his boots.

But the monster chose a different place—a hard and armored place, one covered in a cage of bone.

It reached out an arm and placed a clawed hand on Beau's chest. He had not expected that, and for a few seconds, he froze. Only his heart moved, slamming against his ribs, beating out the rhythm of his terror. The monster could feel it. Its claws tightened, piercing his clothing and his skin, digging in, as if it would tear his heart out. The creature's ears flattened. Its black lips drew back.

Now, Beau told himself. *Do it. Do it now!*

He drove his hands upward, aiming for the monster's neck, hoping to smash its windpipe. He was quick, the strike was strong and well-aimed, and had it hit its mark, it would've done damage—but once again, the creature was quicker. It saw the strike coming.

Beau heard a scream of rage. He felt claws sink into him. Felt his feet leave the ground and his body fly through the air.

Then his vision exploded in a blaze of white.

And he felt nothing at all.

− S E V E N −

The stag is careless. Hunger has made it so.

It steps out from a stand of swaying pines and into a clearing. The beast, hidden in a thicket of frost-kissed bracken, is watching.

Why did the men come to the castle? They should not have. Now the one they left behind will pay the price.

How it envies the foolish stag. It knows nothing of sorrow or regret. It knows nothing of fear. Not yet.

The beast tenses. It crouches and springs. It is ruthless but quick, and howls over its kill. Night creatures hear it and run for their dens. They know what comes next.

The beast will tear out the stag's still-beating heart.

Because it cannot tear out its own.

– E I G H T –

"What's that one, Beau?" the little boy asked, pointing up at the night sky.

They were huddled together in a haystack trying to sleep, but the night was chilly, their bellies were empty, and sleep wouldn't come.

"That's Hercules, Matti," Beau replied. "One of the gods."

"Did the gods make the stars?"

"Yeah. I think so."

"What's that one?"

"Ursa Major. The great bear."

Their father had taught him the names of the constellations. A long time ago.

"What about that one there?" Matti asked, tracing the outline with his finger.

"That's the bear's tail. Some people call it the Wagon. Or the Big Dipper."

"What does the Big Dipper hold?"

"I don't know. Darkness, I guess."

"No."

27

"No?"

"It holds good things, Beau. And one day the gods will pour them down on us."

Beau turned his head and looked at his little brother, struck by the fierceness in his voice. "What things, Matti?"

Matti turned his head and looked at Beau. "Gold coins with chocolate inside them. Oranges. Sugared almonds. And jam."

"*Jam?*" Beau said, with a laugh.

Matti nodded solemnly. He was always solemn. It worried Beau. He tried to lighten the boy's spirits.

"We're going to be a sticky mess if the gods pour jam all over us, don't you think?"

Matti giggled, but then he turned serious again and his gaze drifted back to the night sky. "One day, good things will pour down on us, Beau. And then we won't be hungry and cold ever again. You'll see."

Beau pulled his little brother closer, trying to keep him warm. He wanted to tell him he *would* have good things one day, that he—Beau—would make sure of it, but he couldn't; the lump in his throat wouldn't let him. He followed Matti's gaze and saw clouds move across the stars. He heard bells tolling. Or was it clock chimes? A sense of dread engulfed him. There was something he needed to do, somewhere he needed to be. What was it?

Matti was saying something to him, but he couldn't understand him. His voice sounded far away. He tugged Beau's ear. Then he slapped his face. Playfully at first, and then a good deal harder. Until Beau's cheek stung and his teeth rattled.

"*Ow!*" he said, batting his brother's hand away. "Cut it out, Matti!"

"My name is Valmont, not Matti," said a gruff voice. "Rouse yourself, thief."

Beau's eyes snapped open. Matti's sweet face was gone, and a very unsweet face was leaning over him—a face with whiskers, bushy eyebrows, and a nose that looked as if it had been broken once or twice.

"What the *hell*?" he yelped, throwing himself backward and whacking his head. "Oh. *Ow.*"

"Get up," the man said, straightening.

A dizzying sense of unreality gripped Beau. He shook his aching head, trying to clear it, but the motion only made things worse. A greasy wave of nausea washed over him. *Too much wine*, a voice inside him said. *But where? When?* His thoughts came as slow and thick as a pour of honey.

Willing his queasiness away, Beau pushed up on his arms and looked at himself. He was dressed except for his jacket and boots, and lying on a narrow wooden bed. There was a headboard behind him and a straw mattress under him. A jug of water and a cup rested on a small table next to the bed. Embers glowed in the room's tiny fireplace. Sunlight flooded in through the single window. He looked at the man again. His thick salt-and-pepper hair was cut short. He wore a slate-blue jacket, a white shirt, and black britches. At least twenty skeleton keys dangled from the large iron ring he was holding.

"This . . . this is a servant's room . . . you're a servant . . . is this your room?" Beau asked. "No, you're not real. This is a dream. It must be. I'm still asleep."

He scrubbed at his face with a grimy hand, then winced as his fingers found a large goose egg on his head. The sudden stab of tenderness convinced him that he wasn't dreaming. Sounds and images rushed at him in a blur—a castle, a feast, a beast. His wits returned, and with them came a hot rush of anger.

"That thing . . . that *monster* . . . it threw me into a wall!" he said.

"Monster, eh?" the man said. "Did it jump out of a wine bottle?"

29

Beau realized that he sounded insane. "It came after me . . . I—I hit my head."

"That tends to happen when you guzzle alcohol and stumble around in the dark."

"I *wasn't* drunk. My head hurts like hell! There's a bump . . ."

The man crossed his brawny arms over his broad chest, smirking. "Want me to kiss it better?"

"Why don't you kiss my ass?" Beau shot back.

The cheek of this old toe rag. Locking him up. Taunting him. Lying to him. There *was* a monster. It had chased him. Grabbed him. Nearly killed him. *Hadn't it?*

In the cold light of morning, Beau found he had difficulty believing it, too. What he'd thought was a monster had surely only been a man—a guard in a fur cape, or a huntsman—who'd been trying to scare off a pack of thieves. He'd been exhausted from the long ride, frozen from the beating rain, half-starved, too, and then he'd drunk too much and the alcohol had played tricks on him.

"Get up," the man said. "You've been summoned."

Pride flared in Beau. He was about to tell the man that *he* was no one's lackey, thank you, but he bit his tongue. He was a prisoner, it seemed, and pride wouldn't set him free; cunning would. He sat up all the way and immediately regretted it. His head throbbed. A ragged groan escaped him. He raised his hand to the goose egg again.

"Smarts, does it?" the man asked.

Beau said nothing, but he stopped rubbing his head. The man was no friend, and it wasn't wise to let a foe see that he was hurting. *Wolves only circle the weak*, Raphael always said.

Raphael.

The rest of the night crashed back into Beau's brain like an avalanche. Raphael, Rodrigo, Antonio, the others . . . they'd abandoned him after the bridge gave way. They'd ridden off without so much as a backward glance, leaving him to become a prisoner. Or a dead man.

Why are you surprised? he asked himself. He knew better than to trust other people, even the ones who called themselves family.

It was the worst thing that could have happened to him, and fear's icy fingers clawed at his heart, but then a hot rush of exhilaration melted them as he began to see that the worst thing was also the best thing.

He'd never planned to get on a ship in Barcelona with the others. He'd planned to run away. From his thief's life. From Raphael. He'd planned to ride off one night when the others were asleep. He'd fetch Matti and they'd hole up in some no-name town where no one would ever find them.

He'd tried to leave once. Long ago. But Raphael had caught him. He could still taste the blood in his mouth from the beating, still hear the thief lord's words as he stood over him. *Leave? You're never leaving, boy. I saved you, remember? Now I own you.*

Raphael had saved him. He'd fed him, sheltered him, and taught him, too. Made him one of his gang. Beau would have died on the streets without him. And in return, Raphael had used him. As a lookout at first, then a pickpocket, then an inside man. *My help comes with a price, boy,* he'd said. *Everyone's does.*

Beau reached for his boots and pulled them on. His heart was thumping with excitement. He was almost free. There was bound to be another bridge across the moat or a tunnel under it. All he had to do was wait for his chance, then run.

He shrugged his jacket on. His fingers felt for the ring he'd hidden behind the button; it was still there. Then they dipped into an inside pocket, searching for the letter from Sister Maria-Theresa.

It was gone.

Beau's heart lurched. He felt in the pocket again, then frantically turned it inside out, but it was empty. He searched his other pockets, but the letter wasn't in any of them.

He'd still had it on him when he and the others were riding through the woods last night; he remembered it crinkling inside his jacket. Had he lost it when he'd run from the great hall? Or when the bridge had crumbled underneath him? If so, it was at the bottom of the moat.

He hadn't read it. He had no idea what news it contained. He expected it to say that Matti had gotten better, but what if he hadn't?

"No," Beau said under his breath. He would not allow himself to even *think* that. He would go to Barcelona, letter or no, just as he'd planned. And Matti would be there waiting for him. He *would*.

"What's wrong?"

The big, burly man was standing in the doorway, looking at him intently, and Beau realized his feelings were on his face. Cursing himself for letting his guard down, he said, "I'm hungry."

The man laughed mirthlessly. "An empty belly's the least of your problems," he said as he headed out of the room.

Beau buttoned his jacket and followed him. As he stepped across the threshold, he found himself on a landing at the top of a narrow, spiraling stairwell.

The man was already halfway down it. "Hurry up!" he called over his shoulder. "We're late."

"Who sent for me? What does he want?" Beau asked as he caught up to him.

"*She*. Lady Arabella, the mistress of this castle. You'd do well to remember that. And your place."

Beau bristled at his patronizing tone. "Hey, Fremont . . . that's your name, isn't it? Fremont? Tremont?"

"*Valmont*."

"Who's Lady Arabella? What is this place?"

Valmont tossed him a withering look but said nothing.

The gloomy stairwell led to a gloomy hallway, which led to another stairwell that carried them down into the castle's armory—a cavernous room with narrow windows and vaulted ceilings.

"This way," Valmont said, motioning impatiently as Beau eyed the weapons and armor. "The mistress doesn't have all day. She's at breakfast and doesn't linger there long."

As the words left Valmont's lips, Beau stopped. He'd spotted a row of shields hanging on a wall, all shining brightly. He walked up to one and regarded himself in its reflection. "So she wants to see me, does she? Well, that's no surprise," he said, wiping a smudge of dirt off his cheek.

Valmont stopped, too. He put his hands on his hips. Beau glimpsed him in the shield's silver gleam and winked. "What female would let this"—he gestured to himself—"go to waste?" He ran his hands through his long dark locks. His fingers found a knot. "Got a comb on you, Monty?"

Valmont glared. "Let's *go*."

"You can't expect me to go to your mistress looking like this," Beau said with an insolent grin. "I was thinking about leaving, but maybe I'll stay. Long enough for her to fall in love with me and make me lord of the manor, just so I can throw your ugly ass out in the cold."

Valmont took one of his meaty hands in the other and cracked his knuckles. "*Walk.*"

Beau licked his fingers and smoothed a lock of hair out of his face. He was still grinning as he caught up to Valmont, but as soon as Valmont turned, the smile slid off his face.

It had all been an act—preening and primping, provoking Valmont. Beau hadn't been gazing at himself in the shield's reflection; he'd been casing the room, looking for objects of value, escape routes, an advantage. His dagger was gone; he'd felt for it. The only weapon he had now was knowledge. Even the spartan little room where he'd slept had given him a wealth of information. The angle of the sun's rays pouring in through the window told him the room was on the east side of the castle. The curved walls told him it was in a tower; the long stairwell told him it was a high one. He'd counted the number of steps he'd taken and the number of floors they'd descended so he could retrace his path, even in the dark.

Valmont led Beau out of the armory, down a gallery, through a music room, a study, two sitting rooms, and into the castle's enormous kitchens. Just as Beau thought they'd never get wherever it was that they were going, they emerged in the great hall.

Raised voices greeted them.

"I interrogated all of them, my lady, every last one."

Valmont stopped inside the doorway. Beau, who'd stopped a few feet behind him, edged to his side so he could see who was speaking.

"They all say the same thing—they were nowhere near the gatehouse last night."

The voice belonged to a short, slight, anxious-looking man in a mint-green jacket and tan britches. He was standing by the head of the dining table.

"It would appear, then, that the portcullis raised itself. Is that what you're saying, Percival?"

That voice, young-sounding but commanding, belonged to a woman. *Lady Arabella*, Beau guessed. She was sitting in a chair at the end of the table, her back to a crackling fire. Beau couldn't see her—the man called Percival was blocking his view—but he could hear her words. They were cold and restrained, but anger rushed just below them, like a river under ice.

"I do not know how the miscreant got into the gatehouse to raise the portcullis," Percival said, shaking his head. "The door is kept locked and

34

the key never leaves my sight. Perhaps the thieves somehow breached the walls? Or crawled into the window above the gatehouse?"

"Or perhaps someone is *lying*."

That was a new voice, cold and severe.

Beau craned his neck and saw another woman. She was older and sitting to the younger woman's right. Her hair, piled high atop her head, was jet black. Her face was deathly pale. Her lips were thin and bloodless. Her dress looked like a fine, heavy silk to Beau, and was well cut, but the color was a dull pewter gray.

Other women sat around the table. They numbered about two dozen. Beau guessed they must be Lady Arabella's court.

At first glance, they appeared to be eating breakfast, but as his eyes lingered on them, he saw that one was ripping petals off a flower. A second, shockingly thin, was viciously gnawing at a fingernail. A third used her fork to catapult berries at the others, grinning madly as she did. Her face was greasepaint white, like a clown's, with black-crayon eyebrows, red circles in the centers of her cheeks, and heart-shaped lips.

Beau tried not to stare at them, but their behavior was so strange, he couldn't help it. It was like trying to not watch a hanging. After a moment he looked past them, eyes searching for the golden clock. It was gone, hidden behind the paneled wall again, but he could hear it ticking.

"We *will* find out who did it, Percival, and when we do—" the lady in gray began.

The woman ripping the flower apart cut her off. "Someone *stole* the key, Lady Espidra. How else could he get into the gatehouse?" she said stridently. Beau saw she wore a gown of crimson.

"Surrender it, Percival, you weasel," said the shockingly thin woman, who was dressed in a gown the color of scraped flesh. "You're a liar. A sneak. You can't be trusted."

35

"But the key was not out of my sight, Lady Hesma, I swear it!"

Beau could not see Percival's face, but he could hear the hurt in his voice.

"The key, Percival. *Now*," the woman in gray demanded.

Percival's shoulders sagged. "Very well, Lady Espidra." He dipped his hand into his jacket pocket, pulled out a large brass skeleton key, and placed it on the table. Beau's gaze sharpened; his thief's fingers twitched. It was a master key; he could tell by the shape. It would open every door in the castle.

As Percival stood there, his head bent, the ladies continued to harangue him, like a flock of crows pecking at a corpse. Valmont cleared his throat noisily, silencing them.

"What is it, Valmont?" Lady Arabella asked, her voice tannic with irritation.

"I've brought the visitor, Your Grace."

"*Visitor?*" Beau echoed under his breath. Harsh words sprang to his lips, but he bit them back. If he hoped to charm the mistress of the castle into letting him go, pretty words were needed.

And then Percival stepped aside, and Beau saw a young woman, perhaps eighteen years of age, and for the first time in his life, he found he had no words. None at all.

They had fallen away.

Like coins through clumsy fingers.

– NINE –

She wore a sharply tailored jacket of robin's-egg blue edged with black braid, and a black riding skirt. Her golden hair was pinned up in a neat coil. A pair of flawless pearls dangled from her ears. Her spine was as straight as a sword, her bearing regal.

But it was her face that had robbed Beau of words.

The sunlight, pouring in through the windows, played over its beguiling geometry. He saw the broad planes and angles of her cheeks, the strong line of her jaw, the full arch of her red lips. He saw her beautiful gray eyes—cool and appraising, fiercely intelligent.

And they saw him.

He'd planned to enchant the castle's mistress, to make her heart flutter with silky smiles and satin words, to play her, just as he'd played every other woman he'd ever met. Instead, he was the one who was spellbound.

"Bow, you clotpole," Valmont ordered. He grabbed the back of Beau's neck and tried to shove his head down. His rough touch broke the spell. Beau smacked his hand away and stood tall.

"Approach," Arabella said, with a wave of her jeweled hand. She was no longer looking at him.

"No, thanks," said Beau, balking at her imperious tone. "I'm good where I—unhh!"

A shove from Valmont sent him sprawling. He nearly fell flat on his face but caught himself on a chair. Laughter rose from Arabella's court, but Beau ignored it. He shot Valmont a dirty look, then made his way to the head of the table.

If Arabella had seen him stumble, she gave no indication. Her attention was absorbed by a book. It lay open next to a porcelain cup filled with black coffee. Near the book were platters of tantalizing foods, and Beau's stomach growled at the sight of golden brioche as fat as pillows, flaky croissants oozing chocolate, and apple muffins topped with a rubble of streusel. There were fluffy scrambled eggs flecked with chives, too. Fat sausages slicked with grease. Streaky crisps of bacon.

Arabella closed her book as Beau approached her. He glanced at the spine. *The Ancient Edifices of Athens.*

37

Arabella took a sip of her coffee, put the cup down again, then sat back in her chair and regarded him with her mesmerizing eyes. Beau looked terrible; he knew he did. He'd seen himself in the shield's reflection. He was dirty, sweaty, and rumpled. His hair was a haystack. *Your face is your fortune, boy. And mine,* Raphael often said. If that were true, then he was broke at the moment, and the knowledge of it made him wilt a little under her penetrating gaze.

Finally, she spoke. "What is your name, thief?" she asked, her voice chilly.

Beau lifted his chin. "Beauregard Armando Fernandez de Navarre," he replied. "Beau for short."

"Beau?" Arabella echoed, looking him up and down. "You are anything but *beau*, Beau."

Her ladies laughed. Beau flinched. The insult had cut him, so he did what he always did when someone drew blood—he cut deeper.

"I guess that makes two of us," he said. "Since you are anything but *belle*, Ara-*bell*-a."

It was half a lie. Arabella was beautiful, but her cold, disdainful manner made her less so. Lie or not, though, his words had wounded. Anger sparked in her eyes, but it was gone as quickly as it had come, drowned under ice.

"H-how *dare* you!" Percival sputtered, outraged. "Who do you think you are? You're nothing but a thief! Valmont, take him back to the dungeon!"

Nothing but a thief . . .

The harsh words burst in Beau's ears; their bitter poison dripped into his heart, searing it. How many times had he heard them? From sheriffs and judges, shopkeepers, the schoolmaster, the priest?

A beating's too good for you, boy, you're nothing but a thief . . .

You have no place in my school, boy, you're nothing but a thief . . .

You're not welcome in this holy church, boy, you're nothing but a thief . . .

38

The sound of Valmont's feet striding toward him silenced the voices. Beau shook off the hurt. He had only seconds before the man grabbed him.

"Why am I a prisoner?" he demanded, holding Arabella's gaze. "You've no right to keep me."

Valmont was just steps away when Arabella raised her hand, stopping him. "You are not a prisoner," she said.

"I am *not*," Beau said. "Huh." He tilted his head. "So what am I? An honored guest? I must be. You gave me the tower suite. With a door that locks from the outside."

"You were locked in because I cannot allow a vicious criminal to roam freely in my castle," Arabella said. "I have the safety of my household to consider."

"*Vicious criminal?*" Beau scoffed. "I took a couple of napkin rings!" He pulled them out of his pocket and banged them down on the table. "And I didn't leave the premises with them. Which means I *didn't* steal them. Technically. So let me go."

Arabella poured herself more coffee. "I'm afraid that's impossible."

An image flashed into Beau's head of Matteo, his body racked by a fit of coughing. "Why?" he pressed, a desperate edge to his voice. "Why is it impossible?"

"Because the idiots accompanying you destroyed the bridge!"

The words came not from Arabella but the woman in crimson. She was gripping the arms of her chair, glaring at Beau with such naked fury, he found himself taking a step back.

"That will do, Lady Rega," warned Lady Espidra.

"I can't stay here. I have to leave now, before snow cuts off the mountain pass," Beau protested. "There must be another way out."

"There is not," said Arabella tonelessly, returning her attention to her book.

39

"But this is an ancient castle. Built on the border of Spain and France, two countries often at war."

"Your point?"

"Castles that are likely to be attacked have more than one exit. You're telling me there's no second bridge? A drawbridge? A footbridge?"

"I am, yes," said Arabella, without looking up. "That's exactly what I'm doing."

As she finished speaking, a high, whining scrape was heard. Rega had risen from her chair. Espidra shot her a warning glance and she sat down again, a smoldering look on her face.

Beau's desperation turned into panic. He tried to wrestle it down. Losing his head wouldn't get him any closer to his brother. "What about a tunnel? Running under the castle? How else did the lord of the manor send a messenger for help during a siege? Or smuggle a princess to safety?"

"We have no lords in this castle," Arabella replied. "No princesses, either."

"You're lying," Beau said hotly. "There *is* a tunnel. There has to be."

"*Enough!*" Lady Rega shouted, slamming her hands on the table so hard, her plate jumped. "You want to leave this place? Build a new bridge and walk yourself over it!"

Beau looked at her as if she'd lost her mind. "Build a *bridge*?" he repeated. "Over the *moat*? It has to be a twenty-foot drop!"

"Thirty," Arabella said. She snapped her fingers. "Get him out of my sight, Valmont. Find him work to do. He has a debt to pay. His friends stole half my silver."

"Take him to the stables, why don't you?" drawled Lady Hesma. "Something tells me he'd be good at shoveling manure."

"This way," Valmont said, taking hold of Beau's arm, but Beau shook him off. He strode back to Arabella.

"Tell me where the bloody tunnel is!" he demanded.

40

Lady Rega sprang out of her chair so fast that it fell over, hitting the floor with a deafening crash. She grabbed a heavy crystal goblet from the table and threw it at Beau's head. It missed, barely, and hit the wall behind him, exploding like a firework. The other ladies ducked and screamed.

"You could have killed me!" Beau angrily shouted.

"Stop it, Rega," Lady Espidra commanded. *"Now."*

"Why did you come here? *Why?* You shouldn't have!" Rega bellowed at Beau.

"No shit!" Beau bellowed back.

Arabella looked up from her book. Her eyes found Beau's. "You poor fool," she said. "You don't know what you've done."

Beau shook his head, incredulous. *"I'm* a fool? *I* am? *You're* the fool, girl! Who leaves a portcullis up at midnight?"

At that instant, Valmont, who'd been sneaking up behind Beau, grabbed one of his arms and twisted it behind his back, sending a bolt of agony through his body. What little self-possession Beau still had shattered. "Where *am* I?" he shouted. "What is this godforsaken place?"

"Just that," Arabella replied. "A godforsaken place."

"And you?" Beau demanded. "Who are you?"

Arabella laughed. It was a dry, wasted sound, like cornstalks rattling in the wind. "Godforsaken as well. We are all godforsaken here, thief." She nodded at Valmont. "Take him away."

Valmont shoved Beau forward. It was all he could do to keep his feet under him. Arabella watched them go. As soon as they were out of sight, she turned to Percival.

"This is *your* doing," she said sharply. "You allowed a pack of robbers in to eat my food and steal my belongings. What were you thinking?"

Percival looked stricken. "We didn't know they were robbers when we put food out for them," he said. "We were only trying to be hospitable, Your Grace. To shelter lost travelers."

"That is a *lie*, Percival. I know exactly what you were doing, all of you, and I won't have it. This is a man's life you are playing with. His *life*. I will discover who raised the portcullis, and when I do, he will pay for it. Dearly."

For a long moment, Percival did not respond. He simply stood there, his hands clasped in front of him, struggling to hide the sorrow in his eyes. Then in a tremulous voice, he said, "My lady, you cannot punish someone for holding on to hope."

Arabella squeezed her eyes shut, as if battling a sudden and deep pain. After a moment, she opened them again, rose from the table, and picked up her book.

"You still have hope, do you, Percival?" she asked coldly.

"Most days, hope is all I have," Percival replied.

"How fortunate you are," said Arabella as she left the room. "I myself lost hope. A century ago."

– TEN –

"The kitchen? Perfect. I'll have an omelet, Monty," Beau said. "Peppers and onions, please. Can I get some toast, too?"

"Shut your mouth," Valmont said, pushing him forward.

Fresh pain shot up Beau's arm; Valmont still had it twisted behind his back. They were walking through the castle's kitchen, a room bigger than most of the mansions Beau had worked in. He saw a white-hatted chef stirring a stockpot. A teenaged boy peeled and chopped vegetables; a second one emerged from the larder carrying a sack of flour over his shoulder. A woman, the sleeves of her blouse rolled up, her hair wrapped in a scarf, kneaded dough at a marble-topped table. Her eyes followed Beau.

Valmont gave him another push and this time Beau lost his balance and fell, breaking his captor's grip. He landed gracelessly on all fours, a few feet away from a long wooden worktable and the large willow baskets filled with onions, carrots, and potatoes that stood by it.

"Get up," Valmont ordered.

Beau grabbed hold of a basket's rim and used it to push himself to his feet. His movements were slow; he was weary and hungry. And he was rattled. Badly. By Arabella, who'd told him there was no way out of this place, and by the unhinged courtier who'd thrown a goblet at his head. But he knew he couldn't give in to his feelings; he had to stay sharp.

"Seriously, Monty, any chance of some food?" he asked when he was standing again.

Valmont's stormy expression softened. He motioned to a stool by the worktable. "Sit there," he instructed. Then he turned to the woman kneading dough. "Camille, please fix our guest some breakfast."

As Beau sat, the boy who'd been peeling vegetables came up to Valmont and asked him for help with a sink tap that was stuck. Valmont warned Beau to stay put and followed the boy. Camille wiped her hands on her pinafore, took a mug down from a shelf, poured coffee into it from an enameled pot, and wordlessly handed it to Beau.

"Thank you," he said, taking the mug in both hands. The coffee was hot and bracing and it brought a bit of life back into him.

As Beau drank it, Camille took a roll from a basket and deftly sliced it open. She slathered butter on the halves, then cut slices from a large ham and a wedge of cheese left over from the servants' breakfast. As she worked, Beau's eyes swept over her, then Valmont and the kitchen boy, the chef at his stove, a small boy turning a spit, a lady's maid polishing a pair of boots. He saw everyone and everything except the one thing he was searching for. He didn't believe Arabella. There *was* a tunnel under the castle, there had to be, and the way to it was through the cellar.

So where's the door? he wondered, craning his neck. He looked like a giraffe, but luckily everyone was too busy with their work to notice. Just

43

as he was about to give up, the boy who'd passed by earlier with a sack of flour over his shoulder walked by again, this time with a basket in one hand and a lantern in the other, then disappeared down a hallway.

Beau set his cup down. His heartbeat quickened. *He's going to the cellar to fetch something,* he reasoned. *Why else would he be carrying a basket and lantern?*

"Here."

The voice startled Beau. It was Camille. She'd finished making his sandwich and had wrapped it in a clean kitchen towel. *"Here,"* she said again, holding it out to him.

Beau took it from her and deployed his most devastating smile, one that never failed to set hearts aflutter. He'd gotten nowhere with Arabella, but now, right in front of him, was a second chance. He would flatter the little baker. Charm her. Ask her questions.

"Thank you, mademoiselle," he began.

"It's madame and we both know it," Camille said crisply.

Beau's smarmy smile faded, but he pressed on. "It's kind of you to take pity on a poor prisoner. I'm—"

Camille brusquely cut him off. "Do you think you're the only one?"

Beau tilted his head. He didn't understand her question. And then he did. If he couldn't get out of here, neither could anyone else. Guilt nibbled the edges of his conscience with its sharp rat's teeth. He chased it away. If anyone should feel guilty, it was Arabella.

"Yeah, the bridge . . ." he started to say.

"Yeah, the bridge," Camille mimicked. "The one you and your wolf pack destroyed."

"Hey, we really didn't—"

"Didn't what? Think? Care? Give a damn? No, you didn't. Twenty horses on a rickety bridge . . . What did you expect would happen?"

44

Camille shook her head in disgust. "You don't *give* at all, do you, thief? You just take."

Camille's jibe cut him. Just like Arabella's had. He hadn't let Arabella see that she'd drawn blood and he wouldn't let this mouthy little baker see it, either.

"Oh, ouch. *So* harsh," he said mockingly.

Camille's eyes narrowed. She was about to let loose when Valmont reappeared. "Let's go," he barked, and for once, Beau was happy to see him.

Camille lowered her head and returned to her kneading, pummeling the dough so hard the worktable shook. Beau rose, clutching his sandwich in one hand. He waited for Valmont to grab hold of him again, but the man seemed to give him the benefit of the doubt this time. They walked in silence, a foot or so apart, out the kitchen's back door, through a walled courtyard containing a kitchen garden, sodden and dormant now, and into the stables.

"The stalls need mucking out. Here . . ." Valmont said, handing him a pitchfork. "Get busy. Don't make me regret not locking you up."

As soon as he was gone, Beau tossed the pitchfork on the floor. "Shovel your own crap, Monty," he muttered. Then he sat down on a wooden feedbox, unwrapped his sandwich from the kitchen towel, and tore into it. Like anyone who's ever been hungry, he knew to eat his food quickly, before someone bigger and stronger snatched it from him. When he finished, he wiped his mouth on the towel and leaned back against the wall.

"Any minute now," he said.

A couple of minutes passed. Then five. Ten. Beau sang as he waited, letting his gaze drift. Curious horses peeked their heads out of their stalls, blinking at the noisy newcomer. There was a tack room at the end of the aisle, and he could see a row of saddles through its open door.

There were bound to be plenty of useful tools in there—awls, picks, files, shears. He would help himself.

Footsteps—several sets of them, coming from the courtyard outside—pulled Beau out of his thoughts. "Took you long enough," he said under his breath. Then he shrugged out of his jacket, hung it on a hook, and picked up the pitchfork.

"Where is it?" Valmont thundered as he came barreling through the doorway.

Beau shoved the tines of the pitchfork under a pile of horse droppings, then dumped them into a wheelbarrow, making it look as if he'd been working all along. He feigned a look of confusion as Valmont strode up to him. Two young men, both of whom Beau recognized from the kitchen, stood behind him.

"I know you have it. Hand it over. *Now.*"

Beau leaned on the pitchfork's handle. "You're being very mysterious, Monty. Hand *what* over?"

"Henri, hold him. Florian, search him," Valmont ordered.

Henri, short and stocky, grabbed Beau's arms and pulled them behind his back. Tall, skinny Florian patted him down, running his hands over Beau's torso, dipping them into his pockets, feeling inside his waistband.

"Easy there," Beau protested as Florian patted down his britches. "Maybe take me to dinner first?"

"There's nothing on him," Florian said when he'd finished.

"Pull his boots off," Valmont demanded.

Florian did so, turning each boot over and shaking it. When nothing fell out, he shoved his hand inside them and felt around.

"Mind telling me what we're looking for?" Beau asked.

"You know damn well what we're looking for," Valmont growled. His eyes fell on Beau's jacket. He snatched it off the hook and rifled through its pockets.

"Actually, I don't."

Henri gave Beau a rough shake. "The master key. Percival put it down on the table in the great hall and now it's gone."

Beau whipped around and shoved Henri hard. "Watch yourself," he warned, no longer joking. "I don't have your key. Maybe Lady Touchy threw it at me. Maybe one of the maids swept it up with the broken goblet. Go dig in the garbage." He reached down for a boot and pulled it back on.

"I don't believe you," Valmont said.

"I don't give a snail's left ass cheek what you believe," Beau said, pulling his other boot on.

Valmont, glowering, silently turned on his heel and left. Henri and Florian followed him. A stallion, unsettled by the angry voices, kicked at the back wall of his stall. Beau went over to the animal and petted his neck to calm him.

"Do you know the first rule of thieving, boy? No? I'll tell you: Never get caught with the goods." He leaned in close and whispered in the stallion's ear. "I palmed the key off the table in the great hall when I slapped the napkin rings down. Then I dropped it into the basket of onions in the kitchen." The horse whickered; he tilted his head. "Why, you ask?" Beau scratched behind the animal's ears. His gaze shifted to the stable's doorway; his eyes darkened. "So I can get the hell out of here. Tonight."

– ELEVEN –

The castle opened its eyes at night. It came to life in the darkness.

Arabella heard it. She heard the howls, the laughter, the whispers and wails. Percival always told her that it was just wind whirling through the eaves, or old timbers creaking. As she walked down the dark corridors, she trailed a hand over the ancient stone walls. Her fingers came away wet.

47

"It's just a leak, mistress," Percival would say, but Arabella knew better. The walls had seen what had happened in this place. They'd held so much pain, so much grief, that they themselves were weeping.

Ghosts roamed here, creatures made of memories and regrets. They drifted down corridors and through rooms, trailing sadness in their wake like a courtesan trailing perfume.

And all the while, the golden clock kept time, counting off minutes and hours, days and years. Arabella could never escape the sound. No matter where she went, she heard it ticking, like the castle's monstrous heart.

A gallery window caught her reflection as she hurried past it—the collar of her blue-velvet dressing gown framing her face, her golden hair trailing down her back, her slippered feet passing like whispers over the floor. In the far reaches of the castle, places where no one went anymore, chairs covered with sheets loomed like malevolent specters, their arms outstretched. Suits of armor stood like shadowy sentinels in cobwebbed corners. Portraits of stern ancestors gazed unforgivingly from their frames.

Moving swiftly down one dismal hallway after the next, Arabella tried every handle to every door, making certain that they were locked tight. Now and again, she pressed a palm to a door or leaned her forehead against it, her ears cocked, her body tensed.

Lady Espidra had locked them away. *For your own protection, mistress,* she'd said. She'd never told her where, in case—in a moment of weakness—Arabella was tempted to let them out. They'd been silent in their imprisonment, but now they were restive; Arabella could feel it. They wanted to get out, to roam again, to do her harm. She could not rest until she knew that no door had been left unlocked.

It was as she was hurrying from the east wing of the castle to the west that she heard it—singing. The sound was so unexpected, so completely out of place, so beautiful, that she stopped dead. No one sang. Not here. Not anymore.

Ah, song of the rising sun!

And song of dew!

Ah, song of the waters . . .

It was a man's voice, as meltingly rich as a ribbon of warm caramel. More Spanish than French. Arabella recognized the lyrics; they were from "The Mountains of Canigou," an old song, pretty and sad, that the people of the Pyrenees sang.

The singing grew louder. Arabella realized it was carrying up from outside and hurried to a window. Looking down, she saw a broad-shouldered man walking across a courtyard toward the kitchen, a lantern in his hand.

"Valmont?" she whispered, shocked at the idea of her stern butler singing. But no, it was another man, younger, rangy, following Valmont at an unhurried pace, hands in his pockets, shoulders hunched against the cold.

"The thief," Arabella whispered. Valmont was escorting him back from the stables.

The moon poured its rays over him, painting streaks of silver into his black hair, highlighting the angles of his face, pooling in his dark, unknowable eyes.

"He is an uncommonly beautiful man," said a voice from behind her.

Arabella jumped. She stepped back from the window, flustered. A woman stood in the shadows, just a few feet away.

"You startled me, Lady Espidra."

"The most beautiful of them all, I would say," Espidra added, moving close. Her thin lips curved into a smile of regret. "But unlike the others, he's trapped here, my dear. Because of *you.*"

49

Arabella flinched. Espidra's words scraped her heart raw. "But it *wasn't* me," she protested. "You *know* that. I forbade anyone to raise the portcullis."

"Does it really matter who did it?" Espidra asked. "All that matters is why. And just imagine if he were to find out."

Arabella read the threat under her words and bristled at it. "You are not to tell him. I forbid it."

Espidra pressed a hand to her chest. "*Me?* Never, Your Grace."

Arabella returned to the window, her eyes searching for another glimpse of the thief, but he was gone.

Espidra extended her hand—fingers bent like bare winter branches—and stroked Arabella's hair. "Supper is in an hour. Come, we must dress you."

"Not yet. I am not finished here."

"I shall be waiting," Espidra said, and then she left.

Arabella lingered by the window for a moment longer, then she continued down the dark hall, moving from door to door, making sure each one was locked. The unfamiliar rush of brightness that coursed through her heart just moments ago had drained away. She felt heavy now. Weighted. Like a corpse at the bottom of a lake, staring up through sightless eyes at a dark and faraway sky.

– T W E L V E –

The boy who turned the enormous meat spit walked across the kitchen with a bowl in his hands, his brow furrowed, his steps careful. He was small and slight, only nine or ten years of age.

He was also the filthiest damn kid Beau had ever seen.

A cap that was once white but was now gray with soot covered his head. His cheeks were smudged with spices; his clothing was grimed with batter, butter, gravy, and grease. He looked like he hadn't bathed in a year. Maybe two.

Watching him, Beau thought about his brother, who was only two or three years older. Even when they'd been on their own, he and Matti, sleeping in barns and stables, stealing eggs from henhouses and apples from orchards to stay alive, Beau had tried to keep the little boy clean. He would find a stream to bathe him in, or a horse trough where he could at least dunk his head.

He'd made sure Matti was clean the day he'd taken him to the nuns. He'd been thin and ragged—they both had—but he'd been well-scrubbed.

Matti didn't know why they were at the convent, not at first. When Beau knelt down to tell him, he'd thrown his arms around Beau's neck and wailed. When Beau tried to explain that he needed food, a fire, a warm, dry bed—things Beau couldn't give him—Matti said he'd rather starve than be without his brother.

Don't leave me here, Beau, please, please don't. I want to come with you . . .

Don't cry, Matti. Please don't cry. I'll come back for you. As soon as I can. I promise. I swear . . .

The nuns had taken the boy then, peeling his arms off Beau, and Beau had walked away. It was like cutting out his own heart.

His promise to Matti echoed in his head now.

"*Move*, kid," he said under his breath. He had a bead on the onion basket, all the way across the kitchen, and the dirty spit boy was blocking his view.

Beau was sitting at the baker's worktable. *Again.* After fetching him from the stables, Valmont had placed a meaty hand on his back and shoved him toward a stool. "Sit and stay," he'd said to him, as if he were some mangy mutt.

But Beau didn't want to sit. Or stay. He needed to get to the onion basket and fish out the key he'd hidden inside it. The urge to get over the mountains to his brother was so powerful, it hurt. He felt like a fox caught in a cruel iron trap, so desperate to escape, it would chew its own leg off.

He'd broken into dozens of shops and mansions and escaped undetected. Picked diabolically intricate locks. Slid watches out of the pockets of their owners. All he had to do now was dig a key out of a basket—a simple task, yet seemingly impossible. There were so many people in the kitchen slicing, sautéing, plating, saucing, and garnishing, he couldn't move a muscle without ten of them seeing him.

"Come *on*, kid. Get out of the *way*," he hissed.

But instead of moving out of Beau's sight line, the boy walked up to him and set down the bowl he was carrying. Beau recoiled slightly, expecting any child as crusty as this one was to stink like a dung heap, but he didn't. In fact, he smelled good. Like butter-basted chicken. Roasted chestnuts. Bacon drippings.

"For you. I helped Chef make it," the boy said, a shy pride swelling his skinny chest. He pulled a spoon from his apron pocket, set it next to the bowl, and then he was gone, making his way back to the fiery realm of hot ovens and crackling spits.

Beau looked down at the bowl; it contained beef stew. He didn't want it—his nerves had killed his appetite—but he picked up the spoon anyway. Not eating after working all day would look odd; it might make Valmont suspicious, and Beau could not risk that. He spooned up some stew, blew on it, then shoveled it into his mouth, ready to swallow it down quick. Instead, his eyes widened and his stomach gave a long, growling purr as the meat melted like butter on his tongue. The tender chunks of carrot and potato, the tiny pearl onions collapsing into the dark, winey sauce—they tasted of something more than themselves. They tasted of patience. Of time taken. Of care.

He took another bite and as he did, he was gripped by a memory so strong, it squeezed the breath from him. He saw a woman. She had a smiling face and kind eyes. She was singing to him, her voice warm and low. He could smell her—vanilla, butter, almonds—as she took his face in her hands and kissed the top of his head. Losing her had nearly killed him. But it had taught him, too. He'd learned how to wall his heart up, brick by brick, so it could never be broken again. No one was allowed inside the wall now, no one but Matti.

"Do you want some bread?"

The words tugged Beau back from his past. He looked up and saw Camille sliding a plate toward him. Thick slices cut from a large loaf lay upon it. He thanked her, ripped a slice in half, and dragged its soft, craggy edge through the sauce.

"Rémy can get you more stew," said Camille, nodding in the boy's direction.

"Rémy's his name?" Beau said. "Does he ever take a bath?"

Camille cracked a smile. "He's not fond of water."

She resumed her task—piping icing flowers onto a pair of cakes—and Beau let his gaze settle on her. She was petite, full-figured, and handsome, surrounded by the tools of her trade—a scale, pastry bags, bowls of icing, wooden spoons, spatulas, nutcrackers, and picks. He'd felt the rough edge of her tongue earlier in the day, but her brown eyes were warm and there was a sadness in their depths.

Sad people are kind people, he thought. *Keep her talking. Get her to open up. Maybe she'll tell you something useful.*

"They're pretty," he said, nodding at the cakes.

But before she could thank him for his compliment, a deep voice behind him barked out a command. "Finish up, thief. And see to your dishes. As soon as I've served dessert, I'm taking you back to your room."

It was Valmont. He walked to the other side of the table, picked up a chocolate torte on its porcelain stand with one hand, a chestnut cake with the other, and carried them out of the kitchen.

Beau cursed silently. He only had minutes to get the key but still no way of doing it. He gobbled down the rest of his meal, then carried his dirty dishes to the sink, lingering there for a few seconds to ask the kitchen boys if they needed help, but they shook their heads. His frustration growing, Beau glanced around. Camille was in the pantry. The chef was straining the contents of a stockpot. Rémy was wiping down the spits. The others were all busy finishing service. No one was watching him. His eyes shot to the doorway leading to the great hall. Valmont wasn't back yet but could be at any second. It was now or never.

Beau started walking, his gait slow and nonchalant even as he was fighting down the urge to run. Bit by bit, he closed the gap between himself and the basket, his hopes lifting with every step. Twenty feet . . . fifteen . . . ten . . . he was almost there.

And then the kitchen doors swung open, and Valmont appeared. His eyes skewered Beau. "Where do you think you're going?"

Beau stopped. "I want an onion," he said innocently.

Valmont's bushy brows shot up. "You want an *onion*?"

"I get hungry during the night."

"What about an apple?"

"I like onions," Beau said.

Valmont's scowl remained on his face, but his skeptical expression softened slightly. Beau felt excitement surge inside him. The key was *his*. "Just a small one," he rushed to say. "I can get—"

But Valmont cut him off. "Rémy!" he shouted. "Toss me an onion!"

The boy hurried to the basket, then grabbed a large onion and lobbed it. Valmont caught it and handed it to Beau.

Beau forced a smile as he took it. "Hey, a big one. Thanks."

"Let's go," Valmont said, giving him a push.

Beau's heart sank as they set off; his plans had disintegrated like a sandcastle in the waves. That key, the one he was now walking away from, was his only hope.

After Valmont had searched him earlier and returned to the castle, Beau had decided to have a look around. He'd made his way from the stables to the castle wall, and followed it until he found a set of stone steps notched into its side. They led up to a narrow walkway that ran along the top of the wall. He'd scrambled up the steps, and then he'd run the entire length of the wall. It had taken him over two hours. While he was up there, he'd discovered that Arabella had not lied to him about a bridge.

Outside the wall, the moat surrounded the castle in a long, unbroken ring, and there was nothing—no drawbridge, no footbridge—traversing it. Inside the wall, the castle's grounds appeared to be endless. They held gardens and pastures, barns for livestock, fields, a lake, and a forest. He had stopped at one point, taking in the illogical, impossible vastness, and it had seemed to him as if Arabella's domain was its own universe, contained and self-sufficient, with no need of the outside world. The thought had chilled him to his marrow.

Arabella didn't lie to you about a second bridge, and she might not be lying about a tunnel, either, a voice inside him had said. He'd squashed it. He needed there to be a tunnel.

The path to Beau's chamber was long and winding, and the lantern Valmont carried did little to dispel the gloom that pooled in the hallways and stairwells. They walked in silence, Beau trailing behind his captor, until finally, after about fifteen minutes or so, they reached the small tower room. As Valmont unlocked the door and ushered him inside, Beau saw that the bed had been made. A warm fire burned in the hearth. There was a fresh jug of water on the table and a clean glass. A taper burned in a tin candleholder.

The room was cleaner, warmer, and more comfortable than any in the dank rookeries where he'd lived with the thieves, yet he despised the sight of it. It made him feel as if he were an animal being shut up in a cage.

"If you think I'm so damn dangerous, why not lock me out?" he angrily asked as Valmont bade him good night. "Make me sleep in the stables? If I'm such a risk to everyone's safety, why keep me here?"

Valmont didn't deign to answer, but as the door closed, he muttered something. It was hard to hear him over the rattle of the key in the lock, but Beau was able to make out a few words.

"It's not for our safety, thief. It's for yours."

- THIRTEEN -

Josephine the washerwoman sat deep in her rocker, warming her old bones by the fire.

"After all these years, someone actually manages to raise the portcullis, and *this* is what wanders in?" she said disgustedly. "He's a waste of time. The worst of them all. There's no chance with him. None."

One of the maids, darning a sock at the servants' table, lifted her head.

"He's sneaky and sly," Josephine added. "A liar, a rogue, *and* a thief. All in one."

The maid burst into tears. She threw down her darning and ran from the room.

Lucile, the gardener's wife, a busy, bright-eyed woman, lowered her knitting. "Really, Josephine. Did you have to do that?" she scolded.

"Do what?"

"Dash Claudette's hopes. The poor girl's in love."

"In *love*?" Josephine echoed in surprise. "Who with?"

56

Lucile leaned forward in her chair. Her eyes gleamed in the firelight. "Florian!" she whispered.

"*Florian?*" Josephine said with a snort. "He's a half-wit. Can't she find someone better?"

"And where, exactly, would she do that? At the market? At a village dance?"

Josephine had the good grace to look shamefaced. "Well, I wouldn't pin my hopes on the thief if I were her."

A pall fell over the two women, and the rest of the servants, too. They were sitting in the kitchen as they did every night. The older ones relaxed in cushioned chairs close to the fire, drinking brandy. The younger ones sat around a long pine table, sewing or playing cards, and sharing a pot of hot chocolate.

Percival was the first one to break the silence. "Who did it? That's what I want to know. Who had the . . . the . . ."

"Balls?" Josephine offered.

"*Temerity,*" Percival continued, "to unlock the gatehouse, turn the winch, and raise the portcullis? And how did they get my key?"

Josephine cocked an eyebrow. "How do we know it wasn't *you?*"

The rest of the servants laughed.

"Not our Percival," said Phillipe, still wearing his white chef's jacket. He gave the underbutler a fond pat. "He's as loyal to the mistress as the day is long."

"Maybe it was *you*, Josephine. You're strong as an ox." That was the gardener, Gustave, a bulky man, wearing a woolly sweater and smoking a pipe. He nudged Percival. "She could've done it, you know. Why, just look at her hands . . . each one as big as a ham!"

"You're as stupid as a ham, Gustave," Josephine retorted. "I was sick in bed with a chest cold that night. Slept through the whole thing."

Gustave took a long, thoughtful pull on his pipe. "Valmont?" he said, breathing out a cloud of smoke.

Percival shook his head. "He was with me, playing cards." He pointed at the chef and the head groom in turn. "Phillipe, you can vouch for him. You were there." As the chef nodded, Percival turned back to the gardener. His eyes narrowed. "Maybe *you* did it, Gustave."

"Don't be ridiculous. I'm asleep by nine," said Gustave with a dismissive wave. "Claudette, perhaps? She certainly has a motive—she's in love."

"Claudette? Operate a *winch*?" Phillipe scoffed. "She can barely work an eggbeater."

"I think it was the kitchen boys," said Percival. "They're always up to no good. I asked them, but they denied it, of course."

As Phillipe poured more brandy, Gustave worked his way through the remaining suspects: Martin the farmer, and his daughter, Mirabelle. The huntsman, Jacques. Josette, the other maid. The footmen. The scullery girls.

Gustave had just proposed that Louise the seamstress, bent-backed and so thin she looked as if a summer breeze could blow her away, had done it, when they heard a noise. It was coming from the back door. It sounded like scratching, followed by a hard thump.

Percival jumped. "It's not midnight yet!" he said.

"It's only ten o'clock!" whispered an alarmed Lucile.

"So it can't be . . ." Gustave's voice trailed away.

"Then what is it?" Percival whispered.

Bears roamed within the castle's forest. Mountain lions. Wolves, too. One had killed a ewe just last week.

"Stand back!" Gustave shouted, rising from his chair. He pulled a pair of pruners from his trouser pocket and valiantly thrust them toward the door.

Henri grabbed a cleaver, Phillipe a carving knife. As they all crept closer, there was another loud thump, and then the door banged back on its hinges. Lucile jumped. Josephine gasped. But no slavering wolf, no lumbering bear, appeared. Instead, Camille emerged out of the cold night, shaking leaves from the hem of her cloak, the handle of a willow basket looped over one arm.

"Camille! You gave us a fright!" Gustave angrily shouted, shaking his pruners at her.

Camille looked at him in surprise, then put her basket down. "I'm sorry," she said. "The door was stuck."

"What on *earth* are you doing outside the castle at this hour?"

"Picking spiderbane," Camille replied, hanging her cloak on a hook. "There's a patch of it still alive under the old oak."

"Spiderbane? What do you want with that?" Gustave demanded. "It's poisonous!"

"Valmont sent me for it. He says it's not poisonous if it's mashed with silverstick and brewed into a tea," Camille countered. "He says it soothes the heart."

Gustave's scowl melted into a worried frown. "How is the mistress?"

Camille's eyes found his. "Restless."

"And Valmont thinks he can soothe her with a cup of tea?" Gustave asked, shaking his head.

"I'd better get busy," Camille said, picking up her basket and starting toward the pantry. "Midnight's not far away."

"Midnight's never far away," Lucile said, her eyes on the door.

"Where is Valmont?" asked Percival, his voice fretful.

"Making his rounds through the castle with Florian, checking that everything's locked down for the night," Gustave replied.

"Camille . . ." Percival called.

The baker stopped. She looked back over her shoulder. Her eyebrows lifted.

"Do your best. This is our last chance."

With a brisk nod, Camille was gone.

Gustave watched her go, then turned back to the others. In a hushed, conspiratorial voice, he said, "Maybe it was *her!*"

"Our little baker?" Phillipe said with a laugh. "She makes sweets, Gustave. Dainty cakes and tarts. Why, I have to get the heavy pots down off the shelf for her. Raising a portcullis is a man's work, and a strong one at that. Camille couldn't do it if she wanted to."

Gustave put a hand on Phillipe's shoulder. His blue eyes, rheumy and faded, were full of heartache. "*If*, my old friend?" he said. "There's no *if* about it. Of course she wanted to. We all want to. Who among us wishes to die?"

– FOURTEEN –

You sausage-fingered blockhead! How many times have I told you? A lock is like a woman. To woo her, you must ask, not demand. Listen, not speak. Give, not take . . .

Antonio's voice sounded inside Beau's head as he knelt on the floor of his room, working a silver pickle fork—one of its prongs bent back—into the lock on his chamber door.

Antonio was the one who'd shown Beau how to make the impossibly thin tension wrenches, the slender picks and rakes, and how to use them. He'd taught him how to see inside a lock with his hands instead of his eyes, how to listen as the pins and tumblers spilled their secrets.

Do those things, boy, do them well, and there's not a lock on earth you can't open.

"I *am* doing them well, Tonio," Beau said between gritted teeth, "but even you couldn't open a lock with a crappy little pickle fork!"

The fire had burned low, and the room had grown chilly, yet sweat dripped down Beau's face. He wiped it off with his sleeve, then turned the fork's handle once more, but the metal was too soft. The prong got stuck and wouldn't budge. Swearing furiously, he yanked until it came free, then threw it across the room.

"I'll never get out of here," he groaned, collapsing onto his backside. He'd spent hours working on the lock. It had to be past midnight now. He'd hoped to be on his way long ago, but here he was, still stuck in his room.

The wind howled outside like a vengeful spirit, its long fingers poking and prodding at the old stones of the tower, trying to find a way in. Beau knew this wind; he hated it. It was the same stalking wind that swirled around the convent on the edge of Barcelona. It scoured across his memories now as if it were scouring dirt off a grave, laying bare things long buried.

He squeezed his eyes shut against the images, but they came anyway. He saw thin, pale Matti, hunched over and coughing. The sound of it, harsh and rattling, echoing in his head got Beau up off his rear end. If only he hadn't lost Sister Maria-Theresa's letter. Then he'd know for sure that his brother had recovered.

He shook the tension out of his hands. Cleared his mind. And remembered Antonio's teaching.

Think of the lock as a lover's heart—guarded, wary, full of secrets. It longs to open itself to you, and it will, if you let it . . .

Beau saw his error. In his eagerness to break out, he'd been impatient and clumsy, digging into the lock with his makeshift tools like a thick-fingered dentist trying to pull a rotten tooth.

His candle stood in its holder on the floor next to him. He lifted it and peered at the lock. "You're iron and you're old," he said to it. "You're rusty, too, which means you've been neglected. If Antonio's right, if locks are like hearts, then yours is heavy."

Brow scrunched, Beau set the candle down and pawed through the objects he'd stolen earlier that day from the stables and the kitchen, all laid out on a napkin on the floor. A nutpick looked promising. He inserted the pointed end into the keyhole and turned it. It promptly snapped in half. Groaning, he pulled the broken piece out, then dug through his pile again, selecting a thin iron nail and a tine from a rake.

Patience, lad, patience . . .

Slowly, methodically, Beau worked the lock, prodding, coaxing, listening, until finally one pin shifted into place, and then his breath caught as the rest followed in a metallic symphony of scrapes, pops, and clicks. Few sounds were as beautiful to him as the deep, satisfying *thunk* of a bolt sliding back.

Moving quickly, he knotted the napkin around his tools and tucked the slender bundle into his waistband. Then he pulled the door open— not far, just enough. His thief's eyes had watched Valmont come and go and had noted the precise spot where the hinges creaked. He squeezed through the gap, taking his candle with him, leaving its holder behind.

"*Yes!*" he whispered as he stepped out of his room. There was still time to find the tunnel. With any amount of luck, he'd be long gone when Valmont came to rouse him.

Holding his candle high, Beau crossed the landing and started down the stairs. When he'd taken five or six steps, he glanced back at the door, but the gloom was so thick and the candlelight so faint, he could no longer see it. It was as if the night sensed him and surged toward him like a dark sea, eager to pull him under. He was surprised to feel a shiver rattle through him.

"Get a grip, you infant," he told himself.

He continued down the steep stairway as silently as a shadow, wary of making the slightest sound. The stairs ended in a broad landing on the east wing's third floor. Three long corridors snaked off it. Beau couldn't see them in the clinging darkness, but he'd memorized their locations. He had no idea where the ones on his right and left led, but the one straight ahead would take him to the castle's main stairway, which led down to the entry hall. From there, he would make his way through the great hall to the kitchen and then into the cellar.

He started for it, creeping quietly across the wooden floor.

And that's when he heard the sound, low and blood-chilling.

He tried to tell himself that it was only the wind. Or the rain. Stones settling. Timbers creaking.

But it wasn't.

It was the sound of growling.

– FIFTEEN –

Don't move. Don't flinch. Don't breathe, Beau's slamming heart warned him. *The wolf never runs before the rabbit does.*

So he listened. Like a mouse listens when the cat is near. With his ears, his flesh, his nerves, with every fiber of his being, and his body told him that the beast was crouching in the mouth of the very corridor where he'd meant to go.

Slowly, so slowly it did not look like he was moving at all, Beau raised his candle to his lips and huffed out its flame. He couldn't see the beast; now it couldn't see him, either.

The growling grew louder, more guttural. Beau heard a footstep, then another. It was moving toward him. The muscles in his legs snapped and jumped, telling him to run. Run fast. Run *now*. But he held himself steady. He knew he had only one small chance to escape.

Ten paces back to the staircase, he told himself. *Forty-two steps to the landing . . .*

Raphael had taught him to look for exits. Always. Everywhere. He'd learned to measure distances in his head, to memorize turns and corners and doorways. *Five paces across the landing to the chamber door . . .*

He took a deep, slow, silent breath, filling his lungs with air, and as he did, he cocked his arm back. Then he threw his candle as hard as he could, aiming for the corridor at his left, praying it made it through the archway.

He heard it land and roll along the floor. He heard the beast lunge out of its hiding place after it. And then he heard nothing but his own pounding footsteps as he flew back up the staircase.

He'd left the door to his room ajar, and the fire, still alive in the hearth, threw a sliver of light across the landing. He shot inside his room, slammed the door shut, and dropped to his knees. Frantically, he pulled the bundle of tools from his waistband and shook it open.

As he fumbled the rake tine and the nail into the lock, he heard footsteps on the stone stairs. He heard a growl rise into a snarl. Panic foamed over him like a storm surge. It caused his hands to shake. He dropped his tools.

"Come on . . . come *on*," he breathed, scrabbling them up again.

Go easy, boy . . . Take your time . . .

Antonio was back in his head, steadying his hands.

Soft and slow, like a first kiss . . .

The snarl was rising. The beast was on the landing. Beau's heart was in his throat.

In one last desperate move, he jammed the tine back into the lock and raked it along the pins, nudging the tumblers, and one by one they fell. Instead of the noisy *thunk* he'd made when he'd unlocked the door, this time there was only a soft *snick* as the bolt shot home.

64

A split second later, the beast slammed into the door. The impact sent Beau tumbling backward. As he sat on the cold floor, hands braced behind him, chest heaving, he heard it roar in fury. It hurled itself at the door again. And then Beau heard its snarl trailing away, as if the creature was retreating down the staircase. He held his breath. A long minute passed and then it was silent.

Beau let out a long, ragged exhale and flopped back on the floor, pressing the heels of his hands over his eyes. "You're a liar, Valmont," he whispered.

The beast wasn't a fantasy. It wasn't some figment of his wine-soaked imagination.

The beast was here. It was real.

And it wanted to kill him.

– SIXTEEN –

Lady LaJoyuse cast a worried glance around the breakfast table at her fellow courtiers. They did not look well.

Lady D'Eger, who'd grabbed the basket of muffins and eaten every single one, looked nauseous. Lady Piconisus, pale as a grub, skulked in a corner, refusing to eat anything at all. *The food's been poisoned*, she claimed. Lady Hesma picked at a scab on her chin. Lady Sadindi made a face at her and told her she was disgusting. Lady Rafe stirred spoonful after spoonful of sugar into her tea with trembling hands. Lady Romeser stood by a window, staring silently into the distance. Lady Espidra sat staring straight ahead of herself, fingers drumming on the arm of her chair.

They were all on edge. Because of the thief.

A movement across the table pulled LaJoyuse out of her thoughts. It was Lady Iglut. She'd risen from her chair and was walking toward Arabella.

"Just look at that bootlicker. Slinking around the mistress like a hyena," LaJoyuse hissed to Sadindi. "How I hate her."

Iglut draped an arm over the back of Arabella's chair. Her sleeve was wrinkled; her cuff was grimy. "A *second* helping of bacon, Your Grace? Are you sure that's a good idea?" she asked, her voice an oily gurgle.

LaJoyuse continued to watch her, simmering like a pot of gruel.

"Well, I suppose the dressmaker can always let a few seams out," Iglut added. "Better not to have eaten so much in the first place, but control was never your strong point, was it?"

Arabella's hands, resting atop the table, clenched into fists.

"Oh, what the devil. In for a penny, in for a pound, that's what I always say." Iglut picked up the empty platter. "Why don't we get some more? I'll fetch it myself."

"No, *I* will!" LaJoyuse shouted, unable to bear Iglut's toadying any longer. She shot out of her chair and ripped the platter from her hands.

Iglut gasped. "That was a *wicked* thing to do, Lady LaJoyuse. Though unsurprising, since you are a wicked person."

But LaJoyuse wasn't listening. She was already on her way to the kitchen. *Why does the mistress even tolerate Iglut?* she wondered. She, LaJoyuse, was a thousand times more appealing. She was smarter. Funnier. More stylish. Much prettier.

As she walked into the kitchen, LaJoyuse expected the servants to be in their usual places, grimly going about their work. She nearly dropped the platter when she saw them gathered around a worktable—all except for Valmont—laughing and shouting. Curious, she crept closer and saw what was making them so happy. It was the thief. He had something in his hands.

"Are you *sure*, Josette?" she heard him say. "The coffee bean's under *that* shell? That's definitely your pick?"

He flashed the young maid a smile—a knee-weakening, heart-fluttering, blush-inducing one.

"Yes! Yes!" she squealed, bouncing on her tiptoes. "I'm positive!"

LaJoyuse saw Florian give Josette a longing look. It was the worst-kept secret in the castle that he was in love with her. And that Claudette was in love with him. And that Henri was in love with Claudette.

"Josette's right! That's the one!" Camille called out excitedly. She was standing near the thief, a mixing bowl nestled in the crook of one arm.

Percival, spooning Darjeeling leaves into a teapot, agreed. "There's no question."

"You sure, Perce?"

"I am," Percival replied, fixing Beau with a stern look. "And do *not* call me *Perce*."

The chef—Phillipe—weighed in. "Of course it's the one. I saw it with my own eyes!"

Even the filthy little spit boy piped up. LaJoyuse wrinkled her nose at the sight of him. He was dirty and disheveled, as always. He stank of butter, rosemary, and other things that made her gag. Careful to avoid him, she skirted around the crowd and peeked over the top of Florian's shoulder.

Beau had three walnut shells on the table in front of him, lined up in a row. "All right, then, if you're really, really, *really* sure . . ."

"Yes! Yes! Go on, flip it over!" Josette urged him.

Beau heaved a deep, dramatic sigh. "I guess you've got me this time." Then he lifted the shell. There was nothing under it. "Ha! Got *you*!" he crowed, bursting into laughter.

The servants erupted into a cacophony of good-natured outrage.

"No way," said Florian, shaking his head. "You tricked us. It's not under any of the shells."

Beau smiled. He picked up the shell on his right. The bean was there. A cry rose—the happy dismay of those who have willingly been duped. Shouts of *Again! Do it again!* went up.

This isn't good, LaJoyuse thought. "The mistress requires more bacon," she loudly announced, holding the platter out.

The servants all stood to attention, shamefaced at having been caught playing. Phillipe ordered Henri to see to her request. As the boy took the platter from her, LaJoyuse moved closer to Florian—so close, in fact, that her arm touched his. As it did, his sunny expression darkened.

"Ah, the shell game," she said jovially. "Do continue. I enjoy a good magic trick."

The servants relaxed a little. Smiles returned to their faces.

"Show us how you do it, Beau!" Josette begged. *"Pleeeeease?"*

"That's not a good idea," said Florian, a disapproving set to his jaw. "If Valmont catches us fooling around—"

"Don't be such a spoilsport!" Josette scolded. "Valmont's not here, is he?"

Florian winced; he took a step back.

"Come on, Beau, show us!" Claudette cajoled.

Beau shook his head and said he couldn't reveal his secrets, but the maids kept pleading, and he relented. He turned his left hand over and revealed how he used his ring finger to pin the bean against his palm, then deposit it under whichever shell he liked. He invited her to have a try.

LaJoyuse watched Josette giggling and blushing and looking up at Beau as she clumsily tried to master the trick. She fumbled it again and again until Beau took her hand in his, pressed the coffee bean into her palm, and curled her finger against it.

A small, secret smile played about LaJoyuse's lips. She leaned toward

Florian and placed a hand on his forearm. "My goodness, but he's clever, isn't he?" she whispered.

Florian gave a brusque nod. "Yes, my lady. Very clever."

There was something new in his voice, something coiled and low. LaJoyuse heard it; her smile deepened. "He's fun, too, and God knows we could use a bit of *that* around here. Handsome as well," she added, a purr in her voice. "That *hair*. It's like"—she twined her fingers in the strand of pearls she was wearing—"like a waterfall of midnight."

Florian stiffened; LaJoyuse felt it. "And the body's not too bad, either," she continued. She gave a throaty laugh, then glanced sideways at Florian. "Oh. *Sorry*. That was rather inappropriate, wasn't it? Let's talk about his face instead. Those chiseled *cheekbones*, that *jaw*, and those *eyes*! Like brandy sparkling in a crystal glass. And my word, those *lips*—"

"*Josette!*" The word exploded from Florian.

The young maid turned to him, a quizzical expression on her face. "For goodness' sake, Florian, what is it?"

"We . . . we should go. There's work to do."

"I'm not going anywhere," Josette said with a toss of her head. Within seconds she was laughing with Beau again.

Fuming, Florian stalked off. LaJoyuse's smile was so wide now, she looked like a crocodile. She turned, looking for Henri. "How about that bacon, boy?" she drawled.

Henri had just finished stacking rashers on the platter. He carried it to her for her approval. "Shall I take it to the mistress, my lady?"

LaJoyuse tilted her head and regarded him. "Yes. Come, we'll take it together." As they started for the ballroom, she put a hand on his back, then in a hushed voice, said, "It seems rather unfair that Phillipe made *you* see to the bacon while Florian got to stay and watch the game. Then again, he *is* Chef's favorite, isn't he? It must be hard for you, Henri, being younger than Florian, and not as good-looking, and nowhere near as smart, and rather lacking in the personality department, and also . . . hmm, how shall I put it? *Frumpy.* Not that there's anything *wrong* with that . . ."

To LaJoyuse's delight, Henri's head dropped, inch by exquisite inch, until his gaze was on the floor. "You must resent Florian. Maybe even hate him? *I* certainly would," she continued, her voice sugared with fake sympathy.

"No, I . . . I don't, I . . ." Henri's voice broke. He lifted his head. His expression, always so eager and open, hardened. Something ugly surfaced in his eyes, like blood seeping through a bandage. "Yes, I do. I *do.*"

LaJoyuse smiled. She patted his back, pleased to know that she hadn't lost her touch, but her smile slipped as she walked with him down the corridor. If the thief could make the maids blush and the baker laugh and even get that fusspot of a Percival to crack a smile, what might he do to the mistress?

A fresh volley of laughter from the kitchen carried to her ears. *This won't do,* she thought as she reentered the great hall. Espidra, the rest of the court . . . they hadn't worked so hard for so long just for this interloper to come in and destroy everything.

They'd made a mistake. All of them, even Espidra—the strongest among them. They'd dismissed the thief, but he was different from the others who'd found their way to the castle, and he might prove more troublesome than they'd anticipated. After all, they didn't yet know what he was capable of.

Then again, she said to herself, *he doesn't know what we are capable of.*

The thought brought a smile back to her lips. "Be careful, young Beauregard Armando Fernandez de Navarre," she whispered as her eyes found Espidra. "You have no idea with whom you are dealing."

SEVENTEEN

"I'd take some more coffee," Beau said to Camille, sliding his empty cup across the table.

"Anything else His Lordship requires?" Camille asked, looking up from the batter she was stirring.

Beau smiled at her. "Another brioche? With strawberry jam?"

"Don't you have work to do?"

"The shell game *is* work. Took me years of practice to get good at it."

Camille nodded at the platter of pastries at the end of her worktable. "Help yourself. Coffeepot's on the stove."

Beau did, pleased. The request had been a small test—to see if he'd be permitted to leave Camille's work area and move around the kitchen— and he'd passed it.

He slathered jam on his brioche now like a mason troweling mortar. "This is so good. What do you put in it?" he asked.

A flush of pleasure filled Camille's cheeks at the compliment. "Rose water," she replied. "Just a drop."

She was warming to him. They all were. Because he'd delighted them with the shell game. Charmed them. Made them laugh. People would do anything for you if you made them laugh.

He was counting on that as he made his next request. "Can I have an onion, too?"

Camille gave him a quizzical look. "An *onion*?"

Beau laughed. "Who doesn't like onions?"

"Chopped and sautéed in butter, yes. Whole and raw? For breakfast?" Camille shook her head but gestured at the basket.

Yes! Beau silently shouted. He finished his brioche and walked across the kitchen, nodding cheerily at Phillipe as he passed him. Then Henri. Then Claudette. His cheeks felt like they were going to crack from all the fake smiling. He'd made these people like him, but he didn't like them. They were liars, every single one of them.

There *was* a beast, a brutal, murderous creature. Valmont knew about it; they all did. They must, yet no one spoke of it. Valmont had actually denied its existence right to Beau's face. When Valmont had fetched him from his room earlier that morning, Beau had wanted to lash out at him, to tell him how close he'd come to being torn apart last night, but he couldn't, not without revealing that he'd been out of his room. If Valmont knew that, he'd take away Beau's lock-picking tools and find him more secure accommodations—like a dungeon cell.

After he'd made it back to his room last night—barely—Beau had lain awake in his bed, realizing that it would now be a thousand times harder to escape, understanding that it would take all his skill and all his cunning just to get from his room to the cellar door. Wasting time picking locks with bad tools would get him killed. He needed the master key.

Beau had reached the baskets now. He glanced around quickly, to make sure no one was watching him. Camille was at the bread oven pulling out loaves. Phillipe and Rémy were threading game birds onto spits. The maids were in the pantry. Valmont had been called away from the kitchen but could return at any second.

Beau bent down to the onion basket and thrust his hands down into it, feeling for the key.

But it wasn't there.

He dug deeper, frantically pushing onions aside. His fingers scrabbled through the loose skins, seeking hard metal, but found nothing. A cold dread gripped him. What if he hadn't buried the key far down enough and someone had spotted it? He tipped the basket toward him and was just beginning to sweat when he saw it—a bright glint of brass.

"What the devil are you doing?" a brusque voice barked from behind him.

72

"*Damn* it," Beau whispered, his heart plummeting. He couldn't allow himself to be thwarted again. He had to get that key. Grabbing an onion, he turned and straightened. "I'm eating my breakfast," he said, giving Valmont a guileless smile.

The man was standing a few feet away, holding a heavy iron wrench. Florian and Henri were flanking him.

"*Really*. You're really going to eat that?" Valmont said skeptically, placing one hand on his hip. "I didn't see you eat the last one."

"I ate it. It was my midnight snack," Beau lied. He'd hidden it in a gutter outside his window.

He doesn't believe me. He thinks I'm up to something. Which I am, Beau thought, trying to keep his cool. He had to convince Valmont otherwise. He had to find a way to linger here. "What else would I do with it?" he asked.

"Go on, then," Valmont said, nodding at the onion.

"Go on what?" But Beau knew the answer.

"Eat it."

Beau's stomach knotted, but he gave a nonchalant shrug. "You're the boss."

He leaned back against the table, crossed one ankle over the other, and started to peel away the onion's papery skin, hoping that Valmont would miraculously be called away again and he wouldn't really have to eat the damn thing, but the man didn't budge. He just stood in place, holding his wrench like a club. Florian and Henri, still at either side of him, were goggle-eyed.

Beau finished peeling the onion. He regarded it, turning it this way and that in his hand, then bit into it as if he were biting into a fresh-picked apple.

It almost killed him.

The sharp flesh puckered his tongue; the fumes made his eyes water.

He took another bite, and another, chewing the raw mouthfuls and swallowing them, forcing his stomach not to heave them back up.

"Mmm, *so* good," he said as he finished it, wiping his mouth with the back of his hand. "Nice and juicy."

"I'll be damned," said Valmont.

"Never seen that before," Henri said.

"You boys don't eat onions? You should," Beau advised. "Onions make you handsome."

Josette walked by at that very moment. She overheard Beau's words. "Then you must've eaten a wagonload," she said, tossing him a flirtatious smile.

Florian looked at Beau with envy. Henri looked at the onion basket with hope.

"Mind if I take another one?" Beau casually asked. "Dealing with the copious amount of manure around here makes me hungry."

Valmont ignored the dig. He shook his head as if he couldn't believe what he'd just seen. "Take as many as you want," he said. "But the shoveling can wait. Get busy with the firewood first. These two usually do it"—he nodded at the kitchen boys—"but I need them this morning. Start with the great hall, then the ladies' quarters, then the kitchen. The wood's stored in an outbuilding next to the stables." He walked off. Florian and Henri followed him.

Excitement surged in Beau's veins. He'd gotten himself another crack at the basket. He bent over it again, plunged his hands into the onions, and worked them down to the bottom, where he'd glimpsed the flash of brass. His fingers quickly found the key and pushed it up his sleeve. As he straightened, he put his hand on his right knee and let the key slip out of his sleeve into his boot.

"Ah! Here's a nice one," he said, holding an onion up to admire, just in case anyone was still watching him. He dropped it into his jacket pocket, swiped a cinnamon stick from a bundle on the chef's worktable, and headed outside to find the firewood.

As he walked across the empty courtyard past the sad, dead gardens, he cracked a piece of the cinnamon stick off with his teeth and chewed it, desperate to get the taste of onion out of his mouth. A sudden gust of wind shrieked down on him, making him duck his head. It was late November, and the weather was turning.

That's the winter wolf howling. His fur is made of snow; his fangs are made of ice; his eyes are the gray of a stormy sky. Run when you hear him, boy. Lock the door and shutter the windows. He's bringing his whole pack with him.

Raphael had told him that when he'd first found him. Lying in an alley, his blood staining the snow. Then he'd pulled the knife out of Beau's chest, picked him up, and carried him home.

The wind dropped. It was muttering now. The skies were darkening. The temperature was dropping. Snow wasn't far off; Beau could feel it. A few inches and he could still get over the mountains; a few feet and he'd be trapped in the castle for months.

Beau buttoned his jacket up around his neck and walked on. The horrible feeling of helplessness that had possessed him last night was gone; a grim determination had taken its place.

He had the key. All he had to do now was wait until nightfall. He intended to be up in the mountains by this time tomorrow.

The beast had tried to kill him twice.

He'd be damned if he gave it a third chance.

- EIGHTEEN -

"Good morning, Your Grace."

Arabella, her elbows on the table, her chin resting on her hand, did not look up. She was focused on the game board in front of her. Her eyes roved over it like birds of prey.

And Beau's eyes roved over her, lingering on the jewels she was wearing—the haircomb, the pearls in her ears, the gold necklace, bracelets, and rings. His old mistress's ring would buy his way to Barcelona. He hadn't thought any further than that, and then he'd found himself a prisoner in Arabella's castle, but as he moved through the great hall, he realized that he would need more money once he actually got to the city. And just one of Arabella's baubles would bring enough to keep himself and Matti fed and housed for years. He moved closer to her, flexing his thief's fingers.

Beau tried again. "Um ... good morning, Your Most Excellent Majestyness?"

Irritation flickered across Arabella's features, telling him that she'd heard his greeting, but she still did not return it.

"Good morning, Your Highly Royal Excellentness? Your Most Gracious High-Up Ladyness? Your—"

"Stack the wood and be gone, boy."

The voice was Lady Sadindi's. Beau flashed a smile at her, and in return, he received a look sharp enough to etch glass. He hurried on his way, the muscles in his arms protesting under the weight of the firewood he was carrying.

The other court ladies were with Arabella in the great hall, just as they had been yesterday. "And they're just as weird as they were yesterday," Beau said to himself.

They didn't like him, that much was clear. He glanced at Lady Rafe, who shrank from him, even though he was nowhere near her. Lady Rega, angrily fumbling with tangled embroidery thread, threw him a look that said her troubles were all his fault.

76

Lady Espidra, seated at a spinning wheel, watched him expressionlessly, her sunken eyes following his every step. Beau met them but quickly looked away. There was something in her gaze that unnerved him, something hidden and dangerous.

Beau reached the great room's fireplace and leaned down to deposit the wood. As he did, the logs unbalanced themselves in their leather sling and tumbled to the stone floor, as noisy as a landslide. The ladies, startled, screeched at him like starlings.

"Clod!"

"Bungler!"

"Ninny!"

"Imbecile!"

Arabella, somehow still focused on her game, said nothing. Beau wondered how she could stand to have these women around her. It was clear that they relished the name-calling, the taunting and shaming, but strangely their bad behavior seemed to be almost protective of Arabella, as if they were wary of anyone else coming near her.

Beau hurriedly stacked the wood, then threw a few pieces on the fire. He'd had enough. He'd hoped to engage Arabella and relieve her of a ring or bracelet, but he'd rather lug firewood and shovel manure all day long than spend another minute in the presence of her court. He picked up the sling and headed back toward the kitchen, but as he passed by her again, he saw her reach for a chess piece, then frown and withdraw her hand.

Arabella didn't see her opening, but Beau saw his.

"Good call. Had you actually moved your queen to f6, your opponent would likely have used the Bovordunkian Defense and snared you in the Trockenbunger-Tinklepot Trap," he said.

"Can you *please* be quiet?" Arabella asked, her eyes still on the board. "Chess is hard work. It takes concentration, discipline, and silence."

"Pffft," Beau said. "So what?"

Arabella looked up at him, her focus shattered. *"So what?"* she repeated, ice in her voice. "You just ruined my game and that's all you have to say . . . *So what?*"

Her eyes caught his and held them. They were the silvery gray of a January dawn, and they made him stop dead. They made him catch his breath. They made the whole damn world fall away.

What's with you? Have you never seen a pretty face before? Shake it off, a voice inside him said.

Beau heeded it, playing toward his endgame. He dropped the sling, grabbed a dining chair, spun it around, and sat down at the table across from Arabella.

"I don't recall inviting you to sit," she said.

Beau ignored that. If he wanted to steal something from her, he had to get close to her. "Chess is a complete waste of time," he said, leaning his forearms on the chair's back. "Say you enter into an epic match. You play for eight hours straight. You don't eat or drink. As the hours go by, you become exhausted. Wrecked. You hit the limit of your endurance. And then, after this huge, giant struggle, you win." He pointed at her. "What do you have?"

"A victory," Arabella replied. "Now, if you'd be so kind—"

But Beau cut her off. "No. Nothing. You have *nothing*. You won a game. A *game*. Like checkers. Or tiddlywinks. Who gives a rat's flea-bitten ass? In all that time you just wasted, you could've picked a hundred pockets. Lifted scores of wallets. Nabbed a dozen watches. You could have made yourself a rich man. Or woman," he added.

"I already am a rich woman."

"Yes, you are," Beau said. He leaned across the table, helped himself to a piece of bacon from a platter, and crunched it. "I guess that's the difference between the rich and the poor. The poor work. The rich play games and call it work."

Arabella crossed her arms over her chest. "What a pompous, self-righteous, utterly asinine statement," she said. "Are you actually telling me that what *you* do is work? A thief is the ultimate freeloader."

Beau blinked at her. Her response was not what he'd expected, and it knocked him off course for a moment. He wasn't used to that, to a woman seeing through him, and he didn't know what to do. He opened his mouth, hoping something clever would come out of it, hoping he could recover his swagger.

But Arabella didn't give him the chance. "Show me," she said.

"No, Your Grace! He'll kill you!" yelped Lady Rafe.

"Have you lost your wits?" screeched Lady Hesma.

"Show me," Arabella said again, paying them no attention.

Beau cocked his head, confused. "Show you what?"

"Show me what you call work. Picking pockets, picking locks . . . those sorts of things." Arabella uncrossed her arms; she leaned forward. "You said the rich play games and the poor work. So come on, you insufferable, bloviating windbag, show me."

Beau let out a low whistle. *"Insufferable, bloviating windbag . . ."* he echoed. "I'm half insulted, half impressed. I myself would have gone with nasty-ass little fu—"

"I'm sure you would have," Arabella said. "Profanity is the refuge of the lazy."

"What the hell does that mean?"

Arabella did not acknowledge his joke. "Profanity is dull and unimaginative," she said. "Take a moment. Think. Then say what you actually mean. Were I to continue to describe you, *muck-spouting blockhead* or *shambolic, filching rook* would also hit the mark."

Beau nodded thoughtfully. "I see what you're saying. Were I to describe you, *puffed-up tosspot* or *toffee-nosed biggity pomp* would do the trick."

"Biggity pomp?" Arabella echoed in scornful disbelief. *"Biggity* isn't even a real—" She abruptly stopped talking, eyes darting to the doorway.

Her icy composure had cracked, just for an instant, and Beau had glimpsed a flash of heat underneath it. Discomposure was good; he could use it. His thief's senses sharpened. A huge piece of luck had just fallen into his lap.

"Do you really want to learn how to pick pockets?" he asked, before she could call for Valmont to remove him.

The question hung in the air and Beau's heart dropped. He was certain he'd lost her, but then she pulled her gaze from the door—reluctantly, as if fighting her better judgment—and returned it to him.

"Yes," Arabella said.

The ladies whispered among themselves, scandalized. *This is outrageous! Shameful! Disgraceful!*

"Consider your position, Your Grace," warned Lady Espidra. "He is nothing but a common criminal."

Nothing but a common criminal . . .

For an instant, it wasn't Espidra who was there speaking but the workhouse matron, hand raised, ready to slap him senseless. He shook off the memory. This was no time to become distracted.

Arabella's eyes dropped back to the chessboard. He walked around the table to where she was sitting and held out his hand. She looked at it but did not take it.

"Believe it or not, I actually don't have all day," he said.

After a long moment, Arabella—hands resolutely at her sides—rose from her chair. Beau caught her scent. She smelled like a rich girl: vetiver, leather, linen, books.

"I've seen enough," said Lady Hesma.

She left the room. The others followed her, casting baleful glances behind themselves, clucking their tongues, shaking their heads. Only Lady Espidra remained, sitting by her spinning wheel, as still as a spider.

Beau went to work. *Don't be greedy*, he told himself. *Greedy thieves get caught. All you need is one piece of jewelry. Just one.*

"Um, actually . . . not here," he said to Arabella, frowning in mock concentration. "I need space." He took her arm and steered her toward the fireplace, but when they got there, he stepped around to her other side. "Nope. This is no good, either. How about there?" He pointed at the area between the far end of the table and the doorway. He took her other arm, guiding her past the mantel, ducking around a chair. "I—oh! *Ow!*" He stumbled; his free arm flailed. Arabella whirled around to catch him. She put a steadying hand on his chest, trying to keep him upright. He felt its warmth through his shirt.

"What's wrong?" she asked, her forehead creasing with concern.

"Sorry," he said, wincing. "I stubbed my toe." He leaned into her, forcing her to take his weight. His hands were on her arm one second, her shoulder the next, her waist. He could feel her chest heave as she struggled to support him. "I think I broke it. It hurts like a son of a—no . . . hang on . . . wait a minute . . ." He scrunched up his face and pretended to think. "It hurts like Satan heated his favorite pitchfork in the sulfurous flames of Hades and drove it straight into my mortified muscles, my torn tendons, my suppurating, septic wound, my—"

"I think you've made your point," Arabella said. She staggered a little, straining against his weight, then thrust her body forward again. Beau waited for a few seconds; when he felt her arms quiver, he righted himself.

Arabella let out a long, weary breath as he did. "Are you sure you're all right?" she asked, straightening.

Beau nodded. "This way," he said, continuing on, his arm entwined with hers. When they finally reached the center of the room, he released her.

"Well?" she said, looking at him expectantly.

Beau tilted his head. "Well, what?"

"Are you going to show me how you rob people or not?"

"Hold out your hands."

Arabella hesitated. "Why? So you can take my rings? Will you give them back?"

"What rings?" Beau asked, a grin spreading across his face.

Arabella looked down at her hands and gasped. They were bare.

"*What?* Where did they . . . it *can't* be . . . how did you . . ."

She raised her eyes to Beau. The ice inside them had melted. They were sparkling now with a giddy mixture of awe and joy. She looked like a child who'd just seen the most astonishing magic trick.

"Ha. *Ha!*" she said, shaking her head. "That's impossible. It's incredible. It's amazing. *You're* amazing. Ha."

Beau felt a rush of pride. No one had ever called him amazing. Far from it. It was a strange feeling, foreign and new, and he wasn't sure it suited him. Like the beautiful things he saw in fancy shopwindows, it seemed meant for someone else.

"Where are they?"

Beau took her hands and drew them together in a bowl shape. Then he dipped his hand into his jacket pocket. Out came a ring. He held it up before Arabella's astonished eyes, then placed it in her hands. Three more rings materialized. Her necklace. Her pearl earrings.

It was necessary to make a show of returning her things, to drag it out. That way, it would feel like he'd returned everything.

Arabella stared at the growing pile of jewelry, dumbstruck. Then she looked up at Beau. "How did you do it?"

"By distracting you, misdirecting your attention. Leading you one way, then the other, bumping into you, pretending to trip."

"Teach me," she said eagerly, dumping her jewelry on the table.

"Do not do this," Espidra said tersely. But neither Arabella nor Beau heard her.

"First tell me why you want to learn how to rob people," Beau said. "You certainly don't need the money."

He was still engaging her. Distracting her. Keeping her attention fully on him. Making sure she didn't suddenly decide to put her jewelry back on and notice that one piece was missing.

"I like to learn new things."

"How about a language?"

She waved the idea away. "I speak seventeen."

Beau shot her a skeptical look. "No one speaks seventeen languages. Two if you live in the borderlands. Four or five if you work for a king. But more than that? Only if you're some kind of genius."

Arabella looked away. "Yes. Well." Then she raised her eyes to his again. "Teach me. This is your job now. Or would you rather stack firewood?"

Beau considered her offer, then he held up a finger. "First lesson . . . the things right in front of you are the hardest ones to see."

Arabella tilted her head. "I don't understand."

Beau moved toward her. When he stopped, his face was only inches from hers. *Glad I swiped that cinnamon stick*, he thought.

"Here I am, standing close to you. A bit too close."

"A bit," Arabella said, clearly uncomfortable.

"You see my face, but what can't you see? My fingers, hovering by your wrist. Why? Because you're distracted by my extreme gorgeousness."

Arabella snorted.

"You're so taken by my soulful brown eyes, melting like chocolate in the sun, so warm that you could bathe in them . . ."

"If I bathed in chocolate."

"And my strong, noble nose . . . my full mouth . . ."

"That never seems to close."

"Where are my hands all this time, Arabella?"

"I—I don't know."

"Because you're distracted."

"I certainly am *not*."

Beau stepped back and held his hands high. Three bracelets were threaded between his fingers.

"Wait . . . *what*?" Arabella cried, delightedly outraged.

"The other thing you have to learn is to make your hands clever and fast," Beau said. He walked to the table, put the bracelets down, and picked up a ring. "See if you can take this from my pocket without me noticing. Don't worry about being fast yet. Go slow. Use small, light movements."

Arabella nodded, excited now. She waited for Beau to prepare himself and turn around, then she pounced on him. Her movements were so clumsy, she may as well have been trying to stuff a brick in his pocket. At first, she nearly pushed his britches down—he grabbed his waistband just in time—and then, as she tried to get her hand out again, she tugged them up too high.

"Ooof! *Ow!*" he gasped.

Arabella pulled her hand free. "Sorry," she said, wincing.

"Remember: *small, light* movements," Beau said, fixing his britches. "I'm not supposed to feel anything."

He turned his back to her again. Arabella took a deep breath and slid her hand in his pocket once more. This time, his britches stayed up.

"That's better."

Encouraged, she grabbed a handful—but not of jewelry.

Beau yelped. "Ow! *Hell!* It's the ring you want to make off with, not my left butt cheek!"

Arabella's hands came to her mouth. "I'm so sorry!" she said, flustered. "I'm not . . . I—I never meant to—"

Beau held up his hand. "Apology accepted. I *do* have a great ass, but focus, Bells, *focus*."

Arabella's cheeks flushed bright pink. "My name isn't *Bells*, and I—"

"Try again. Pretend I'm a rich man who's had one too many. I'm strolling through the Palais-Royal in Paris. It's midnight, the party's just getting started. There's music. Dancing. Acrobats are performing. I'm watching a beautiful aerialist high up on a trapeze. She's a goddess. I can't take my eyes off her. Here's your big chance . . ."

He turned once more, then felt a slight pull at the back of his britches, like a fish tugging at a hook. A second later, Arabella was holding up the ring and crowing.

"Ha! *Look!* I did it! I *did* it!"

"Much better. But you used too many fingers. I felt them." He took her hand in his and smoothed it flat. "Pointer and middle are all you need." He folded her other fingers, and her thumb, flush against her palm. "Use them like a pair of tweezers," he instructed. Then he reached around behind her and plucked the comb from her hair. "See? Easy!"

Her lush tresses tumbled around her shoulders.

"My hairdo!" she cried.

"It's more of a *hairdon't* now."

"Give it *back*," she said, swiping the comb from his fingers. She put it between her teeth, twisted her hair up, then fixed it in place. It looked like a squirrel's nest. "What?" she said, reading Beau's amused expression. She pushed a stray tendril out of her face.

"Maybe you should leave it down. It looks nice down."

He plucked the comb from her hair again and put it in her hand. And then, because they were standing so close, but not talking anymore, and it was a little awkward, he smiled at her.

It was his seducer's smile, shrugged on like an old sweater. He didn't even think about it. He'd used it on every woman he'd ever known. It was a slow-burn grin, full-lipped and full of promises.

It was effective, devastating.

It was a mistake.

Arabella yanked her hand away. She stepped back, looking as if she'd tasted something bad, something bitter.

"Bells?" Beau said, somewhat uncertainly. "Ready for the next lesson? Picking locks? We'll need—"

She cut him off. "My name is Arabella. And I'm finished, thank you."

"But—"

She turned in a circle, frantic, her eyes scanning the room.

"I am here, child. I am always here."

Arabella gave a soft cry of relief as she found Espidra. She did not appear pleased, though, to see her lady-in-waiting. The light went out of her eyes; her shoulders slumped.

"Tell Valmont I shall take my dinner in my chambers today," Arabella said to her, then she left the room, hands knotted, heels pounding across the floorboards.

Espidra rushed after her. She caught up with her right before she disappeared through the doorway. "Foolish girl. I warned you," Beau heard her say as she put a thin arm around Arabella's shoulders. "Go to your chambers. I shall join you there with a nice pot of tea."

Arabella nodded, and then she was gone. For a second time, Beau's silver tongue failed him. He didn't know what to say, what to do. He felt like a champion marksman who'd picked up his rifle one day only to find he no longer had any idea how to hit a target.

"Arabella, hang on, I didn't . . . I wasn't—" he called after her, but it was too late.

Flirting with you, he was going to say. *Toying with you. So I can get what I want from you.*

He'd rattled Arabella and he didn't know why. Which rattled him. She mystified him. Intrigued him. Why did she want to pick pockets? How had she learned to speak seventeen languages? He found himself remembering the excitement in her voice. The warmth of her touch. The light in her eyes. And missing them.

Drop it, he told himself. He'd had fun teaching Arabella. He'd enjoyed showing off, but he had a bigger goal in mind than a silly flirtation. And he'd gotten what he wanted—one of Arabella's rings.

He'd kept it back as he'd piled the rest of her jewelry into her hands, and in her excitement, she hadn't noticed its absence. He doubted she would; she had so many others. The band was simple, but the setting contained three sapphires. He and Matti would be warm and well fed this winter.

He was just about to leave the great hall when he heard the voices again, voices that were always inside his head, telling him he was nothing but a thief. And then he heard a new voice. Talking over them. Silencing them. *Her* voice.

That's impossible. It's incredible. It's amazing. You're amazing . . .

Beau glanced at the pile of jewelry still sitting atop the table, where Arabella had left it, and the strangest desire gripped him—the desire to return the stolen ring. The desire to be something more than a thief.

Cursing his own foolishness, he pulled the ring from his pocket, walked over to the table, and dropped it on top of the other jewels. As he did, a voice spoke.

"Monsieur Beauregard . . ."

Beau jumped. His eyes sought the speaker and soon located her. It was Espidra. She was standing in the shadows of the doorway. He'd had no idea she was still there.

"I believe I have something of yours." She pulled a small, crinkled envelope from her bodice and held it out to him. "I found it earlier this morning. Under a rug in the entry hall. You must have dropped it in your eagerness to leave us."

It was all Beau could do to not snatch the letter from her hand. "Thank you, Lady Espidra," he said as he took it.

Espidra acknowledged his thanks with a dip of her head and left the room. As soon as she was gone, Beau ripped the envelope open. As he read the letter, dread drained the color from his face.

2 November 1785

Dear Beauregard,
I received your letter and write back in great haste.
Matteo's illness has taken a turn for the worse. It is consumption. I am so sorry. We are doing what we can, but he needs a doctor and medicine, and we are a poor order and cannot afford them.
You must come for him immediately. Our abbey, already damp and cold, grows more so as winter approaches and makes his condition worse. With proper care, he might have a chance. Without it, he will not live to see Christmas.

Yours,
Sister Maria-Theresa

The child watched from the corner of her cell as the woman sat down at the table.

"Another visit? So soon? You must be worried."

"Not worried, *bored*," said Lady Espidra, placing a carved rosewood box on the table.

The child took a seat across from her guest. She smiled sweetly, then said, "What shall we play? Canasta? Whist? How about *bridge*?"

Espidra's thin lips thinned even more.

"Find out who did it yet?" the child taunted.

"No, but we will."

"The visitor is ruffling feathers. He certainly ruffled Lady Rega's. I heard the carnage all the way down here."

"Don't be so smug," Espidra chided, opening the box. "You don't have much longer. You're fading fast."

The child held her hands up in front of her face. She could see Espidra through them. "Be careful what you wish for," she said as she lowered them. "You need me. You can't exist without me."

"Nonsense. I can't wait to be rid of you," Espidra retorted.

She reached into the box, pulled out a folded game board, and opened it. A neat grid of half-inch squares had been carefully drawn upon it. Happy little hand-painted cherubs frolicked in fluffy white clouds around the grid's border. They blinked their eyes now, startled by the light. Some chattered or giggled; others flew around the board. Espidra handed a small stand carved from bone to the child. She placed a second one down on her side of the board. Then she pushed a cloth sack across the table. The child opened it and pulled out an ivory tile. It had a letter drawn on it.

"*A!*" she crowed.

Espidra snatched the bag back and pulled out a Z. Glowering, she tossed the tile back into the bag, shook it, drew out seven new tiles, and put them in her stand. After the child had done the same, Espidra took a small hourglass from the box, turned it upside down, and placed it on the table. Glittering bloodred sand flowed through it.

"Rega's a problem. Always was," the child said, rearranging her tiles. "But you know that, and you use it. You use *her*."

"Nonsense. She's Arabella's creature."

The child frowned ruefully. "The old Arabella wanted nothing to do with her."

"What *did* the old Arabella want?" Espidra asked archly. "Shall I tell you?"

"No."

"Far. Too. *Much*."

The child rolled her eyes.

"You know it's true," Espidra insisted. "She refused to be what girls should be."

"And what is that?"

"Sweet, gentle, and kind. Also? Forbearing. Unselfish. Obliging. Accommodating. Forgiving. Uncomplaining. Self-sacrificing. Gracious. Submissive . . ."

"Are you finished?"

"I'm just getting started. Understanding. Undemanding. Amiable. Trusting. Docile. Untroublesome. Agreeable. Amenable. Sympathetic. Empathetic. Caring. Self-effacing. Soft-spoken. Peaceable. Compliant. Compassionate. Patient. Tractable. Unoppressive. Even-tempered. Mild. Charming. Obedient. And nice."

Sighing, the child picked up several of her tiles and began to lay them down on the grid. "Funny thing, isn't it? Men want the whole world, and because they want it, they take it. Caesar, Alexander, Tamerlane, Attila,

Charlemagne, Ashoka, Genghis Khan . . . and soon a new man, a short one . . . Bonaparte. But a woman? She is not allowed to want things, never mind take them. She must not take the lead, take initiative, or take charge. She must not even take a piece of cake." She placed her last tile down and brightened. "There! Seven letters. One hundred and seventy-four points." The little cherubs, seeing the word, clapped their pudgy hands.

"*Floruit?* That's not a word," said Espidra.

"It is. In fact, it's one of my favorite words. It comes from the Latin *florere*, which means to bloom, to flourish, to be at the peak of one's powers. Rather like me."

Espidra snorted.

"Are you challenging it?" the child asked, reaching for more tiles. "If you do and you're wrong, you lose your turn."

Espidra's lips cinched tight, like the strings of a miser's purse. She picked up one of her own tiles, put it back down again, then picked up another.

"Here we go . . . *doomed!*" she exclaimed, laying her tiles down to incorporate the *o* in *floruit.* "That's one of *my* favorite words. It means likely to have an unfortunate and inescapable outcome. Also rather like you. That's what . . . let's see . . . one hundred and fifty-two points."

The cherubs looked at the word. Their smiles faded. Their wings drooped.

The child regarded her opponent with a look of contempt. "You're like some poisonous mushroom, feeding on broken things. No wonder you've grown so strong."

"Tsk tsk," said Espidra, reaching for the bag of tiles. She turned the hourglass. Then she and the child battled across the game board for over an hour, until all the tiles had been used and their scores were tied.

"Shall we play again?" the child asked, sitting back in her chair.

Espidra was quiet for a moment, then she said, "Have you given my offer any consideration?"

"Not for a second."

Espidra's gaze hardened. "You try my patience, girl. Leave. While you still can, or it will not go well for you."

The child leaned forward, her gaze equally flinty. "Where are the others?"

"How should I know? Gone? Dead? Not here, at any rate."

"I don't believe you. I think you locked them away, too."

"Think what you like; the clock is ticking. *Au revoir*."

The child watched as Espidra stood. As she crossed the room. As the heavy iron door swung open, then slammed shut.

The child's glow, already wan, dimmed. She looked down at the board and picked out seven letters from the words there—E-S-P-I-D-R-A—and began to rearrange them.

The painted cherubs watched her, curious at first, but they fearfully flew away and hid behind the clouds when they saw what she had spelled out.

DESPAIR.

– T W E N T Y –

Beau felt like he was climbing into his own grave.

The stone steps that spiraled down into the cellar were narrow and steep. The smell that rose from the cellar's depths was a mixture of damp earth and old wood.

Spiders, centipedes, and other things with too many legs scuttled over the walls. But the worst thing was the darkness. It swirled around Beau like a dense fog. The weak flame of his single candle did little to dispel it.

But Beau didn't let the darkness slow him. He flew down the treacherous steps, heedless of the danger. When he'd read Sister Maria-Theresa's letter, he'd had to muster every ounce of self-control he possessed not to bolt for the cellar door right then and there. It had been agony waiting for nightfall, for the servants to leave the kitchen hearth and go to bed, for the castle to grow quiet. Christmas was only a few short weeks off and he was a long way from Barcelona.

He'd waited to leave his room until he heard the golden clock in the great hall strike eleven, hoping that the servants would be asleep by then, and the beast in its den, wherever that was. He didn't know when the fearsome creature rose and prowled, but the two times he'd seen it had been just after midnight. Letting himself out of his room with the master key, he'd crept through the castle, expecting to hear footsteps behind him at every turn. By the time he'd reached the cellar door, he was drenched in sweat.

"Hang on, Matti. Just hang on," he whispered now as he reached the bottom of the stairs. "I'll be there soon."

All he had to do was find the tunnel. He'd been in the cellars of the rich. He knew that there would be several rooms containing foods that had been salted, fermented, and sugared, plus a wine vault, and that it wouldn't take him long to walk through them.

Then he raised his flickering candle high and saw that he was wrong. Arabella's cellar didn't comprise a few rooms; it was vast. He was standing at the threshold of the castle's wine vault, and it was as big as a church. Giant wooden barrels were stacked three high in its center. Casks of brandy, cognac, and port lined its walls.

"Every man, woman, and child in France could get drunk in here," he whispered. He walked to one of the barrels in the center of the room, wiped away dust, and saw the name of a château branded into the wood. With a clutch of recognition, he realized that he knew the place.

It bordered the lands of the merchant whom he, Raphael, and the others had robbed, but the château was a ruin; it had burned down fifty years ago.

"Must be an old vintage," he murmured.

Cobwebs kissed the top of his head as he left the vault and made his way along winding passages and in and out of doorless rooms. In one chamber, hams, each as big as a small child, hung from the ceiling, and salamis dangled as thick as vines in a jungle. He grabbed one and stuffed it inside his waistband, like the dagger he used to keep there. He had no idea how long it would take him to get from the castle to the nearest town, and the salami would keep hunger at bay.

In another room, rounds of salted butter sat atop blocks of ice, and cloth-wrapped cheeses lay nestled on shelves. He glimpsed cones of white sugar and slabs of chocolate, pots of honey, candied chestnuts, pickles and chutneys, tins full of costly spices, crates of tea, and sacks of coffee beans.

"There's enough food here to last a century," he said as he hurried out of one room and into the next. His words unnerved him. He'd uttered them as a joke, but they weren't—they were true: There *was* enough food here to feed Arabella and her servants for a hundred years. Why would anyone need so many provisions?

It was yet another question that would never be answered, but Beau had no time to dwell on it. He guessed he'd wasted a good half hour already, wandering from room to room. He started down yet another corridor, but when he reached the end of it, he once again found no door, no gate, no gaping earthen mouth—just another room.

Panic scuttled through his thoughts like a mouse through hay. Just how big was this cellar? How many rooms would he have to walk through? What if he didn't find the tunnel and was still down here when dawn broke?

Half walking, half running now, Beau entered another room, this one filled with root vegetables in bins and glass jars of preserved fruits. Flustered, he never saw the turnip sitting in the middle of the floor, perhaps knocked from a shelf by one of the kitchen boys. His foot came down squarely on top of it. It rolled to the left, pitching him to the right. He lost his balance and hit the floor with a bone-jarring thud.

His candle flew out of his hand and landed in a crate of potatoes. It guttered briefly, then snuffed out.

Darkness filled Beau's eyes; dampness filled his nose. He was lying face-down on the dirt floor. His knees and elbows had taken the brunt of his fall; they were throbbing. Fear's rancid breath chilled the back of his neck. His candle was gone; he could see nothing. He rose to his feet shakily, took a few steps, and smacked his shin against something hard. As he bent down to rub the fresh pain away, he whacked his head against a shelf. There was a clinking sound, and a second later, a smash. A sweet scent rose.

"One less jar of applesauce in the world," he said through gritted teeth.

He turned the other way, hands out in front of him, flailing at the darkness. His sleeve caught on something. An instant later, a pumpkin tumbled to the floor.

"Stop. Calm down. Think, Beau. *Think.*"

Beau took a deep, balancing breath, and saw that all was not lost. If Valmont or Florian came looking for him, he could hide. The cellar was a dark, twisty rabbit warren. He could crawl behind the casks of port or tuck himself under the cheeses. They'd never find him.

And then, tomorrow night, when everyone was asleep again, he would make his way back to the stairwell, head to the kitchen for another candle, and resume his search. He didn't relish the thought of bedding down with the mice and the bugs, but he'd endured worse.

In the meantime, he was in no danger of starving down here. He could help himself to any delicious thing he desired. As if on cue, his stomach squeezed. He pulled the salami from his waistband and took a big, anxious bite.

That's when he heard the weeping.

– TWENTY-ONE –

Beau couldn't see in the darkness, but he could hear.

Whoever was crying was not far away.

Beau's first panicked thought was that it was the beast, but he quickly dispelled it. The beast growled, snarled, and roared; it didn't weep. Was it one of the maids? A kitchen boy? Had they heard him? Would they tell the others?

Beau tucked the salami back into his waistband, and then, like a night creature, he let his ears navigate him toward the sound.

Hands stretched out in front of him, he took a few careful steps. His fingers found the doorway. He felt his way out of the room and along the walls of another corridor. A sudden emptiness under his hands signaled the entryway to another room. He walked through it, ever deeper into the cellar. He turned into another room, but the weeping grew fainter, so he turned back and retraced his steps until it grew louder.

Two more rooms, another corridor, a sharp turn, and then he saw it— a thin crack of light, about two feet wide, running along the floor.

Beau stopped, surprised by the sudden glow. He walked toward it and his outstretched hands found rough wood. The light was seeping out from under a door, and the sobs, high and thin, were coming from behind it. His hands found the knob and slowly turned it, but the door was locked. His experienced fingers moved over the keyhole; they told him it was the type of lock that could only be turned from the outside. Whoever was behind that door had been locked in.

Warring impulses clashed within him. The person inside the locked room was a prisoner and clearly needed help, but he wasn't in a position to give it. The only one he needed to help was Matti. But the prisoner had a candle or a lantern. If he could get hold of it, maybe he could still find the tunnel.

Beau's hand dipped into his pocket and pulled out the key. He would open the door; that was enough help. Then he would take the prisoner's light and go. His help came with a price. Everyone's did.

Quickly, so that he could keep the element of surprise on his side, Beau inserted the key into the lock, turned it, and wrenched the door open. He tensed, ready to fend off an attack, but except for a few pieces of furniture, it appeared that the room was empty. He took a step into it, and as he did, something grabbed his ankle.

Beau yelped. He jerked his leg hard, trying to break free, but whatever had hold of him only tightened its grasp, digging deeper into his flesh. He looked down and saw that a hand was circling his ankle. A child's hand, small and grubby.

A ragged breath trailed out of Beau. His fear trickled away and fury took its place. Why was a child locked away in a cold, damp cell? Who had done this terrible thing? The beast? Images rose in his memory—of his brother, of the cruel workhouse matron. He pushed them away.

Then slowly—holding the key in one hand and raising the other to show he meant no harm—he knelt down and peered at the child.

A girl peered back. She was sitting on the floor of the cell. Her dirty blond hair fell across her eyes. Her cheeks were tearstained. She was covered in grime, yet her face glowed with a pale, flickering light. She reminded Beau of a candle flame, buffeted by the wind.

The girl released Beau. She scrambled to her feet and backed away, trembling. She was wearing a pink dress. Its hem was ragged, its collar torn, its skirts smudged with dirt. She was small, no more than four feet tall, and Beau saw now, to his amazement, that her whole body glowed with the same pale light that infused her face. The light he'd seen spilling out from under the door hadn't come from a candle or lantern; it had come from her.

Her eyes, huge and fearful, met his. "It's not safe here," she whispered. "She's coming."

"Who's coming? And who are you?"

The child didn't answer. She took a few hesitant steps toward Beau, who was still crouched down on one knee. "Don't let her find you," she said. "She's dangerous. She locked me in here."

"Who's *she*? Espidra? One of the court ladies? Why are you so afraid of her?"

Quick as a snake, the girl darted past Beau and out of the cell. She was so fast, and so nimble-fingered, he didn't realize she'd snatched the brass key from his hand until he saw it in hers.

"Hey! Give that back!" he cried, getting to his feet.

The little girl shook her head. She was no longer weeping, no longer trembling. She was backing down the hallway now, grinning, and Beau saw it had all been a ruse.

"Later, alligator," she said, twiddling the key between her fingers. "And, hey . . . thanks!"

- TWENTY-TWO -

So this is what it feels like to be dumb, Beau thought. *Huh. Now I know.*

The child had tricked him, well and truly. It was so shocking, so completely disorienting, that for a long, painful moment, he did not know what to do.

"Wait. Hey. Stop. *Stop!*" he shouted after her.

"Not a chance."

98

"I want my key back. *Now*," he thundered, pulling his dagger from his waistband.

He expected her to be terrified at the sight of the blade, to toss him the key immediately. Instead, she snorted laughter. "Or what? You'll make me eat a charcuterie plate?" She nodded at his weapon.

Beau glanced at the knife he thought he was holding and saw that it was, in fact, a salami.

"Son of a—"

"Can I get a piece of cheese with that?" the little girl taunted. "Some quince paste?"

Beau threw the salami down. "I want that key back," he growled. "You stole it."

"That's rich coming from you," said the girl. She dropped the key into her skirt pocket.

Desperation stabbed at Beau. He tried a new tack. She was just a child, a child who'd been cruelly imprisoned in the darkness. He would show her some fake sympathy.

"Who locked you away down here, little girl?"

"Lady Espidra."

"When?"

The girl tilted her head. "Mmm, about a hundred years ago."

"A hundred years ago," Beau said flatly.

"Give or take a decade."

"Little girls shouldn't tell fibs."

"Neither should grown men. They also shouldn't steal stuff."

Beau's entire body went cold. "How do you know—"

She cut him off. "I'd love to stay and chat, but I have work to do. I'd advise you not to linger down here, either. Ta-ta."

And then she turned and ran, taking her light with her. The darkness wound Beau in its tentacles again.

"Wait!" he shouted, starting after her. "Don't go!"

The little girl had a strange effect on him. She drew him like a beacon, and he found he couldn't bear to lose sight of her. She would lead him out of the darkness. Back to the stairwell. To the kitchens. If he was lucky, there would still be time to snatch another candle. To find the tunnel and escape from this horrible place. To get to Matti and make him better. He could do these things. All of them. He *would* do them. Nothing could stop him.

But the child was diabolically fast, and he had to run to keep her in his sights. She sped through rooms and down hallways, rounded corners at breakneck speed. She reached the stairwell quickly and dashed up it, taking two steps at a time.

Beau emerged in the kitchen a few seconds after she did, panting for breath, and found her standing in the middle of the room, her head tilted, listening. As he started toward her, she whirled around, pointed at the long worktable, and said, "I'd duck under that if I were you. Right about . . . *now.*"

"Valmont? Percival? Is anyone here? Camille?" a voice called from a corridor. "Her Grace is unsettled. She requires a pot of tea."

Beau ducked under the table just as Lady Espidra and Lady Rega entered the kitchen. He heard them stop dead and gasp. Balancing on his fingertips, he leaned forward, the better to see them.

Espidra, her eyes impossibly wide, reached for Rega and gripped her arm so tightly, her nails pierced Rega's skin. Blood seeped up under their sharp points. Astonishingly, Rega seemed not to feel it. Her gaze was fastened on the girl; her expression was murderous. Lady Hesma had followed them into the kitchen. She stumbled backward now, shielding her eyes with their hands, as if the child's wan, flickering light blinded her. Behind her, half a dozen other ladies whispered and hissed like a nest of vipers.

"You," Espidra said. "How did you get out?"

"I'll never tell," the girl said with a wink.

"Seize her! Take her back to the cellar!" Espidra shouted at Rega.

"I think not," the girl said.

In the blink of an eye she jammed the key into the cellar door's lock, turned it, and then she was gone, running out of the kitchen through a doorway.

Beau's heart hit the floor. His chance at freedom was gone, too. The cellar door was locked now. How could he resume his hunt for the tunnel without the key? He tried to see which way the child had run, so he could follow her, but a table leg blocked his view. He could still see Espidra, though. Her face was as pale as bone. Her hands were shaking.

She wasn't furious, like Rega. She wasn't shaken, like Hesma.

Espidra was terrified.

– TWENTY-THREE –

Beau raced down the narrow corridor in the castle's west wing, tearing past room after room. All their doors were locked tight.

And then he turned a corner, and they were not. In the hallway ahead of him, every single one had been unlocked and flung open. He could see inside them; the hallway was lit by lanterns resting in wall niches.

Someone was nearby; he could hear footsteps. Was it the girl? He tensed in the darkness, listening.

A split second after the girl had bolted from the kitchen, Espidra had recovered her composure and ordered the court ladies to spread out through the castle and search for her.

Beau waited until they'd all left the kitchen, then he'd bolted off, determined to find the child before they did. He'd been careful to avoid the women, and as he looked at the doors now, he wondered who'd opened them. The child? One of the ladies?

Beau knew he couldn't stand there forever. He'd have to make a move, even if it meant risking discovery. Eyes sweeping back and forth, ears attuned to the slightest sound, he took a few quiet steps. He made it to the first door, on the right side of the corridor, and peered inside. It was empty. He inched to the second room, on the left. It, too, was empty. He moved lightly, willing himself to be invisible. He'd made it halfway down the hallway when the golden clock in the great hall begin to toll the hour—midnight. The echoing chimes were an alarm that should've stopped Beau in his tracks, and then sent him running for safety, but he was so desperate to recover the key, he didn't even hear them. He walked on, and just as he was crossing the doorway to the last room on the corridor, a figure came hurtling out of it and crashed into him with such force that he went flying sideways and landed on the floor.

Groaning, he raised his hands in surrender. Whoever had knocked him down was big and powerful. It had to be Valmont. He waited for the man to shout at him, to grab him and march him down to some dank, dark cell. But as he lifted his head, he saw that it wasn't Valmont; it was *her*, the little girl. She was staring at him, her face frozen in an expression of alarm.

"*There* you are, you little weasel!" he shouted, scrambling to his feet.

The girl backed away from him. Her head swiveled toward the staircase; she was listening to the clock.

"Don't you dare run off again," Beau said. "You stay there. Right—"

"Go, you dunce! Get out of here!" she hissed, waving him away.

Beau blinked. "What did you just call me?"

"Hide! *Hurry!*"

"I'm not going anywhere, kid. And neither are you. Not until you give me back the key."

The last chime sounded. The little girl shrank against the wall.

Good, Beau thought. *I've scared some sense into her. Maybe she'll behave herself now.*

102

He waited for her to apologize, to hand over the key. But she did neither.

"It's coming," she said, a tremble in her voice. Her eyes were glued to the stairwell.

"It? You mean Espidra?" Beau asked. "I'm not scared of—"

The girl held up a hand, silencing him. Her fear puzzled Beau. She hadn't seemed overly frightened of Espidra only moments ago, when the two had met in the kitchen. If anything, Espidra had seemed frightened of her.

A second later, footsteps sounded overhead, poundingly loud.

The little girl hurried to Beau; she took his hand in hers. "You need to *go*," she said slowly, as if speaking to a child. "Get back to your room. Lock the door."

The footsteps grew louder. They were no longer overhead; they were on the staircase now.

Quick as a minnow, the little girl darted off again. She turned back to him once, terror in her eyes.

"Run, Beau," she said. "*Run.*"

– TWENTY-FOUR –

Lady Rafe, flinching, trembling, constantly looking behind herself, clutched Lady Espidra's arm.

"The little wretch. She's searching for her sisters. Of course she is. We have to find her before she finds them. They're stronger together, you know they are. They—"

"Stop jabbering, you dolt, and look for her!" Espidra snapped, shaking her off. "She's probably hidden herself in some dark hole like the filthy little rat that she is."

Espidra was carrying a silver-topped walking stick; she poked it viciously under furniture and into corners as she spoke.

Rafe, whimpering, looked behind a door. Then she pushed aside a pair of dusty draperies, gulping spasmodically. "It's all h-h-his fault, the thief's. I j-j-just *know* it."

Espidra's frown deepened. Rafe was right; the thief had something to do with this. Too much had happened since his arrival—the disappearance of the master key, the child's sudden liberation—to be mere coincidence.

He'd upset the balance of things in a way that no other visitor to the castle ever had. He disarmed Arabella. Engaged her. Challenged her. His influence would have to be curbed. Permanently. Espidra had given him back his letter, after steaming it open. She hoped the urgency he must be feeling would lead him to do something rash. Something stupid. Like getting himself killed.

Both he and the child were threats to the order Espidra had imposed, and she did not take kindly to threats. She knew that Arabella had long ago stopped wanting things she couldn't have. Or had she? Was there still some small secret part of her that had not given up?

In the early days, Arabella had yearned for the girl, keeping her always at her side. But then the girl started to come and go, like a beautiful butterfly—here one moment, carried off by the breeze the next—and the days without her were torture for Arabella.

Espidra saw this. She, more than any of the other court ladies, saw her mistress's torment.

As the years passed, as visitors came to the castle and left it again, the child's absences grew longer. But no matter how long she stayed away, Arabella always welcomed her back with open arms, covering her with kisses, making her promise that she would never leave. The vicious little liar broke her promises, though, over and over. And when she left, Arabella would lie in her bed for days, facing the wall, refusing to eat or speak.

Espidra was the only one Arabella would allow near her then. She was the one who sat next to Arabella through the long, dark hours, stroking her brow. She was the one who persuaded Arabella that it was better to do without the child than to have her heart broken again and again. It had taken her time to poison Arabella against the child, but once that had been accomplished, it had been easy to persuade her to lock the girl away.

Once she was gone, Espidra had raised up the ladies she favored—Rega, Iglut, and Hesma among them—and had banished the ones she did not.

Espidra and Rafe continued their search now, moving from a music room to a portrait gallery, opening cabinets, ripping sheets off furniture, until they finally found themselves in a corridor with other members of the court.

"The little wretch is not in the north wing. I searched every inch of it," Iglut said. She sat down on a chair, kicked a slipper off, and rubbed her foot. "I can't *believe* you made us search the whole castle, Espidra. I'm exhausted. My back hurts. I'm cold. You have no consideration. None at all. In fact, you—"

"Where are the others?" Espidra demanded, cutting her off.

"LaJoyuse and Sadindi are still searching," Iglut replied.

"And Rega?"

"She's in the south wing. I heard furniture breaking, so I didn't get too close."

"The girl will find the others before any of you find her!" Espidra shouted, enraged. "She'll set them free! She won't stop until she does!"

"Don't chide *us*, Espidra," Hesma shot back. "This is *your* fault. You should have been more vigilant. More conscientious. You were foolish and lazy. You should have anticipated—"

"Oh, do shut up, Hesma," Lady Elge said. "Our little escapee is just a foolish child. We'll find her before too long. There's no cause for worry." She smiled, showing a mouthful of crooked teeth. "Let's keep looking, why don't we?" she added, leading the others out of the room.

As soon as they were gone, Espidra began poking in corners again. Elge was wrong. There was every cause for worry.

In all the world, there was only one who could best her, only one who could defeat her.

That treacherous wretch of a girl.

– TWENTY-FIVE –

"Kid! Hey, kid, stop!" Beau shouted.

He started running after the girl, determined not to let her get away again. But she disappeared down the corridor, turned the corner, and was gone, all in the space of a breath.

Beau ran harder, desperate to keep up with her. As he rounded the corner, his heart leapt. She was just up ahead. He was about to shout again, but before he could, he heard pounding footsteps coming from the hallway behind him. They grew loud, faded, then grew loud again, and he knew that whoever was making them was running into each room, searching it.

The girl stopped at one door and pulled something out of her skirt pocket. It was the key. Beau could tell by the way her hands shook as she fumbled it into the lock that she heard the footsteps, too. The door opened just as he caught up to her. Wordlessly, she grabbed his arm and dragged him inside. Holding a finger to her lips, she quickly closed the door, relocked it, and dropped the key into her pocket. Then she took a step back. Listening. Watching. Waiting.

"Who are we—"

"Shh!"

Running from? Beau mouthed.

The girl didn't reply. Her gaze was glued to the door. Beau debated snatching the key from her pocket, but she'd likely put up a fight, and he didn't want whoever was out in the corridor to hear them. He didn't want to be here, wasting precious time, when he could be in the cellar, maybe even halfway down the tunnel by now, but he had no choice.

As the girl stood by the door, waiting and listening, Beau looked around and saw that they had ducked into someone's private chambers. He was standing in what appeared to be a sitting room, but it looked like it hadn't been entered for years. A moth-eaten wool rug covered the floor. Silk draperies hung in the windows, their hems tattered, their silver embroidery fraying. The flowered wallpaper had yellowed. Strips of it had peeled away in places and now lay on the floor in sad, dusty curls. An archway led from the sitting room to another chamber.

Beau cast a glance at the child, worried she might open the door and make a run for it, but she was still standing motionless, her hands clenched.

Letting his curiosity get the better of him, Beau walked through the sitting room, noting a delicate slipper chair, its seat covered with a stack of books; a silk shawl draped over the back of a sofa. His eyes came to rest on the mantel. When he saw what was hanging above it, he stopped in his tracks.

The portrait's frame, like everything else in the room, was covered in dust and darkened by time, but the face on the canvas was as fresh, and as striking, as the day it had been painted.

Beau stared at it, struck by the girl who stared back at him. She seemed familiar, but he didn't know her. Twelve years old or so, she had a regal, self-possessed bearing, but her smile was lively and challenging. Her blond hair, gathered in a loose ponytail, hung over one shoulder. She wore a moss-green jacket with a high collar. Her gray eyes were large and expressive; a fiery intelligence burned in their depths.

With a sudden shock of recognition, Beau realized that he *did* know the girl.

"It's *her*," he said, pointing at the portrait. "Hey . . . hey, kid, that's Arabella."

The little girl turned around, tossed him a withering look, and said, "I stand humbled by your blazing powers of perceptiveness."

– TWENTY-SIX –

Beau did not appreciate being mocked by a child.

"That's no way to talk to your elders and betters," he whisper-shouted.

"Then it's a good way to talk to you since you're neither," the girl whisper-shouted back.

Beau walked over to her. He knelt down and put his hands on her shoulders, ready to tell her that this stupid game had gone far enough. The girl looked at one of Beau's hands, then the other, then she lifted her eyes to his. The look in them was scalding.

Beau sheepishly removed his hands, then peppered her with questions. "Who are we running from? Why were you locked up? What's your name?" His frustration made him loud.

"Be quiet, you fool!" the girl ordered.

Beau lowered his voice. "Just tell me one thing . . . are these Arabella's rooms?"

"*Were.* They were Arabella's rooms. She doesn't come here anymore."

She returned her attention to the door and Beau returned his to the mantel, trying to reconcile the chilly, brittle, grown-up Arabella to the girl in the portrait.

He thought back to that morning, to his pick-pocketing lesson. He'd seen flashes of the painted girl then—an excited smile, a sparkle in those gray eyes. And though he didn't want to, he remembered more: the way Arabella smelled, the feeling of her arm entwined with his, the heat of her hand on his chest.

A moment later, he found himself walking into her bedroom, almost against his will. *What are you doing? Why are you wasting time?* a voice inside him demanded. *Admiring the decor isn't going to get you out of here.* But Beau found he didn't have an answer.

The chamber contained a four-poster bed, a tall mirror leaning against one wall, a desk, a bureau, cabinets, a broad window seat, but what amazed him was the sheer number of books it held. The walls were lined with shelves, all containing leather-bound volumes. A sharp stab of longing pierced his heart. He had never coveted any of the things he'd stolen for Raphael—not jewels, not silver, not even gold coins, but he hungered, always, for books.

Beau ran his fingers over a row of spines. *Le Vau* was stamped in gold on one; *Wren, Palladio, Mansart* on others. They were architects. He'd heard their names mentioned in the grand homes where he'd worked. He moved on to history, philosophy, plays and novels and poetry. His fingers stopped at a small volume of Shakespeare's sonnets. He pulled the book off the shelf. Its red leather cover was worn smooth in places where hands had held it.

He opened it and read, and found himself transfixed by the beauty of the poems. There were stanzas he softly read aloud, just to feel their rhythm on his tongue, and others he read silently, just to feel their weight in his heart.

Beau wanted the book desperately and for an instant, he thought about slipping it inside his jacket, but he put it back. Some things were too valuable to steal. Pulling himself away from the shelves, he continued his explorations. On the far side of the room stood a delicate walnut desk, its surface littered with rolled papers, a crystal inkwell, a quill, and a leather portfolio.

A fine cloud of dust rose into the air as Beau flipped the portfolio open. He waved it away. His eyes fell on drawings of buildings—France's Notre-Dame cathedral, the Fasil Ghebbi castle in Ethiopia, and Kukulkan, a pyramid in the Yucatán.

Beau knew that people's private chambers were their sanctuaries. They kept the things they loved in them—portraits, letters, jewels. It seemed that Arabella didn't love those sorts of things; Arabella loved buildings. A shock of excitement coursed through him at the realization. Maybe there was a drawing of her own castle here. An elevation, a cross section . . . something that would show him where the tunnel was.

He picked up a cylinder of paper and unrolled it, but it showed drawings of Beijing's Imperial City. He threw it down in frustration. He unrolled another, but it depicted the library of Ephesus. These weren't what he needed. He looked up and spotted a large wooden chest. It was pushed up against a wall and secured with an iron padlock—which told him there was something valuable inside it. Using a letter opener and a small screwdriver that he found in a desk drawer, he had the lock open in minutes, but the chest's contents were not what he was expecting.

"What *is* all this junk?" he muttered, pawing through a jumble of protractors, compasses, T squares, and rulers. He closed the lid, then he ransacked the rest of the room, pulling out drawers, opening cabinets, but once again, he found nothing that told him anything about the castle. He sat down on the bed and groaned. Another dead end. The night was waning, the hours were slipping away, and he was no closer to escaping.

He heard his brother's voice, full of fear, echoing in his head. *Don't leave me here, Beau, please, please don't . . .*

And his own voice answering. *Don't cry, Matti. Please don't cry. I'll come back for you. As soon as I can. I promise. I swear . . .*

Anger coursed through him, driven by fear—fear that he would be too late, that Matti would die thinking he'd broken his promise. He got to his feet, grabbed a pillow, and drop-kicked it across the room. It hit the wall with a heavy *whump*. He did it again. He was about to do it a third time when his foot got tangled in the voluminous folds of the satin bedspread. Struggling and swearing, he managed to extricate himself, but as he did, there was a sudden flash of brightness. He bent down, squinting at the bedspread, and realized that the underside was heavily embroidered with what looked like miles of silver thread.

Mystified, he yanked the cover off the bed and spread it out on the floor, tugging at folds, pulling at corners, until it was fully open. Then he took a step back, amazed by what he was seeing.

Stretched out on the floor before him was a magnificent city, twinkling like stars in a midnight sky. And at the top, in the right-hand corner, a single word was stitched.

Paradisium.

– TWENTY-SEVEN –

Beau had seen fancy needlework before.

He'd seen lace collars that cost more than most people earned in a decade. Silk frock coats embroidered with roses so lifelike, it looked as if petals would fall from them. Gowns embellished with gemstones and pearls. But he'd never seen anything as beautifully made as the needlework before him.

Using a variety of stitches—some small and straight, others swirling and twining—the embroiderer had created a diabolically detailed architectural drawing. In the center of the dark blue satin stood an elegantly columned city hall, with wide stone steps and a soaring tower. In front of it was a tree-lined square with a fountain in its center. The glimmering silver city also boasted a university, with domed and spired buildings, a hospital, a school, a market hall, shops, and cafés.

Beau knelt down and ran his hand over the stitches. *Who made this?* he wondered. *Arabella? Why would she want to hide it?*

At that instant, a movement caught his eye. A flash of blue from across the room. Beau froze; he lifted his gaze. The mirror stood there, propped against a wall. He looked directly into it.

There was someone in the glass.

Standing right behind him.

– TWENTY-EIGHT –

Beau sprang to his feet and whirled around, ready to fight.

But no one was there.

He took a hesitant step toward the middle of the room. He was *certain* someone had been standing there . . . right *there*, in the center of the rug. Was he seeing things now? Running a shaky hand through his hair, he spun back toward the mirror.

The silver glass was alive with motion.

Images danced before his eyes, shadowy, flickering, lit from behind—like pictures in a magic lantern show. He saw a streak of blue again, then bold flashes of crimson, yellow, rose, and green. They blurred together like paints running in the rain, then came into sharp focus.

Beau's mouth opened in surprise. The cracked mirror showed Arabella. She was sitting at her desk, her head bent, her hair up in a messy twist. Books and compasses, rulers, pens, and paper littered the desktop. She was drawing.

His gaze swept over her, taking in the furrows in her brow, the set of her jaw, the light in her eyes—not hard with disdain as they usually were, but blazing with the intense concentration of an artist lost in a world of her own making.

Behind her, on the bed, lay half a dozen open boxes. Colorful gowns spilled out of them, one more beautiful than the next.

A worried-looking Josette eyed them. "Mistress, your mother will be here soon," she said. "She will wish to know which gown you intend to wear to the ball, and you haven't even tried them on!"

"Mmm," Arabella said absently, roughing in the windows of a building with a piece of graphite.

Josette held up a corset. "*Please*, mistress, you must—"

"Oh, Josette, stuff the ball!" Arabella said. "It's a bore and I hate—"

The sound of brisk footsteps carrying into Arabella's chambers from the hallway cut her off. Her eyes widened in panic.

"Help me put these things away! Quickly!" she whispered, wiping the gray smudges off her hands with her robe.

Together they hid the rulers and compasses in drawers, then jammed the papers and books under her bed. When the door to her chamber opened, Arabella was holding her corset in place as Josette tightened the laces.

"Good morning, Mother . . . Aunt Lise," Arabella said, forcing a smile as two women, both tall and imperious, both possessing the same gray eyes and blond hair as Arabella, strode into the room.

"Josette, when you've finished here, tell Valmont he needs to change this seating plan for the ball's dinner," Arabella's mother said, handing the maid a piece of paper. "He has me sitting next to a mere *baron*. What can the man be thinking?" She turned to her daughter. "I just saw the dance master, Arabella. He told me you did not attend your lesson this morning."

"I forgot. Forgive me, Mother," Arabella said.

"Oh? And what were you doing that was so absorbing?"

"I was . . ." Arabella's voice faltered. She glanced frantically around the room. Her eyes fell on the bed. "I was trying to decide between all of these beautiful gowns!" she said brightly.

The duchess raised a skeptical eyebrow.

Arabella winced. "Mama, what does it matter?" she asked placatingly. "I *know* how to dance."

"That corset's far too loose," the duchess said, her critical eyes raking over her daughter. "Fix it, Josette."

Josette quickly unknotted the corset's laces, tugged at them, then planted her feet and pulled hard. A gasp escaped from Arabella. She pressed her hands to her rib cage as her lungs struggled to find their new shape. Josette reknotted the laces, then stood back.

Beau grimaced. The corset looked so tight, he half expected to hear Arabella's ribs break. And then he did hear a crack. But it was made by the duchess. Something had broken under her foot.

"What on earth is *that*?" she said, bending down.

A slender piece of graphite lay on the rug, in pieces. The duchess picked them up. Her face hardened as she realized what they were. She turned her palm over, letting the pieces fall back to the floor, then grabbed the bed skirt and yanked it up. Her sharp eyes roved over the books and papers hidden behind it. She released the fabric and turned to her daughter.

"I should have known," she said, her voice frosted with anger. "Must I remind you, Arabella, that many wealthy and powerful young men will be at the ball, and that each one is looking for a *wife*, not a stonemason?

You are not a milkmaid, free to come and go as you please. You are a duke's only child and heir."

Arabella looked at the floor, her hands fidgeting at her sides. Beau could see that she was battling to contain her emotions, trying to bite back her words, but they slipped out anyway.

"I would rather find a teacher than a husband," she said. "And I would rather study architecture than try on dresses."

The duchess's expression darkened. "Must I also remind you that I do not want a repeat of past behavior?" she continued. "In fact, you will be on your very best behavior or there will be consequences." She snapped her fingers at the maid, then pointed at Arabella's books. "Josette, take those things downstairs. Tell Valmont to burn them."

Arabella's head snapped up. "No! Mama, please!"

"You've no one but yourself to blame, Arabella. I warned you time and time again. You don't need books and compasses to find a husband; you need a sweet, obliging manner and the right gown."

Josette knelt down, dug Arabella's books out from under the bed, and carried them from the room. Arabella watched her go. And Beau watched Arabella. He saw her lose her battle for control as her emotions overwhelmed her, like floodwaters surging over a dam.

"Mama, you are cruel! I want to learn how buildings are made. How towns and cities grow. How people live and work and play in them," she said, her voice rising, "and instead you demand that I waste my time at a boring ball chatting and smiling and simpering at men who are duller than death!"

Two bright splotches of red appeared in the duchess's cheeks, but her voice—when she finally spoke—was steady. "How dare you speak to me like that." She took hold of her daughter's arm and steered her to her mirror. "Look at yourself, Arabella. *Look.*"

Arabella raised her eyes to the sliver glass. They were brimming with tears.

"Nostrils flaring like a bull's . . . face as red as a rooster's comb . . . voice as shrill as a hyena's . . . bristling like some vile she-boar," the duchess said, disgusted. "A girl who cannot control her emotions is no better than a beast."

A raw, painful silence fell upon the room. Lise was the first to break it.

"What a lovely frock, my dear," she said, picking up the blue gown. "Any man who sees you in it will fall head over heels in love and immediately ask for your hand."

Defiance sparked in Arabella's unhappy eyes. "I would rather he ask for my heart first."

Lise shook her head. She glanced at her sister and with a troubled smile said, "The girl has a fiery spirit."

"Fires that burn too hot are quickly doused," said the duchess.

Lise held the gown out. Arabella sighed. She stepped into it, then threaded her arms through its sleeves.

Lise fastened the row of buttons that ran down its back. "No one likes an opinionated girl, Arabella," she said gently. "Or a loud girl. Or an angry girl. Or a difficult girl."

"How about a sad girl?" Arabella asked lifelessly.

Lise shuddered. "Those are the worst of all."

"Then what type of girl shall I be, aunt?"

"A charming girl. A congenial girl. A girl who's always cheerful, always positive, always smiling. A girl who talks about gardens and concerts and horses and flan."

"*Flan?*" Arabella echoed in disbelief.

Lise nodded sagely. "Flan is safe and uncontroversial. Have you ever known a flan to spark a heated discourse?"

"No, aunt," Arabella said, her shoulders sinking. "I have not."

After trying on the blue gown, Arabella tried on the rest. The duchess declared the blue to be the most flattering, then swept out of the room. Lise followed her and Arabella was left alone, staring at herself in the mirror.

She seemed smaller to Beau. Diminished. Defeated. The anger had drained from her face and underneath it was anguish, raw and aching. As he watched, she stepped closer, touched a finger to the silver glass, and drew a smile on her own reflection. The small, sad gesture pierced Beau's heart. Without even being aware of what he was doing, he stretched out his hand and pressed it to the glass, his fingers meeting hers. He forgot that she couldn't see him, forgot that she was just an image in the glass.

"As it turns out, the duchess was right: There *were* consequences."

The voice, coming from the doorway, made him jump. It was the girl.

"The duchess took away most of Arabella's things, but she found a way to keep drawing. To keep dreaming." She took a few steps into the room, gazing wistfully at the glimmering city still stretched out across the floor.

"Did Arabella make this?" Beau asked.

The girl nodded. She walked to the dusty draperies and traced the outline of shadow flowers with her finger, and as she did, her pale glow brightened. "At night, she would unpick the silver thread from these panels and use it to create her city. She would work through the small, lonely hours, when everyone else was fast asleep. The only ones who ever knew about it were the maids, but she gave them coins to keep her secrets. She found a way. And it was enough." Her light dimmed. "Until it wasn't."

"Why? What happened?"

The child was about to answer when a wild, earsplitting shriek of rage cut her off. It was followed by a loud thump on the door.

"Quick! We have to hide!" she whispered, trembling now. She grabbed Beau's hand and tugged him toward the windows.

There was another thump. It was harder. Louder. Beau heard it, and finally realized exactly who, or rather what, was chasing them.

"That's not Espidra is it, kid?" he said, panic clutching at his insides.

As the words left his lips, the door exploded open with a splintering crash. A second bloodcurdling shriek filled the room. The little girl grabbed his hand again, and this time he didn't pull free. There were cabinets under the window seat. Their fronts were made of filigreed brass panels. The girl opened one and frantically motioned for him to follow. The cabinets were wide and deep, and both Beau and the girl were able to fold themselves into the dark space. They pulled the doors closed just as whatever had made those blood-chilling sounds stalked into the room.

Beau sucked in a gasp as he saw it, then whispered two words.

"The beast."

– TWENTY-NINE –

The child dug her fingers into Beau's arm, silently warning him not to make a sound. Not to move. Not to breathe.

The creature's eyes were blazing with rage. Its mouth was a gash of red. Powerful muscles rippled under its fur. Its nostrils flared as it scented the room. Then it threw its head back and roared, and Beau felt the child shrink against him. He covered her shaking hand with his own, squeezing it.

The beast lurched around the room, searching for them. When it couldn't find them, it smacked a stack of books off a table. They hit the floor in an avalanche of noisy thuds. Instead of placating the creature, though, the destructive action only increased its rage. It upended a chair.

Toppled the nightstands. It picked up a table and smashed it against the wall.

Then it started across the room, toward them. Beau felt the child stiffen with terror. He knew that if the beast came any closer, if it peered down at the filigreed doors, it would see them. His heart was crashing against his ribs; he could hear its frenzied beat, and thought for certain the beast would hear it, too. But halfway across the room, the creature stopped and trained its gaze on the bedcover, heaped on the floor.

It flattened its ears to its skull, bared its teeth, and leapt on the heap, but when it realized that the child was not hidden in it, its eyes filled with a murderous fury, and it charged out of the room.

Beau waited until he heard its roars and shrieks fade down the hall. Only then did he dare crawl out of his hiding place. He prided himself on his steely nerves. He'd been in tight spots many times. He'd been chased and beaten. But he'd never, *ever* been as frightened as he had by the creature that had come through the door. His legs felt as if they had no bones. His thoughts were disordered. He had trouble speaking.

"Wh-what *is* that thing? How . . . who . . ."

The little girl followed him out of their hiding place. Beau noticed that her light had faded to a flicker. She looked as if she would snuff out with the softest huff of breath.

"I have to go now," she said.

"No, you can't. I need that key. I need to find the tunnel."

"There is no tunnel."

Beau shook his head. "That's not true. It *can't* be."

The child gave him a pitying look. "Be careful, Beau. I'm the one the beast wants, but it will tear you to bits, too, if it finds you." And then she darted off.

Beau was too dazed to chase her, but he called after her, as loudly as he dared. "Wait! Stop. *Please.* Tell me your name. Who are you?"

Just before she disappeared through the doorway, the child glanced back at him, and with a tremulous smile, said, "Hope."

– THIRTY –

Arabella watched as Beau dropped a silver spoon into his jacket pocket. "Take it," he said, flashing her a grin as he turned away.

"All right, I will," she said. *But not yet*, she thought, glad he could not see her seeing him. *Oh, not yet.*

He stood, one hip cocked, his long hair tied back, his face in profile. Her eyes lingered on his nose, with the bump in its bridge, his soaring cheekbones. They traveled downward, taking in the set of his shoulders, the graceful flare of his back.

"I was thinking maybe sometime today?"

"I'm cultivating the element of surprise," she replied, wishing she could stop time and stay here, in this moment, forever.

A second later, as she pulled the spoon from his pocket, he caught her hand, startling her into a cascade of giggles.

"Got it!" she crowed. "I was as smooth as silk. Silent, too."

"*Silent?* You may as well have set off fireworks," he said, not letting go of her hand.

She looked into his warm brown eyes, so full of surprises. At his smile, so full of promises. And for an instant, for one single instant in an endless century, she was happy.

And then another sound rose over their laughter—as measured, as inexorable as the ticking of a clock. Arabella looked up, and her blood ran cold as she saw who was walking toward them.

The clockmaker.

"No!" she cried, her heart filling with fear. "Please. Not him. Not *him*."

She gripped Beau's hand and started to run, heading for the nearest doorway, but when they reached it, they found that Lady Iglut was blocking it. She wore a gown the color of mustard; its lace collar was yellowed, its hem grimy. Her pallid face was pocked with livid sores.

Arabella spun around and ran for another doorway, pulling Beau after her. But Lady Hesma appeared in it. She glared at them balefully, her arms wrapped around her body like a straitjacket. Her nails, curved and sharp, dug into her sides.

Reeling, Arabella ran for the last doorway, still gripping Beau's hand, but Lady Espidra stood in it, looking down at the floor. Until she heard them approach, and then her head jerked up and Arabella saw that she had nothing where her eyes should be, just two black, gaping holes.

Arabella screamed. And sat bolt upright.

Frightened, disoriented, she looked around wildly and saw that she was not in the great hall with Beau; she was in her bedchamber. Alone. Gray morning light was pouring in the window. She had fallen asleep in her chair.

"It was only a dream . . . it wasn't real," she whispered, pressing a hand to her heaving chest. Relief flooded through her, but it was quickly doused by dread.

Nothing is more real than a dream, a voice inside her said. And she knew the voice was right. Dreams were powerful. They were mirrors to the soul. In her dream, it had felt like the early days again—days when the child was constantly by her side. Arabella shook the memory from her head. It was dangerous to want those days back. The child was safely locked away and had been for decades. All three of them were. In the thin light of morning, she knew the thief was doomed, just like the rest of them. And there was nothing she could do about it.

Arabella's heart clenched at the thought. She closed her eyes against the searing pain of it. *"This* is not my fault," she said brokenly. *"You* are not my fault."

Oh, but it is, the voice said. *And he is.*

Arabella got to her feet, desperate to escape the voice. She would go riding. She would have the groom saddle her stallion, Horatio, and gallop through the woods. The wind rushing in her ears would drown out everything else.

She hurried down the curving staircase in a swirl of skirts and ran out of the castle. When she reached the stables, she discovered that the groom was in the hayloft, throwing down bales. She saddled Horatio herself, then headed for the forest, urging the horse into a gallop before they'd even left the stable yard.

The old wives said there was no rider on earth fast enough to outride death.

Maybe not.

But she meant to try.

– THIRTY-ONE –

A gust of wind whirled through the stable yard, rattling the barn doors.

It muttered and cackled like a witch in its low, raspy voice, taunting Beau. Telling him that a storm was coming. One that would bring snow and ice. One that would keep him here.

A hammer in one hand, a bag of nails in the other, he ignored it, so the wind tried again, rising and keening until its voice was that of a child's—high and frightened.

Please don't go! Don't leave me, Beau!

Beau knew the voice wasn't real; he knew it was only his worried mind playing tricks. But knowing it didn't help. He still saw Matti standing by a window, waiting and hoping and wishing for him to come. And he saw him turn away, crushed, when day after day after day, he didn't. He still felt as if the keening wind had reached inside him and wrapped its pitiless fingers around his heart.

Hunching his shoulders against it, Beau knelt down and furiously nailed two planks together, end to end. When he'd finished, he hurried to the stable's workroom, grabbed two more planks, and did the same thing. Then he lapped one end of a newly elongated plank over the other one, nailed them again. He was hurrying and distracted, and the hammer came down on his thumb. Yelping in pain, he shook his hand and let out a string of very unspecific curses.

Arabella wouldn't be pleased, he thought after the throbbing dulled a little. Well, he didn't give a hummingbird's fart what Arabella thought. Because of her, he'd spent the whole day building the world's crappiest bridge. Dusk was coming down now, and he wasn't even close to being finished.

He'd come up with the idea last night, after Hope had left him. After he'd raced back to his room and locked himself in. There was no tunnel—she'd convinced him of that—so he'd had to devise another way of getting out: a skinny plank bridge.

The distance across the moat looked to be about forty feet. The nailed-together planks were each ten feet long. Beau planned to make six in all, to give himself ten extra feet on each side of the moat. He'd connect the planks with more nails and some rope, then push the sixty-foot length through the gatehouse and across the moat. Then he'd stabilize the castle-side end of his homemade bridge with counterweights he'd found in the gatehouse and just hope really hard that the other end bit into the bank on the far side and anchored itself there.

And that was the easy part. If he actually managed to get his rickety contraption stretched across the moat, and it actually held, he would then have to walk across it. Across a six-inch wide, sixty-foot long, bouncy-as-hell length of wood cobbled together with rusty nails and some mouse-gnawed rope.

The plan was insane, and he knew it, but it was the only one he had. He picked up the hammer and started to work again, but as he did, the door banged back on its hinges.

"Blasted wind . . ." he muttered, standing up to close it.

But it wasn't the wind. It was Valmont. Percival was with him. They didn't look happy.

Valmont's eyes traveled from the hammer in Beau's hand to the planks on the floor and the nails scattered around them. He gave a gusty snort and started toward him. Beau braced himself for a fight. He'd had enough. Of Arabella and her creepy court. Of the sticky-fingered kid. And of murderous monsters who came out at midnight.

"Back off, Monty. You've no right to stop me. You're a pack of liars. All of you. You—"

But Valmont cut him off. "Shut up," he said, taking the hammer from Beau's hand and throwing it down. "Come with us."

"Where to? The dungeon?"

"No, the moat."

"Why should I?" Beau asked warily.

"So you don't kill yourself," said Percival.

The two men turned to go. Beau followed them. They walked in silence until they reached the gatehouse and its moat-side archway.

"Why are we here?" Beau asked, his gaze sweeping down to the murky water. A few slime-covered rocks jutted up from its depths, but nothing seemed to live in it.

Valmont picked up a large stone that had tumbled from the gatehouse wall and tossed it into the moat. It hit the water with a deep, noisy splash. For a long moment, nothing happened. And then one of the rocks moved. It tilted back, and Beau saw a face staring up at him from the water. Its

124

skin was a gangrenous green; its eyes were milky with decay. Fungus crawled over its lips. As Beau stared at the thing, his belly tightening in horror, it growled at him through blackened teeth.

"Wh-what *is* that thing?" he said, taking a hasty step back.

As the words left his lips, the water began to roil and froth around the creature. A second monster surfaced, and then another, until there were dozens of them, all groaning and thrashing. He saw a man whose skin hung off his bones in a tattered curtain. He saw a fish swim in and out of the eye sockets of another. An eel slithered through the rib cage of a third.

"If you still want to build a bridge, make sure it's a strong one," Valmont said, and then he left.

Percival remained. Together, he and Beau watched the sad, sullen creatures, some of them still growling and snapping, others clawing uselessly at the air until, one by one, they submerged again.

Beau stood rooted to the spot, the image of the creatures' awful faces, the sound of the horrible gurgling that rose from their throats, still with him. One wrong step on his ridiculous bridge and he would be in the water with them.

"Percival, what *are* they?"

"Soldiers. Mercenaries. Anyone who tried to attack the castle."

"Are they alive? Dead? Both?"

Percival hesitated, then he said, "There are things here, Beau, things you do not understand."

"Then explain them to me."

"They protect us," Percival said, nodding at the moat. "They protect Arabella."

Beau gave a bitter laugh. "*Please.* Arabella doesn't need protecting. Arabella is as tough as a rock."

"Spoken like the ignoramus you are."

The vehemence with which Percival spat the words shook Beau. "I know all that I need to know about Arabella," he said unconvincingly.

"You know *nothing*," Percival shot back. "Nothing of the baby who toddled into the butler's pantry to stack cups and saucers until they were taller than she was. You know nothing of the girl whose parents took her to Paris to buy her gowns, but who slipped away to see Notre-Dame instead. Or how her parents found her outside the cathedral, sketching the towers, the windows, the flying buttresses. You know nothing of the young woman who wished to build things."

Beau's own anger kindled now. He remembered Arabella's cutting words when they first met and how coldly she'd dismissed him after he taught her how to pick-pocket. "You're right, I don't," he said. "The Arabella I know treats people badly. She uses them."

Percival's jaw tightened at Beau's words. He looked away, turning his gaze to the forest beyond the moat. It was some time before he spoke again.

"Long ago, when I was a boy, there was a judge who presided over this realm, appointed by the old duke, Arabella's grandfather. His first decree was that every town must erect a jail and a gallows. Every thief, no matter if he stole a sack of gold or a loaf of bread, was hanged. A woman who talked back to her husband was fitted with a scold's bridle. Adulterers were branded with an *A*. The stocks were never empty. Blood ran in rivulets from the whipping posts. Bodies rotted on gibbets.

"The judge made himself our moral compass. He and his family never missed church. They dressed plainly and behaved respectably. But once, when I grew older and worked in a shop, the judge's wife came in to buy gloves. As she pointed to a pair, her sleeve rode up and I saw that her arm was covered with bruises. The laundress, who knew everyone's business, said the judge beat her. And his children, too. There were more stories. People said the judge swindled business associates and maligned rivals."

Percival's eyes found Beau's. "I've always wondered . . . when the judge gave his harsh orders—to duck a slanderer in a cold pond, to hang a thief—who, exactly, was he condemning?"

And then with a brisk nod, he left, and left Beau standing in the gatehouse. Though it was freezing cold outside, Beau's cheeks burned. Surely, that old fool wasn't comparing him to that awful judge?

Unbidden, an image of Arabella, as she looked in her portrait, came to him. He saw her lively eyes. He saw her straight back, the proud set of her shoulders, the defiant tilt of her head. The person she was now was so different from the one in the portrait. What had happened to change her? Who had robbed her of what she'd possessed in that portrait: pride and passion?

Why do you care? he asked himself. *She doesn't care about you. She made you a prisoner. And if you don't get that bridge built, you'll remain one.*

Another gust of wind howled down, skittering sleet across the cobbles, forcing Beau to hunch into his jacket, sending him back to the stables. As he hurried inside, a sudden fury, red and ravenous, gripped him. He kicked at the bag of nails. He kicked at a cobbled-together plank over and over again, raging at Miguel and Arabella, raging at sheriffs and matrons and schoolmasters, raging at his own foolishness, until he'd kicked what he'd built to pieces.

And then, his chest heaving, his face flushed, he looked at the planks he hadn't kicked apart. They were a joke. They wouldn't hold up under him. They wouldn't hold up under a cat. They'd dip and bow and dump him straight into the moat. He knelt down, defeated, and picked up the nails he'd kicked across the floor. He knew nothing about building things. His good-for-nothing father hadn't taught him. Neither had

Raphael. The only thing he knew how to do was steal. And that wasn't going to help him now. It wasn't going to get him any closer to Matti.

"What am I going to do? What the hell am I going to do?" he shouted.

As if in answer, Percival's voice floated back to him. *You know nothing of the young woman who wished to build things . . .*

The nails fell from Beau's hands. He got to his feet and started walking. By the time he got outside, he was running.

He didn't have to know how to build a bridge.

Because he knew someone who did.

– THIRTY-TWO –

Lady Sadindi looked down her long, elegant nose at Beau.

He was standing in the doorway to Arabella's private chambers. In his arms he carried a large, lumpy bundle knotted up in a sheet.

"The mistress is taking tea. She has spent the day riding and is tired," Sadindi said with a sniff. "You cannot come in now. Or, actually, ever."

"I don't care if she's taking tea, a bath, or a nice long piss, I need to see her," Beau said, muscling his way inside Arabella's chambers.

"Stop! You can't just . . . now, see here, boy!"

Beau disregarded Sadindi's squawks and walked past her into the sitting room. Arabella was reading by the fire, wrapped in a warm woolen robe, surrounded by her ladies. A silver tea tray had been placed on a table between her chair and the fireplace. A book lay open on her lap. She lifted her head at the sound of his approach.

"Lady Sadindi?" she started to say. "What's going—"

Beau didn't give her the chance to finish. He walked up to her and dropped his bundle at her feet. It hit the floor with a noisy crash.

"That should be just about everything you'll need," he said. "Except for this."

He reached into his pocket, pulled out a tightly stoppered bottle of ink, and banged it down on the table. As he did, something on the tray caught his eye—a small, pretty cake topped with lemon icing and a candied violet. He picked it up and popped it into his mouth.

"Do help yourself," Arabella said archly. "Would you like some tea, too? Here, let me pour it for you. Sugar? Cream?"

Beau, still chewing, held up a finger. He swallowed, then said, "Cream. No sugar."

Arabella scowled, clearly unhappy at having her bluff called. She picked up a cup and saucer from the tray, poured his tea, stirred in some cream, and handed it to him. Beau nodded his thanks, then slurped it noisily.

Eyes narrowed, Arabella waited for him to finish. When he finally did, she said, "Now, would you like to tell me why you threw a bag of garbage at my feet?"

"You're going to build me a bridge across the moat. I brought you everything you need to get started."

As he spoke, Beau knelt down and unknotted the sheet's four corners. Compasses, protractors, pens, books, a T square, an adjustable triangle, a French curve, several rulers, and a roll of drafting paper lay jumbled in the center of it.

Arabella gasped. Her carefully constructed mask cracked and fell away. In its place was a smile, radiant and full of joy. It only lasted for an instant, though, before anger took its place.

"Where did you get these things?" she demanded.

"From your old chambers."

Lady Rega, sitting nearby, jumped to her feet. She snatched the teapot off the tray and hurled it to the floor. "How dare you! How *dare* you!" she shouted as it smashed. "You have no business in there!"

"Prying in other people's things! You should be ashamed of yourself!" Hesma scolded.

Espidra said nothing. She merely watched, her expert fingers working an embroidery needle, her eyes jumping from Beau to Arabella and back again.

"You—you trespassed. You invaded my privacy," Arabella said. "You—"

"I don't give a sparrow's rank worm-burp about your privacy. Because of you, I'm trapped in this ugly pile of rocks. I need to get out of here. You're going to help me."

Pain surfaced in Arabella's eyes at his words, and Beau thought he'd actually pierced her armor, but he was wrong.

"I'm afraid you've made a mistake," she said coldly. "I have no idea how to build a bridge." She turned to Lady Iglut. "Call for Valmont."

Iglut scurried to the bellpull and yanked it frantically.

"That's horseshit, Arabella," Beau said. "You *do* know how. I saw your books and all your tools. I saw the coverlet, too."

Arabella, outraged now, drew in a long breath. She looked like a cobra puffing itself up to strike, but Beau didn't give her the chance.

"Plus?" he continued. "Percival told me you studied the greatest buildings in the world. He said you went to Notre-Dame and sketched it. If you can figure out a flying butt, you can—"

"*Buttress*, you ass," Arabella hissed. "A flying *buttress*."

Beau tapped a forefinger to his chin. "Hmm. A bit imprecise, don't you think? Surely you could come up with something more descriptively specific to the current situation than *ass*."

"Where the devil is Valmont?" Arabella shouted, her composure shattered now.

Iglut ran to the doorway to look for him.

"But whatever," Beau continued. "My point is . . . if you know all about cathedrals and temples and pyramids, you know about bridges. So build me one. It doesn't have to be a big deal."

Arabella laughed in disbelief. "It doesn't?" she said. "Oh, good. I was worried."

"A narrow little footbridge will work. All it has to do is not fall down."

At that moment, Valmont came barreling into the room. "What is it, Your Grace? What's wrong?" he asked.

And then he saw Beau and the tangle of tools on the floor.

"Remove him, Valmont," Arabella ordered. "And then send the maids to clean this rubbish up. Have them burn it."

Her last sentence was not spoken so much as spat. Directly at Beau. An angry Valmont grabbed his arm and hustled him out of the sitting room, but just before they reached the doorway, Beau shook him off. He turned back to Arabella, caught her molten gaze, and held it. She was his last chance.

"You got me into this mess," he said to her. "You can get me out of it."

Arabella held his gaze, then she bent down, picked up the wooden rulers, the French curve, the drafting paper, and threw them on the fire.

- THIRTY-THREE -

The old wives are silent.
Because no one wants to be saved anymore.
That's only for the weak.
And everyone's so strong now.

The old wives are tired,
Of telling you pretty stories.
The ones you never asked for,
Are the ones you most need to hear.

About a knight in tarnished armor.

And an ice queen who melted.

About a handsome prince who lies in wait,

With sharp teeth and long claws.

The old wives are gone now.

To sit with the witch.

And drink with the woodcutter.

And wait for you in the woods.

– THIRTY-FOUR –

"*Do* stop pacing, child. How are we to arrange your hair? Or dress you for supper?"

Arabella waved Espidra's words away.

"What *nerve* he has," she said, stalking back and forth. "Barging in here . . . making his ridiculous demands . . ." She stopped dead in the middle of the floor. "Build a bridge . . . a *bridge*?"

"With what?" Lady Rega snorted. "Your bare hands?"

Lady Iglut, standing in the doorway of Arabella's dressing room, held up a silk gown. "Mistress," she began in her gurgling, lugubrious voice. "Percival has set your table. Valmont has decanted your wine. Phillipe's food is growing cold. The fire is burning down. The candles, too. Florian waits by your chair. Soon the flowers will wilt."

"Yes, Lady Iglut, I'm coming, I'm *coming*," said Arabella, a flush of contrition coloring her cheeks. She hadn't meant to keep her servants waiting.

Still simmering, still muttering, she walked into her dressing room. A tall mirror stood in one corner. The glass seemed to sense the tumult inside her and respond to it. Colors swirled inside it, beckoning to her. Images took shape.

Arabella recoiled as she saw the silver glass coming to life. A destructive impulse fired inside her. She wanted to pick up a vase, a figurine, a doorstop, *anything*, and smash the silver glass to pieces, but it was pointless. She could not break the mirrors. How many times had she tried?

Though she did not want to, Arabella stood in place, as she had a thousand times before, watching the story—her story—unfold, foolishly hoping for a better ending. The glass showed her a sparkling scene—a formal ballroom, all gilt and crystal, where roses spilled out of vases and candlelight flickered over powdered and rouged faces.

A girl came into focus. She was wearing a blue gown. Jewels dangled from her earlobes and neck. Her hair was styled high on her head; not a tendril was out of place. Everything about her was contained—her body, her gestures, her voice. She moved about the ballroom with a porcelain set to her face, a brittleness to her bearing. She looked like the spun-sugar decorations set atop fancy cakes, as if she would crack into pieces at a touch.

The duke, her father, had visited her in her chambers before the ball, with a warning. "I expect nothing less than perfect behavior tonight, Arabella. I have a list of suitors for you as long as my arm: a Sardinian duke, a German viscount, an Austrian baron, a Romanian prince . . . But if you do not control yourself, I'll be lucky to marry you off to a ratcatcher."

The ball's purpose was to find her a husband, but she did not want one. She wanted stone and mortar. Joists and rafters. She wanted to raise walls, build towers, send spires up to pierce the sky. But she'd realized it was an impossible dream; her parents would never allow it, and she was tired of fighting them, tired of disappointing them, so instead, she chatted and danced and smiled.

Young men introduced themselves. An earl squired her around the cathedral-sized room, regaling her with stories of his hobby—stamp collecting. A baron danced with her and talked about his spaniels the whole time. After listening for a full hour to a duke with a passion for fishing lecture her on the differences between the common bream and the silver bream, Arabella declared she was overheated and excused herself to get a glass of punch. She found it challenging to get a word in—about gardens or concerts or horses or flan, as her aunt had advised—but her companions didn't seem to mind. The less she spoke, the more they could.

As she arrived at the refreshments table, she spotted her father, his back to her, deep in conversation with the Italian ambassador.

"I wish your lord were here," she heard him say. "I would value his counsel in a political matter concerning my duchy."

"Perhaps I can be of assistance, Your Grace?" the ambassador offered.

The men moved closer to each other. Arabella, intrigued, leaned in, the better to listen to their conversation, but the men created a wall of their bodies, shutting her out. She could still hear them, though.

"My people grow restive. There have been incidents of rebellion," her father said. "My tax collectors have been beaten. Gallows smashed. Grain stores looted."

"Because you tax your people harshly to build a giant golden clock, Papa," Arabella said. To herself. Or so she thought.

"What a load of rot," drawled a male voice.

Arabella turned. A young nobleman stood nearby, holding a cream puff between his thumb and forefinger. He was tall, like Arabella, and coldly handsome, with light brown hair tied back with a ribbon, bored blue eyes, and an indolent smile.

"Do you know the advice I would give?" he asked, through a mouthful of pastry. "Round up the ringleaders, hang them, and leave their bodies for the vultures."

Arabella winced at his cruel words. "Do you always proffer unsolicited advice, sir?" she asked.

The man snorted laughter. "Do *you* always eavesdrop on other people's conversations?"

He finished his sweet, then frowned at some cream stuck to his thumb. He looked around; his eyes fell on Florian, who was carrying a heavy silver tray of sugared fruit to the table. "You, boy . . . come here!" he barked.

"My lord?" Florian said as he approached, huffing under the weight of the tray.

The man wiped his hand on Florian's sleeve. "On your way. Shoo," he said, waving the boy off.

Arabella stared at him, speechless, then anger surged in her, washing away her shock. She opened her mouth, ready to tell this arrogant oaf exactly what she thought of his atrocious behavior. But before she could, the young man gave her a curt bow and said, "I'm forgetting my manners. Allow me to introduce myself . . . Constantine, prince of Romania."

At that very instant, just as the prince was bowing, Arabella's father walked past them, still deep in conversation with the ambassador. He glanced at her, and her feelings must've been on her face, for his eyes suddenly darkened. She saw the warning in them, and it brought her up short.

"It is a pleasure to meet you, Your Highness," she said, pushing her emotion down. "My name is—"

"Arabella. Yes, I know. You're too softhearted, Arabella. There's only one thing to do with rebellious peasants—end them."

Talk about gardens, a panicked, shrill voice inside Arabella warned. *Talk about kittens. Talk about flan.*

But she didn't listen to it.

"My father's people do not need ropes around their necks; they need food on their tables," she countered. "Two years of rainy summers have led to poor harvests. There's no wheat to make their bread, no hay to feed their animals."

Constantine laughed. "My darling girl, you do not understand power. Allow me to explain it to you: Give the peasants too much and you will teach them to want things they should not. That is how revolutions are started."

"People only rebel when they have nothing," Arabella retorted. "Have you ever seen a king start a revolution?"

"I suppose *you* have devised a way to deal with an unruly populace?" Constantine asked.

"I believe I have, yes."

Arabella expected him to laugh at her again, or walk away. Instead, he said, "Tell me, do."

Ball guests, intrigued by the sight of the duke's young daughter lecturing a prince, drew near.

"My solution is to give our people the tools they need to better themselves," said Arabella, with conviction.

"And those are?"

"Schools and hospitals. Good roads. Proper plumbing."

"Plumbing?" Constantine wrinkled his nose.

"An unappealing topic, yes," said Arabella earnestly, "but an important one, as science tells us that clean drinking water and well-maintained sewers reduce outbreaks of disease."

Carried away by her vision, Arabella did not hear the arch comments from women, whispered behind silk fans. She did not notice the men frown with distaste. Thrilled to have an audience for her ideas, she mistook Constantine's interest for enthusiasm.

"These ideas are ambitious, I know," she continued, the words tumbling off her tongue. "I would start with the village closest to our castle and use it as a proving ground."

"And what would you call this model city of yours?" Constantine asked. "Have you a name for it? Utopia, perhaps?"

The crowd laughed raucously. Too late, Arabella saw what the man had done. He'd asked her questions, he'd drawn her out; he'd coaxed her to share the dream that lived in her heart—not because he thought it had merit but to ridicule it.

Shame and embarrassment seared her, yet she persisted. "No, not Utopia," she said. "Paradisium."

Constantine arched an eyebrow. "And what would make it a paradise, my lady? The fact that you would live there?"

Another wave of laughter engulfed Arabella. She leveled her chin at him and said, "No, my lord. The fact that you would not."

Hushed gasps rose from the courtiers. Snorts and snickers followed.

Constantine gave Arabella an acid smile. Then he said, "I was under the impression that the duke's daughter was a young lady of marriageable age. I was mistaken. She is young, but she is no lady." And then he was gone.

Arabella stood by herself for a moment, mortified by all the eyes on her. It had happened again. Though she'd tried so hard to control it, her emotion had burst out of her, flailing and howling like some vile jack-in-the-box. Remorse gripped her. Word would get back to her parents; she'd let them down yet again. She desperately wished she could behave as they wanted her to, but she didn't know how. It was impossible not to feel her feelings. It was like willing her heart not to pump or her lungs not to draw air.

"Arabella, there you are! I've been looking all over for you!"

Arabella turned and saw her mother making her way toward her, cheeks flushed. Her heart sank. She braced herself for the tongue-lashing that was about to come her way.

But the duchess was smiling.

For once she looks happy to see me, Arabella thought. *I wonder why?*

She didn't have to wait long to find out.

"I've found you a husband!" the duchess said excitedly. "I was talking with an old, dear friend. Her family lived close to mine in Paris before she married, and she married *very* well, and it happens that she has a son, just a few years older than you are, and we think the two of you would make a *perfect* match!"

Arabella was tired. Her head hurt. She didn't want a husband now any more than she had when the ball had begun, but it was so rare that she made her mother happy, so rare that the duchess looked at her with anything like approval, that she smiled brightly and did her best to look eager as she asked, "Who is it, Mother?"

The duchess gripped Arabella's arm and in a breathless voice said, "His Royal Highness, Prince Constantine!"

The real Arabella stepped back from the mirror now. She squeezed her eyes shut. When she opened them again, the images in the silver glass had faded. She stood perfectly still for a moment, nails digging into her palms, trying not to remember her story's next chapter.

She had asked for forgiveness a thousand times. But it did not matter. She would never forgive herself.

– THIRTY-FIVE –

Beau regarded the row of doors yawning open in the dark corridor before him.

It was the kid. Who else could it be? She was at it again. Searching for something, or someone.

"Hey, kid! Pssst! Hey, Hope!" he called out.

He held his candlestick high and took a few tentative steps down the corridor, peering around the first door he came to. The room—a bedroom—was torn apart. Had Hope been in there? Was she still? Moonlight spilled in through a high bank of windows, washing the chamber in silvery light. Beau blinked, momentarily blinded after the deep gloom of the corridor, then stepped inside.

"Hope? Are you in here?" he whispered, but he got no response.

He'd let himself out of his own room moments ago and was on his way to Arabella's old chambers to find books on bridges. He'd heard nothing from her after he'd gone to her rooms to demand she help him build one. When morning came, he would go to her again and dump the books on her floor. He'd gather up her notebooks and dump those, too. Drawings. Scrolls. Parchments. Anything and everything. He'd make such a nuisance of himself that she'd give in and help him, if only to get rid of him.

The clock struck eleven. Its sinister chimes, echoing throughout the castle, reminded Beau to get moving. After his last run-in with the beast, he was determined to be back in his room by midnight. He was just about to leave the ransacked bedroom when he noticed the tall wardrobes standing at the back of it. Their doors were open and costly gowns spilled out of them. There were jackets richly embroidered with gold thread, fur capes, coats of satin. Above the garments, plumed hats, muffs, and dainty silk shoes stood lined up on shelves.

Beau moved closer to the wardrobes, his thief's instincts driving him. Maybe there was something here of worth. He still had his old mistress's ring stitched into his coat, but was it valuable enough to buy Matti's health back? He crossed the room in a few quick strides, then reached into a wardrobe, but as he grabbed a jacket off its hanger, the fabric disintegrated in his hands. He threw it on the floor and took hold of a cape, but tufts of fur came away. He snatched at a skirt, a gown, a cloak, but every garment he touched was moth-eaten, ancient, ruined.

"What's with this?" he muttered, baffled. Why would Arabella keep all this threadbare clothing?

He remembered, with a creeping unease, the dust-covered furniture in her old chambers, and the strange claim Hope had made—that she'd been locked away for a hundred years.

Shaking the feeling off, Beau hurried to another wardrobe, but again he came up empty-handed. He turned in a slow circle, hoping that he'd somehow missed a trunk, a chest, a small jewelry box tucked up on a shelf.

That's when he saw her.

A woman.

Slight. Stooped. Standing in the shadows.

– THIRTY-SIX –

Panic stole Beau's breath. How had he not noticed her? She was only a few yards away from him.

If she screams . . . his mind yammered. *If she runs or calls for Valmont . . .*

The woman was standing across the room, to the right of the windows, her back to him. Beau saw that she was holding a silk cape in one hand, stroking it with the other.

His mind worked fast. *Is she a maid? One of Arabella's ladies-in-waiting?* he wondered.

"Oh, hey. I'm sorry if I startled you," he said nonchalantly, trying to make it seem like his presence here was no big deal, like he always walked around the castle on his own late at night.

The woman said nothing but inclined her head toward him. A pale shaft of moonlight caught her hair. Beau saw that it was styled high on her head, and so white and flossy, it looked as if it were made of cobwebs.

"So . . ." he said, giving her a dimple-deepening smile. "Have you seen Valmont? I've been looking for him for . . ." He laughed. "I don't even *know*! An hour?"

The woman's head swiveled. She turned toward him jerkily, like a marionette in the hands of a clumsy puppeteer. Moonlight raked across her body now, but her face was still shrouded by shadow. Beau saw that she was skeletally thin. The way her tattered gown hung off her shoulders, like a ragged coat off a scarecrow, unsettled him.

"You serve the mistress, no? The lady Arabella," he asked, his voice rising a little.

The woman released the cape she was holding, letting it drop to the floor. "I am Lady Garconera, and I serve the *true* mistress here," she said haughtily, drawing herself up to her full height. "We *all* do." She laughed then. It was high and screeching, and Beau found himself taking a step back.

As he did, the woman swept a bony hand out before her. "Brocade, satin, velvet, lace . . . Have you ever seen such finery?" she asked, taking a step toward him, her skirts sweeping through the dust on the floor.

Beau strained to catch a glimpse of her face, but the shadows kept it hidden.

"Everything she owned was exquisite, but it was just a veneer—heaven knows the outside didn't match the inside—but what does that matter?" the woman asked. "Sparkly surfaces are all this world cares about."

She passed under the high windows, still moving toward him. As she did, the moon's rays finally revealed her fully. Beau's heart lurched. He wanted to run, but horror held him captive.

Her face was a mosaic of broken mirror shards; her lips a slash of rouge; her eyes jeweled buttons. Her towering hairstyle didn't merely look like cobwebs, it *was* cobwebs, and as she came closer, it started to shudder.

As Beau watched, still rooted to the spot, a slender, bent black leg poked out from the sticky white strands, feeling for purchase. It was

141

followed by another, and another, and then a large black spider crawled out. As the creature made its way down the side of the woman's face, she smiled, revealing a mouthful of sharp, shiny, broken-off scissor points.

And then she lunged.

Beau's thief's reflexes saved him. He twisted to his right and ducked her clawlike hand. Then he ran, crossing back over the threshold and skidding into the hallway. He reached back for the doorknob and slammed the door shut behind him. With trembling hands, he ripped his bundle of lock-picking tools from his waistband and shook it open. The tools clattered onto the floor.

"Come on . . . *come on*," he whispered, grabbing the pickle fork and screwdriver and jamming them into the lock.

Jangling laughter carried to him from the other side of the door. He twisted the fork frantically, hoping it would catch, but it scraped uselessly over the lock's innards.

A split second later, there was a loud, shuddering crash as the woman threw herself against the door. Beau scrambled for the knob, desperate to hold the door closed. As his hand closed on it, a movement to his right caught his eye.

He turned his head and saw the child. Hope. She was running.

Straight toward him.

– THIRTY-SEVEN –

There were two children. Beau saw that now.

The second one was rounder and sturdier. Her dress was blue, and every bit as dirty and tattered as Hope's.

As they saw Beau, they slowed to a fast walk. "Go. Get out of here!" Hope said to him, while the other little girl turned and walked backward, keeping her eyes on the end of the corridor.

"I can't!" Beau said. As he spoke, the creature inside the room gave the door a vicious kick, making it rattle in its frame. "Help me. Grab the knob and hold the door closed so I can lock it!"

"No time," said the second girl.

"But there's a woman in there . . . a *thing*! She tried to kill me!"

"What's chasing us is worse than what's chasing you, I promise," said the second girl as she and Hope passed him.

"*Wait*, damn it, I need your help!" Beau was about to say more, but a scream of fury coming from the darkness at the end of the corridor cut him off. "Who is *that*?" he asked, a note of weary exasperation in his voice. "It sounds like Rega. Is she going to try to kill me, too?"

"Stop talking, blockhead, and run," said the girl in the blue dress.

She shot off then, with Hope right behind her. Beau watched them go, unsure whether to let go of the doorknob or keep holding it. Another scream decided him. He let go, scooped up his tools, and ran, catching up with the children as they turned down another hallway. They were fast, but Rega was faster. She was gaining on them; Beau could hear her shrieks growing louder.

The hallway dumped Beau and the girls out in a wide gallery. Paintings of battle scenes adorned the walls. Suits of armor stood in the corners. A console table, draped with a tapestry, was pushed up against one wall. Another corridor, long and stick straight, led out of the gallery. With a sinking heart, Beau realized that Rega would catch up with them before they got halfway down it.

Hope realized it, too. She pulled off one of her shoes and threw it into the corridor. Then she streaked to the table and grabbed the edge of the tapestry.

"In here! Hurry!" she whispered.

The girl in blue dropped to her knees and crawled under. Beau skidded in behind her. Hope darted in after them and released the cloth.

An instant later, Rega pounded into the room. All three held their breath. They heard Rega stop, then chuckle deep in her throat.

"You can't run forever," she said.

Beau heard footsteps again, loud then fading. Then silence. He heaved a ragged sigh and leaned back against the wall. Hope flopped against a leg of the table and closed her eyes. The other girl raised the tapestry and peered out from it.

"The idiot took the bait," she said. "The coast is clear. Let's go."

"Wait a minute . . . you're not going anywhere," Beau said. "Not until you give me the key back."

"No way in hell," said the other girl. "We need it. We have to find one more of us."

Her voice was a child's, but her words were weary and jaded.

"Who are you?" Beau asked.

The girl, still peering out from under the tapestry, didn't reply.

"She's my sister. Her name is Faith," said Hope.

"Hope and Faith? That's so cute. But I want the key."

Faith dropped the tapestry and turned to him. "And just what do you think you're going to do with it?"

"He thinks he's going to find a tunnel," Hope said.

Faith snorted. "There is no tunnel."

"Yup. Told him that."

Beau's frustration, stoked by fear, was mounting, but he summoned his patience. He reminded himself that his two companions were only children. They couldn't be expected to know about castles and their construction.

"There *has* to be a tunnel," he said. "When castles are attacked—"

Faith cut him off. "*This* castle, begun by the Normans in 1058 and enlarged in the early fifteenth century by Filippo Brunelleschi, resulting in the high Gothic expression that characterizes it, was built of granite," she said. "Unfortunately, unbeknownst to the original architects, its foundations were sunk into a deep deposit of schist, a rock that's crumbly and unreliable. Kind of like you. In fact, if you were a landmass, you'd be full of schist. But I digress. The original builders attempted to dig a tunnel under the castle and moat, but soon discovered that it could cave in at any second and promptly stopped digging. So. Like I said . . . no tunnel."

Beau's mouth was open. He closed it. Then opened it again. "You're a *child*. How do you know all that?"

Faith shot him a mocking glance. "Who do you think you are? Don Quixote? Think you're just going to swashbuckle your sorry ass out of here? Your friends broke the bridge. And there's no tunnel. You're sunk, boy."

"Boy? *Boy?* I'm nineteen years old, you mouthy little troll. Twice your age!"

"Heh. Is that what you think? You haven't figured this out yet?" She turned to her sister.

Hope held up a hand. "Stop talking, both of you. We need to listen. In case you haven't noticed, there's a homicidal maniac on the loose."

Faith snorted. "Only one? Must be a slow night."

Anger, frustration, fear, confusion—they finally all burst from Beau. "Who are you, really? Both of you? And who's Rega?" he demanded.

"Rega?" Faith said, perplexed. She looked to her sister for an explanation.

Hope rolled her eyes. "It's an anagram. They use them to hide who they really are. Arrogance started it. She thinks it's clever and mysterious."

Beau looked between the two girls. "Wait, I don't get it . . . Lady Rega is not Lady Rega?"

"She's Rage," Faith replied.

"That's a nickname? What the other ladies call her?"

"No, that's what she is."

"An angry woman . . ."

Faith took Beau's face in her hands. "They. Are. Not. *Women*. They are monsters. They destroy everything they touch." She released him.

"I—I don't understand," Beau said, feeling hopelessly stupid.

Hope started to explain. "They are Arabella's emotions . . ."

Faith finished. "Come to life."

– THIRTY-EIGHT –

Beau looked at the sturdy, glowy little foulmouthed kid sitting only inches away from him and laughed. "No way in hell. I don't believe it. I don't believe *you*."

Faith shrugged. "I get that a lot."

A dizzying sense of unreality gripped Beau. He pushed it away. "How can emotions come to life? Emotions aren't real."

Faith snorted. "Have you ever actually felt any?"

"Yes, I have. But mine, like most people's, live on the inside," Beau said. "They don't come out and walk around the place, wearing fancy dresses."

"Arabella isn't most people. And this castle isn't most places," Faith said. "I imagine even you have gathered that by now. There's a bit of dark magic at work here."

Beau shook his head. The sense of unreality deepened. He felt as if he were stepping further and further out onto ice that he thought was frozen hard, only to hear it crack under his feet. What Faith had just said . . . it wasn't true. It *couldn't* be. There was no such thing as magic. Then again, how else to explain the beast? The two children's otherworldly glow? Arabella's gruesome court?

146

"So all her ladies-in-waiting—" he began.

"Are not ladies. Far from it."

"Hesma? Iglut?"

"Shame and guilt," Hope replied. "Didn't you ever wonder? I mean, come on . . . *Hesma? Iglut?* Pretty unusual names."

Beau gave a sheepish shrug. "I thought they were Swedish."

Hope closed her eyes. She pinched the bridge of her nose.

"Who are the others?" Beau asked. "Rafe . . . R . . . A . . . F . . . E . . ." He snapped his fingers. *"Fear!"*

"I am awed to be in the presence of such genius," said Faith.

"LaJoyuse . . . Sadindi . . ."

"Jealousy. Disdain."

"Espidra . . . wait, don't tell me." There was a layer of dust where the floor met the wall. He started drawing letters in it. When he figured it out, he slowly drew his hand back, shuddering. As if Espidra herself had dragged a sharp fingernail down his spine. "She's the boss here, isn't she?" he asked.

"She is," Hope said. "That wasn't always the case. We used to be."

"What happened?"

"Espidra's hold over Arabella grew; ours waned," she explained. "We fought hard, but she fought harder. Arabella fought, too. Day after day. Until the days became years, and the years became decades."

"Decades . . ." Beau echoed.

"Nearly a century now," said Faith.

"You're not joking, are you?"

Hope shook her head.

"Arabella, you two, the others . . . you've all been here for a *century*?" Beau spoke the last word in a whisper.

Hope nodded.

Beau closed his eyes. He pushed his hands through his hair. "But that's not *possible*," he said.

"Except that it is," Faith said.

"So you're, what? A hundred and ten years old?" Beau asked, opening his eyes.

"Mmm, a *little* bit older," Hope said.

"And Arabella?"

"Arabella is not one of us," Faith explained. "She is a human being, trapped in time."

"But how—"

"Arabella's heart broke. A hundred years ago. And Espidra found the cracks. She found a way in," said Hope.

"Like the creeping mold that she is," Faith spat.

"She locked us away," Hope continued. "Me in the cellar, Faith in the attic." Hope smiled at her sister. "I just found her. We have much to talk about." She turned back to Beau and covered his hand with her own. "Beware of Espidra," she warned. "Never let her touch you. Don't even let her near you."

Faith started to crawl out from under the table. Hope followed her.

"Wait! Where are you going?" Beau asked.

"We have another sister. We think Espidra locked her away, too."

"Who is she?" Beau asked.

"Love."

"We're trying to find her," Hope said.

"We *will* find her," Faith asserted.

"And then what?" asked Beau.

Hope gave him a grim smile. "And then we're going to kill Espidra. The three of us together."

Beau recoiled. "Whoa, kids. Slow down," he said, shocked. "That's murder you're—"

Faith cut him off. "Before she kills Arabella."

Beau, shaken, said, "Is that what Espidra wants? To kill Arabella?"

Hope started to answer him, but before she could, the tablecloth was yanked up with a sharp snap. A face peered down at her—skeletal, sunken-eyed, lips pulled back in a rictus grin.

"Rega! Come quick! I found them!"

It was Lady Rafe. Her voice sounded like a cemetery gate, its hinges shrieking in the wind. She backed away, still holding the tapestry in one hand, pointing at the table and the fugitives under it with the other.

"Rega! Reeeeega!" she shrilled.

"Shut your mouth, you ghoul," Faith said, crawling out from under the table. Hope was right behind her.

Faith snatched the cloth from Rafe, pulled it off the table, and threw it over Rafe's head. As she did, Hope charged her and knocked her down. She hit the floor with a tumbling crash.

Hope whirled around to Beau; she pointed past him. "Take those stairs to the third floor," she whispered. "Turn right at the top, then follow the main corridor. It'll take you to the tower. *Hurry.* I don't think Rafe saw you, but if she does, she'll tell the others."

And then the two girls raced off, heading down the corridor into the darkness. As Rafe moaned and thrashed, feebly trying to extricate herself, Beau crawled out from his hiding place and peered down the corridor after them. He saw the two children feel for each other's hands. Their light glowed a little brighter as their fingers locked. He took an uncertain step in their direction, trying to decide whether to give chase or retreat. The sound of footsteps, pounding down the hallway, finally got him moving.

A few moments later, Beau was safely back in his tower room. Panting, drenched in sweat, he strode over to the window and opened it. As the cold winter air rushed over him, he took a deep breath and wondered—not for the first time—if he was losing his mind. In the space of an hour, he'd encountered mayhem, maniacs, and magic. And it wasn't even midnight.

Worst of all, he'd failed to get to Arabella's old chambers, failed to get the books he'd planned to use to pressure her to help him build a bridge.

He heard Faith's voice echoing in his memory. *She is a human being, trapped in time . . .*

Unbidden, his heart clenched with sadness for Arabella. And with pity. He didn't want to feel these things, but he couldn't help it. What was it like for her, to be made a prisoner in this place for a century? Was that why she wouldn't build him a bridge? Because she was lonely after a hundred years and wanted company?

But that makes no sense, Beau reasoned.

When she'd first summoned him from his tower, she'd been furious that he and his fellow thieves had destroyed her bridge. And right before that first meeting, he'd overheard her angrily interrogating Percival, telling him that she would find out who had raised the portcullis and let the thieves in, and when she did, that person would pay for his disobedience.

No, Arabella had made it very clear that she did *not* want him here.

Beau closed the window but remained where he was, looking out of it into the deep winter night, troubled by yet another unanswered question. "Somebody raised that portcullis," he said to his reflection in the glass. "Which means somebody wants you here . . . but who?"

– THIRTY-NINE –

Camille knew she should not be in the great hall.

Not this late at night.

Stepping lightly, she climbed up onto the track that arched in front of the golden clock and walked to the doors on its left side. She set down the candle and basket she was carrying, pulled a knife from her pocket, and slid its blade into the thin crack between the doors. A few twists at the latch, and they were open. Wedging her foot between them, she picked up her things and slipped inside the clockworks.

Careful not to disturb anything, she made her way through the figures, skirting around some, dipping under others, until she reached the one she wanted—a smiling baby girl sitting on the ground, her hands pressed together in a clap.

"There you are, my princess!" she said, kneeling down by the baby. She reached into her basket, fished out a pretty circlet of flowers and herbs, and settled it on the child's head. "There's lavender for devotion, thyme for courage, and rosemary for remembrance." Then she kissed the baby's cold porcelain hand. "I miss you, my darling girl. Every minute of every day. And I love you. So, so much."

Camille had brought a tiny cake, too. She placed it in the child's lap. She knew the mice carried away the sweets, but she liked to pretend that the little girl ate them.

"I hope you like this one. It has all your favorite flavors in it: vanilla, raspberry, and lemon, and it has a butterfly on top. Do you see? I made it out of meringue and rose petals." Her voice caught. Tears spilled from her eyes. "Forgive me, my little one," she said, trying for a smile. "Mama's tired tonight."

Camille had risen early that morning, as she always did to begin the day's baking, but instead of going to bed early, as she knew she ought to, she'd stayed up to bake her daughter's cake. A figure of a tall man holding a bridle in his hands stood behind the child. Camille leaned her head against his legs and closed her eyes.

She never meant to fall asleep, and when the huge clock started chiming the hour—eleven o'clock—she startled awake with a gasp.

"Oh no!" she whispered, frantically grabbing her basket. She kissed the child once more, then scrambled to her feet and picked up her candle.

Stumbling, slipping, banging her head on one figure's arm, catching her foot against another's skirts, she made her way back toward the doors, hoping that Lady Arabella had stayed in her chamber tonight. But as she burst through the doorway and jumped from the track to the floor, her hopes were dashed. Her mistress was sitting in a chair, a look of extreme displeasure on her face. Her ladies were standing behind her.

Camille looked down at her feet. "I-I'm sorry, Your Grace," she stammered. "I was only—"

"Speak up!" Espidra ordered. "Why are you here? The mistress permits no one to be here so close to midnight except for her court."

"I brought a cake," Camille said softly. "To give to the baby."

"A cake? For a clockwork child? What a useless gesture."

Camille had been contrite, but as she felt the sting of Espidra's harsh words, her remorse evaporated. Espidra was a poisonous weed, sending her vines everywhere, choking off every bright emotion that tried to send up shoots.

Camille raised her head. "It was for my *child*," she repeated, struggling to keep her anger in check.

Espidra made a noise of disgust. "This is what those vicious little monsters, Hope and Faith, do. They upset the help," she said to Arabella.

The last shreds of restraint Camille possessed gave way. "Do you think you're the only character in this story?" she asked Arabella, her voice rising. She pointed at the clock. "My *husband* is in there . . . my *child*!"

"You wasted your efforts," said Espidra. "The clock winds down. The curse cannot be broken."

Camille ignored her. "Help him, mistress," she said, her eyes still on Arabella.

"How dare you. Remember your place," Espidra warned.

Camille whirled on her defiantly. "Or what, Lady Espidra? You'll lock me up? Throw me in a cell like you did to the children? Go right ahead. You're right—the clock is winding down. In a matter of days, the castle crumbles. I die. My husband dies. My baby girl . . ." Her voice caught. With effort, she continued. "My baby girl *dies*. So to hell with my *place* and to hell with *you*." She turned back to Arabella. "He wants you to build him a bridge. Do it."

"Why would she do that? Only a fool would make such a pointless gesture," said Iglut.

"But the little baker *is* a fool," Hesma taunted.

"Camille," Arabella said, "even if I could build a bridge—which is an absurd supposition because I cannot—the second it's in place, he will cross it and leave us. Nothing will change. Not for us. The curse will not be broken. We will all still die."

"Do it because you care for him."

Espidra blanched. "Is this true?" she asked, looking from Camille to Arabella.

Arabella quickly turned away. "Of course not," she said.

"Have those two demons found Love?" LaJoyuse shrilled. "Have they freed her?" She turned to Espidra. "You locked her away, didn't you?"

Espidra was silent.

Rafe pressed her hands to her cheeks. "Lady Espidra, you *did*, didn't you?" she asked in a tremulous voice.

Espidra gave a stiff, unwilling shake of her head. "She was too quick. She escaped."

"So she's still *here*?" Rafe whispered.

"No, she left the castle. Nearly a century ago."

"How do you know?"

"Because I searched for her," Espidra snapped. "For decades. In every room and corridor and alcove. She is *not* here. I promise you."

Rafe exhaled. She lowered her hands.

Camille rushed to Arabella and knelt down beside her chair. "You care for him, I know you do. I see it in your eyes. You love him, mistress. And when you love someone, you help him."

"Camille, I *don't*—"

"Don't be ridiculous!" Espidra cut in. "Even if the mistress did love the thief, which she does *not*, love cannot build a bridge over a moat. It would take a hundred men, with pillars and ropes and winches. It would—"

Camille straightened. "Do not speak of love, Lady Espidra," she said, her eyes blazing. "Do not hold that word in your mouth when you do not hold it in your heart." She swept her finger in front of her, pointing at all the ladies in turn. "Not *one* of you knows anything of love. Love does not run. It does not turn tail. Love never, *ever* gives up."

Arabella shrank back. From Camille, from all that she was asking. "I can't help him. I can't help anyone," she whispered.

Lady Romeser stepped forward, gaunt and stiff. "The mistress is very sorry, Camille. For your husband, your child. But even so, nothing can be done."

Camille ignored her and addressed Arabella. "I know you're sorry, mistress, but I don't care. I'm sick of sorry. You wallow in your pain. You wallow in our pain. You cloister yourself with your ladies, day after day after day. My God, don't you think we all have remorse?"

Arabella closed her eyes. Bitterness moved across her face like spilled ink across parchment. "I imagine that mine is rather deeper," she said.

"Of course you do," Camille said, a caustic sear to her voice.

Arabella heard it. She opened her eyes. "The clockmaker cursed me," she said hotly. "*Me.* For the terrible thing I did."

"You have no idea what I've done. What any of us has done."

Arabella laughed mirthlessly as she rose from her chair. "What have you done, Camille? Scorched some jam? Burned a cake?" she asked, walking away from her, from her court, the clock, everything.

"I cheated on my husband."

The room was perfectly quiet, except for the ticking of the giant golden clock. Arabella stopped. She turned around.

"Twice. With your dance master."

Lady Elge giggled behind her hand. "That's a bit more than *I* needed to know."

"Claudette steals chocolate from the cellar," Camille continued. "Valmont kicked Henri. Josette likes stringing Florian along. Josephine filches wine. Martin keeps back a pint of milk from the morning milking and drinks it all himself."

"For God's sake, Camille," Arabella said. "All of this is nothing compared to—"

"You? Your mistakes? Your regrets?" Camille approached Arabella. "Leave your high tower, mistress. Step down into the mud with the rest of us. With the fools. The cowards. The bad-tempered and jealous. The heartbroken. We are all like you. Can't you see that?"

"It's no use, Camille. It's over. All is lost. I am lost," Arabella said, and the sorrow in her voice made Camille catch her breath.

She took Arabella's hands in her own. There was a surprising strength in those small fingers.

"Try, mistress. *Try*. Do all that you can. Help him. And you won't be."

- FORTY -

Maybe the court ladies are right.

Maybe Camille is a fool.

Baking cakes for a clockwork child. Trying when everyone else has given up. Defying despair.

But here's the thing . . . It's not so bad to be foolish. In fact, foolish people are vastly underrated.

Only a foolish person saves a broken-winged bird who will never fly again.

Only a foolish person hands a bunch of daisies to an angry old man.

Only a foolish person gives her nice new coat to a beggar girl.

The world doesn't need more clever people. There are plenty of those to go around. You see them everywhere—sidestepping the broken and the lost, sneaking off behind a tree to eat their muffins so they don't have to share them, busily dodging everyone else's pain.

What the world needs is one thing only—more hopelessly foolish people doing shockingly foolish things.

– FORTY-ONE –

Arabella had sent everyone away.

She stood by herself in the great hall now, trying to decide where to go. It was late, nearly midnight, and come morning, she would have to make a choice. Her head told her to go to her own chambers, but her heart was telling her to choose a different path through the castle, one that would lead her to a tower room.

She was at a crossroads, and she knew that they were lonely places, thresholds between one world and another. Thieves and murderers were buried there. Witches, too. Staked through the heart so that their restless spirits could not wander. Valmont always said that the devil lingered at crossroads, ready to lead mortals astray.

"What do I do?" she cried out in torment, her voice echoing through the hall.

As if in answer, the mirror over the mantel shimmered. Arabella watched as it became a window, showing her another time, another Arabella.

That Arabella was standing in the great hall, too. She looked different yet so much the same—alone, unsure, so full of longing. She had ventured downstairs, as she did every night on soft, stockinged feet, and was standing in the shadows.

The golden clock was only half-finished. It had no dial yet, no bell, no track with figures moving along it, just a diabolically complex amalgamation of gears, wheels, springs, and strikes. A man, his sleeves rolled up, stood in front of the immense works, adjusting the tension of the chain that suspended the clock's weights.

Arabella's eyes moved from him to the shiny sheets of gold, all neat in a stack, that would be used to face the clock. Earlier in the day, from the window of her father's fine carriage, she'd seen a thin child picking grains of wheat out of the dirt of a newly harvested field. She wondered now what just one of those gleaming sheets could do for that child, for her entire family. Arabella hated the clock, this folly of her father's, made solely to show off his wealth. Yet she couldn't help but marvel at it, too, for it was a feat of balance and precision. There was wonder on her face as she watched the clockmaker work. And envy.

She stayed in the shadows, not wanting to be seen, until the clockmaker—adjusting a spring—said, "Since you're here, you might as well make yourself useful. Would you hand me those pliers, please?"

Arabella didn't move, mortified at having been found out.

"I won't tell your parents, if that's what's worrying you."

Relieved, she bent down, picked up the pliers off the floor, and gave them to the clockmaker. "What a magnificent machine," she said.

The clockmaker's lips cut a smile into his face at the compliment. "Thank you," he responded, reaching inside the clockworks with the pliers. "But it's not finished yet. I must still fabricate the case."

157

"I wish you wouldn't," Arabella said, watching as he straightened a bent tooth on a gear. "Nothing is more beautiful than the works you've devised. I never tire of watching them."

As she finished speaking, she glanced down at her hands, clasped in front of her. A diamond on her left ring finger glittered in the lamplight. It was as big as a molar and every bit as grotesque.

The clockmaker glanced at it. "I heard about your engagement. You must be very happy. Prince Constantine is a marvel of engineering himself, no? Handsome, tall, powerful, rich—everything a woman could want."

"When will the clock be ready?" Arabella asked, ignoring his question. "The prince admired it, and my father wishes to make a present of it to us on our wedding day."

"In three or four months, I should think," the clockmaker said. His eyes found hers over the top of his glasses. "Or never, if that is your wish."

"Why would I wish that?" Arabella asked, a quizzical expression on her face.

The clockmaker set his pliers down. "I overheard the king. After the parties and the negotiations. After the marriage contracts were signed. I heard him tell his son that the young woman was a good match, a beautiful girl from a wealthy family. Though perhaps a bit spirited. But she would learn her place. 'She will be a queen one day,' he said. 'And queens, like children, should be seen and not heard.'"

Arabella brushed some imaginary lint from her skirt.

"Is this what you want, child? To never be heard?"

"It does not matter what I want," Arabella answered, repeating words her mother had spoken to her. "I am not a milkmaid, free to come and go as I please. I am a duke's only child and heir."

"Surely it matters to you?"

"You are impertinent, sir," Arabella said, turning to leave.

"People are always offended by the truth," said the clockmaker, wiping his hands on his apron. "I see you, Arabella. I see the movement of your heart as surely as I see this clock's. Do you?"

Arabella whirled around, her eyes flashing. "What would you have me do?" she asked.

"Listen to that heart."

"That's exactly what I am *not* supposed to do. I'm supposed to box my heart away and bend to others' wishes. Those who know better—my parents, and soon, my husband."

"You must do one thing and one thing only—become the person you were meant to be. No matter how daunting that task may be. Otherwise, your life is not a life; it is merely a long, protracted death."

"You do not understand, sir. I have a duty."

"To whom?" the clockmaker asked. "Your father, who taxes his people cruelly to pay for this giant golden plaything? Your mother, who slowly squeezes you to death to fulfill her own ambitions? Is your duty to them, Arabella? Or to the girl who wishes to build schools and hospitals? The girl who devised Paradisium?"

The color drained from Arabella's face. "How do you know about Paradisium? Why are you asking me these questions? Who are you?"

"I am the clockmaker, child. The master of hours. The keeper of time."

Arabella backed away, frightened by the man and his words, frightened by the longing they stirred in her. "I cannot do what you ask," she said.

"Cannot or will not?" challenged the clockmaker. "You have listened to too many voices, all telling you that you cannot, should not, must not pursue your heart's desire. But who are they really talking to, Arabella? You? Or themselves? Disregard them, child. They are nothing but squawking crows, deathly afraid that someone else might achieve what they themselves are too frightened to attempt."

"But how?" Arabella asked, with an incredulous laugh. "What shall I do? Pack my books? My sketches? Leave my parents, this castle, everyone and everything I've ever known?"

"If that's what it takes, yes," the clockmaker replied. "I would advise packing a few of your jewels, too. A passage to Rome or Venice, a room when you get there, fees for a teacher—these things cost money."

Arabella let his words sink deep into her consciousness like stones falling through water. For a brief, beautiful moment, she saw herself in Venice, sketching the Doge's Palace, studying the spires of the Basilica, walking over the Rialto Bridge, and her heart leapt with joy.

But then she heard it—a voice that had been whispering to her from an even deeper place. A voice that had grown louder ever since Constantine had humiliated her at the ball. It was dry and rasping, like a snake slithering through dead grass. *Don't be ridiculous, you foolish girl. You're not smart enough to hold your own in a classroom of men. Not tough enough to command the armies of masons and carpenters it takes to build a castle. Not talented enough to come up with designs as magnificent as the palaces and cathedrals you admire. Who on earth do you think you are? All of this is nothing but—*

"A pretty dream," Arabella said aloud. "That's all it is. All it ever will be. I must return to my chamber now. Good night, sir."

"Good night, Lady Arabella," the clockmaker said ruefully. "Sleep well. And remember this—the whole world is ready and willing to tell you no. Do not join their cowards' chorus."

Arabella rushed from the room. Outside the doorway, she stopped, tears brimming in her eyes. She blinked them away, desperate to quell the storm of emotion brewing inside her before it led her, once again, into trouble. Looking down at the ring on her finger as if it were a cancer on her hand, she said, "It's too late, Clockmaker. I already have."

The mirror shimmered again, then it hardened back into cold silver glass. And Arabella felt herself harden with it, as she always did, unable to escape the past and its quicksilver pull. One day, very soon, it would pull her so far under, it would drown her.

She could not save herself, or those who shared the castle with her, but maybe she could save the thief before time ran out. Maybe he did not have to drown with them.

– F O R T Y - T W O –

Soft morning light washed over Beau as he slept.

One of his arms was flung across the bed, one leg was hanging over it. He was snoring. Drooling, too. He needed a shave.

And still, he was so beautiful.

Arabella's eyes drank him in. She wished she could stroke the dark hair cascading over his pillow, run her fingers over his full lips. Press her own lips to the patch of skin showing in the V of his shirt.

Stop, she told herself. *It's not right to stare at a sleeping man who doesn't know he's being stared at, and would be appalled if he did.*

"Ahem," she said.

But Beau did not wake.

Arabella bit her lip. "Monsieur Beauregard Armando Fernandez de Navarre? Pardon me . . ."

Beau rolled over onto his back and snored louder.

Unsure what to do next, Arabella self-consciously tucked a tendril of hair behind her ear. It had escaped from the scarf she'd tied around her head—a scarf that was a marked departure from her usual attire, as was the old, plain jacket she was wearing over a scruffy sweater, the linen work skirt, and the battered, flat-heeled boots. She was holding a scroll of paper.

"Beau. Beau? *Beau!*" she called.

But Beau snored on.

"Really," she huffed. "I don't have all day." She strode over to him then and gave him a shove. "Do wake *up!*"

Beau's eyes snapped open. A split second later, he was on his feet, fist cocked.

Arabella yelped; she jumped back. "Is that how you say good morning?" she asked warily.

She'd been badly startled by his reaction, but she wondered at it, too. What had happened to him to make him so ready to fight before he was even awake?

"How did you get in here?" Beau asked, lowering his fist.

"I asked Valmont for the key to the door," Arabella replied.

"But it's the middle of the night."

"Hardly. It's past seven. The sun's coming up," she said briskly. "And we have work to do. But perhaps you'd like to get dressed first?"

Beau looked down at himself. His shirt was wrinkled. His underwear sagged in the butt. One foot was covered by a sock; the other was bare. Blushing a little, he stalked over to the chair and snatched his britches off it. He stepped into them, then sat down on the bed and pulled on his boots.

Arabella, impatient, knelt down on the floor by him and smoothed open the rolled-up paper she was holding. There was no time to waste.

"I drew this last night," she said, pointing at the sketch she'd made. "There are still problems to solve, but it's a start."

Beau leaned in close to her. His expression sharpened as he saw what she'd drawn. "It's a bridge . . ."

"How astute you are," she teased.

But he did not seem to be in the mood for banter. He was different this morning, serious and unsettled. As if something had spooked him.

"Why did you change your mind?" he asked, touching her arm, making her turn toward him.

His beautiful eyes were wide and searching, and Arabella had to look away before they saw too much.

To save you, she thought. "Because I can't resist a challenge," she said.

"No, because you want me gone," he countered.

Arabella didn't like where the conversation was going, so she changed it back to the bridge. "If we start fashioning the pilings this morning, we might be able—"

"Arabella . . ."

"Yes?" she said, still not looking at him.

"I *know*."

Dread skittered across her heart. "Mmm?" she said lightly, her gaze on her drawing. "What do you know?"

"I know who your court ladies are. I know what they are. I found out last night."

Arabella sucked in a sharp breath. "How do you know?" She was still looking at her drawing, but she no longer saw it.

"Two children told me . . . Hope and Faith."

"No, that can't be true. It *can't*," Arabella said, feeling sick to her very soul. "You saw them?"

Beau nodded.

"Where?"

"Here. In the castle."

"They escaped. I knew it. I *felt* it." She let out a moan, then buried her face in her shaking hands.

"Arabella? What's wrong? Are you afraid of them?" Beau asked, putting a gentle hand on her back. "Why? They're just children, just innocent kids."

163

Arabella laughed bitterly. She lowered her hands. "Believe me," she said, "they are neither children nor innocent."

"But I don't believe you," Beau said. "Not you or Valmont or Camille. Not anyone in this whole damn place. How can I? You've lied to me all along."

His words scalded her. "I'm sorry. You must have wondered—" she started to say.

"*Wondered?*" he echoed, incredulous. "Yeah, you could say that. I *wondered* why your ladies-in-waiting look like they stepped out of a nightmare. Why your moat is filled with the living dead. Why some wolf creature from hell roams the castle at night. And why you don't look a day over eighteen when you're well past a hundred."

Arabella winced at the sarcasm in his voice, and the anger underneath it. "There are things, Beau . . . things it's better you do not know."

Beau bristled at that. "Better for who?"

"For *you.*"

He started to argue with her. "No way. That's not good enough."

"It's going to have to be. You think you know things. About my ladies. About me. You don't. You know *nothing.* Keep it that way."

She meant her words to sound like a command; instead they sounded like what they were: a frightened, desperate plea.

"But I want to know."

Something in his voice—kindness? Pity?—broke her.

"No!" she cried. "You don't. You *don't.*"

"All right, all right, calm down, Arabella. I'm sorry. I didn't mean to upset you."

"I am going to help you build a bridge," Arabella said, trying to keep her voice level. "And then you're going to walk across it and keep on walking. Across the moat, through the forest, and over the mountains, without looking back. Say you will . . ."

"Arabella, I don't—"

"*Say it, Beau!*" Arabella shouted, slamming a hand down on the floor.

Beau pulled away from her, unnerved. "*I will.* There, I said it. Are we good?"

Arabella nodded, still upset, still scared, ashamed at her outburst, but relieved that he'd stopped pressing her.

An awkward silence descended on them. Beau was the one who broke it. He looked at the drawing again, more closely this time. "Will it work?"

Arabella drew a deep breath, trying to steady her hands, her voice, her stuttering heart. "It might," she replied. "Then again, we might both fall into the moat before we even get the first piling sunk. I guess we'll find out, won't we?"

She rolled up her drawing and stood. Beau did, too. Another awkward silence fell. This time, Arabella broke it. "Get some breakfast," she said, forcing a smile. "Then meet me by the gatehouse. We have a lot to do."

"I will," he said. "And hey, thank you for helping me. It's good of you to build me a new bridge, seeing as I helped break your old one."

And then he hugged her.

It was the kind of hearty, thumping hug someone would give a friend, or a horse, or a very large dog. At first, Arabella stiffened, surprised by the gesture, but his nearness thawed her. Her hands found his back. She closed her eyes and felt his cheek pressed against hers, the prickle of his stubbled chin. She felt the rhythm of his breath rise and fall, and the warmth of him enfolding her.

It was the first real embrace she'd had in a hundred years, and it was over all too soon.

"Sorry," he said as he released her. "I probably shouldn't rumple the royalty."

Arabella's legs shook so hard as she left his room, she thought her knees would buckle. She took a few steps down the stairwell, nearly stumbled, and caught herself against the wall. Sobs clawed their way up from her heart to her throat.

Deep inside her, something shifted, something so seismically deep, so irrevocable, that she had to bite back a cry. Her hand went to her chest; she felt the tumblers of her locked heart fall, one by one by one, and it terrified her.

Hope and Faith were free. And Espidra had admitted that she hadn't locked Love away. She'd said that Love had left the castle. But what if she was wrong? What if she was here, and Hope and Faith freed her?

"Damn you, thief," she whispered. "What have you done?"

− FORTY-THREE −

The princess in the glass coffin isn't really dead.
She's just pretending.
She likes it inside the glass. It's quiet and safe. She can
    watch the world go by through half-closed eyes.

The ugly stepsisters like being single.
They tangle their hair into nests and wear their dead
    father's shoes.
They rub ink on their teeth, then grin at the prince and
    laugh when he runs.

And Rapunzel? She could leave her tower anytime she
    wanted to.
All she has to do is cut off her braid and tie it to a chair.
Don't think she hasn't thought about it.

But like the others, she stays.

Because she's afraid she will never be loved.

And more afraid that she will.

– FORTY-FOUR –

Arabella stood on the threshold of the gatehouse, staring across the moat, her brow furrowed.

Beau stood next to her, as pacey as a racehorse, every nerve in his body crackling with impatience. He wanted to make a start, to *move*, to pick up a hammer and nail things together, to build the bridge.

But Arabella was still figuring out how to do that without getting anyone killed.

"For my plan to work, much depends on the tensile strength of the wood," she said, and then launched into a lecture on load-bearing force, center of mass, deflection, and several other terms he didn't understand.

As she talked, Beau shifted his weight and accidentally nudged a rock off the threshold with his foot. It hit the water with a deep *plunk*. A few seconds later, a dozen gruesome faces surfaced, snarling and snapping. More joined them, drawn by their noise, until the moat was a boiling froth of rotting monsters.

"Did you have to rile them?" Arabella asked. "I can't hear myself think."

Beau didn't reply. He just stared. At a jawless dead man with a salamander crawling out of his eye socket. He wanted to ask her how it was possible for a dead man to be swimming around in the moat, growling at them. He wanted to ask her so many things, but she'd made it clear she would not answer. His questions made her angry, which didn't bother him. They also made her scared, which did.

He wished he knew why she was frightened of Hope and Faith. He wished she trusted him enough to tell him. Worst of all, he wished he knew why he wished these things. Why did he care? Arabella, her life, this place, the other people in it—they weren't his concern. Matti was his concern; his only concern.

"You're certain about this idea of yours? The wooden pilings? The boards?" he asked, frustration simmering in his voice.

"Not at all."

"Why can't we just throw a rope across? I could hand-over-hand it across the moat. I'm strong enough."

"Who's going to tie the rope off on the other side?"

"Somebody."

"That's a bit vague."

"Somebody's bound to walk through the woods doing something on their way from someplace to somewhere," he huffed.

Arabella gave him a sidelong look that told him he was being silly and unhelpful.

"What if we tied a rope to an arrow?" he ventured. "And shot the arrow into a tree?"

Arabella considered this, then said, "An arrow fired from a longbow—which has a draw weight of about one hundred and fifty pounds—traveling at about, oh, say one hundred and seventy feet per second over a distance of, mmm . . . I'd guess forty yards . . . would almost certainly generate enough force to pierce a tree trunk, but would it be enough to embed itself deeply? And even if it did, the rope would only be attached to the arrow's shaft." She glanced down at the monsters again. "Do you really want to trust your life to a slender piece of wood?"

"What if we made an arrow out of metal, like a fireplace poker? And fired it out of a gun?"

"That's called a harpoon. Have you got one?"

Beau's frustration boiled over. He leaned his head back and let out a long, loud groan. They'd been standing here for half an hour and had made no progress. He was not one inch closer to Matti. Every minute that ticked by felt like a sharp-toothed harrow dragged across his heart.

Arabella, unmoved by his noise, continued to concentrate on the space between the castle and the far bank, then she said, "During his conquests of what we now call Germany, Julius Caesar built a thousand-foot wooden bridge across the Rhine. Did you know that?"

"No. But whatever he did, let's do that."

"He had the forests of Gaul to plunder for timber and forty thousand men to cut it down. They built enormous pile drivers on the riverbank, moved them into the water, then drove supports deep into the riverbed. Then they connected the supports with horizontal beams, laid decking across them, and marched to the other side. And they did it in just ten days." She turned to Beau. "We can do a modified version."

"Now who's being silly?" Beau asked.

"I really think we can. I based my drawing on the simple, elegant foot-bridges constructed from bamboo by the rural peoples of India. They work the same way as Caesar's bridge, essentially, but are a lot easier to build."

"Arabella? We don't have any bamboo."

"No, we don't. We'll have to use oak planks instead. They don't have as much give, but they'll still work . . . I think."

"You *think*," Beau said, glancing at the monsters again.

Arabella unrolled her drawing. "You see, if we just—" Before she could finish her thought, a frigid gust ripped the drawing from her hands. It held the fluttering paper aloft over the moat for a few seconds, then dropped it into the water. The monsters tore it to pieces.

"Hey, there's a good omen," said Beau.

Undeterred, Arabella reached into one of the braziers at the side of the archway and pulled out a piece of charcoal. Then she walked into the gatehouse. Its inner walls, protected from the weather, were a light, smooth gray. She went to one and started to sketch.

"We drive the pilings in diagonal pairs, to form Xs. It shouldn't be too hard, not as long as there's a deep enough layer of mud to drive into. The first pair goes in here"—she slashed an X across the wall—"about a foot from the gatehouse. The next pair goes in three feet from the first." She slashed another X across the wall. "We can't space them out any farther because each support must double as a work platform from which to construct the next pair, since we don't have the luxury of movable pile drivers . . ."

Excitement colored Arabella's voice as she spoke. Her movements, always measured and contained, became big and sweeping. Her exertions flushed color into her pale cheeks. Her eyes, their depths always hidden, now danced like quicksilver.

Beau watched in quiet astonishment as she sketched, frowned, erased a mistake with her sleeve and started again. It seemed to him as if a butterfly had suddenly emerged from its cocoon and shaken out its magnificent, shimmering wings.

She kept talking, kept drawing, turning to him every now and again, but he wasn't really sure that she saw him. She saw something else, something he could not. She saw lines and angles, forces and counterforces, tension and balance. She saw elegance, beauty, and strength.

And for the first time, for the very first time, Beau saw her.

- FORTY-FIVE -

There was a gasp, a shout, a splash, and then, "Oh, you bloody little bastard! You rotten monster! Damn it! Damn it all straight to hell!"

Beau shot Arabella a look. "That's a bit imprecise. Think about it. Say what you mean. That's what somebody once told me."

"Condemn this godforsaken botch most forcefully to the sulfurous depths of the underworld and stuff it straight up the devil's backside!"

"Much better," Beau said, biting back a smile.

What had just happened wasn't funny, but Arabella was. When she was angry, he'd discovered, she swore like a fishwife.

She was staring into the moat now, her hands on her hips, her gaze on the pieces of hewn timber floating on the water's surface. "We can't keep losing them," she said. "We don't have an infinite supply."

It was nearly four o'clock. Since early morning, she and Beau, joined by Florian and Henri, had been trying to sink a wooden pole into the moat's mud in order to fashion the initial pair of pilings for their bridge. On the first attempt, they didn't drive the pole deep enough, and it toppled over. On the second attempt, they hit a rock and the pole popped up like a cork before falling into the water. On the last attempt, they'd succeeded in getting one piling anchored, but the second had slipped and crashed into the first one with such force that both toppled over, nearly taking Henri and Florian with them.

"We're losing the light," Beau said, looking up at the sky. A few snowflakes drifted down. "It's getting colder and we're getting tired. Maybe we should stop for the day."

Though Beau was worried about wearing Arabella out, the idea of ending the day with nothing to show for it but four poles floating in the moat was deeply dispiriting to him. Every day without progress was another day that Matteo didn't get the help he needed.

Arabella, however, was not worn out in the least. "I'm not ready to call it quits," she said. "We need to know that this will work. If it doesn't, I'll have to come up with a new plan. Tonight."

"Or tomorrow."

"Or tonight," Arabella said forcefully.

Beau cocked an eyebrow. "Why, Your Grace, if I didn't know better, I'd say you wanted to get rid of me."

"Time's wasting. You said you need to get over the mountains before snow closes the pass, didn't you?" Her words were terse and clipped, and Beau heard the anxiousness behind them. Was it on his behalf? Or her own? He didn't have long to wonder about it, though. Arabella walked away briskly, motioning for him to follow.

She's so different, he thought, watching her move through the gatehouse to the courtyard where Henri was working on more poles. Her headscarf had slipped off long ago. She'd hastily scraped her hair together in a ponytail and had tied it with a piece of twine. Her skirt was streaked with dirt. She'd ripped a hole in her jacket.

But the change in her was more than a change of wardrobe. She not only looked different; she *was* different. Beau's eyes lingered on her, seeking out what, exactly, had altered. It was her face, he decided. So often closed and inscrutable, it was now as open as the sky. When she was stymied by a problem, frustration darkened it like clouds crowding out the blue. But after the problem was solved and the path forward revealed, the satisfaction Beau saw there felt like the sun emerging.

Beau was still watching her as she leaned down by Henri and Florian, who'd just finished sharpening a pole. And then it hit him: *This is Arabella happy.* For some reason he could not explain, and was not sure he wanted to, her happiness touched him.

"People have done this without pile drivers. We can, too," she said to the boys, watching as they picked up the heavy pole, carried it through the gatehouse, and lowered the sharp end into the water.

"Angle it to the left a little . . . That's it . . . Now hold it in place," she instructed, then she turned around. "Beau? Are you ready?"

Beau snapped out of his reverie and picked up a sledgehammer. After making sure that Arabella was out of the way, he swung it high and brought it down on the piling with all his might. It was hard. He had to aim well and at an angle, and then drive the hammer home with every ounce of his strength. Over and over he swung, hitting the top of the piling squarely, driving it deeper into the mud. The impact sent shock waves up his arms, and though it was cold, sweat poured down his body. Finally, when the top of the pole was about two feet above the gatehouse's threshold, Arabella signaled for him to stop.

He did so gladly, panting as he stepped back, resting the sledgehammer on the gatehouse's floor. The muscles in his arms were trembling; his back ached. Snowflakes, coming down harder now, lodged in his hair and eyelashes.

Arabella grasped the piling with both hands. She pushed against it. It didn't move. Then she tried to pull it toward her; it still didn't budge.

"Yes!" she crowed. "It's solid!" She glanced at the sky; dusk was starting to fall. "Let's get the second one in and tie it to the first. Then we can start tomorrow's work with one pair in place."

Just as before, Florian and Henri sharpened one end of a long wooden pole, then held it steady while Beau hammered it. The second piling was sunk quicker than the first. Arabella tested it again, and it held.

"Hurray!" she cheered. "We did it! I knew we could! We'll just lash the two poles together, and then we're done for the day."

She ran back into the gatehouse and emerged a few seconds later, running, with a coil of rope.

What happened next might not have happened if the sun hadn't been setting, and the snow hadn't been picking up, and the temperature hadn't been dropping.

Arabella's foot hit a patch of snow-dusted ice. She skidded, dropped the rope, and pitched forward.

There was a scream, a fluttering of skirts, and she was gone.

FORTY-SIX

"Arabella, *no!*"

Beau lunged for her, trying to grab her arm, her sweater, her skirt, *anything*, but it was too late. He saw her hit the surface of the moat. Saw the gray water close over her.

"No. Nonononono . . . come on, Arabella, you can swim, can't you?" he babbled, frantically scanning for her. But there was no sign of her. For once, he didn't think. Didn't calculate. Didn't weigh the risks or count the gains. "I'm going down," he said, grabbing a coil of rope. "The water's ice-cold. She won't last more than a few minutes."

"Where is she?" It was Florian. He and Henri were kneeling down at the edge of the threshold now.

As he spoke, Arabella surfaced, gasping and spitting.

"There!" Henri shouted, pointing a few yards to the left of the poles.

"Arabella!" Beau shouted. "Swim to the pilings!"

She nodded. Her strokes were jerky and clumsy and frothed the water around her. Beau looped the rope around his waist and knotted it. He glanced down again. Arabella had reached the pilings. She tried to hug one, but her hands slipped.

"B-Beau, th-th-throw me a rope," she shouted.

She was half-frozen. Her clothing was waterlogged. Beau knew she'd never be able to pull herself out of the moat and up the side of the castle wall, not without help.

"I'm coming to get you!" he shouted. "I'll be right there! Hang on to the . . ."

His words trailed away. He wasn't looking at her anymore. He was looking past her.

"Arabella, *shh*. Don't talk. Don't move."

"P-p-please . . . Beau . . . it's so *cold* . . ."

"Arabella. Be *quiet*."

"B-B-Beau . . . th-the rope . . ."

"Damn it, Arabella, shut up! They can hear you! They can *feel* you!"

Arabella, shaking now, gave him a confused look, then swiveled her head in the direction of his gaze. Beau heard her gasp. She turned back to him, her eyes pleading.

"I will get you. I promise. Just. Stay. *Still*."

Fear's talons dug into Beau like a hawk's into a rabbit. He knew he had only minutes to save her life. "Henri, distract them! Throw something! Anything!" he ordered. "Just throw it away from her!"

Henri ran into the gatehouse and came out with the broken windlass handle, a chunk of rock, pieces of a broken jug. He dumped them on the threshold, then started pitching them out over the water as far from Arabella as he could.

Beau tested the knot in the rope he'd looped around himself, then handed the rest of the coil to Florian. "Feed it through that." He pointed at an iron ring in the wall by the archway. "Then take up the slack. Hurry."

Florian did so, pulling the rope through the ring hand over hand as fast as he could.

"Good. Now let it out bit by bit."

As Florian gave him some slack, Beau backed out over the threshold, feet balanced on the edge, then made his way down the wall, step by careful step. It was difficult; thick vines grew up out of the moat and over the wall, tangling his feet. He glanced over his shoulder as he descended and saw that many of the monsters were no longer moving toward Arabella. They were thrashing in the water, swinging their horrible heads toward the splashes Henri was making.

Many, but not all.

He glanced at Arabella, but she wasn't looking at him anymore. She was looking at the thing a yard away from her, the thing with no eyes and no lips, with worms writhing in what was left of its cheeks.

Everything inside Beau told him to hurry, but he knew if he slipped and lost his footing, he'd lose precious seconds dangling uselessly until he regained it again.

"Oh God. Please, no . . ."

It was Arabella. Beau risked another look at her. The monster was only a foot away from her now. It was twisting its head as if it could smell her.

Henri stuck his fingers in his mouth and blew a shrill whistle. "Hey! Up here, beautiful!" he shouted. "Look what I have for you!"

The monster stopped. It tilted its fearsome face.

And then Henri, holding a twenty-pound iron counterweight, held it out over the water, in the small space between Beau on the wall and Arabella clinging to the piling, and with a hastily whispered prayer, he let it drop. It hit the creature's skull with a wet, crunchy thunk and plunged it under the surface.

A moment later Beau was in the water next to Arabella. She was shaking so hard she could no longer talk. Tension on the rope around Beau's waist kept him afloat.

"Henri! Throw down more rope!" he shouted.

Henri, still looking over the edge of the threshold, nodded. He disappeared, then quickly reappeared with a new coil. Holding on to one end, he tossed the rest to Beau, who caught it and looped it around Arabella's waist. His fingers, already numb with cold, were stiff and clumsy. It took him several tries to tie a knot, but he finally succeeded.

"You've got to walk up the wall. Like I just did," he told her. "Florian and Henri will pull you. They'll take most of your weight. It's hard, but you can do it."

Arabella nodded. Beau guided her to the wall and helped her get her body turned so that her feet were flat against it. The snow was coming down harder now; it scratched at his eyes.

"Henri, Florian, pull her up!" he shouted.

The two boys had fed their end of Arabella's loop through the iron ring in the wall, just as they had Beau's rope. They pulled on it now, and Arabella started up the wall, inch by slow inch, water sheeting from her sodden clothing. Her progress was slow but steady, and then, halfway up, her right foot slipped. She fell forward and hit the wall hard, then hung there helplessly.

"Come on, Arabella! Get it together!" Beau hissed up at her, casting a nervous glance behind himself. He wasn't sure what would get him first, the monsters or the killing cold.

With a wrenching effort, Arabella righted herself. Slowly, she closed the distance between herself and the ledge, her limbs shaking with exertion. When she finally got close, Florian reached over, grabbed the back of her sweater, and heaved her to safety.

"Your turn, Beau!" Henri shouted. "Now. Right *now.*"

Beau saw the boy's eyes on something behind him. He didn't have to look to know what it was. As soon as tension bit on his rope, he swung his legs up, planted his feet on the wall, and started to climb.

He hadn't taken more than two steps when he felt a bony hand close on his leg. It yanked hard and Beau slipped. He banged into the wall, dangling, both legs kicking at the creature. More of the monsters came, growling and swiping at him. He kicked harder, trying to keep them off.

As he did, pebbles rained down on him from above. He looked up.

Florian had skidded forward, sending the debris over the edge of the threshold. He'd righted himself, but his face was red with exertion. Henri, right behind him on the rope, was struggling against the deadweight.

"Climb, Beau! We can't hold you much longer!" Florian shouted.

Beau kicked hard. His foot connected with a skull. The fingers gripping his ankle uncurled. His scrabbling feet found purchase. He brought his legs up underneath him and started upward again.

Step by step, Florian and Henri moved back from the ledge. Limbs trembling, tendons standing out in their necks, they managed to hold firm while Beau made his way up the wall. After what felt like an eternity, he reached the ledge, then threw himself over it.

"G-g-good job, boys," he said. His teeth were chattering convulsively; his body felt as if it were made of ice. He tried to unknot the rope around his waist, but it was frozen hard, and his useless fingers could only fumble at it. Florian quickly cut it away with a knife.

"Wh-where's—" Beau started to say, but before he could finish his question, his eyes found her. She was lying on the floor of the gatehouse, curled into a shivering ball.

"Arabella!" he shouted, stumbling toward her.

She opened her eyes. They looked faraway and unfocused. "S-s-so cold," she stuttered.

"Henri, is the spit in the kitchen going?" Beau asked as he hauled Arabella up into a sitting position.

The boy nodded.

"Stoke up the fire under it. Florian, tell Valmont what happened. Get towels ready. Blankets. Hot broth. *Go*."

Florian and Henri set off running. With the last of his strength, Beau picked Arabella up in his arms and stumbled through the gatehouse.

Then he ran. Not for his life, not this time.

For hers.

FORTY-SEVEN

Beau shot through the open door.

Florian and Henri had made so much noise as they'd stumbled into the kitchen that all of the servants and court ladies had come running.

"This is all *your* doing," Espidra hissed at Beau now as he carried a motionless Arabella across the room to the blazing open hearth where meats were roasted. "Where are you going? Take her upstairs to her chambers!"

"There's no time," Beau said. "Florian, how's that broth coming?" he called over his shoulder.

"Almost ready!" Florian shouted back as Phillipe ladled rich yellow chicken stock into a mug.

Beau set Arabella on her feet. She swayed, then slumped to one side. It was like trying to stand a marionette up.

"Arabella!" He slapped her face lightly. "Wake up!"

Arabella jerked her head away with a mewl of protest. She tried to bat his hand away, but he grabbed her chin.

"Stand up. Raise your arms," he barked.

Arabella complied as best she could, and Beau grabbed the hem of her sodden sweater, yanked it over her head, and threw it on the floor. Next, he unbuttoned her blouse and pulled it off. A long row of buttons ran down the back of her skirt. He didn't stop to fumble with them; he just grasped the waistband and ripped it open. The skirt fell to the floor.

"Step out of it, that's it," he said. "Move closer to the fire." As she did, he kicked the sodden skirt away. "Where are the blankets?" he bellowed.

At that very instant, Claudette came running into the kitchen, her arms piled high with linens. Josette followed her, carrying a robe and slippers.

Beau snatched a blanket and held it up, shielding Arabella from her servants' gaze. He averted his own eyes. "Get her underthings off."

"Now see here, this is most indecent!" Hesma shrilled.

"Put a cork in it, gargoyle," Beau said.

Hesma squawked like an angry hen.

"Hurry, ladies, *hurry*," Beau urged the maids. "Are her things off?"

"They are," Josette replied.

"Rub her down with the towels. Go easy on her ears, fingers, and toes. She might have frostbite."

The maids did as he bade them, toweling the damp off Arabella's skin and a bit of warmth into her body.

"Put the robe on her, and the slippers," Beau said as soon as they'd finished. "Henri! Bring a chair over here. Lay a blanket over it."

Arabella stood hunched over, hugging herself, still shaking uncontrollably. Beau guided her to the chair and sat her down. He grabbed the edges of the blanket and folded them around her. He draped another blanket over her head and shoulders, then knelt down and wrapped a third one around her feet. Florian appeared with a mug of broth and handed it to him.

"You need to drink this," Beau said, offering the mug to Arabella. "Can you hold it?"

Arabella nodded. "Th-th-thank you," she said, sloshing a bit of broth as she took the mug. She blew on it, then sipped it. Another shiver moved through her. "I can still see that thing," she said. "It's the last thing I remember. What happened after . . ."

"I jumped in after you, but Henri the monster killer saved the day," Beau said, smiling up at the boy.

Henri grinned with pride.

"Did he?" Arabella asked. She turned toward the boy. "Thank you, Henri. I—"

180

"Where the devil is he? I'm going to tear him to pieces. I swear to God, I am!"

Valmont's deep voice boomed into the kitchen. His body followed. He arrived at the hearth and his gaze moved from Arabella's wet clothing, strewn all over the floor, to Arabella herself, hunched over the fire. He pushed his sleeves up, knotting one hand into a fist.

"It's over for you, thief," he growled.

Arabella stopped him. "Valmont, no," she said. "It was my own fault. Beau saved my life."

Valmont looked skeptical, but he lowered his fist. Beau stood up. He wanted to explain to Valmont what had happened. Instead, he almost fell over. Florian grabbed hold of him, steadying him.

"Beau, what is it? What's wrong?" asked Arabella, alarmed.

"I'm not sure," Beau said, looking down at his hands. His fingers were blue. His hands were trembling. From the second Arabella had plunged over the edge of the gatehouse and into the moat, he hadn't thought about anything but saving her. Now his teeth were rattling in his head. His legs felt weak. His entire body started to shake.

"Give him a blanket. Hurry," Arabella said to Florian.

As Florian wrapped a blanket around Beau's shoulders, Arabella stood and made Beau sit down in her chair.

"Henri, stoke up the flames," she said. "Help him get his wet things off."

As Henri tugged at Beau's boots, Percival hurried into the room. "I shall have your supper delayed, Lady Arabella, and have a hot bath drawn for you," he said.

Arabella rose, clutching her blankets around her. She turned to Beau. "If you can forgive me for nearly getting both of us killed, I would like you to join me."

Beau's eyebrows shot up. "In the bath?"

Florian and Henri snorted laughter. The maids bit back giggles.

181

Arabella cleared her throat. "No, *not* in the bath. At my table. For supper."

It was as if Arabella had shot off fireworks in the kitchen. Everyone in the room, all the servants, all the ladies, had collectively sucked in their breath as her words hung, glittering, in the air.

And Beau, who had jumped into deep, icy, gray water, who had faced down hellish monsters without so much as a single thought for his own safety, was suddenly afraid.

It was so stupid, what he'd done. Why had he done it? Why had he risked his life, his *life*, for a girl who wouldn't even do him the courtesy of ever giving him an honest answer—about herself, her castle, the creatures in it? He didn't know, and now he felt trapped. Everyone was looking at him. *Do they think I should be dazzled by Arabella's offer? Grateful for it?* he wondered. *Like some peasant invited to milady's table?*

Well, he wasn't. He'd saved her life, yes, but only because he needed her. She was going to build a bridge for him. So he could get to his brother. That was the reason, the only reason.

Espidra was looking at him as if she suspected that he was more than dazzled, more than grateful. It felt as if her shadowed eyes could see into his heart, to the strange new feelings that had taken root there.

"No, thank you," he said. "I'm not hungry."

His refusal hurt Arabella. He could see that. Her eyes narrowed in a wince, but she forced them wide again.

"Of course," she said smoothly, striving to save face. "I'm sure you're exhausted from your heroic actions. I shall see you in the morning." She stood then and left the kitchen. Her maids and ladies followed her.

The glitter in the air winked out. Beau felt the servants who were left in the room give a big, collective sigh, exhaling hope like acrid smoke.

Beau felt irritated by their expectations. It came out in his voice. "Any chance of a bath for me, Monty? Maybe some dry clothing?"

Valmont shook his head. "I'll give you a bath, all right. I'll throw you right back in the moat."

Percival stepped in. "We'll have one drawn for you in the servants' quarters," he said. "Stay by the fire for now or you'll catch your death."

Beau nodded; he pulled the blanket up around his neck. He was colder than before.

The temperature had dropped in the room.

To somewhere below freezing.

– FORTY-EIGHT –

"Beau! Beau? Hey, *Beau!* Percival says your bath is ready."

Beau startled awake, unsure of where he was. Then he saw Florian's face hanging over him, and he realized he'd fallen asleep in front of the fireplace. He rubbed his eyes, then slowly stood, ready to head to the servants' quarters.

"Oh, but wait! I forgot. There aren't any towels," Florian continued. "Claudette used a ton of them to dry off the mistress. Percival said to ask Josephine for some."

Beau rolled his eyes.

Camille looked up from the batter she was mixing. "Josephine's in the mistress's chambers," she said. "Go to the linen press, Florian. There are more stacked there."

Florian hurried off, and Beau walked toward the baker's worktable. "Could I get a hot cup of coffee?" he asked. He needed something to beat back the tiredness or he'd fall asleep in the bathtub.

Camille set about filling a mug for him from the pot that always seemed to be warming on the stove.

"Here you go," Florian said, reappearing with two towels. He handed them to Beau. He glanced around, then leaned in close to Beau so

Camille couldn't hear him. "I think you were a little hasty, turning down that supper invitation."

Beau groaned. "Not you, too."

"Chef is in the larder, cutting some nice thick fillets."

"Thanks, Florian. But that would be a big mis-steak."

"Huh?"

"Never mind."

Tucking the towels under one arm, Beau picked up the mug Camille had placed on the table for him. He wanted to thank her, but she was all the way across the kitchen now, talking with Phillipe. He gulped down a mouthful, closing his eyes as its warmth spread through his chest.

"Hey, macarons! This is my lucky night!"

Beau's eyes snapped open. Faith was standing there, her fingers hovering over a tray of Camille's treats. Hope was with her. Faith picked one of the sweets up and bit into it. "You certainly are a stupid ass," she said as she chewed.

"Nice to see you, too," said Beau, putting his mug down.

"Can't you smell the smells? Phillipe's cooking up a storm." She finished her treat, walked to the stove, and dipped her finger into a pot. "Mmm!" she said, licking her finger. "This sauce right here? It's some *serious*—"

"You should have supper with Arabella," Hope said to Beau.

Beau stubbornly shook his head. "No."

"Why?" Faith pressed. "Because you're mad that she hasn't told you everything you want to know? Like she should just hand you the key to her soul? You can't steal every key, boy. Some you have to earn."

"You're four feet tall," Beau said. "Stop calling me *boy*."

"You going to have supper with her? You have to eat, don't you? And it's steak night!"

Beau hesitated, unsure now. These two obnoxious children had a way of doing that, of shaking him out of his closed-door certainties and pushing him into the realm of possibilities.

"I've never dined with nobility. What would I do? Behave like a courtier? I don't know how," he admitted. Then, hating that he'd showed even a modicum of vulnerability, he grinned and flippantly said, "Guess I could always be the charming, devastatingly attractive lady-killer that I am."

"How about being a friend, Beau?" Faith said. "Why don't you try that?"

Before Beau could reply, they heard footsteps.

"Bye!" Faith whispered. She snatched another macaron, then ran out of the kitchen.

Hope lingered. "Guilt never built a bridge. Or saved a life."

Beau felt a chill move through him. It was as if Hope had seen deep down inside him, to the real reason he didn't want to join Arabella—because he felt that he shouldn't be sitting in a grand dining room, eating fine food, when his little brother would be lucky to get a bowl of hot soup.

"How do you know—"

The footsteps drew closer.

"Kindness is a rare gift in this world, Beau. Take it when it's offered."

"I don't need her kindness. It's not going to help me."

"Who said anything about you?"

And then she was gone, too.

Percival strode into the kitchen. Rémy trailed him. They were carrying platters. As they set them down, Percival said, "Why are you still here? Your bath is getting cold."

Beau nodded. He started toward the servants' staircase. But then he stopped. And turned around.

"Hey, Perce?" he said.

"Do not call me—"

"Tell Chef he's got two for supper."

– FORTY-NINE –

Word has spread among the servants.

Their mistress and the thief are having supper.

Camille stirs batter for a torte. She uses the finest chocolate, ground coffee beans, candied chestnuts, and mixes in a pinch of paprika. Everyone knows that the spice sparks passion.

Lucile, the gardener's wife, wraps her red wool shawl around her shoulders and ventures to the greenhouse to snip blooms for the table. She chooses camellias for longing and roses for love.

Claudette, Josette, Florian, and Henri ready the great hall as if God Himself were coming to dine. They polish the table. Wind the music box. Lay out the very best porcelain.

And Phillipe the chef begins to cook. He does not know if he will be alive in a week's time, but he knows that food is love.

For a hundred years, he has cooked chicken soup for his old friend Valmont, who coughs too much from too many years spent breathing gunpowder on battlefields.

For a hundred years, he has roasted shank bones for Josephine, whose back aches from lifting wet sheets. The rich marrow does her good.

For a hundred years, he has made duck with sour cherries for Percival, the love of his life, who is creaking to a halt before his very eyes. His joints grow stiff; his gait grows slow. He tries to hide these things behind sharp creases and sharper words, but Phillipe sees them.

He fights for them, all of them, at his giant iron stove like a general fighting a war.

186

He fights powerful enemies: sorrow, grief, hopelessness, despair. He fights with powerful weapons: onions, garlic, butter, and salt.

But for some time now, he has been losing the battle.

He knows this. He sees it in Gustave's stooped shoulders. In Claudette's tears. In Camille's heartbroken eyes. He sees it in the castle's dusty corners, in all the rooms that are never entered anymore, in the vases that stand empty of flowers.

Arabella gave up. Long ago. He himself is close to giving up. He does not know how to fight on. It calls for more strength than he thinks he has.

Then he picks up a white truffle he's been saving, raises it to his nose, and inhales its earthy scent. It brings back a memory of the first dinner he ever made for Percival, such a long time ago: tagliatelle with cream, white wine, and whisper-thin slices of truffle.

He'd been a young chef at a duke's Paris mansion, and the truffle had cost him a week's wages.

Bertrand, the baker, said he'd lost his mind. "What does a fungus know about love?" he'd scoffed.

"More than you do," Phillipe had replied.

He'd surprised Percival, who was then a valet, late one night. It was just the two of them in the cavernous kitchen, with the platter of pasta, half a bottle of champagne left over from the duke's dinner, and candlelight.

Percival had never tasted a truffle, and Phillipe can still see the look on his face as he tried it. He'd chewed his first bite and swallowed it, then he'd leaned across the table and kissed Phillipe full on the lips.

"I fell in love that night," Percival always says.

"With me?" Phillipe always teases. "Or a truffle?"

Phillipe regards the fat little jewel in his hand. It worked once . . . could it work again?

Though it hurts to hope, he lights the big stove once more. He heats a pot of chicken broth, fetches a bag of rice, a chunk of Parmesan. There isn't enough time to make fresh pasta, but risotto's good, too.

Valmont walks into the kitchen carrying a silver tray. Percival is right behind him with a wine decanter. They stare at the truffle.

"It won't work," Percival says with a sigh.

Phillipe shoots him a look. "I won't give up. I *can't* give up."

"But they do not love each other. They do not even like each other. It's pointless."

"What, exactly, is pointless?" Phillipe asks, his voice rising.

"All of it. Everything. We've tried, Phillipe, haven't we? Over and over and over—"

Phillipe slams the pot he's holding down on the stovetop and gestures at Valmont. "Our old friend there is not pointless!" he shouts. "Gustave and Lucile and Josephine are not pointless! The maids are not! Even *Florian* is not pointless! We matter, Percival. Each and every one of us. This is our story, too."

Percival's chin quivers. His eyes fill with tears. The sight melts Phillipe's anger. He crosses the room and touches his forehead to Percival's. "You are not pointless. You are my life," he says ferociously. "And I will fight for you until the clock winds down. Until the walls around us crumble to dust. Until I draw my last breath."

Percival nods. He wipes his eyes and touches Phillipe's cheek. Then he turns and leaves the kitchen.

Phillipe watches him go, then picks up his grater. This will be the best truffle risotto ever made. It will be so delicious, so beguiling, the thief will not know what hit him. It's only when he finishes grating the Parmesan that he realizes Valmont is still there. He is leaning against the table, a look of pain on his face.

Phillipe's brow creases with worry. "What's hurting you now, old friend?" he asks. "Your shoulder? Your knee?"

Valmont shakes his head. He taps his chest.

On the left side.

Where his heart is.

– FIFTY –

Beau eyed his reflection in the mirror, turning this way and that.

He had never even seen such a beautiful piece of clothing, never mind worn one. Slipping the frock coat on was like pulling a length of midnight around himself. The indigo silk gleamed in the candlelight; its silver buttons, set with sapphires, sparkled.

Beau pinched one between his thumb and forefinger, inspecting it. "What do you think one of these would go for, Perce?"

"I would not know. I am an underbutler, not a fence," Percival sniffed, running his hands over Beau's shoulders, smoothing the fabric. He looked over the top of his spectacles; his eyes met Beau's in the mirror. "However, I do know that there are six buttons down the front of this jacket and three more on each cuff. And they had all better still be there when you hand this back to me."

"Where did this come from? Was it yours?"

Percival laughed. "Goodness, no. It belonged to the duke, Arabella's father." He stepped around to Beau's front and adjusted the jacket's collar. A wistful smile curved his lips. "In his younger days, he cut quite a dashing figure."

Beau wore tall black leather boots, britches of ivory, and a shirt of soft white linen under the coat, ruffled at the neck and cuffs.

Percival tugged on one of the shirt cuffs now, coaxing the ruffle to fall just so. "Good clothes are important. They make you want to stand up straighter. Hold your head higher. They make you want to be—"

"*Better,*" Beau finished softly. The word had come unbidden.

Percival stopped fussing with the cuff and looked at Beau, squinting slightly, as if he was seeing something he hadn't seen before. "Yes," he agreed. "Better."

He circled Beau one last time, then said, "It's time to go."

Beau nodded and followed him, telling himself that he was only doing this to be polite, to stay on Arabella's good side. Until they finished the bridge, he needed her help.

But the truth was something different. He wanted another key now— the key to the mystery that was Arabella. He wanted to turn it and see what it unlocked. He'd never wanted such a thing before; he'd never allowed himself to. He'd learned long ago that it was better not to want things. That way, it didn't hurt so much when you didn't get them.

The tall double doors to the great hall were closed. Percival grasped the handles and threw them open, and Beau found himself amazed, just as he had been the first time he'd set foot in the castle. Flames crackled in the fireplace, throwing warmth into the room. White roses and camellias, entwined with ivy, cascaded from vases. Elegant tapers flickered in silver candelabra. The music box played a slow, lilting tune. Everything looked even more beautiful than it had that first night.

Except for the head of the table. Which was a spectacular mess.

Arabella was seated there, amid scrolls, books, quills, and an inkwell. She'd cleared a space to work by pushing the tablecloth, candlesticks, vases, plates, glassware, and cutlery into a heap. Her head was bent. She was drawing. Again. With an almost manic intensity. It puzzled him.

Beau saw that she was wearing a silk gown of deepest emerald. Its collar rose high in the back. Its bodice, heavily embroidered with gold thread and pearls, ran in a straight edge from shoulder to shoulder, narrowing at her waist. Her gleaming hair had been swept up and anchored with a pearl comb. A deep blue shawl had settled in the crooks of her arms.

How beautiful you are, he thought.

And then he felt fear turn his bones to sand, and he wished with all his heart that he had not done this. He wished he could turn around and leave. But it was too late.

Percival cleared his throat. "Pardon me, Your Grace . . ." he began.

"Put it down anywhere, Percival," Arabella said, not bothering to look up.

"I cannot, Your Grace. *It* is not a platter. *It* is Monsieur Beauregard."

Arabella looked up. *"Beau?"* she said. Before she could stop herself, her mouth, her eyes, her whole face broke into a smile.

"That supper invitation still good?" he asked.

"Yes, of course," Arabella said.

Beau stood rooted to the spot. Until Percival cleared his throat. Then, remembering himself, he snatched a rose from a vase, swept Arabella a bow, and handed the bloom to her.

"Oh, you shouldn't have," she said with a tart smile, taking it.

"Yeah, well," he said self-consciously. "I tried to get you a bouquet in town, but all the flower shops were closed."

Arabella snorted and Beau's shoulders relaxed a little. They were back in their familiar rhythm of taunts, goads, and semi-insults.

"Sit down . . . sit *here*." She gestured at the chair on her right, then frowned at the mess she'd made.

Percival frowned, too. He looked downright tragic. "I shall help you, my lady," he said.

"No need," she said, pushing the tablecloth and vases and salt cellars and mustard pots down the table in a rumple of bunched linen and clanking silver. "There," she said, satisfied. "Now there's plenty of room."

Percival sighed, then extricated two place settings and arranged them in front of Arabella and Beau.

"You were working on the bridge?" Beau asked her.

"Yes. And I think I've figured out how we can sink the second set of pilings," she said, nodding at her drawing.

"You did? That's great, Arabella," Beau said excitedly, but his excitement faded and panic took its place as he sat down and eyed all the cutlery. He had been in many great halls before, but always as the servant, never the served.

"Perce," he whispered out of the side of his mouth. "The *silverware*."

"You must not steal *that*, either," Percival said, giving him a stern look.

"I'm not *going* to. I forget which fork is for what!"

Percival's expression softened; he patted Beau's back. "Work from the outside in."

The advice did little to calm Beau, but luckily, Percival had a stronger remedy at hand—a bottle of champagne chilling in a silver bucket. He produced two crystal flutes, then looked for a suitable place to set them.

"Oh, Percival, don't fuss," Arabella scolded. "Plunk them anywhere."

Percival nudged Arabella's drawings aside, and a stack of books as well. Then he put the two glasses down and poured. When he finished, he wiped the lip of the bottle, set it back in its ice bath, and left for the kitchen.

Arabella picked up her glass. "Here's to not being eaten by moat monsters."

Beau touched his glass to hers. "Cheers," he said, and then he downed half of it. He was, to his deep annoyance, strangely shy around her. He was never shy around a woman. *Never*. He chugged the rest of his champagne.

"All warm and dry now?" he asked.

All warm and dry now? a voice inside him mimicked. *You sound like someone's grandmother.*

"I am, thank you," Arabella said. "What about you?"

"A hot bath set me right." He gestured at his ensemble. "Percival found these for me."

"I remember that jacket," Arabella said, with a wistful smile. "It was my father's favorite."

Beau wasn't sure what to say. "He's not here anymore?"

Arabella didn't reply, but her eyes filled with sorrow and Beau guessed he must've died.

"But he's always here. In your heart, I mean, right?" he quickly said, grimacing at his own insensitivity. "I'm sorry, I shouldn't have brought up a hard topic. Seems I'm good at doing that."

At that moment Percival returned, a white linen cloth folded over one arm, and Beau was happy to see him—and to change the subject. Percival was followed by Florian and Henri. The boys were both carrying domed plates. Florian set his down before Arabella; Henri placed his in front of Beau. At a nod from Percival, they lifted the domes.

"Vichyssoise with a garnish of crème fraîche and caviar," Percival said. Then he leaned in close to Beau and whispered in his ear. "That's cold potato soup to you."

He poured a crisp white wine, perfectly chilled, then he and the kitchen boys left. The awkwardness Beau had introduced by bringing up Arabella's father had been dispelled, but as he stared at his bowl, a new unhappiness took its place. Nothing about the dish—not *cold* nor *potato* nor *soup*—sounded appealing. Potato soup was what he, Raphael, and the others ate when they didn't have a penny. He edged his soup spoon into his bowl, lifted it to his lips, and got a wondrous surprise. The soup was like poured satin on his tongue. It tasted of a rich, long-simmered stock, earthy potatoes, fresh cream, and black pepper. The caviar was a salty exclamation point.

"This is amazing," he said. He quickly swallowed another mouthful. "Arabella, you have to taste it."

193

"Mmm, yes," she said absently, stretching one arm toward the drawings Percival had shifted. She made no move to pick up her spoon.

"No, really. It's *so* good," he said excitedly, carried away by the pleasure Phillipe's food gave him. "You have to try it. Here . . ."

He dipped the spoon back into his bowl, filled it, and held it out to her. But in his excitement, he tilted the spoon and spilled its contents down the front of her beautiful green bodice. It looked as if a seagull had flown over her.

Beau sucked in a breath, appalled at himself. How could he be so clumsy? What was wrong with him tonight?

"Oh no. I'm so sorry," he said in a rush. "Here . . . I'll fix it."

He dipped a corner of his napkin into a pitcher of water, then rubbed briskly at the spot, determined to remove it before it left a stain. He was so absorbed in his task, he didn't notice Arabella stiffen or see the look of mortification in her eyes.

"Beau?" she said, her voice rising a little.

"Don't worry. Seriously, Arabella, I've got it. Stain's almost out, and—"

Arabella cleared her throat. "Beau, that's my cleavage," she said. "Could you not?"

Beau froze. "Oh my *God*." His eyes widened in horror as he realized what he'd done.

Arabella slowly pushed his hand away and picked up her own soup spoon.

Beau balled up the wet napkin. Then smoothed it out again. Then folded it over. "I—I don't even know what to say." He didn't recognize himself. He was always as smooth as silk around women. He made *them* flustered. But tonight he was as fumbly and awkward as some squeaky-voiced, knock-kneed fourteen-year-old.

Percival saved him again. He appeared with the decanter of white wine, refreshed their glasses, then directed Florian and Henri to remove their plates.

"What's next, Percival? Do you know?" Arabella asked as Beau took a large gulp of his wine.

"I'm afraid I don't, Your Grace. Phillipe only tells me when the dish is ready to be served."

"That's a shame," Arabella said. "Our guest likes to be kept abreast of things."

Beau snorted but managed not to spew his wine across the table. Percival glanced between Beau, who was blowing his nose in his napkin now, and Arabella, who was affecting an expression of wide-eyed innocence, and then he set off for the kitchen, a look of confusion on his face.

"You are evil," Beau said, when he could speak again.

"So I've been told," Arabella said.

Percival had left the decanter of wine on the table in his haste to fetch Beau a new napkin. Arabella picked it up and filled Beau's glass. Any lingering strangeness between them was now gone.

"We didn't get as much done today as I'd hoped," she said, a regretful note in her voice.

"I guess not, but the pilings we did manage to set into the moat are there to stay," Beau said. "How do we get the next pair in, though? That's the challenge."

Arabella, having given up digging through her drawings, gathered up her silverware and Beau's. She laid a butter knife horizontally on the table. "As I mentioned, I think I've figured it out. Say this is the gate-house's threshold . . ." She placed two forks, crossed, a few inches above it. "And these are the first pair of pilings . . ."

Beau leaned in, elbows on the table, chin on his hand, watching her as she explained the logistics of setting the second pair of pilings. He liked how unguarded she became when she spoke about building things. How she wrinkled her nose, squinted her eyes. How she leaned back in her chair, drumming her fingers on the arm, then shot forward, excited by a breakthrough.

"So the biggest problem we'll have tomorrow is stability—our own," she said. "We'll need to fashion some sort of platform in the notch of the first pair of pilings, to support us while we set the second pair." She frowned at the diagram she'd made, then sketched out a couple of ideas. "What do you think?" she asked when she finished.

But Beau hadn't really heard her. He was too taken by the fire in her eyes and the passion in her gestures.

"Beau . . . *Beau?*" She was slapping the table in front of him with her palm.

"Hmm?"

"Have you listened to a word I said?"

Percival saved him. "Chateaubriand with truffle risotto and steamed asparagus," he announced, reappearing with Florian and Henri.

When they'd set the plates down, he poured an old red, so dark it looked black in the candlelight, then the three returned to the kitchen.

It was all Beau could do not to tear into his meal. The fillet, beautifully seared on the outside; the yellow béarnaise sauce lapped over it, redolent with the scents of butter and tarragon; the heady perfume of the truffled rice—it made his stomach squeeze with hunger. But he knew he must not start before his hostess, so he waited until Arabella began, then cut into his beef and lifted a piece to his lips.

"Oh. Wow. I mean, *damn*," he said.

Phillipe's food was casting its spell over Beau and Arabella. When they'd finished their entrées, Percival brought out dessert—a towering chocolate torte, filled with layers of coffee buttercream, chocolate ganache, and chestnut meringue. After that, there were cheeses—crumbly ones, gooey ones, moldy ones, smelly ones. Sugar-frosted cherries. Figs soaked in brandy. Tiny meringues. Cognac.

After nearly two hours at the table, Beau leaned back in his chair and groaned. "If I eat one more bite, the buttons will pop off this coat." *And if I have one more drink*, he thought, *my head will pop off my neck.*

Arabella laughed. "That coat looks good on you. In fact, you could pass for a young nobleman in it." She sat back in her chair, took a sip of wine, and said, "Why don't you?"

"Why don't I what?" Beau asked, puzzled.

"Pretend to be a count, or an earl. Get yourself invited to balls and shooting weekends at the grand châteaux. Maybe even Versailles. Why not? You could rob much more efficiently that way."

Beau smiled, surprised to learn that Arabella had a mischievous side, and intrigued by it. He leaned forward, elbows on the table. "Never pegged you for a criminal mastermind, Bells."

Arabella leaned forward, too. "Think about it. Where are the biggest diamonds likely to be? Around the neck of some country squire's wife? Or dangling down the décolletage of a grand duchess?"

"You have a point."

"I'd have to train you first."

"*You* train *me*?" Beau said with a snort. "In what?"

Arabella, smiling impishly, said, "Court etiquette. Titles. Pecking order. For example, at a state pageant, who immediately precedes the king . . . a duke or a viscount? At a bird hunt, when may a count hand a prince his gun?"

"Hmm."

"You can pass yourself off as a nobleman from a distant country—that way you can be forgiven for a bit of awkwardness—but at the very least you'd have to know how to shoot pheasants, pass tea cakes, talk about nothing, and dance."

"I know how to dance, Arabella."

"Do you? The minuet? A contra dance?"

"Maybe not those," Beau conceded.

"I'll teach you," Arabella said. She shrugged off her shawl and hurried to the music box. "This thing plays different types of music," she said.

She opened the side of the music box, replaced a small brass cylinder with another one, then walked to an open area. Beau met her there as dull, stately music began to play, suddenly feeling a little off-kilter, a little self-conscious in his borrowed clothing. He'd made too much of the food. Overindulged in the wine. Just like the know-nothing street kid he was. Expensive clothing, fine wines, court dances—they belonged to the world Arabella lived in, a world he could only ever visit. Arabella curtsied to him; he bowed to her. She moved to his side, then lifted her arm. He stared at her, not knowing what to do, his awkwardness growing. But then she took his arm and lifted it, too, then placed her hand over his, smiling. Her smile was real. Her skin was silken; her touch was soft and warm, and it calmed him immediately.

"Step and slide, step and slide . . . yes, that's it," she instructed. "Head up, chin high. Arms out . . . no! Not like a *stork*, like *this*."

Beau sighed. The music was slow; the steps were complicated.

"Hands graceful. Right, now turn," Arabella prompted. "No, *no* . . . toward me . . . and away again. That's it. Now I rest my hand on yours and we promenade. Our steps are light . . . *light*, Beau! And turn once more . . . very good. Now repeat."

Beau's shoulders slumped. "Repeat? You mean we have to do that again? I am going to die."

"Will you stop?"

"I am. I'm dying."

Arabella released Beau's hand. She took a step back from him, her own hands on her hips. "Of what?"

"Boredom."

"It's a pavane, Beau. It's a refined and elegant court dance."

"It's a funeral march," Beau said sulkily.

"What happens if you're invited to a ball given by the Dowager Countess von Bismarck and she asks you to be her partner?"

Beau shrugged. "I won't go."

Arabella lifted an eyebrow. "That would be a shame. The countess owns the biggest pair of ruby earrings I've ever seen."

Beau decided to turn the tables. "What if *you* find yourself at the Slaughtered Lamb, dancing with Raphael, Lord of the Thieves," he challenged her. "He's stolen the key to the innkeeper's strongbox. You could take it from him—you're Paris's best pickpocket—but first you have to get close to him. And the thief lord loves to dance. But *not* a pavane."

"I guess I'd miss my chance," Arabella said ruefully. "All I know are court dances."

"Then you're lucky I'm here," said Beau, brightening.

He shrugged out of his borrowed coat and draped it over a chair. Then he loosened the silk cravat around his neck.

"I'll teach you a real dance," he said. "A gavotte. A rigadoon. A true bumpkin throw-down. We just need the right music."

He walked to the music box and rifled through the cylinders. The names of the songs they played were printed on them, but he didn't see what he wanted. He frowned, stymied, then snapped his fingers. "Come on!" he said, taking her by the hand and pulling her to him.

"Where are we going?"

"Dancing."

Almost every servant was in the kitchen when Beau and Arabella burst through the door. They didn't have time to curtsy or bow before Beau shouted, "Lady Arabella wishes to dance. Hey, Perce! Can you play anything?"

"Well, yes. Yes, I can," Percival said, after he got over his surprise. "The violin."

"Go get it!"

Perce? Arabella mouthed at her underbutler.

Percival rolled his eyes.

"Florian, you play anything?" Beau asked.

"The accordion," Florian proudly replied.

"Why am I not surprised," Beau said. He shooed Florian off to get the accordion, then turned to the others. "How about a guitar? Anyone play the guitar?"

Valmont cleared his throat. "I've been known to strum a few chords on occasion."

"I have a tambourine," Henri offered.

As they, too, hurried to fetch their instruments, the rest of the servants finished what they were doing—washing dishes, damping the fires, wiping down the oven. By the time everyone was assembled and tuned up, the whole company had taken their aprons off, and cakes and brandy had been set out at Arabella's request.

Percival and Valmont played together on occasion, but the four had never attempted it, and their first few tries were abysmal.

Beau covered his ears with his hands. Then he spun around on his heel and marched over to the musicians. "Stop, stop, stop!" he said. "Not fancy music. Real music. Anyone know 'The Fisherman and His Nice Long Pole'? No? How about 'The Highwayman's Sweet Little Pistol'?"

Percival looked at Valmont; Valmont looked at Percival. They shook their heads.

Beau huffed an impatient sigh. "Give me that, Monty," he said, reaching for his guitar. He held it against his body, fingered the frets, and began to strum. "This one's called 'The Hangman's Limp Rope' . . ."

"I've never heard of it," said Percival.

"That's because I made it up. Now pay attention ... it goes like this," Beau said as he started to sing the funny, bawdy tavern song and accompany himself on Valmont's guitar.

His beautiful voice and quick fingers worked magic. At first, the servants traded glances, surprised by Beau's talent. Then, within seconds, they were laughing and clapping and singing the chorus. Henri faux-curtsied to Florian, who bowed in return, and the two started to dance, Henri taking mincing steps, Florian twirling him around. By the time Beau finished the song, to a burst of cheers and applause, even Arabella was clapping.

Valmont, Percival, Florian, and Henri all pulled up chairs and sat down. Then they began to play Beau's song. Bit by bit, it gathered steam.

"Pick it up, boys! It's a party, not a wake," Beau shouted. "One, two, three! One, two, three!" He clapped his hands in time.

Martin, the farmer, jumped up on a chair and called out steps. Gustave and Lucile started a promenade. The old gardener grasped his wife's hands, twirled her around, and escorted her down the line. Josette, red-cheeked and laughing, her skirts flying, joined in with Claudette. Camille curtsied to little Rémy. Phillipe bowed to Josephine.

"*That's* what I'm talking about!" Beau shouted. He locked arms with Arabella, and they joined the line of dancers. "Follow me!"

Arabella made a few mistakes but was soon able to keep up. As they reached the end of the line, broke apart, and started back to the top, Henri put down his tambourine and broke into a vigorous hornpipe, to the cheers of all the other dancers.

Arabella clapped with delight. "Top that, Beauregard Armando Fernandez de Navarre!" Her gray eyes were sparkling.

"Bells, you're not daring me, are you? Because that would be *such* a bad move."

Arabella nodded. "I'm sorry—"

"You should be."

Arabella grinned. "—that you're such a scaredy-cat."

Beau pretended to be insulted. The musicians picked up their tempo, goading him. Beau took their dare and launched into his own hornpipe, his feet moving even faster than Henri's had. For his grand finale, he pirouetted, stubbed his toe, stumbled, fell backward, and landed in Valmont's lap with a loud *whump.*

Valmont's guitar exploded. The chair collapsed. And then the two men found themselves flailing around on the floor like a pair of upside-down turtles.

"Blast and damnation! Get *off* me!" Valmont bellowed.

"*Ow,* Monty! Stop pulling my hair!"

"Let go of my foot!"

Josephine and Lucile giggled so hard at the sight, they started to wheeze. The maids shrieked with laughter. Percival bent over double, and Phillipe laughed until he had tears in his eyes. Arabella pressed a hand over her mouth, but even she couldn't smother her mirth; it burst out of her.

And Beau, who was still on the floor on his hands and knees after crawling off Valmont, watched her, awestruck. He'd heard her laugh before. Mirthlessly. Mockingly. Acidly. This was real laughter— spontaneous, unfettered, joyous. Full and sparkling, like a rushing silver stream in springtime. And beautiful. So beautiful.

As she was.

Her color was high. Her eyes were shining. Tendrils of silken hair had slipped from their knot and now framed her face.

And suddenly, Beau wanted her. With a longing like he'd never felt in all his life. He wanted to hold her, to kiss her, to tell her how lovely she was. He quickly looked down, before anyone saw his feelings. Before she did. He knew all too well that such a bright and beautiful creature was not meant for him, but it would kill him to hear her say so.

He got to his feet, then helped Valmont up. Arabella promised Valmont that she would replace his guitar with one from the castle's music room. Then she asked Percival to fetch more brandy from the cellars. As she did, a visible shiver ran through her. She was flushed from dancing, but the ovens had been turned off, the fires had burned down, and the cavernous kitchen had grown chilly.

"I'll get your shawl, mistress," Josette said.

Arabella waved her offer away. "Thank you, but I can do it."

"I'll go with you," Beau said. "I left your father's coat there. Percival will kill me if anything happens to it."

Percival overheard him. "I certainly will," he said.

When they reached the great hall, Beau could barely see to look for the coat. Most of the candles had melted; the rest were guttering stubs. They gave only a soft half-light.

"Poor Valmont," Arabella said, picking up her shawl. "Not only did you break his guitar, I trod on his foot during the gavotte. Everyone moved so fast! I couldn't follow the steps that happen right before the jump." She put the shawl down again, raised her skirts slightly, and looked at her feet. "Step out and close. Step out and close. Cross, touch . . . cross, raise, then skip?" She looked up at Beau.

"Almost," Beau said, walking toward her. "It goes like this . . . "

He showed her the steps. After two tries, she executed them perfectly.

"Good, but go a little faster," he said, picking up the tempo.

"I need music," she protested.

"No problem," Beau said, taking her hands. He began to sing "The Hangman's Limp Rope" again as he led her through the steps, but made up new lyrics.

Hey there, Arabella, who's that handsome fella?
The one with such a pretty face, he makes the ladies sigh.
He's smart as a professor, and such a snappy dresser . . .

Arabella, twirling under his arm, cut in before he could sing the next line.

Hey there, Beauregard, you make these dance steps very hard,
You've trod on my feet so many times, they look just like a duck's.
Hate to be a fuddy-duddy, but my toes are very bloody,
If you don't learn to step lightly, they surely will be f—

"*Arabella!*" Beau admonished, cutting her off.

"What?" Arabella said innocently, as they promenaded side by side.

Beau gave her a look. "You were about to say a very bad and unimaginative four-letter word. One that begins with *F.*"

"I was about to say *flat*," Arabella retorted. "I can't imagine what *you* were thinking."

Beau's mouth twitched with mirth. He spun her in a circle, and they continued dancing and singing made-up lyrics, making each other laugh, until they ran out of lyrics and stopped, heaving for breath, standing only inches from each other, still holding each other's hands. Not laughing anymore.

Let go, a voice inside him said. *Right now. She doesn't want this.*

Beau released her. Before he embarrassed her. Before he embarrassed himself.

But Arabella didn't move away.

Instead, she looked up at him, her eyes asking him.

Wordlessly, he answered.

And then she kissed him.

FIFTY-ONE

When Beauregard Armando Fernandez de Navarre kissed a woman, he only ever thought of stealing.

His mind was never on her; it was always a hundred other places, trying to figure out how to get a key out of her pocket, or slip a bracelet off her wrist, or sweet-talk the location of the master's strongbox out of her.

Now, for the first time—for the only time—in his life, he thought nothing, he only felt.

He felt the sweet heat of Arabella's lips on his, the taste of her, brandy and bitter chocolate.

He felt the warmth of her body pressed against his. And he felt doors open in his heart that he knew he'd never be able to close again.

Nothing, not bullets or knives or jail cells, scared him as much as this. He broke the kiss, fear overwhelming him, and took a step back, fighting down the panic, the urge to save himself, to walk out of the room, to walk away from her, without looking back.

Arabella's eyes were questioning at first, then hurt filled them, and he couldn't bear it. He took her face in his hands and kissed her again, but as he did, a noise rose behind them, the sinister ratchet of clock weights traveling up their chains.

The golden clock came to life. Gears, cogwheels, and pawls engaged. A door opened near the large silver bell. The mechanical clockmaker emerged with his hammer and started ringing the hour—midnight.

The chimes, bright and insistent, sounded like an alarm. They pushed at Beau's consciousness, intruding, trying to warn him of something. He blocked them out; he didn't want to hear them. He only wanted to stay like this, his lips pressed to Arabella's, his hands buried in the silk of her hair. But before he knew what was happening, Arabella pulled away from him, stumbling backward, her eyes wild with fright.

"What's wrong?" he asked, confused.

She didn't answer. She just kept backing away, her eyes on the clockmaker, her hands raised, as if to push him from the room.

"Arabella?" he pressed.

And then it hit him. Midnight.

"My God, the beast," he said.

Arabella shifted her gaze to him, but her eyes were far away. He wasn't even sure that she saw him.

Beau knew the vicious creature would be coming out to prowl the castle at any second, if it wasn't out already. They were in terrible danger, both of them. The servants, too.

"It's all right," he said, reaching for her. "I'll get you to your room. You'll be safe there."

Arabella's eyes focused on him, then grew large with fear. In a strangled voice, she whispered one word.

"*Run.*"

– F I F T Y - T W O –

"I'm not leaving you. I won't let it hurt you. Take my hand, Arabella."

But Arabella's gaze was inward now. She seemed to not even hear Beau. He started toward her, determined to get her out of harm's way, but before he'd taken three steps, she cried out, then doubled over.

"Arabella, what's wrong?"

"Don't touch her!" a voice boomed from behind him.

Beau whirled around; it was Valmont. He barreled toward Beau, reaching for the iron ring at his hip, and fumbled a skeleton key off it. Percival was close on his heels. Their faces were pictures of barely contained terror.

"Something happened to her . . . she's hurt," Beau said.

"Get away from her," Percival commanded.

Beau was shocked by his callousness. "But she's in pain!"

"Leave, you fool!" Valmont thundered. He pressed the key into Beau's hand. "Get to your room. *Now.* Lock yourself in."

"I'm not going anywhere! She needs help!" Beau shouted. "*Look* at her!"

Arabella had sunk to her knees, keening. She was in agony.

Valmont grabbed Beau by the back of his jacket, strong-armed him to the doorway, and threw him into the entry hall. Beau stumbled, caught himself on the edge of a table, then turned and ran back, but the doors slammed shut on him.

"Yeah, Monty? You think so?" he said.

He ran up the broad stone staircase, sprinted across a landing, veered through a narrow corridor, and hurtled down the servants' stairs into the kitchen. A moment later, he was striding back into the great hall, fury snapping in his eyes.

"Beau, *no!*" Percival shouted, rushing at him.

But Beau, agile as a panther, ducked him. He ran to the pitiful figure, now crumpled in a dark corner. "Arabella, talk to me," he demanded, taking hold of her arm. "What's going—"

A rolling scream of pain and rage ripped through the air, and the next thing Beau knew, he was lying on his back, his head throbbing where it had smacked against the stone floor. He pushed himself up and looked around. Arabella had flung him clear across the room.

"Why . . . *how* . . ." he mumbled, dazed.

"Stand up, Beau. Slowly. Very, very slowly. Then walk back to the kitchen and hide. It's your only chance," Valmont said quietly.

"Arabella," Beau said, ignoring him. "Talk to me. Please."

A growl rose, and then Arabella emerged from the darkness slowly, deliberately, like a stalking predator. Horror seized Beau as he met her gaze. Her eyes had grown round, the pupils impossibly large. Her canine teeth had lengthened into powerful, curved fangs that shone whitely against her darkening lips.

Her hand shot out and wrapped around the back of a chair. Only it was not a hand; it was a furred paw, tipped with knifelike claws. Her clothing was gone; it lay in shreds behind her. Thick fur covered her body, and though she stood on two legs, her back was arched, and her limbs bent.

As the last stroke of midnight echoed and died, Beau raised his eyes to hers, to the woman he had just held in his arms, and found himself staring into the face of the beast.

– FIFTY-THREE –

Arabella was a nightmare come to life.

A silver skein of saliva dripped from her jaw. The velvet fur of her snout was furrowed; her lips were drawn back in a vicious snarl.

But it was her eyes that made Beau's guts tighten. There was nothing there. No mercy, no pity. Just cold calculation. She was studying him, the way a wolf studies a stag to figure out the best way to bring it down.

Closer and closer she came, head low, eyes boring into Beau. *Don't bother running*, they said. *You won't make it.*

But Beau didn't believe she'd attack him. Not until the very last second.

It was as if an invisible tether had snapped. She hurtled into him, snarling, teeth bared. He had just enough time to get his arm up and protect his throat. Her claws missed their target and slashed through cloth and skin instead, drawing blood. The impact sent Beau sprawling. As he hit the floor, the beast careened toward a wall, but with a predator's sinewy agility, she managed to spin herself around before she hit it. Her eyes narrowed in fury; her ears flattened to her head. She readied herself to charge again.

Beau didn't have time to get up before she was on him. "Arabella, it's me . . . *me* . . ." he shouted, bracing his hands against her shoulders.

She lunged at him, teeth snapping only inches from his face. As he struggled to hold her off, he was dimly aware of voices around him. They were shouting at her. Valmont had an iron poker. Percival had grabbed a log from the stack near the fireplace. Beau heard Camille yelling, too. She'd snatched a carving knife from the table. They were all trying to help him, trying to draw her off.

"Stop, Arabella, *please*," Beau rasped. "Before you kill me."

His words did what shouts and weapons could not. With a roar not of anger now but anguish, Arabella backed away. For an instant, the human girl—scared and tormented—surfaced in the depths of the beast's silver eyes.

Beau got to his feet. "It's all right. You don't have to be afraid," he said.

Arabella hesitated. Beau could feel her listening to his words. He could feel her wanting to believe them. But then she shook herself, like a wolf shaking off water, and with a last, agonized roar, she was gone. Out of the great hall. Through the castle's massive doors. And into a swirling snowstorm.

Beau, holding his wounded arm, watched her go. Then he turned to the others.

"Arabella is the beast? *Arabella?*" he asked, his voice raw.

Percival nodded.

Inside Beau, rage ignited. He strode up to Valmont. "You lying sack of—"

"Watch your mouth, boy," Valmont warned.

"You owed me the *truth!*" Beau shouted, shoving him.

"I owed you *nothing*, thief," Valmont spat, his hands tightening into fists.

"Stop it!" Camille shouted, getting between them.

Beau stepped back, shaking with fury. "Where did she go?" he asked Camille.

"To the forest. To the darkness," she replied. "It's dangerous when she turns. She barely knows herself, barely knows us. She's lost now. Until morning nears. Until the light changes her back."

Beau grabbed a napkin off the table and quickly tied it around his arm as a bandage, then he headed for the doorway.

"Where are you going?" Valmont demanded.

"To find her."

And then he was gone, too, running down the long servants' hallway to the kitchens. He stopped by the door to yank a heavy, hooded coat off a hook and snatch a pair of gloves out of a basket. He grabbed a lantern burning atop a table, then he stepped outside. The storm wolf howled down as if it had been lying in wait for him. The wind tore at his clothing. The snow blinded him.

He took a few steps, shielding the lantern as best he could.

Before the storm wolf closed in, and swallowed him whole.

– FIFTY-FOUR –

Some say that fairy tales are windows that show us a make-believe world. Full of impossible creatures.

But they are wrong.

Fairy tales are mirrors, not windows. They show us this world. They show us ourselves.

Come close, take a look, right here in the silver glass . . . That's not an ugly stepsister, an evil queen, a bad fairy you see in there.

It's you.

Snatching the glass slipper away. Rigging the beauty contest. Leaving sharp objects lying around.

It's you.

Lost in the forest. Locked in the candy house.

Alone. Afraid. And angry, so angry.

Because a wicked stepmother cut out your heart.

Because a careless father left you to the wolves.

Come closer to the mirror, child. *Closer.* What do you see?

Troll? Witch? Ogre? Beast?

Hunt the beast, the old ones say. *Kill the beast.*

But what if you *are* the beast?

– FIFTY-FIVE –

Arabella had kissed him.

She'd stood close to him, so close. And then she'd asked him, and he'd answered yes. And her lips had felt like everything he'd never known he wanted. And her body, pressed to his, felt like home.

And then she'd tried to kill him.

Beau could feel his own blood now, wet and warm, soaking through the napkin into his sleeve. He needed a real bandage. A fire. Shelter. He needed to return to the castle before he froze to death. But he would not, not until he found her.

Tearing winds drove snow into his face, forcing his head down. Deepening drifts clutched at his legs. It was all he could do to keep the struggling flame of his lantern alive.

And yet, he trudged on, driven by a white-hot fury that no snowstorm could cool.

The wind whirled around him, taunting him with her words. *There are things, Beau . . . things it's better you do not know . . .*

"You're a liar, Arabella!" he yelled back.

What he didn't know had gotten him three ragged slashes across his arm. He was all done with not knowing things.

Was Arabella a flesh-and-blood woman? A stalking beast? Was she the contained, icy girl he'd first met, a girl who could draw blood with a word or a glance? Or the girl he'd danced with, a girl with fire in her lips?

Beau was going to find her, and beast or girl, she was going to tell him the truth.

As he walked on, deeper into the dark woods, the wind died little by little and the snow lightened enough that he no longer needed to shield his eyes against it. He shook his hood off and looked around, raising his lantern high.

"Arabella!" he shouted. "It's me, Beau!"

There was no reply. Beau ventured farther, scanning the white drifts for tracks.

"Arabella, come out! I want to talk to you!"

As the words left his lips, he glimpsed it—a dark blur flashing through a stand of pines.

Beau's guts tightened with fear. His calls had summoned a creature, but not the one he wanted.

A black wolf emerged from the trees and stopped a few yards from him, head lowered, eyes glinting. It was joined by five more.

They were real beasts, not enchanted ones.

But every bit as dangerous.

– FIFTY-SIX –

The pack moved out of the trees. They looked like shadows in the lantern's weak light. Their leader advanced toward Beau in a crouch. The others fanned out, surrounding him.

Beau knew he was in serious trouble. He'd run out of the castle and into the forest armed only with his anger. It was an unforgivably stupid move. If he died out here, Matti died, too. He turned in a circle, stamping his feet, swinging his lantern, yelling, trying to make himself look bigger than he was, but the wolves kept coming, closing in, tightening the noose.

He never saw the silver one. He only heard the creature's feet, whispering through the snow behind him in the instant before it sprang.

The impact knocked Beau to his knees. He dropped his lantern; it hissed out in the snow. He struck at the silver wolf, and the creature backed away. The darkness emboldened the others, though. One ventured close and lunged. Beau saw it coming out of the corner of his eye, kicked at it, and felt his boot connect with its snout. It yipped and fell back. A third loped forward and snapped at his shoulder, but he moved, and it missed his flesh, burying its teeth into the cloth of his coat instead. He was yanked sideways. His arms flailed above his head. The silver wolf saw another opening and lunged for Beau's belly but missed its mark and sank its teeth into his leg.

Beau bellowed in pain. He battered the wolf with his fists, but it wouldn't let go. He heard snarling, snapping, and then a roar so loud and full of fury, it shook the snow from the pine boughs. Were the wolves fighting one another now? He could see so little in the darkness, but he heard the leader howl loudly, and an instant later the silver wolf released him and retreated into the shadows with the rest of its pack.

Beau flopped back into the snow, his breathing ragged. Blood from his wound ran into the whiteness, weakening him. It looked as if he were lying in a field of crimson poppies, misshapen and obscene. He didn't know why the wolves had run off, but he knew he had to get back to the castle before he lost more blood. Already the cold night was stiffening his limbs. It would creep into his torso next and turn his heart to ice.

He tried to drag himself up into a sitting position, but a sickening bout of dizziness caught him and pulled him back down. He stared up at the sky, hoping to find a star to focus on, so he could stop the horrible spinning in his head. Instead, images whirled together in his brain, in a blur of color and sound.

He saw a winding city street. A nun, her head bent, a rosary twined in her fingers. He heard the sound of a wet, hitching cough. A church bell ringing.

"Get up, get *up*, you useless bastard," he rasped, his voice breaking.

But he couldn't. His body had been through too much. His strength was seeping out of him, along with his blood. Tears leaked from his eyes. He had time to whisper a few last words to the sky before the darkness closed in.

"I'm sorry, Matti . . . I'm so, so sorry."

– FIFTY-SEVEN –

So this is death, Beau thought.

It wasn't as bad as he'd feared. He was warm, at least. And lying on something soft.

Am I in heaven? he wondered.

Would he find his mother here? What would he say to her? How would he tell her that he'd failed her, that he'd left Matteo all alone?

He forced his eyes open, searching for her face, for the brown eyes he'd known, so warm, so full of kindness. Instead, he saw a pair of gray eyes looking down at him. Soft as a gull's wing, full of worry.

"Arabella?" he rasped. His throat felt as if someone had rubbed it with sandpaper. "Am I . . . am I *alive*?"

"Had enough of malingering, Sleeping Beauty? Time to get your scrawny backside up."

Beau turned his head and saw a whiskered face staring down at him, too. It was wearing a cantankerous expression.

"Looks like I didn't make it to heaven," he said, his voice still a croak. "Looks like I'm in hell. With Satan himself."

Valmont straightened, affronted. "I cleaned you up, thief. Stitched you, washed you, stayed up half the night with you."

"Didn't know you cared, Monty."

Valmont turned to Arabella. "I shall have breakfast sent up, Your Grace," he said crisply, then he left the room.

"You've hurt his feelings," Arabella admonished.

Beau closed his eyes. He didn't give a damn about anyone's feelings. They'd lied to him, all of them, and their lies had nearly cost him his life. After swallowing a few times to ease his parched throat, he spoke again. "How did I get here?" he asked.

"Valmont and Florian. They went out after you, found you in the woods, and carried you back," Arabella replied.

"But the wolves . . ."

"I took care of them."

She poured a glass of water and handed it to him, explaining as she did that she'd run from the castle deep into the forest, but then she'd heard the wolves howling and him shouting, and she'd returned and fought the animals off.

Should I thank her for that? Beau wondered. He didn't. He forced his eyes open and looked around. He was lying in a four-poster bed, in a large, well-appointed chamber. He sat up, grimacing at the throbbing chorus of pain coming from his arm and leg.

"Why am I not in my tower room?" he asked, his voice still gravelly.

"This one is closer to the kitchen," Arabella explained. "It's easier to carry hot water here, as well as medicines and poultices to fight off infection."

He looked at her then. She was sitting in a chair by his bed, wearing a night-robe. It looked as if she'd just come in from the woods. Her tousled hair hung loose around her shoulders. Leaves and tiny twigs were stuck in it. She met his eyes, then looked down at her hands. They were knotted in her lap.

"You saw me. The first time I tried to escape," he said. "I made it down the tower stairs to the landing. You chased me . . ."

"I only meant to scare you. To keep you from roaming the castle and learning its secrets." Her eyes met his. "If there's anyone you should be angry with, it's me, not Valmont. For chasing you. For attacking you in the dining room. For the gouges in your arm. I—I can't always control it. I'm sorry, Beau. So sorry. For everything. Florian, Henri, myself . . . We'll get the bridge built for you. I promise. Valmont will help, too. And Martin and Gustave and anyone else who can sharpen a pole or swing a sledgehammer."

As she spoke, a few of her ladies assembled in Beau's chamber and clustered together, whispering behind their hands, shooting curious glances at him.

"I think he's going to die," Lady Rafe predicted. "Of some dreadful infection. Sepsis, perhaps. Gangrene. Or rabies."

Lady Sadindi wrinkled her nose. "Let's hope he does it quickly and doesn't make a smelly mess."

More members of the court entered the room, crowding in through the doorway. They were followed by Josette, who was carrying a breakfast tray. There was so much chatter that no one noticed the two small girls who snuck in behind her and hid within the draperies.

Josette set the tray down on a table, then curtsied and left. Arabella rose, assembled a plate for Beau, and placed it on his night table. Her ladies watched her every move with busy, bright-eyed interest.

"I'll go now. You must rest," Arabella said, turning to go.

There was something evasive in her voice, skittish in her manner.

"No," Beau said.

Arabella halted in the doorway. "Is there something wrong with the breakfast? Something else you'd like?"

"Stop it, Arabella."

She nodded as if she'd been expecting this. "What do you want, then?" she asked.

"The truth."

Arabella gave a bitter laugh. "Where would I even start?"

She'd asked the question of herself, not him, but he answered it nonetheless.

"I saw you. In the mirror in your old chambers. With your mother and aunt. You were trying on gowns for a ball. Start there."

- FIFTY-EIGHT -

Arabella sat down on the edge of Beau's bed.

So many questions were pushing at his tongue; she could see it. How could she answer them? As soon as she did, she would lose him. He would hate her when he found out, as all the others had. To see him pull away from her, to see his beautiful eyes fill with fury . . . it was more than she could bear.

"Secrets are secrets for a reason," she said, breaking his gaze.

"I saw you turn into a beast. Right in front of my eyes. I saw you with fur and pointy ears and sharp teeth." His voice rose as he spoke, his anger getting the better of him. "I *kissed* you, Arabella. Right before you tried to kill me. So enough with your secrets."

Part of Arabella longed to tell him, longed to unburden herself to him. But a bigger part was afraid to, and the words stuck like burrs in her throat.

Just then, Lady Elge bounced into the room on the balls of her feet, her face painted with her customary clown's makeup—red circles in the centers of her white-greasepaint cheeks, high black eyebrows, heart-shaped lips.

"Why, isn't *this* a lovely gathering?" she exclaimed, looking all around at Beau, Arabella, and the members of the court.

"Oh hell no," Faith said, stepping out from behind the drapes.

"Watch out for Elge, Beau, she's a maniac," Hope said, joining her sister.

Arabella heard the girls. She turned toward them as if turning toward an executioner.

"Be careful, mistress!" Rafe cried, cringing behind Lady Rega. "God only knows what they'll do!"

Rega snarled at the two girls, advancing toward them.

Faith pulled a dagger out of the folds of her skirt and pointed it at her. "Make my day," she said. Rega stepped back.

Glancing furtively at Beau, Lady Piconisus approached Arabella. She wore a gown the color of creeping ivy. Her hair was an oily black. Her skin was the bloated, translucent white of something that lived under a rock.

"It was *him*," she whispered in Arabella's ear. "*He* let them out. *He* stole the master key. I *knew* it. I knew it all along."

Arabella turned to Beau, stricken. "*You* let them out?"

Beau's own anger, smoldering, ignited. "Damn it, Arabella, I'm asking the questions now!"

Elge rushed to Beau's bedside. She put an arm around his shoulders. He tried to pull away, but she held him fast. "Don't. You. *Worry!* Not for one little-ittle-wittle *second!*" she said in a singsong voice, tapping Beau's nose with her finger. "If she won't answer you, I'll find someone who will!"

She released him and grinned—with so much force, her cheeks fractured like a dropped vase. Beau blanched at the sight. Elge giggled at his reaction, then dashed off into the herd of court ladies.

"Hesma? Iglut? Where arrrrre you two?" she called out, disappearing into the crowd. "Come now, ladies, this is no time to be shy. Ah! Here we go!"

A moment later, the crowd of courtiers parted and Hesma stumbled forward, shoved by Elge. Like a rodent pulled from her den, she tried to burrow her way back to safety, but Elge wouldn't let her.

"Ah, ah, ah!" she scolded, wagging a finger. She whirled Hesma around and gave her another shove.

Hesma was wearing a colorless sack of a dress, which made her look more like a prisoner than a lady of the court. Elge prodded her in the back, directing her toward Beau. When Hesma reached him, hunched over and wringing her hands, she started to talk, but her voice was so low and quavering, he had to lean in to hear her.

"No, Hesma. Stop," Arabella demanded. She'd gotten to her feet; her fingernails were digging into her palms. "Stop."

Elge turned to Arabella. "He has a right to know, don't you think?" she asked, her lunatic's grin hardening into something darker.

"You have no right to tell him. I've forbidden it."

"I know that, but so what? I'm going to betray you! We all are. It's what we do!" Elge trilled. She turned back to Hesma. "Come on, you silly! Speak up!"

"It's all because of her!"

It was Iglut, not Hesma, who'd spoken. She was pointing at Arabella. As the court turned to her, she shrank into herself, lowering her head. She spoke again, but her words were muffled by her hair, which was hanging across her face.

Elge rushed to her. "Darling, we can't hear you! We can't see your pretty face!" She brushed Iglut's greasy hair back and tucked it behind her ear, revealing a face that was anything but pretty. Iglut's eyes were dull, their gaze darting and furtive. Her cheeks were dotted with scabs. Her lips were bitten raw.

"*She* did it," Iglut said, staring balefully at Arabella. "She was always a beastly girl."

"What are you talking about?" Beau asked.

"You are not to speak of it!" Arabella shouted.

Elge fixed her mistress with a bright, vicious gaze. "That's not really fair to him, is it?" she said in a low, stagy voice, hooking her thumb at Beau. "I mean, wouldn't *you* want to know if you were—"

"For God's sake, *stop*," Arabella cried, her voice breaking.

"As you wish," purred Elge. "I won't say another word."

"But *I* will."

Espidra walked to Arabella's side and placed a withered hand on her shoulder. Arabella sagged at Espidra's touch, helpless. Tears welled in her eyes.

"A hundred years ago," Espidra said, "Arabella killed someone."

"A young man," said Hesma.

Espidra smiled. "Prince Constantine."

– FIFTY-NINE –

Beau's heart felt as if it were made of glass.

And Espidra's words had opened a crack in it, thin and spidery. He pushed against them, not wanting to believe what she had just said. "That's not true. It's not, Arabella, is it?" he asked.

Arabella closed her eyes and nodded, and the crack widened.

"When you . . . when you were a beast?" Beau said, remembering the sharp claws, the curved fangs.

"Oh, no," Iglut cut in. "When she was still very much a girl."

"And this Constantine . . . who was he?" asked Beau.

"Arabella's *fiancé*. Never in your *life* did you *see* such a *man!*" said Elge breathily. "I mean, you're not *bad*, Beau, and *I* certainly wouldn't kick you off the couch, but the prince?" She rolled her eyes as if she'd just eaten the most delicious bite of cake. "He was as handsome as a god."

"And stinking rich," said Lady D'Eger, snatching a roll from Beau's breakfast tray.

"The duke and duchess decided he would be Arabella's husband," Iglut explained. "They wanted an alliance with a royal house."

Elge tugged on Beau's sleeve and directed his attention toward a mirror on a nearby wall. "Strong magic happened in this place," she said dramatically. "So strong that it etched itself into the looking glasses. Now they replay it for Arabella, so she never, *ever* forgets. It's part of the curse!"

"Curse?" Beau echoed.

Elge pressed a hand to her chest. "*Yes!*" she said. "The direst curse *imaginable*! It happened at the stag hunt."

"Enough, Lady Elge."

It was Lady Romeser. She was wearing a gown the color of crushed plums. Her face, her hands, every visible inch of her skin, was mottled by bruises, some old, some fresh.

"She does that to herself, you know," Elge whispered to Beau, smothering a giggle.

"Take a seat, Elge," Romeser said. "I won't ask you again."

Elge's shoulders slumped. "You ruin *everything*," she huffed as she walked to a chair, scuffing her feet the whole way.

"Before a royal wedding, tradition decrees that families of the bride and groom celebrate with a stag hunt. Arabella's father hosted it," Romeser explained, walking to the mirror. She pointed at the glass. "Look there . . ."

"No," Beau said. "I won't." He turned to Arabella. "Unless you say I can. You. Not them."

He understood something now that he had not before—that he was gazing at memories that lived deep within Arabella. And that viewing them was an intimate act.

Arabella's eyes were still closed. The tears she'd held back now spilled down her cheeks.

Hope approached her, guarded by Faith; she touched her hand. "You can do this," she whispered to her. "You *can*."

Arabella opened her eyes.

And breathed one word. *Yes.*

– SIXTY –

"I visited with the Duchesse d'Orléans yesterday," declares the Marquise d'Alençon, "and she had the most charming new tea service!"

"Have you seen Lady Louise's pretty riding hat?" asks the Comtesse de Marignac. "I *must* find out the name of her milliner."

"If you ask me, hydrangeas have no place in an herbaceous border," the Baronne de Beauvais says with a sniff.

Arabella is in the castle's stable yard, seated on a placid mare. Her smile is painted on, like a fairground puppet's. She wears a riding suit of pink trimmed in black, for the prince finds pink most becoming. Stiff petticoats rustle under her skirt. A starched-linen corset encases her torso, its laces pulled so tight they creak.

She no longer grits her teeth at small talk, and only occasionally digs her nails into her palms. And if her heart breaks every time she passes a castle or cathedral . . . well, what does it matter? It's hidden away in a cage of bone where no one can see the cracks.

The prince sits atop Horatio, Arabella's own magnificent stallion, as it is deemed unseemly for a princess-to-be to ride such a spirited animal. Jealousy sparks in her eyes at the sight of them, but she douses it before anyone notices. Her father is laughing this morning; her mother is smiling. She will not ruin their happiness.

"A glass of port here!" Constantine bellows, snapping his fingers in the air. "God's truth! Where is that blasted boy?"

Henri, carrying a bottle and glasses on a tray, hurries to the prince and pours him a drink. Constantine snatches it from his hand. Henri bows. As he turns and walks away, Constantine leans out of his saddle and boots him in the backside.

The boy goes sprawling. The tray hits the courtyard's cobblestones with a dull clang. The bottle and glasses smash. As he struggles to his feet, his face scraped raw, a braying laugh fills the courtyard.

The lords and ladies of the court know better than to stand there in stony-faced silence while a prince whoops and howls. There are only snickers at first, then giggles, then full-throated guffaws.

Arabella's painted-on smile slips. Anger threatens. Alarmed, she closes her eyes and takes a few shallow breaths; the whalebone in her corset does not allow for deep ones. She hears Constantine, her betrothed, the man she will spend the rest of her life with, bark at Valmont to polish a smudge off his boot, shout at Florian to tighten Horatio's girth strap, and order Percival off like a kitchen boy to fetch a plate of cakes.

When she opens her eyes again, her smile is back in place. She chats with the duchess about teapots, relieved to feel only what she has trained herself to feel—nothing.

. . .

The riders are all mounted now. The hounds are brought from the kennels. They bark and bay, impatient to be off. The hunt will soon begin. But then Horatio whickers unhappily and kicks at another horse. The horse shies and its rider nearly topples off.

"Slacken his reins," Arabella whispers.

She knows that the stallion is headstrong and proud and does not suffer fools.

He is a horse fit for a prince, but the prince is not fit for the horse.

Constantine pulls harder on his reins, trying to keep Horatio under control, jerking the bit cruelly. Nostrils flaring, Horatio tosses his head and dances in circles, trying to spin the monster off his back.

The Austrian archduke laughs as Constantine tries to keep his seat. Wounded pride flames into anger on Constantine's handsome face, branding his cheeks red.

"The girth is too tight, you fool!" he yells at Florian, striking him with his crop.

Arabella pales as she watches him. She presses her lips together, knowing she must say nothing. She forces her face to hide what she's thinking: How could a man so beautiful be so hideous?

The prince strikes Florian again. This time, the crop opens a gash across his cheek.

Arabella gasps. "Stop it!" she says. The words break free from her lips against her will, but no one hears them. They are drowned out by the groom's cry, the prince's shouts, the horse's frantic whinnies.

Arabella needs to make herself heard. She takes a breath, but her corset is so tight, it's a struggle to draw enough air to speak, never mind shout.

The duchess, mounted next to her, grabs her arm, sinking her nails in. "Keep *quiet*. It's not for you to upbraid the prince."

But someone will, Arabella desperately hopes. *Someone will stop him. His brother, his father . . . someone.*

Horatio stamps his feet frantically. Grooms and servants scatter. The prince lashes into him mercilessly. The defenseless animal gives a piteous cry.

And deep down inside Arabella, something shatters.

"Dear God!" she cries, taking up her reins. "Will nobody stop him?"

The duchess snatches her reins. "Stay where you are, you foolish girl!" she commands.

But it's too late.

Arabella rips her reins out of her mother's hand and touches her heels to her horse's sides.

"Stop! Stop it, you brute!" she shouts.

She raises her own crop, aiming to knock the prince's out of his hand, but poor Horatio does not know that. He sees her coming toward him and his terror only grows.

It happens so fast. It only takes a heartbeat, but for Arabella, it will last a hundred years.

The stallion rears. The prince tumbles from the saddle. There's a sharp crack as he hits the cobblestones. He twitches, then groans. The breath leaves his body. He lies there, perfectly still, his eyes empty, his blood seeping into the cracks between the stones.

- SIXTY-ONE -

Arabella lurches out of her saddle. As courtiers gasp and point, she stumbles, rights herself, falls on her knees by the broken prince.

She grabs his hand, chafes it, tries to wake him. His blood stains her skirts.

She cannot catch her breath. Emotions swirl through her like a storm. She claws at her rigid bodice, at the cruel corset underneath.

Sharp fingers dig into her shoulder. The duchess is behind her. "Dear God in heaven, Arabella, what have you done?"

Arabella's lungs are heaving for air. She tries to get herself under control but cannot. She's been held down for too long. Courtiers are shouting, now, condemning Arabella. The prince's retinue lift his body and carry it inside the castle. The duke tries to help, ordering his servants to their aid, but they are coldly turned away.

"Do you see now?" her mother hisses. "Do you see what happens when girls do not contain themselves? The prince is *dead*. Our lives are over. We are ruined."

Her mother is right. She should've kept quiet. This is all her fault. She claws at her chest. She is suffocating.

There's a harsh *riiiipppp* of cloth tearing. Her jacket and corset have split along their seams. Air rushes into her lungs. She takes a deep breath, then utters a ragged cry, overcome. Her emotions are wild from having been caged for so long.

And then there is another tearing sound—deeper, louder, more fearsome than the rending of cloth.

It is the tearing of Arabella's soul.

- SIXTY-TWO -

Arabella remains on her knees, her forehead touching the cold ground, her fingers digging into her ribs.

For a long moment, there is only silence; then it is broken by the rhythmic, ringing *pok-pok-pok* of heels on the cobblestones.

A woman emerges, spectral and imperious, wearing a gown the

color of ashes. She parts the crowd as she makes her way across the courtyard.

Arabella raises her head. Her cheeks are tearstained. Her eyes are hollow.

"I am Lady Espidra," the woman says as she approaches her. She gestures to the grim retinue trailing her. "And this is *my* court."

The duchess, always perfectly in control, starts to fray. "Who summoned you here?" she asks, confused by the new faces.

"Why, Lady Arabella did," Espidra replies, with a wintry smile.

The duchess points at three small, glowing girls standing at a distance from Espidra's court. "And those children? They are with you?"

Espidra follows the duchess's gaze; her smile congeals. "Not for long," she says.

Lady Elge steps forward. "Go! Shoo!" she says to a few straggling members of the prince's retinue. "Leave this place. While you still can."

Spooked by Elge's too-wide smile and her glassy puppet's eyes, the courtiers do as they're told, stumbling over themselves in their haste, but the duke is outraged by Espidra's presumptuousness and starts to bark commands.

Espidra holds up a hand. "You misunderstand, Your Grace. You are no longer in charge here. *I* am."

"Valmont! See these women out!" the duke bellows. "I will *not* be ordered about in my own—"

Espidra approaches the duke; she puts a clawlike hand on his shoulder. At her touch, he collapses inward like a rotting apple. She presses down, and with a soft, surprised sigh, he drops to his knees. Then she walks to the duchess and renders her powerless, too.

The duke and duchess's courtiers, afraid now, back away as Espidra turns her soulless eyes on Arabella. "*A girl who cannot control her emotions is no better than a beast* ... isn't that what your mother told you?" she taunts.

Like a jackal, she circles Arabella, and as she does, she begins to speak in rhyme. The color drains out of Arabella's face as she realizes what this is. An incantation. A spell. A curse.

> *A girl who'd rather break than bend,*
> *Has caused a prince's bloody end.*
> *So selfish, willful, awkward, wrong,*
> *To her, all shame and guilt belong.*
> *Be what you are, a feral beast.*
> *On creatures wild and furry feast.*
> *Spend forever more in woods so deep,*
> *Among the moss and dead leaves sleep.*
> *To make your penance even worse,*
> *I'll wrap this castle in the curse.*
> *And doom for all eternity,*
> *Each and every one I see,*
> *To a fate far worse than death.*
> *Alive, though they do not draw breath.*
> *Clockwork figures, each a mime,*
> *Imprisoned, captive, slaves of time.*
> *Next hope and faith I shall efface,*
> *As I your foolish dreams erase.*
> *And with my court work hand in glove,*
> *To bring about the death of love.*
> *That's how I kill a mortal's soul,*
> *And take my baneful, bitter toll.*
> *Ah, how I relish my dark task.*
> *Was silence all that much to ask?*

"*No!*" Arabella screams, sick with fear. "Please! I didn't mean to hurt him! *Please!*"

But Espidra merely laughs.

"Help my child . . . someone, please! Do not let this be the end of her!"

It is the duchess. She has somehow struggled to her feet and is staggering toward Espidra.

Espidra fixes them with a smile of feigned sorrow. She offers the duchess her hand, and as the duchess takes it, she gasps. She tries to back away, but cannot move. It's as if her feet have been fastened to the ground. Small, frightened cries escape her as she fights to free herself.

"What have you done?" the duke shouts, rushing at Espidra.

But his body seizes before he can reach her. A sound rises, a grinding, metallic whine, as if someone is winding a music box. Or a clock. The duchess's body stiffens. The duke freezes in place. Their eyes turn shiny, like a trophy animal's. Circles of painted color bloom on their cheeks.

The courtiers and servants are transfixed by fear now, unable to tear their eyes from the grotesque transformations. Espidra moves among them with a bright, malicious glee. She taps a countess, pats a maid, runs her hand over the head of a child. Everything human, warm, and alive drains away at her touch until one after another, they all become clockwork figures.

Too late, those whom she has not yet touched realize what is happening. They try to run, but the courtyard gates slam shut.

Only Arabella, still on her knees, does not try to flee. "Please do not punish these people for my transgressions," she begs.

Her words are cut off by a new voice. "Lady Espidra!" it booms. "I command you to stop!"

Espidra whirls around. Her face crumples into a hateful grimace. She knows this creature. She envies his might, covets his power.

The one who spoke proceeds into the center of the courtyard. The tapping of his walking stick over the stones sounds like a metronome.

Arabella looks at him through a blur of tears. And knows him.

He is the clockmaker.

– SIXTY-THREE –

"You have overstepped yourself, Lady Espidra," the clockmaker says. "Once again."

Arabella rises. She stumbles to him. "Help us! Undo this curse, I beg you!"

The clockmaker takes her hands in his. His bloodless lips part and he speaks an incantation, too, but it is too little, too late.

> *Child, what have you summoned here?*
> *A demon named Despair, I fear.*
> *A heartless creature, dark and dire,*
> *Whose hands will light your funeral pyre.*
> *I cannot stop what she's begun,*
> *Or turn back what's already done.*
> *But some things I can yet put right:*
> *A beast you'll be, but at midnight.*
> *The souls imprisoned in the clock*
> *Must stay. Their fates I can't unlock.*
> *To those not yet held captive there,*
> *I shall, for now, entrust your care.*
> *Despair's foul curse can't be unspoken,*
> *But there is one way it can be broken.*
> *Mend what you have torn apart.*
> *Pick up the pieces of your heart.*

Seek kindness, trust, a hand extended,
Till one you shunned is now befriended.
Cross the bridge, unwind the years,
Escape this prison of your fears.
That's how you will break this curse,
And undo this infernal verse.
And when to love you finally learn
You will be loved in return.
But a warning now, to one and all,
As you fight against Despair's dark pall . . .

The clockmaker is about to speak the last few lines of his poem, but before he can, there is an explosive crash and glass shards rain down on the floor. Arabella stands behind Beau, her chest heaving. She has thrown an inkwell at the mirror, but it—not the mirror—has shattered, covering the silver glass in black ink. It drips from the frame and pools on the floor.

The mirror looks as if it's bleeding.

– SIXTY-FOUR –

Arabella, laid bare, spoke.

"No more, thief. You have my story now. And your answers."

Elge, unable to contain herself, scurried back across the room to Beau and sat down with a *whump* beside him. "Can you *imagine* the guilt? The shame?" she whispered exultantly.

Arabella closed her eyes. Her hand clutched at her robe, fingers knotting in the fabric. Her chest spasmed, as if someone had just plunged a knife into it.

Iglut turned the blade. "All those people trapped like insects in amber.

231

I think they see. I think they feel. Imagine being immobilized in a clock-work body, fully conscious, but not able to move or speak."

LaJoyuse nudged Iglut aside. "Arabella bore up stoically at first," she said to Beau. "She had hope. After all, the clockmaker said the curse could be broken if she learned to love. Every time a man crossed over the drawbridge, every time he came into the castle, she hoped he would become her suitor. But they all left again as soon as they discovered the real Arabella. And who could blame them? Who could love a beast? She tried her best to recover, to carry on, to never lose hope or faith. But after failing again and again to find love, after watching those around her suffer, knowing all the while that *she* was the one who caused their suffering . . . well, it became too much. Hope was no longer a comfort to her; Hope was a torment."

"So Espidra locked me away," Hope said. "And my sisters, too."

"And when we were gone, Arabella gave up," said Faith. "She lowered the portcullis and that's where it has remained."

"Until now," Elge said, clapping her hands like a child. "Until *you*."

"Now? Me?" Beau said. "I—I don't understand."

"Oh, don't you?"

And then he did, in a shock of realization so strong, so visceral, he felt sick.

"Becauuuuuuse . . ." Elge prompted, elbowing him in the side.

"Because," Beau said, his voice barely a whisper, "*I'm* the latest suitor."

– SIXTY-FIVE –

Beau reeled.

He felt as if he'd been hit by a runaway carriage and left for dead.

"Leaving the portcullis up wasn't an accident. It wasn't a mistake," he said woodenly. "You trapped me here on purpose."

"No, Beau, that's not true!" Arabella said vehemently.

But Beau barely heard her denial. "You ordered the portcullis to be raised, like a hunter setting a snare. You laid out a feast in the great hall as if you were laying bait. And we?" He laughed bitterly. "Raphael, Antonio, all the rest . . . we were the stupid rabbits that hopped right in. And I'm the stupidest of them all. I was supposed to save you, right? To fall in love with you and break the curse."

"I *didn't* do it," Arabella protested, her voice catching. "I *swear* I didn't."

Beau shook his head, furious now. Why had he trusted her? Why had he let her into his heart? He knew better. She was no different from the other women who'd used him. Women who'd seen him as nothing but a pretty face, an amusing diversion.

"Who did, then?" he asked. "Your servants? *Please.* For some reason, they're as loyal as lions to you." The pain of her betrayal snatched away his words. It was a moment before he could speak again. "Looks like you're a thief, too, Arabella," he finished. "But you took more than I ever did."

Hope stepped forward. She pulled Elge off the bed, away from Beau, then regarded him, her eyes beseeching.

"*Don't.* Don't look at me like that," he said to her. "She's not my problem. Nobody in this hell house is my problem." Then he threw back the covers, swung his legs over the side of the bed, and stood up. The hem of his shirt dropped as he did, covering him to his thighs.

A constellation of puncture marks from the wolves' teeth dotted one of his calves. Ugly stitches seamed the gouges Arabella's claws had made in a forearm. A groan of pain escaped him as his legs took his weight.

"What are you doing?" Arabella cried. "Lie down or you'll pull out your stitches!" She turned to Elge. "Call for Valmont!"

Beau ignored her. "Where's my jacket? My britches?" he demanded as Elge tugged frantically on the bellpull.

"They're being repaired. They were torn and bloodstained," Arabella explained. "Percival found you some old clothes to wear."

"Where are they?"

Arabella hesitated but, seeing he was determined, pointed to a neat pile of clothing atop a bureau.

Fighting off light-headedness, Beau quickly dressed. He pulled on his boots, relieved to see that the leather on one had only been punctured, not torn. Valmont entered the room as he was buttoning his jacket.

"Yes, Your Grace?" Valmont said.

"Please, Valmont, tell him he shouldn't be up. Make him see sense," Arabella pleaded.

Beau, fully dressed now, was heading for the doorway, but Valmont intercepted him, ready to strong-arm him back to bed.

"Get out of my way," Beau said, shaking him off. "I'm not going back to bed. And you're not locking me in. Not today, or tonight, not ever again. If you're still so worried that I'll murder you in your sleep, you can damn well lock me *out*." He cast a scathing glance around the room at the court, the servants. "You're all as guilty as your mistress is. You all knew, but not one of you told me the truth. Not one."

And then he left, and left them all staring after him. Within a few minutes, he was outside the castle. The day was clear but brutally cold. He made his way to the gatehouse slowly, his gait stiff and shambling, anger still simmering in his blood.

A brisk wind swirled dead leaves across his path as he walked. They sounded like ghosts whispering as they rasped over the cobblestones. From deep within him, a memory surfaced from years ago. He was standing at the edges of a Christmas market in a busy town square, watching the shoppers. They were red-cheeked and laughing. They were warmly dressed and well fed, buying presents for their families and friends. Couples walked arm in arm. Parents held their children's hands.

As Beau had looked at them, something dark had unfurled inside him. He'd blown on his hands to warm them, then he'd delved into the crowd like a shark among herring.

When he got back to the thieves' hideout, he'd walked up to Raphael, who was sitting by the fire, and divested himself of his loot. He pulled out billfolds and coins, watches, rings, bracelets, snuffboxes, pillboxes, even a few silver buttons, and dumped all of it in the thief lord's lap. It took him five full minutes to empty his pants pockets, coat pockets, the insides of his boots.

Raphael's eyes had lit up in amazement at the swag Beau had brought him. He was so pleased, so proud of his protégé, that he handed him a shiny gold coin to keep for himself.

But Beau gave it back. He didn't want it. Raphael didn't understand; none of the thieves did. Beau hadn't robbed those people of coins or a pocket watch. He'd robbed their smiles, their happiness. He'd grabbed at the love between them, trying to snatch it away. If he couldn't have any, why should they?

As he entered the gatehouse now, the memory drifted away. He couldn't wait to get out of here. What an ass he was, playing at being a builder. Playing at being a nobleman. A lover. He was nothing but a thief. That's all he was, all he ever would be. Hadn't the whole world told him so?

He picked up a hammer, gritted his teeth against the pain from his wounds, and got to work. He had a bridge to build. He was nobody's damn savior.

- SIXTY-SIX -

"Why the ever-loving hell did you do it?" Faith shouted at Arabella.

But Arabella, still standing by the mirror, did not answer her.

235

Sadindi walked over to Faith and looked her up and down. "I could grab you and lock you away myself. You're really small."

"So's a grenade, sister. *Move*," Faith said, holding up her dagger again.

Sadindi stumbled out of her way and Faith stalked up to Arabella. "You cut the clockmaker off before he could finish his spell!" she yelled. "You stopped Beau from hearing the most important part. Did you forget what happens? Hang on a minute, I'll remind you."

She snatched a napkin from the breakfast tray and wiped the ink off the mirror. The clockmaker was still visible in the glass, and as they watched him, he spoke a few more lines.

You no longer have eternity,
The clock counts down a century.
In a hundred years, the curse will end.
Make haste. Godspeed. Farewell, my friends.

"That century is nearly over, Arabella," Faith said as the image in the mirror faded. "You have only a few days left. Five, to be exact. You know what that means, don't you? If you don't break the curse in the next five days, you die." She pointed at servants. "*They* die." She gestured at Hope, at all the ladies-in-waiting. "*We* die."

As the words left her lips, the sound of hammering was heard, muffled and distant, carrying up to the chamber's windows from the gatehouse.

Faith grabbed Hope's hand and started toward the kitchen.

"Where are you going?" Arabella asked.

"To tell him," Faith called over her shoulder.

"No, I forbid it!" Arabella shouted. "You heard what he said. He doesn't love me. In fact, he hates me, and I won't be the cause of another death. There's a chance he can make it out of here, a chance he can live. If he knows the truth, he might try to stay. To break the curse out of pity for

236

us. But if he's still here when the clock strikes midnight at the end of the fifth day, *he* dies."

The hammering grew louder. Every blow felt as if it were driving nails straight into her heart.

Espidra joined Arabella and took her hand. "The bridge you've begun is amazing, child," she said. "A wonder, built of nothing but scraps and ingenuity. Bridges are good *sometimes*. But they're risky structures, too. They so often collapse. Walls are better, in my experience. So broad and strong. So impenetrable. So *safe*." She laid a shriveled hand on Arabella's back. "I know you have feelings for the thief. Do not give in to them. It will only end badly. You've always been such a selfish girl. It's how you ruined your life and everyone else's. Don't ruin his, too. For once in your life, be your better self. If you truly love the thief, let him go."

She would've said more, but at that very moment, a croissant, slathered with strawberry jam, hit her squarely in the back of her head. It stuck there for a second, then dropped to the floor with a thick, wet *splat*.

Espidra whirled around. Faith was standing there, stocky arms crossed over her chest, smiling defiantly.

"You threw that!" Espidra growled. "How dare you!"

"You talk too much, windbag," Faith said. She looked at Arabella. "This is your last chance. You know that, right?"

Hope took Arabella's hands. "Beau should know the truth," she said.

Fierceness resurfaced in Arabella's gaze; she pinned Hope with it. "If you breathe a word to him, I will throw myself into the moat. I swear it."

"But you'd kill yourself," Hope said.

Arabella nodded; she pulled her hands free. "Better yet, I'd kill *you*. No more pain. No more suffering. No more Hope."

Hope swallowed hard. "Do you hate me that much?"

"You have no idea."

"Why?"

"Because you are cruel. Crueler than all these monsters put together," she said, gesturing to her court. "You made me believe. Over and over again. You made me believe there were such things as forgiveness, redemption, love . . . even for me. You made me believe that there was a way out of this."

"There *is*," Hope insisted.

"Is there?" Espidra asked archly. "Tell me, girl, have you found your other sister yet?"

Faith shot Hope a warning glance. It was quick and furtive, but Espidra saw it.

"I didn't think so," she purred. "Love's the only one of you that had enough sense to leave this place."

"I want your word that you will tell him nothing more about the curse, both of you," Arabella demanded of the two girls.

Hope looked as if she was going to argue, but Faith grabbed her and pulled her toward the doorway, still brandishing her dagger. Hesma, Iglut, and LaJoyuse had been slyly edging closer, trying to surround them.

"You have our word," Hope said as Faith tugged on her arm. The girls ran out of the chamber, slammed the door shut, and locked it with the master key.

"That will slow them a little and give us some time to hide," Hope said, pulling her sister through the great hall, toward the main staircase.

"We blew it," Faith said, putting her dagger back in its sheath. "Everyone's doomed."

"Hardly! What just happened in there was wonderful! It was the best possible outcome!" Hope said.

Faith blinked at her sister. "Have you lost your mind?"

"Think about it . . . Arabella betrayed herself. She showed us what's really in her heart. She doesn't want any harm to come to the thief. She

238

would rather that he leaves this place, and she dies, than that he stays, and he dies."

Faith thought about it. "You believe she really cares for him?"

Hope nodded. "I do. In the past, she'd do anything, say anything, to make a suitor fall in love with her. To break the curse. To save her own skin. But she never loved them, not truly."

Faith brightened a little. "I think we can work with this."

"We can, but we need Love's help. We need to find her, and we don't have long," Hope said as they started up the stairs.

Faith's brightness dimmed. "We've looked everywhere. What if Espidra's right? What if she's really gone?"

Hope cut her off. "She *is* here. I can feel her," she said. "Don't lose faith."

− S I X T Y - S E V E N −

All the fairy-tale girls are liars.

Do you think it's the wolf Red Riding Hood is so afraid of? That's just a lie she tells her mother to avoid a beating. It's her own heart that terrifies her. It's her longing to talk to a silver-tongued stranger, her wild desire to follow him into the woods.

It isn't the evil queen who frightens Snow White. Or the forest. That's just what she says to the seven kindly men so they'll take her in. It's a belief, gnawing deep inside her like a cancer, that she has no choice but to accept the poison she's offered.

Cinderella tells the worst lies of all. Informing her stepmother, her stepsisters, lords and ladies, and anyone who will listen all about her happy ending. Smiling until her face aches. What she never tells anyone is just how badly those glass slippers hurt. How they dig bloody grooves into her heels and crush her toes. How they keep her from running. From stamping and kicking. How all she can do now is walk. How all she will ever do, for the rest of her life, is walk—slowly, sedately, and two steps behind.

If you want to know a person, don't ask to hear their truth.

Listen to their lies.

– SIXTY-EIGHT –

"It will be dark soon."

Beau stopped sawing and looked up. Camille was standing there, wrapped in her blue cloak, the handle of a willow basket looped over one arm.

"I brought you supper."

"Thanks," he said, returning to his work.

Florian and Henri had gone inside an hour ago, but Beau had not returned to the castle since he'd learned the truth about Arabella early that morning. He didn't want to see her. And she must've felt the same way, for she had not joined him in the gatehouse, choosing to send advice and instructions through Valmont instead. He'd worked, only stopping to take a drink of water or eat the sandwich Rémy had brought at midday. The work, his wounds—they were taking a toll. Exhaustion smudged dark circles under his eyes, pain etched lines in his brow, but he refused to rest. Resting wouldn't get him across the moat. It wouldn't get him to Matti.

Rega kept him company now, amusing herself by throwing rocks at the moat monsters. He didn't mind her being near, for he was consumed by anger. At Espidra and her gruesome court. At Valmont, Percival, and the other servants. At Arabella. Most of all, he was angry at himself. For believing things he had no business believing. For wanting things he had no business wanting.

He'd been a fool to think Arabella might care for him. He'd known love once. Long ago. It smelled like rosemary and clementines. It tasted as sweet as San Juan cakes. It felt as warm as the Catalan sun. Losing it had made him a feral thing, lonely and guarded and wary of traps, and that's how he would stay.

"I fixed a plate of chicken for you," Camille said, trying again to make conversation. "With roasted potatoes, gravy, rolls . . ."

Beau was about to ask her if she could just leave the basket when Rega turned around sharply and sniffed the air. She dropped the rock she was holding and ran out of the gatehouse, looking as if she'd just smelled a week-old corpse.

Camille watched her go. "She hates the smell of roast chicken. They all do." She turned back to Beau. "The work's going well?"

"I'm getting close," he said. "Should be done in a few days."

"Ah," Camille said. She lowered her head.

"Is something wrong?" Beau asked, glancing up at her.

Camille set her basket down. Her eyes were bright with emotion. "You don't care about anyone, do you? Except yourself."

"Whoa. Where did that come from?" Beau asked, sitting back on his heels.

"You love her."

"Who?"

"Oh, please."

"I don't know what you're talking about."

"Why are you so angry?"

"Maybe because she trapped me here?"

Camille made a noise of disgust. "She didn't trap you. She told you as much."

"I don't believe her."

"Well, you should. Because she didn't do it."

"Oh, no? Who did, then?"

"I did."

Beau snorted laughter.

Camille jutted her chin. She crossed her arms over her chest. "I stole Percival's key from his room one night when he was bathing," she said. "I opened the gatehouse door and returned the key before he finished. Later that night, I took the plow horse from the barn, harnessed him to the windlass, and raised the portcullis. A few hours later, you and your friends rode into the courtyard."

Beau studied her face. He put his saw down. "You're not lying, are you?"

Camille shook her head.

"Damn it, Camille, *why*?" he shouted.

"Because my baby daughter is a clockwork figure, and my husband, too!" Camille shouted back. "Because I want them back! Is that a good enough reason for you?"

The look in Camille's eyes—a mixture of sorrow, rage, and fear—was so raw, Beau had to look away.

"I'm sorry, I am. But I can't pretend—"

"But you're *not* pretending. You love her, but you won't admit it. Because you're a lone wolf, right? Love is for fools, and you're no fool. You're too tough, too shrewd." She gave him a smile, one that looked like it had been soaked in vinegar. "I have news for you: You're *not* tough. You're a coward."

Beau raised his hands. "Hold up, Camille . . ."

But Camille did not hold up. "You think love is for weak people, but you're wrong. Love is for the strongest. The bravest. The fiercest." She looked up at the gatehouse ceiling for a moment, blinking her eyes. Then she looked at Beau again. "When I was eleven years old, my mother got sick. Cancer."

"That's rough, I—"

"Shut up and *listen*," she said. "The disease was a monster with knives

242

for teeth, and it devoured her. My God, how she screamed. And when her throat was too raw to scream anymore, she bashed her head against the wall until her blood ran down the plaster. She cursed my father, a good and gentle man. She called him names I would blush to repeat. All because he could not stop the pain. Nothing he had—not brandy, not wine—could help her."

Camille swallowed hard, then continued. "My father was no doctor; he didn't know what to do. Sometimes he blundered and made things worse, and then he would hold his head in his hands and weep. He tried so hard. He held ice to her parched lips. He kissed her hands. He held her and sang her lullabies . . ." Camille's voice quavered. "And at the end, when her eyes were two black pits, and her face was just a skull with skin stretched over it, he told her she was beautiful, the most beautiful woman he had ever seen. He told her how happy she had made him. How proud he was to be her husband. He promised to take care of us and told her she mustn't worry. He was scared to death. He was angry and lost and heartbroken, but he smiled, and he kissed her cheek, and he told her it was all right to go." Tears slipped down Camille's cheeks. "That . . . *that*, Beau, is love." She wiped her face with her palms, then hurried out of the gatehouse.

"Camille, wait . . ." Beau said, starting after her.

But she was already gone.

He was sorry. Sorry for Camille. For her mother and father. Sorry for her child and husband and everyone else inside the clock. But she was wrong. He couldn't help them. He couldn't break the curse.

He felt guilty, too. Remorse settled in his bones like a sickness as he remembered how awful he'd been to Arabella. He hadn't believed her when she'd said she hadn't trapped him. He'd yelled at her, accused her of something she hadn't done, and then stormed out.

Beau turned from the archway and got back to work. There would be others. He would build this bridge. For himself, yes, but for them, too. That's how he could help Camille and her family, Valmont and Percival, all of them. That's how he would make amends to Arabella. Other men would cross the bridge, and one of them would fall in love with her.

He picked up his saw again. His hands were blue from the cold. His body ached. And there was still so much to do. He would have to lay the plank across wobbly pilings. He would have to brave moat monsters as he did it. And then, if the bridge held, if he made it across to the other side, he'd have to brave storms and wolves as he crossed the mountains.

But he would do it. He would face all those monsters, and more, rather than face the one thing that terrified him above all.

His traitorous, treacherous heart.

- S I X T Y - N I N E -

Beau didn't mean to fall asleep.

It wouldn't have happened if he hadn't pushed himself so hard. If he hadn't been so weary. And hungry. And cold. And stubborn.

He'd sat down close to the small fire he'd built on the gatehouse's floor and leaned back against the wall, meaning to close his eyes for just a few minutes.

Two hours later, he'd fallen so far down the black well of sleep that he didn't hear the chimes of the golden clock carry faintly across the court-yard as they struck the hour—midnight.

It was a soft, dry crunch that woke him. The sound of footfalls on dead leaves.

His eyes snapped open and instinct kicked in. He was instantly alert, every sense prickling with alarm. He looked around but could see no one. Had he only imagined the sound? His fire had burned down; just a few embers were left. Time had passed . . . how much? His eyes flicked to the archway. Snow raked the darkness. A sickening plunge in his belly told him that it was too late. He should have left the gatehouse hours ago. He should have made his way to the safety of the stables and locked the door.

Calm down, toddler, he silently told himself. *There's no one here but you.*

And then he saw the glow of the embers reflected in a pair of silver eyes and realized he was wrong. *She* was there, on the other side of the gatehouse, crouched in the shadows.

For the briefest second, he thought about bolting, but knew he could never outrun her.

His eyes darted around, searching for something he could use as a weapon. But the hammer . . . the saw . . . the planks . . . they were too far away. He didn't even think about shouting for help. It was pointless. No one would hear him.

He was alone with the beast.

And utterly defenseless.

– SEVENTY –

Arabella emerged from the darkness, vulpine and wary.

In one hand, she clutched a dead rabbit. In the other, a squirrel and two chipmunks. Blood darkened her muzzle. She licked it away.

Her silver eyes stayed on him, watching him, gauging him, as she paced back and forth by the glowing embers.

Trying to decide whether to kill me or not, Beau thought.

She snorted, deep and gusty, warning him to keep his distance, then dumped her kills on the floor.

Slowly, so that he did not spook her, Beau stood and gathered up scraps and offcuts from the planks he'd sawed earlier and placed them on the embers. Wisps of smoke rose. Thin fingers of flame curled around them.

Arabella sat down by the fire. She picked up a chipmunk and bit off its head, cracking the skull between her teeth. She finished it in two bites, then ate the squirrel. As she tore through fur and crunched on bone, her eyes left Beau and lighted on the charcoal sketch of the bridge she'd made two days ago on the gatehouse wall.

It was the first time Beau had found himself able to sit with her, not run from her. It was the first time he could simply take her in. She was a miracle. Powerful. Fierce. Magnificent. Her fur was a rich, dusky gray. Her eyes were the color of a winter moon. She smelled of silver creeks, the north wind, snow.

He stretched out a tentative hand and touched the fur on her arm. Arabella's eyes darted back to his. Her ears flattened. The velvet across her nose wrinkled. Her fangs flashed.

But Beau wasn't afraid. Words he had discovered in her old chamber, in a book of sonnets, rose to his lips. Words that had lodged in his heart. "'What is your substance, whereof are you made, that millions of strange shadows on you tend?'"

The ferociousness on Arabella's face softened to surprise. Her eyes widened, and Beau saw an aching vulnerability in them. She quickly looked away, unused to seeing wonder on a human being's face, he guessed. Unused to seeing anything but fear.

"Sonnet Fifty-Three. My favorite," she said, her eyes fixed on the fire. "I didn't know you read Shakespeare."

Beau blinked in astonishment. "You . . . you can *talk*?"

"Of course I can talk." She stood up on her hind legs and started toward her sketch, but halfway there, she turned and held up a clawed finger. "*Don't* touch my rabbit."

"Wouldn't dream of it."

She nodded, then, looking a little shamefaced, she said, "I guess you could have a leg if you'd like."

246

"I'm good."

Arabella cast one last possessive glance at her kills, then continued to her drawing. She tilted her head, taking it all in, tracing lines with a curved black talon, then she rubbed out a section of it with her paw. After a brief search, she found the stub of charcoal she'd used to make the sketch and started to redraw the rubbed-away lines.

"The pilings are too close together," she said. "We have to place them farther apart, or we'll never finish."

We, Beau thought. She said *we*, not *you*. She wanted to help him. Even though he could not help her. The realization made him feel achingly guilty, yet again, for blaming her for something she had not done. They hadn't talked, not since he'd stalked out of the castle. Maybe it was time they did.

"Arabella . . ." he began. "I'm sorry. I was wrong. About the drawbridge. I believe you. I know you didn't do it."

Arabella stopped sketching but did not turn around. "What changed your mind?"

Beau opened his mouth to answer her, then realized he might land Camille in trouble. He quickly cast about for words that weren't quite the truth but weren't a total lie, either. "Time," he finally said. "To cool down. To think things over."

Arabella nodded and Beau continued. There was something else he wanted to talk about.

"Listen, about . . . about the—"

That kiss, he was going to say. The one you gave me. The one I gave you. But she didn't let him.

"The planks?" she asked. "Have you laid any between the pilings yet? I think we'll still be able to get away with a thinner one across longer stretches. It'll have more bounce to it, but hopefully not enough to dump your thieving ass in the moat."

247

"Not having my thieving ass dumped in the moat would be good," Beau said, biting back a smile at her language.

After working a shard of bone out of her teeth with a claw, Arabella rubbed away another section of her sketch and redrew it, talking about span and pitch, which Beau did not understand. But he did understand one thing—she didn't want to talk about the kiss they'd shared. And he was relieved; at least that's what he told himself. It was easier to keep their conversation limited to solving problems of surface strength. To glance over problems of tension, and to avoid moats and the hard, dark things that lurked in them.

"I'm consulting everything I can find on footbridges," Arabella continued. "I'm worried about the far end of our bridge. The forest side appears to be higher than the gatehouse side. What if we get there and we're well below the grade? What do we do then?"

Beau thought for a moment, then said, "Balance a ladder on the decking?"

"Not unless you care to go swimming again," she said. "I've been looking at pictures of Venetian bridges to see if I can solve that problem. The Venetians did what we're trying to do, but a million times better. They sank pilings through the silt and mud of the lagoon, then connected them with planking, too. Then they put layers of limestone over the planks to serve as a foundation for the buildings. It was hard, ugly work, and yet, out of wood and mud and rock, those builders created one of the most beautiful cities in the world."

"An entire city built on the water," Beau said. "It doesn't seem possible."

"A Venetian ambassador once told me stories about his home. He made it come alive—the palaces and the art, the music and the masquerades, the smell of salt air, the songs of the boatmen . . ." Her voice trailed off. When she finally spoke again, her words were raw with longing. "Can you imagine the beauty of it, Beau? That's why builders build,

248

isn't it? Why they try to make their castles and cathedrals touch the stars. So that we might stand on the shoulders of the past and see forever."

Beau looked at her and thought, *This sad, brilliant creature has been a prisoner here, too. For far longer than I have.*

The enormity of it, of years spent living in this grim place, cut off from the world, hit Beau hard. *How lonely it must've been for her*, he thought. *What agony for a mind so bright and searching.*

"You'll break this curse, Arabella. You'll go to Venice one day. I know you will," he said, his voice suddenly husky.

Arabella gave him the ghost of a smile. "Perhaps." She looked at her sketch again, frowning with worry. "There's still so much to do, and we only have four days left." Then, as if catching herself, she quickly added, "To stay ahead of winter, I mean." She winced and scratched furiously behind one ear. "Fleas. Such a nuisance. I have to drown the little bastards in a hot bath every morning."

Beau laughed. He liked this beast-Arabella. She was frank and funny. Foulmouthed. Greedy and rude. And smart. So damn smart. Just like the other Arabella.

Still clutching her charcoal, Arabella walked to another wall now, one without any sketches on it. "I wish I had time. And winches. A granite quarry. Horses and wagons. And two hundred masons," she said. "What a bridge I could build then."

She started drawing, not a rickety plank walkway made of scraps but an arched marvel, wide enough for two carriages to pass over at the same time, with railed walkways and iron lampposts.

Beau asked her questions as she drew, one after another, just so he could hear the passion in her voice as she answered them. Once again, lost in work, in conversation, and in each other, Beau and Arabella forgot the time.

Until Beau, feeling his lack of sleep, yawned. Until he rubbed his face with both hands, trying to scrub away his weariness. Until his stomach growled for food.

"I wonder if Camille's up yet," he said. "I could really use a cup of her coffee. And a warm croissant or five."

Arabella turned to him and blinked, as if he'd called her out of a trance. Then she swiveled her gaze to the archway. It was still snowing, but the darkness was beginning to lighten.

"Oh no. Oh, blast. Beau, give me your shirt. Quick!"

He looked at her askance. "My shirt? Why?"

"Just *give* it to me," she demanded.

Beau shook his head. He did not want to remove his shirt. Not in front of her.

"Here," he said, reaching for his jacket. "Take this."

"It's too short. I need your shirt."

"No."

"For God's sake, Beau!" she shouted, her eyes huge with panic. "I don't have time to argue!"

"You can't have it. It's, um, it's really cold. *I'm* really cold."

"In about sixty seconds, *I'm* going to be really cold. Since I'm going to be completely naked. Please, Beau, for decency's sake, give me your damn shirt!"

– SEVENTY-ONE –

"Turn around."

"Is that what this is about?"

"Are you the only one who's allowed to be modest?"

"Fair point," Arabella said, turning her back to Beau "But I still need that shirt. Right now."

She stretched her hand back and, a few seconds later, felt him press his shirt into it. Clutching it, she ran for the far side of the gatehouse, ducking behind the windlass in the nick of time.

An instant later, her agony began. She'd borne it every night for a century, and yet the intensity of it always broke her. Everything that was too big and too much—the long bones of her limbs, her teeth, her snout, her powerful muscles—pulled back into themselves. She felt as if her entire body, every inch of flesh, every sinew, blood vessel, and nerve, was being folded into a too-small box. She bit back her cries, not wanting Beau to hear them, and then, just when she thought she would go mad from the pain, it was over, and she was her human self again, compressed and contained.

She took a few steadying breaths, then shrugged into Beau's shirt. It had no buttons, just a V at the neck, and it slipped easily over her head. The cuffs hung down over her hands and the hem fell to her thighs. She wasn't warm, but at least she was covered.

"Th-thank you," she said to Beau as she stepped out from behind the windlass, her teeth chattering.

"You should get inside, before you freeze to death," he said. He had put his jacket on. It was made of leather, soft and worn, with a collarless neck.

"You should, too."

"I have to see to the fire."

"I'll wait for you."

He shook his head. "There's no need."

Arabella gave a self-conscious nod, confused. A moment ago, he'd apologized to her. She hadn't expected it, and it pleased her deeply that he believed her, but now a wall had come down between them again. He wouldn't even look at her and she had no idea why.

"All right," Arabella said, trying to hug some warmth into herself. "I'll see you inside."

251

Beau made no reply. He leaned forward, poking at the fire, and as he did, the front of his jacket sagged open, exposing his neck, a bit of his chest, the curve of his left shoulder.

He hurried to close the jacket up again, but he wasn't fast enough.

Arabella stopped dead when she saw it.

She stared. She couldn't help herself.

Beau saw her looking. He awkwardly tugged his jacket back into place, blood rushing to his cheeks, and Arabella felt as if she'd seen something she shouldn't have, something he would never have willingly revealed.

Look away, a voice inside her said. *Look at the sketch. At that pile of rope over there. The floor. Anywhere but at him.*

But she didn't.

"Guess you were right, weren't you?" he said. "I am anything but *beau*."

Arabella did not answer him. She took hold of his jacket, then, asking him with her eyes, she pushed it back off his shoulders. It settled in the crooks of his arms.

Arabella caught her breath. Gently, she touched one of the scars. "Do they still hurt?"

Beau nodded.

"What happened?"

He shook his head. "It's in the past. It should stay there."

"Tell me."

Beau stood very still for a moment, and Arabella knew he was fighting with himself, weighing whether to trust her or not. For a split second, she saw indecision in his eyes, and a raw vulnerability, but then his face hardened. He wrenched his jacket back up. A second later, he was across the gatehouse, heading for the doorway.

"Beau, wait . . ."

Beau stopped but did not turn around.

"Gustave makes a salve. It eases pain. It might help."

"I don't need Gustave's salve. All I need is a way out of here."

As he walked out of the gatehouse, his footsteps sounded final, irrevocable, like the slamming of a dungeon door. Arabella stared after him, afraid she'd gone too far, pushed him too hard. Afraid this was the end.

Until a child stepped into the gatehouse and, in a small, quiet voice, said, "Don't let it be."

Arabella looked at her. It was the first time they had been alone with each other in a very long time.

"Go to him. Hurry. The clock is winding down."

Arabella shook her head. "He hates me."

"He hates himself," Hope said. "You have much in common."

"Here you go again, promising so much."

"I give possibilities. Turning them into certainties is your job."

Arabella stood, looking fearfully at the archway. Then Hope gave her a little push. It was all she needed. She kept going, through the archway, and into the courtyard, her steps growing quicker, until she was running.

– SEVENTY-TWO –

Into the castle and up the staircase Arabella raced.

By the time she reached the tower, she was breathless. She stood in front of Beau's door, still wearing his too-big shirt, and knocked on it. But he didn't open it. She turned the knob, but it was locked.

"Beau? Beau, I know you're in there. Open the door," she said, banging on it with the flat of her hand.

There was no response.

"This is childish, Beau."

Still no response. "Coward!" she shouted, giving the door a kick.

Worried, always, about the ticking clock, Arabella sat down, her back against the door, unsure what to do. A moment later, she heard the sound of pounding feet. She looked up and saw Faith running toward her.

"Why are you sitting on the floor?" she asked breathlessly.

Arabella gave her a wan smile. "As usual, your sister has made me a glittering promise and left me empty-handed," she replied.

"Want some cheese with that whine?" Faith asked.

"I'm not whining!" Arabella said, insulted. "I just—"

Faith cut her off. "The thief wouldn't let a locked door stop him."

"He knows how to pick a lock. I don't."

"Then you're lucky I came along," Faith said. She reached into her pocket and pulled out the master key.

"*You're* the one who stole it?" Arabella asked indignantly.

"Not exactly. I got it from someone . . . someone who *re*-stole it."

Before Arabella could question her further, new voices spiraled up the stairwell.

"Lady Arabella? Are you there? What's come over you? This behavior is beneath you! He's a common criminal!"

"Come away from that door! Before he opens it and bashes you over the head with a chair!"

"Ugh, here they come," Faith said. She hurried across the landing and skirted behind a table. "You can do this. Believe in yourself!"

Arabella stood a little taller, heartened by Faith's encouragement. "Do you believe in me?" she asked.

Faith shrugged. She tilted her hand side to side. "Ehhhh," she said, and then she ducked down. A few seconds later, Arabella's court arrived on the landing, as bumptious as a bag of rats.

"He doesn't want anything to do with you, can't you see that? No one does!"

"He only kissed you because he felt sorry for you."

"You're going to make *such* a fool of yourself."

Arabella turned away from them toward Beau's door, clutching the key tightly in both her hands. She tried to work up her nerve to turn it, but it was impossible to feel courageous when all she could hear was her ladies' words. For a hundred years, their poisonous voices had echoed in her ears. She longed to hear another voice now—her own.

"Be quiet!" she ordered, whirling on them.

Sadindi recoiled, shocked. She pressed a hand to her chest. "A lady *never* raises her voice," she scolded. "It's shrewish and unbecoming, and . . . and—"

"I told you to stop."

Sadindi stepped back. She looked smaller. "Lady Espidra shall hear of this," she threatened.

Rafe clutched Sadindi's arm tightly. She started to whimper.

Sadindi shook her off. "Oh, do stop sniveling!"

Rafe began to howl.

"Rafe? Is that you making all that noise?"

It was Hesma. Iglut shambled along behind her.

"Who made her cry?" Hesma demanded. "It was you, Sadindi, wasn't it? You are *such* a witch."

Sadindi raked her eyes up and down Hesma. "Where did you get that gown, darling? Steal it from a beggar?"

Hesma gasped. She called Sadindi a bad name. Sadindi called her a worse one. LaJoyuse, Elge, and Rega joined them. The squabbling grew louder. Arabella let it. She squared her shoulders and turned away from them. Then she put the key in the lock, turned it, and pushed the door open.

Beau was lying shortways on his bed, his feet on the floor, staring up at the ceiling. "You're invading my privacy," he said.

"I guess that makes us even," Arabella said. She strode across the room and flopped down next to him.

"I didn't invite you into my room, much less ask you to lie down on my bed," he said, not taking his eyes off the ceiling.

Arabella turned her head toward him. "I invited myself. Since it's my room. And my bed."

With Beau trying his best to focus on the ceiling and Arabella focusing her attention on Beau, neither of them heard the court ladies slip into the room and take their places like spectators in the Colosseum, eager for the blood sport to begin. Faith quietly darted in behind them.

Arabella was frightened, but she drew on her new reserves of hope and faith and tried again. "How did you get those scars?"

"Arabella, I don't want this."

"You know everything about me, Beau. *Everything*," Arabella said. "And I don't know anything about you. You demand that I share my secrets but hoard your own."

"You know what matters—that I'm a thief."

Arabella thought of how he'd jumped into the moat to save her. How he'd taught her to pick pockets. To dance again. To laugh again. She thought of the lines from the sonnet he'd spoken to her, and how they made her feel, for the first time in a hundred years, that she was something more than a monster.

"Beauregard Armando Fernandez de Navarre, you are so much more than a thief. Can't you see that?"

She reached for his hand, afraid he would pull it away, but he didn't. Then she asked him again how he got his scars.

"You don't give up, do you?" Beau said. He was quiet for a long moment; his gaze was somewhere else, somewhere in the past. Then, finally, he spoke. "I stole a man's wallet. He caught me and tried to stab me to death."

Arabella felt her heart crack into pieces. "When did—" she began, but then she lost her words, swallowed hard, and tried again. "When did it happen? How old were you?"

Beau closed his eyes. "Ten."

– SEVENTY-THREE –

Beau kept a box of memories inside his head, full of treasures. Sometimes he would take the box out and turn them over in his mind, as if they were bits of sea glass or polished pebbles—the small stone house, sunlight streaming in through its windows; a bowl of clementines on the table; the sound of a woman singing.

They were his and his alone. He had never shown them to another soul. Now Arabella was asking to see them. It would be easier, he thought, to hack through his own rib cage and show her his beating heart.

Tears were welling in her eyes, turning them into shimmering silver pools. "Tell me," she said.

"The man had come out of a bar, drunk. I thought he'd be an easy mark, but he felt me take his wallet and pulled a knife. When it was over, I was on the ground with a blade in my chest. Somehow, he missed my heart."

Beau's gaze was still on the ceiling; Arabella's, too. They didn't see another court lady walk in—one who had not walked freely in the corridors of the castle for decades—Lady Campossino.

Tall and strongly built, she wore a sky-blue gown and no jewelry. Her long brown hair trailed down her back. She sat down on the only chair in the room. The other ladies recoiled at the sight of her like a nest of cobras that had spotted a mongoose.

"What happened next?" Arabella asked.

"Raphael found me. He took me in. Patched me up. He saved my life.

When I got better, he told me it was good my face had been spared, for it would be his fortune. He taught me everything he knew—how to pick pockets and locks, how to rob shops and houses. I worked on the streets of Barcelona for years. Until things got too hot for us, and we left for the countryside of Spain, and then France. I was fifteen, and I started working as a kitchen boy in the houses of the wealthy. I was tall. The maids always thought I was older than I was. A few lovelorn looks, some stolen kisses, and they'd tell me anything. Where the silver was kept, the jewelry, the strongbox."

He opened his eyes and turned his head toward her. "So there it is. My story."

Arabella wiped her eyes with the heel of her hand. "Liar. You've told me nothing. You were only ten years old when you stole the wallet. Why were you on your own? Where were your parents?"

Beau drew in a breath. This was exactly what he'd feared—that Arabella wouldn't stop. That she'd try to dig up all the dark things he'd buried.

"Beau," she pressed.

His breath came out in a rush; his words followed it. "My mother died in childbirth. The baby, a girl, died with her," he said. "My father was heartbroken. He started drinking. He fell off a bridge one night and drowned. I was nine. My brother, Matteo, was three. There was no one to take us in, so we were put in a workhouse. They separated us and beat us for any reason, or no reason at all. I heard him. I heard Matti screaming as they hit him. He was so little, Arabella . . ." Beau's words fell away. His throat worked. It was a long moment before he could gather himself. "One night, I took him. And ran."

Lady Orrsow entered the room quietly. The others motioned for her to join them, but she would not. She stood alone, barefoot, her white

258

hair trailing down her back, tears trailing down her cheeks.

Hesma pointed at her and giggled. Campossino heard her. Shaking her head, she walked over to Hesma and said, "That's enough."

"A nine-year-old and a three-year-old on their own?" Arabella said. "How did you survive?"

"We stole eggs from henhouses," Beau replied. "We drank milk from cows in the field. Pulled carrots out of gardens and apples off trees. We slept in barns. But then the weather turned, and it got harder to find food. Matti was always hungry, always cold. He needed to be warm and dry. So I took him to a convent in the city's old quarter and begged the nuns to look after him. They were a poor order and said they couldn't, but I promised I would pay for his keep. I stole the money. By myself, at first. Then with the gang. I kept back coins. Raphael never found out."

"Where is Matteo now? He must be, what . . . thirteen years old? Has he left the convent?"

"He's still there. He's sick. It's consumption."

Arabella paled at his words. She knew that people with consumption rarely got better. "I'm so sorry, Beau."

"Don't be, Arabella. Don't be sorry," Beau said fiercely. "He's going to get better. He *is*. I'm going to take him away. I promised my mother I would take care of him. I've broken every other promise I've ever made, but I won't break that one." He sat up, agitated now, and leaned forward, his forearms on his knees. Shafts of morning light played across his face, emphasizing the new hollows in his cheeks, the faint lines in his forehead. "He cried so hard when I left him. Sometimes I still hear him. Calling for me. Begging me not to go. It never fades. It only ever gets worse."

"What do you mean?"

Beau looked at her, his eyes deep wells of pain. "My parents were poor," he said, "but my mother wanted more for us. She sold the only thing she had of value—a little gold bracelet—to pay the fees for me to go to school. I still see her. In my memories, my dreams. She's heartbroken at what I've done. At what I've become."

"Beau, what happened to you and Matti wasn't your fault," Arabella said.

"Pffft. It certainly *was*," Iglut said, under her breath.

Campossino heard her. "Do I need to explain to you what *stop* means?" she asked.

"I just . . . I wish things had been different," Beau said brokenly.

As he spoke, Iglut told Campossino where she could go. Sadindi slapped Orrsow. Orrsow, outraged, knocked Sadindi to the floor. Hesma shoved Romeser. And then a loud, heated brawl erupted as the ladies vied for dominance.

Arabella, watching in distress as they noisily pummeled one another, felt violently whipsawed between emotions. One moment, fury gripped her. Then hysterical laughter burbled up, only to be replaced a second later by a stark and crushing grief. *"I wish things had been different,"* she said with a heavy sigh. "That's an understatement, Beau. It's the understatement of the year. No, make that the century. One hundred long, helpless, hopeless, joyless, terrifying, stultifying, gray, and rotten years. Oh, if only things *had* been different. Why can't we go back in time?"

She struggled to rein herself in, but the dam burst and then, like a raging flood down a dry riverbed, racking sobs came.

Beau, worried, took her hand and squeezed it. Arabella squeezed back, weeping. After a moment, when the flood lessened to a trickle, she looked down at their entwined hands and in a faltering voice said, "I know you won't be the one to break the curse. I know that you don't have . . . feelings . . . Goodness, this is awkward . . . I know you don't love me. But I promised I would do my best to get you out of here, and I meant it, but there's no time to waste. The sooner you leave, the sooner you can get to your brother."

There was a shadow in Arabella's voice, something that did not want to be seen. Beau heard it and puzzled at it. He might have pressed her on it if he hadn't been trying so hard to hide something himself.

"Beau? Did you hear me?" she asked, releasing his hand and standing. "We should go. There's so much work to do. Beau? You've gone quiet. Is something wrong?"

Beau looked up at her. "Yes, Arabella," he said. "Something is wrong. You are wrong. I *do* love you."

– SEVENTY-FOUR –

In Beau's small chamber, silence descended.

The ladies stopped fighting. They stood motionless.

All except for Hope, who'd joined Faith. She elbowed her sister now and said, "Look! *Look!* It's Joy," nodding at the courtier who'd just arrived, a ginger-haired woman, freckled and smiling, her lush curves skimmed by a lavender gown. No one had seen her for a century.

Arabella stood as motionless as the rest of her court. All she could hear was the crashing of her own heart. How had this happened? Hope and Faith had not found Love, and yet Arabella knew what she was feeling was real. Was Espidra wrong? Was Love actually somewhere in the castle? Arabella closed her eyes, suddenly convinced that her ladies were playing a cruel trick. Afraid that if she moved, or spoke, if she so much as breathed, Beau would deny what he'd said. He'd say she'd misheard him. He'd laugh at her.

Seconds passed. Half a minute.

And then Beau spoke again, hurt edging at his voice. "Usually, when someone puts their entire heart on the line, they get an answer back. Even if it's not the one they want to hear. Even if—"

"What did you say?" Arabella asked, her voice barely a whisper.

Beau looked at her, incredulous. "I'm so sorry. Am I keeping you up?"

"No."

"Were you not listening?"

"I *was* listening. But I can't . . . I can't quite believe . . . Did you—"

"Tell you I love you? Yes, Arabella. I did."

"*Me . . .*"

"Yes."

"But are you sure you meant *me*?"

"You just want me to say it again."

Arabella opened her eyes and looked at him. "Yes, Beau. I do. More than I've ever wanted anything in my entire sad, weird, awful mess of a life."

But there was more heartbreak than joy in her eyes as she spoke. She was like a poor creature that had spent so long in a cage, it couldn't remember what freedom felt like.

Beau saw her anguish. He stood up and cupped her face in his hand, running his thumb over her cheekbone. "I love you, Arabella. I'll say it a thousand times if you need me to. If that's what it takes to break the curse." His eyes searched hers. "Did we break it? Is it over now?"

Arabella shook her head. "Not yet. There's one more thing we have to do. *Cross the bridge, unwind the years . . .*"

"*Escape this prison of your fears,*" Beau finished.

Then his lips were on hers, and she felt the warmth in his kiss. And the wanting. And a promise, one that felt like the scent of woodsmoke on a winter night. Like a fast horse in a dangerous forest. Like making it home just before dark.

"I love you, Arabella," he said. "I love you and we're going to finish building the bridge, and then we're going to walk across it together." He paused, then hesitantly added, "At least, I think we will."

"Think?" Arabella echoed, doubt shadowing her newfound happiness.

"Yes, think. I'm kind of flapping in the wind here," Beau said, feeling helpless.

"I don't understand."

"Do . . . *you* . . . love . . . *me*?"

Arabella fixed him with a stunned look of disbelief. "Yes, of course I love you. Don't you know that?"

"Funnily enough, I don't. Given that you've tried to kill me several times."

"I was afraid to show it. Afraid for you, most of all. That you'd be stuck here, doomed like the rest of us." She touched his face, needing to tell herself again and again that he was real, that this was real. "And afraid for myself. Afraid that you'd see my feelings and mock me for them."

Beau stood up. He ushered all the ladies out of his room and closed the door. Then he pulled Arabella into his arms and kissed her until neither of them could breathe.

"Ask Percival for another shirt," she said, reluctantly breaking the kiss. "And then get some coffee. We're going to need it. We have a bridge to finish."

After one last kiss, Arabella left him, rushing past her court, hurrying to her chamber.

From deep within the castle, the golden clock chimed the hour— eight o'clock—reminding her that time was running out. That there were so few days left. She almost turned around then and there. She almost ran back to Beau and told him that he hadn't heard the worst part of the clockmaker's poem—that there was an end to the curse, and it was almost here. He would understand; she knew he would. But a small, frightened voice inside her, scarred from a century of sorrow, refused to trust love. For she had been told for so long that girls who felt too much, and thought too much, and said too much, did not deserve it. That voice told her to keep quiet. It told her that Beau might feel angry if he knew. That she might lose him.

And so Arabella made a terrible mistake. She listened to it.

– SEVENTY-FIVE –

Camille patted the beautiful orange pumpkin Gustave had just brought her. She reached for her cleaver.

"What will you make with it?" he asked.

"A charlotte. For supper tonight," she replied. "Filled with a spiced pumpkin mousse and edged with chocolate ladyfingers."

"Mmm! I'll be your taster!" Josette said, piling still-warm croissants onto a tray for Arabella and Beau's breakfast.

The kitchen was filled with a bustling sense of excitement. Word had traveled through the castle—thanks to Hope and Faith, who were gifted at the art of eavesdropping—about what had happened in Beau's room.

"Love . . ." Valmont had said skeptically, his bushy eyebrows drawn together, as the servants had huddled around the two girls an hour ago.

"Yes," Hope had replied.

"*Love* love?" Lucile had asked.

"Yes!" Hope had crowed.

"L-O-V-E?" Florian had added.

"Florian, you know how to spell!" Faith had said, fake clapping. "Want me to teach you some more four-letter words?"

"She's here, then. Somewhere. Your other sister?" Valmont had asked the girls. "No one has seen her."

"She must be," Hope had replied. "Arabella has fallen in love, hasn't she?"

"We just haven't found her yet," Faith had said.

"But we will. We *will*," Hope had added, as if trying to convince them all. And herself.

"Do you know what this means?" Percival had asked, his voice hushed.

"It means Lady Arabella will cross the bridge. And the curse will be broken," Phillipe had replied. "It means we will live."

Percival had squeezed the kitchen rag he'd been holding until his knuckles turned white. He looked at Phillipe. "Do you remember?" he asked him. "The little stone cottage in the forest?"

Everyone remembered. The two had bought the cottage with their hard-earned savings, hoping to retire there one day.

For a long moment, Phillipe could not reply. "I do," he'd finally said, exchanging a look of longing and hope with Percival that had been a century in the making.

All the servants hoped, though it frightened them to do so. They hoped they would walk out of the castle and across the bridge, too. They hoped they would never again hear the golden clock ticking away the minutes, hours, and years of their lives. But others in the castle had not greeted the news with happiness.

Lady Hesma and Lady Elge burst into the kitchen in a swirl of gray and red now, shrilling at the servants. One was carrying a length of rope, the other a pair of iron shackles.

"Where are they? Sticking their grimy fingers into the batter? Filching sweets?" Elge demanded.

"The children that you seek are not here, Your Ladyships," Percival replied, his voice seething with contempt.

Elge heard it. "Watch yourself, old boy," she cautioned. "We're still in charge here. How would *you* like to spend some time locked away in the cellar? I can arrange it."

As she spoke, Rémy approached them, carrying a platter of breakfast sausages. He was as filthy as ever, spattered with fat, smudged with ash, trailing the scents of sage, thyme, and nutmeg.

Elge's clumsily rouged lips collapsed into a grimace as he passed by. She clutched the large, garish pearls around her neck, then began to convulse like a cat with a hairball. "Dear God, the *stench!*" she cried.

Rémy came to a stop. He looked at her uncertainly.

Hesma pounced. "Yes, that's right. She's talking about *you*, you smelly guttersnipe."

The little boy flinched. His cheeks colored under the grime.

Hesma saw his humiliation; her eyes glittered cruelly. "You *stink*. You're filthy and disgusting. Don't you ever wash?"

Rémy's eyes filled with tears. He backed away like a puppy that had been kicked. Camille's grip tightened on her cleaver.

"Come on, Rem. Chef needs some eggs."

It was Henri. He motioned the boy over to Phillipe's worktable, took the platter from him, and set it down. Rémy rubbed his eyes with a balled fist.

Henri knelt down by him. "Chef also needs potatoes and onions. Can you help me carry them?"

Rémy nodded.

"Good man," Henri said, clapping him on the back. He set off, with the little boy trotting close at his heels.

"Happy, Lady Hesma? You made a child cry," Camille said.

"*Happy?* Goodness no. I'm euphoric!" Hesma replied.

Camille raised her cleaver. "Get out of here. Before I toss you out. In pieces."

Hesma gasped. Elge's head swiveled in Camille's direction. Her doll eyes narrowed; her grin widened. "Poor thing, you really think this is it, don't you?" she said. "The grand, soaring happily ever after? Just because Hope and Faith are running around the castle like two escaped lunatics. But you're forgetting something . . . Love is not here. Has anyone found her? No. Whatever Arabella and the thief *think* they feel for each other—attraction, infatuation, lust—it is *not* love."

Camille brought her cleaver down on the pumpkin with such force that it split cleanly in two.

Elge looked at the raw, fleshy halves, rocking back and forth on the table. Her fingers fluttered nervously with a button on her dress. "Come, Hesma," she said. "We're distracting the help."

The two ladies flounced out of the kitchen and started down the corridor toward the great hall but stopped to listen as the servants' voices carried after them.

"We can't give up. Hope and Faith are strong," Camille said.

"They've survived all these years," Percival added.

"Maybe they'll be enough," said Josette.

Elge clutched at Hesma's arm, jubilant. "Did you hear the wonderful worry in their voices? The awesome anxiety? The fabulous fear?"

Hesma arched an eyebrow. "I hear the asinine alliteration in yours."

Elge kissed Hesma's greasy cheek, leaving a smear of lip rouge, then grabbed her arm and pulled her along. "Mortals are *such* fools," she said. "They break their own hearts again and again and again, then stand amid the shattered pieces and declare that love conquers all." She burst into screechy laughter. "Four days, Hesma, my dear. Just four more days. Then the clock will run out, the castle will crumble, and *we* will win."

- SEVENTY-SIX -

Espidra watched them, Arabella and Beau.

They were sitting at the dining table, cups and plates scattered about, heads bent together. They were feverishly poring over a revised drawing Arabella had made for the last section of the bridge.

Espidra had been informed about the little talk that had taken place a few days ago in Beau's room. The dark blood that ran through her veins simmered as she saw other ladies of the court—ladies who had been banished to the shadows—reemerge: Compassion. Pride. Vulnerability.

The curse ended tomorrow night when the clock struck twelve, and the bridge was nearly finished. What if the thief truly managed to break the curse? It would spell the end of her.

No, it won't happen, Espidra told herself. *It can't.*

She knew the terms of the curse: Arabella must learn to love, and be loved in return. But the third wretched sister had not been found. Because she was not here; Espidra was certain of that. The thief was a mere crush, a passing fancy. Arabella did not love him. It was impossible.

Espidra leaned over to Iglut, who was reading a book, and whispered, "I need a few minutes with him. Alone." She nodded at Arabella's water glass, which had been pushed close to the edge of the table. "See what you can do."

Iglut rose and closed her book. "It's chilly this morning, Lady Espidra," she said. "I'm going to fetch a shawl. I won't be a moment."

Iglut walked toward the table, stopped by Arabella, and gave her a quick curtsy, as was customary. As she rose, however, and continued on her way, she tripped. Her book went flying. Her body lurched forward. It looked as if she would fall to the floor, but at the last moment, she managed to catch herself on the edge of the table . . . and knock Arabella's water glass into her lap.

Arabella gasped as the cold water soaked through her clothing.

Iglut gasped even louder. Her hands came up to her mouth. "I'm so sorry, Your Grace! I'm so clumsy. So hopeless. So bad at *everything*."

"Enough, Lady Iglut," Arabella said, standing. "It's just water." She looked at Beau. "I'm going to change. It'll only take a minute. I'll meet you at the gatehouse."

Beau stood, too. He took one last bite of a roll and washed it down with a gulp of coffee. Then he put his jacket on.

Espidra joined him. "How fortunate that clumsy Lady Iglut did not ruin your drawing. Is it final?" she asked lightly.

"We hope so," Beau replied, eyeing her mistrustfully.

Espidra's gaze settled on the drawing. "My goodness, but that bridge is narrow." She looked up at him. "Will it really be strong enough to hold you both?"

Beau started to roll the drawing up. "What, exactly, are you asking me, Lady Espidra?"

Espidra placed a hand on his arm. At her touch, the sparkling light in his beautiful eyes dimmed. The color in his cheeks faded. And his pulse, so strong and surging, weakened a little.

"I would like to see this marvelous bridge of yours," Espidra said. "Come, let us walk to it together." Her shawl had settled in the crooks of her elbows. She pulled it up around her neck, then threaded her arm through his.

The two proceeded through the great hall, out of the castle, and across the snow-covered courtyard. Espidra remarked on the chilly wind and the scudding clouds, and predicted a clear, sunny day, a good day for building.

They walked through the gatehouse, and as they reached the far threshold, she released Beau's arm. Her eyes roved over the crossed pilings, marching in pairs halfway across the moat, the narrow walkway.

"I must say, it is ingenious. Well done, Monsieur Beauregard." She turned her face to his. "I know the plan. Tomorrow you cross, no? Bright and early?"

"No, at midday," said Beau. "So the sun can melt any ice on the planks."

269

Espidra shook her head regretfully. "Ah, my hopeful young friend. You may think you can help her, but you cannot."

"I have already helped her," Beau said defiantly. "And she has helped me."

Espidra's eyes turned as hard as obsidian. "I will not relinquish Arabella to you, not without a fight. I know who she is. I know what she's capable of. And despite that, I care for her. I'm the only one who truly ever has."

"I care for her, too, Lady Espidra."

"Do you?" Espidra turned her gaze to the far side of the moat. "Imagine for a moment that the two of you actually manage to break the curse and return her to her former state. Then what? A storybook ending?"

Beau's jaw tightened. Espidra saw it and went for the kill.

"I don't think so. And neither do you. Oh, you may *want* to be the knight in shining armor, riding in to save the damsel, but you can't be. Because deep down, you know that you're not good enough for her. She is learned, cultured, refined. A member of the aristocracy. And you?"

She laughed scornfully and as she did, her face changed, melting and morphing. And suddenly it wasn't Espidra standing in front of him but the sheriff, after he'd just locked him inside a jail cell. Beau wanted to run, but horror froze him to the spot. Espidra opened her mouth to speak and the words came out in a man's voice.

A beating's too good for you, boy, you're nothing but a thief . . .

Her face changed again, this time to the schoolmaster's.

You have no place in my school, boy, you're nothing but a thief . . .

And then the priest's.

You're not welcome in this holy church, boy, you're nothing but a thief . . .

"N-no . . . *no*. It's not true . . ." Beau stammered, shaking his head, but his protest was weak. Espidra's words had drained the fight out of him.

"They were right, weren't they?" Espidra murmured, assuming her own form again. "You really are nothing but a thief, Beauregard. A

270

no-account boy from the slums. Your neck should've been broken by a noose years ago. I have no doubt that it soon will be."

Beau's eyes had dulled. His shoulders were slumped. Espidra squeezed his arm tightly, and led him closer to the threshold. One step, then another, steering him not toward the narrow plank walkway of the bridge but to the right of it, where there was nothing—except a sheer drop into the moat.

"Arabella needs love to break the curse, yes, the love of a *good* man. If you truly do care for her, be that good man. For once in your life, do the right thing. When tomorrow comes, and you get across that bridge, leave her."

Beau's gaze dropped to the ground. He tried to push back at the hopelessness that had immobilized him. "You . . . you're . . ."

"Right," Espidra finished, walking him closer to the edge. "I always am. I see you, Beau. I see the man you really are—sly, devious, selfish— and I know you'll never escape that man, no matter how much you try. It's too late. You've done too much damage. Caused too much harm."

And then Beau caught his toe on something and stumbled. He looked down. It was a dead rabbit.

"What the devil is that doing here?" Espidra muttered, kicking it aside.

She tugged on Beau's arm again; they were only two steps away from the edge now. But this time, Beau, still staring at the rabbit, didn't move.

"Come along," she coaxed silkily. "Just another step . . ."

Beau was resisting, struggling, trying to dredge up a few last scraps of strength. Espidra had seen it before, many times. Mortals often made one final, futile attempt to escape before they succumbed to her. It reminded her of a gazelle trying to pull free from the lion's claws, a mouse running from the owl's shadow. So noble. So brave. So absurd.

She waited for Beau to realize that it was hopeless, to give in. But he didn't; he straightened his back and lifted his head. It took a great force of will. It cost him; she could see it did. Dread convulsed her shrunken heart. She waited, silently urging him to fail. Instead, there was a rush of blood to his cheeks. Fire ignited in his eyes. He shook her touch off like a dog shaking off mud.

"You're right, Lady Espidra," he said. "I'm no good. But Arabella *is*. And she deserves more than dead rodents, and this place, and you. She deserves a chance to prove it." He picked up the rabbit, walked to the threshold, and threw it into the moat. "If you'll excuse me, I have a bridge to build," he said in a voice granite-hard with determination.

Espidra backed away, aghast. Then she turned and hurried from the gatehouse to the castle. For the first time she saw the possibility of her own failure.

For Espidra had done something she rarely did; she'd made a mistake. The thief was clever. He'd taught Arabella how to steal.

And the first thing the beastly girl had stolen was his heart.

– SEVENTY-SEVEN –

It is midnight, and Arabella runs.

Under the pale silver moon. Across the white fields. And into the woods.

In pursuit of a stag.

Her powerful limbs carry her through creek beds. Her broad paws crash through the eggshell ice. The shock of cold water makes her gasp, then laugh.

She barrels through bracken and briar, under pine boughs, past boulders.

The resiny tang of evergreens, the musty loam of the forest floor, the mineral scent of new-fallen snow—these perfumes are finer to her than costly civet or ambergris. They call to her blood. They spur her on.

Here in the woods, unlaced and unseen, the beast inside her is free to want. To chase what she desires and take it. Without shame. Without guilt. Without apologies.

Today, after dawn's light, she will shed this heavy pelt forever. She will banish her dark and difficult court and never look upon their faces again. She will walk out of the castle and over that bridge. Today, the curse will be broken.

And yet, as she leaves the forest with leaves in her fur and dirt under her claws, as the gray dawn rises over the trees, it is not the morning sun's rays in her eyes that cause her to blink.

It is her own tears.

– SEVENTY-EIGHT –

It was the last time.

The last time Beau would ever walk in the shadows. That last time he would sneak through someone else's house. The last time he would pick a lock.

He was going to be a better man from here on out. For Arabella. And for Matti.

"I swear it," he whispered.

But they had to break the curse first. *Today*. Arabella had driven herself, and everyone around her, mercilessly yesterday, trying to get the bridge finished. When Beau had asked her why she was so anxious, she'd mumbled something about snowstorms. They'd worked hard and had almost finished late last night, but then midnight came, and with it the beast, forcing them indoors. Beau had been tense yesterday, too, but for a different reason—Espidra. She meant to stop them. She had tried to kill him two days ago, and he had no doubt that she'd try again. Which was why he was moving so stealthily through the castle now, just after dawn, determined to avoid her. He was dirty, sweaty, and

273

bleary-eyed. He left his room shortly after midnight and had snuck back to finish the bridge with Espidra's words echoing in his head. *I will not relinquish Arabella to you, not without a fight.* He believed her; Espidra was not a kidder.

The lock's tumblers fell. The god of thieves was with him. He opened the door a crack, praying its hinges wouldn't squeak, then squeezed into the room and closed it.

A smile came to his face as he saw her, the pale light of morning washing over her. She was sprawled out facedown in her enormous bed, her head hanging off one side, arms dangling to the floor, legs tangled up in the sheets, one bare foot on a pillow.

He started toward her, sidestepping the muddy tracks on the floor. The dead leaves. The half-chewed chipmunk. He had to wake her. They needed to go. Before the household was up. Before Espidra could make good on her threat.

He had to be careful, though. If he frightened her, if she screamed, Espidra, Hesma, and the rest of the ghouls would come running.

"Arabella!" he whispered.

Nothing.

"Arabella, wake up!"

A grunt. Some snoring.

Beau looked back nervously at the door. "Come *on*, Arabella . . ." He moved across the room quietly and tickled the bottom of her foot.

"Erf. Blerg. Hahaha."

"Ara*bell*a!"

Arabella sat up and turned around. Her eyes widened. She inhaled deeply, ready to let out an earsplitting scream.

"Shhh!" Beau whispered, clapping a hand over her mouth. "It's me!"

Arabella slapped his hand away. "What are you *doing*?" she hissed. "You scared me to death!"

"We need to go. Right now."

"That's going to be hard," she said blearily. "Given that the bridge isn't finished."

"It is. It's done. I worked through the night. Laid the last boards just before dawn. I didn't want anyone to know. Didn't want Espidra to find out. She's going to try to stop us, Arabella. I know she is. A few days ago, I lied to her. I told her we'd be leaving at midday. She isn't expecting us to leave now. Which is exactly why we're going to."

Arabella sat up in her bed and blinked, gathering her wits. The neckline of her shift had slipped down over one shoulder. Her hair tumbled down her back. Her cheeks were flushed. Beau couldn't take his eyes off her. She saw him looking at her.

"Do you want to kiss me as much as I want to kiss you?" she asked.

"More. But if I do, we'll never leave this room."

"On the other side, then."

"Yes, on the other side. A hundred times, I hope. But now you need to get dressed. *Quick*, Arabella."

Arabella slipped into her dressing room. Then almost immediately stuck her head out. "Beau, what do I wear?," she called out. "What do we do once we get to the other side?" They had both been so busy building the bridge, neither had thought about what would happen after they crossed it.

"I have to go to Barcelona, to Matti," Beau replied. "But I'll come back to you, Arabella, I swear it."

"I'm coming with you."

"You can't," Beau said. "It's a long, hard trip over the mountains in winter."

"You're talking to a girl who spends her nights outside in the snow and eats rodents for breakfast. I can manage the mountains."

Beau wanted to protest, but he saw the determination in her eyes, and

275

he knew that this was an argument he would lose. He saw something else there, too—kindness. Arabella knew what his little brother meant to him and she wanted to help reunite them. He hadn't known kindness, not for a very long time, and he had to swallow once or twice before he said, "Thank you."

Arabella dressed quickly in warm clothing and leather boots, put a few gold coins in a small leather pouch, and a few moments later, they were sneaking out of her chambers, hands clasped.

"I know a shortcut," she said, leading the way.

Beau followed her, wary and tense, his eyes sweeping the hallways. They didn't have far to go, and there was no reason to think they wouldn't make it. No one would expect them to be up this early. The court ladies would all still be asleep. Yet Beau knew better than to underestimate Espidra.

She was like a viper under dead leaves. A scorpion. A poisonous spider.

Something you didn't see coming until it was too late.

− SEVENTY-NINE −

"Take some rolls!" Camille whispered, pressing a warm, cloth-wrapped bundle into Beau's hands. "Do you want some jam?"

"Camille, what are we going to do with rolls and jam?" Beau whispered back.

"Eat them?" Hope ventured.

"You should never go anywhere without rolls and jam," Faith advised.

The five of them were standing in the kitchen, trying to keep their voices down. Camille had made sure both Beau and Arabella had warm hats, scarves, and mittens, too.

"The sun's already up. Soon the court will be, too. We need to *go*,"

Beau said. "What happens when a curse is broken, anyway? Is there lightning or something?"

"I don't know. I've never broken one before," Arabella said.

"They'll come back to us, the ones in the clock. That's what will happen," Camille said. "You come back to us, too, mistress," she added, taking Arabella's hand.

"I will, Camille," Arabella said, covering the baker's hand with her own.

A thump was heard from overhead. Everyone's eyes flicked up to the ceiling.

"It's Percival," Camille said. "He'll be on his way down soon. He makes a tea tray for the mistress and carries it to her chambers."

"Lady Espidra takes it from him," Arabella added. "She meets him at my door. If he's up, it's later than I thought. She'll probably be there now, wondering where—"

"Lady Arabella!" Espidra's voice, shrill with alarm, carried from the great hall. "Percival! Valmont! Where is the mistress? She's not in her bed!"

"Time to go!" Faith whispered, grabbing Hope's arm and heading for the back door.

"Go, mistress! Hurry! I'll stall her," Camille whispered.

Beau and Arabella started after the two girls, but then Arabella stopped and turned back, Camille's words echoing in her ears. *They'll come back to us . . . the ones in the clock . . .*

"It was you, wasn't it?" she said to her. "You're the one who raised the portcullis."

Camille nodded, bracing herself for Arabella's anger.

Instead, Arabella threw her arms around her. "Thank you!" she whispered in her ear. And then she was gone, running out the back door after the others. Toward the gatehouse. And freedom.

EIGHTY

"This is the big moment," Beau said. "I'll go first and check for any weak spots. After I'm across, you start out."

He was talking too much. He was nervous. Arabella could see it.

"We'll be fine," she said. "It's strong enough to hold us. It held you and Henri and Florian as you built it."

"Barely," Beau said, worry in his voice. He glanced at the far side of the bridge. "Right, then. I'm off. But there's one thing I want to do first . . ."

He folded her into his arms, and time stopped for Arabella. She closed her eyes, feeling his warmth, the rise and fall of his chest, the beat of his heart under her hand.

"It's my last chance to hug the beast-girl," he whispered. "I'll miss her."

He held her for a beat longer, and then he was gone, making his way across. He stepped carefully, holding his arms out for balance, Camille's parcel of rolls clutched in one hand. There was no railing to stop his fall. There was nothing but the pilings and the thin boards stretched between them. Arabella could hear them, creaking and popping under his feet.

"Go. Keep walking. Don't stop," she whispered, urging him on.

The monsters in the moat heard the groaning of the boards; they felt the vibrations of Beau's footsteps. One by one, they surfaced, their tortured faces contracted in snarls of malice, their bony hands clawing at the air.

Arabella's heart jumped into her throat once, when a board whined, then sagged frighteningly low, but Beau got across it and then, miraculously, he reached the other side. He stepped onto the far bank, set his parcel down, then turned around.

Arabella saw a broad, beautiful smile spread over his face. He looked back at her, beckoning. "It didn't fall down! Can you believe it? Come on, Bells! Walk across!"

Arabella felt a hand slip into hers. She looked down. Hope was standing there.

"Go," the little girl said.

Faith was standing next to her. "And hurry," she added, nodding at the bridge. "All the faith in the world isn't going to keep that piece of junk standing."

Arabella raised Hope's hand to her lips and kissed it. She hugged Faith. Then she started walking. The first few steps were easy. The decking barely moved under her feet. But as she made her way farther along, the boards started to bounce. She had to put her hands out at her sides, as Beau had, to keep her balance. She took another few steps, and then a gust of wind blew down, rattling the bridge and throwing her off-balance. Her arms windmilled; her stomach did, too. She stopped, took a breath, regained her equilibrium, and continued.

"Keep walking! You're doing fine!" Beau shouted.

A few more steps, a few feet gained, and then Arabella made the mistake of looking down. The dark gray waters seemed to rush up at her; one of the monsters opened its black maw wide. Dizziness gripped her; she lurched to one side.

"Arabella, hey! Look up! Look at me!" yelled Beau.

The sharpness in his voice snapped her out of her vertigo. She pinned her gaze on him, steadied her breath, and kept walking. If she looked up, not down, if she kept her eyes on him, she could do it. Two more feet gained. Five more. Her heart leapt with joy. She was actually crossing the bridge.

But her happiness was short-lived. For when she was exactly halfway across the bridge, she found that she could no longer move forward. Not a step, not an inch.

It wasn't because the bridge's height made her feel dizzy. Or that the groaning, thrashing creatures below it scared her. It was because a wall, invisible and impenetrable, was blocking her way.

Arabella felt as if her heart had tumbled out of her body and fallen into the moat, to be ripped apart by the soulless things there. She lowered her head, fighting back tears. "What a fool you are," she said to herself. "A fool to have hoped. A fool to have believed."

She loved Beau. With all her heart. But he didn't love her. He'd only said he did. Out of pity, perhaps. Or maybe out of greed. After all, he was a thief, wasn't he? If he truly loved her, the curse would be broken; there would be no wall between them.

"Come on! Don't stop, Arabella! Keep walking!" Beau shouted.

"I *can't*," she cried.

This was just how it had happened all the other times. A wall, halfway across. Stopping her. Turning her around. To the heartbroken servants. To the figures in the clock. To the bleak prison that was her life.

"Of course you can! Just don't look down. Look at me!"

Arabella lifted her face. "It didn't work. It was never going to work. But you knew that, didn't you?"

"What are you talking about? You're halfway there! Just keep going!"

Arabella shook her head. She raised her hands over her head and slapped at the air above her, but her hands didn't *whoosh* through it. They stopped suddenly, forcefully, smacking loudly against a barrier no one could see.

Beau stared at her, bewildered. He took a few steps forward. "No. *No.* Just stay there, Arabella. I'm coming to get you."

And then he was thundering back across the narrow planks. She saw them bow and pop as his feet passed over them. One pair of crisscrossed pilings swayed forward, torquing the decking. Her heart squeezed with fear. If she didn't stop him, right now, the loose pilings would topple; the decking would collapse underneath his feet. He would fall into the middle of the moat, where no one could help him. The monsters would tear him apart.

She had to make him turn back.

"Stop, you fool!" she shouted at him, backing away from the invisible wall. "You'll bring the whole bridge down! You'll kill us both!"

But he was already at the halfway point. "I'll get to you!" he shouted, pounding his hands against the wall. "I'll find a way around this thing!"

Arabella forced a hard laugh out of herself, and harder words. "Don't bother. Of course there's a wall. Of course we didn't break the curse. Did you think for a moment I could fall for *you*? You're nothing but a thief."

Her words hit Beau like an arrow to the heart. "What are you saying?" He shook his head, wounded and confused. "This isn't you. You're upset . . ."

"Oh, but it is me. What you see is what you get, Beau—a beast, inside and out. Don't you understand? I just played along. To get you to build a bridge. To get you to leave. How else could I get rid of you?"

"Arabella . . ."

Her nose wrinkled. *"Go,"* she snarled.

The hurt in Beau's eyes deepened. He hauled off and punched the wall. Again and again. Until his fist was bloody. And then he turned and walked away from her. He stopped when he reached the other side of the rickety bridge, just for a moment, as if he might turn and speak to her again, but he did not. He started walking instead. Toward the dark forest. The trees welcomed him, then closed around him. And he was gone.

"You're free," Arabella whispered. Relief flooded through her, but it was followed by a rush of sorrow so searing, she dropped to her knees on the bridge. Sorrow for Valmont and Percival, Camille, her parents, and everyone else inside the castle who longed to be free of the curse, but never would. She felt no sorrow for herself, only a deep desire to have it over with. After a hundred years, all she wanted was relief. From the guilt. The remorse. The despair. Espidra was right, she was always right: Love had abandoned her.

She felt a hand on her shoulder. "Come, child," said a hollow voice.

Arabella nodded. She rose. The clockmaker was standing behind her, slender and elegant in his black suit. He led her back to the gatehouse. When they were both inside it, he turned, raised a pale hand, and made a swirling motion. In the moat, the waters started to churn. The monsters swarmed to the pilings. Some pushed against them, some pulled. Others knocked their skulls into the pilings over and over again, until they shuddered and swayed, and the ropes binding them snapped, and they pitched into the moat, bringing the walkway down with them.

Arabella watched as the clockmaker destroyed her work. She watched until the last board had toppled end over end into the water. Until the last piling fell, and nothing was left of what she and Beau had built together.

And then she followed the clockmaker through the gatehouse, across the courtyard, and into the castle.

She glanced back once, just once, before the heavy wooden doors slammed shut behind her.

– EIGHTY-ONE –

You knew death was coming.

You saw in his eyes what he meant to do, long before you saw the knife.

But what could you do? She was a queen, and he was a huntsman.

And you? You were a girl. And no one can ever let that be.

He thought it was over when he threw down his knife, but you knew it was only beginning.

You ran to him as he swung up into his saddle, pleading, clutching at his reins, but he kicked you away.

You stood there weeping as he rode off. Then panic set in. You screamed yourself hoarse.

The first night was the worst. You'd never known such darkness. Such loneliness. Such fear. You learned so much as you tried not to die.

What was safe to eat. Where to find water. How to hide from things that snuffle and grunt.

You walked out of those woods long, long ago, but part of you is still there and it always will be. Forever lost. Forever hungry. Forever afraid.

There are times when you wish the huntsman had been brave enough to follow his orders.

There are times when you think the queen had only been trying to be kind.

Turns out she knew something you didn't: No one can break your heart if you haven't got one.

- E I G H T Y - T W O -

It served him right.

How many people had he stolen from? How many had he lied to and tricked?

As Beau trudged through the snowy woods, his own court of emotions tormented him. He felt raw. Angry. Bewildered. Broken.

Arabella had told him that she loved him. What he had felt when she touched him, when she kissed him—that was real. She wasn't a good enough liar to fake that. No one was.

But then her words came back to him, and he knew it was only wishful thinking . . . *Did you think for a moment I could fall for you? You're nothing but a thief* . . .

She didn't love him, that was a fact. If she did, she would've been able to cross the bridge. That invisible barrier was real, too. He'd felt it with his own hands. His despondency deepened as he remembered how Hope and Faith had searched for their sister, but had not found her. Of course they hadn't. What would Love want with the likes of him?

Winded, Beau stopped walking for a moment, leaned his head back, and stared up at the lowering sky. Words from the clockmaker's poem drifted back to him.

And when to love you finally learn
You will be loved in return.

When Arabella truly loved, she would be free. But she didn't, so she wasn't. Maybe next time. When a better man came along.

Beau wished he could just hate her. That would make things so much easier. But he didn't hate her; he loved her and missed her and wanted her here, by his side. He missed brainstorming with her late at night at the great hall's table, a pot of hot coffee and a plate of cakes nearby. He missed hammering and banging and building their crappy bridge. He missed celebrating each time a piling stood up, and swearing—precisely and creatively—each time one fell down.

Once, he'd thought that picking a diabolically difficult lock or breaking into a well-guarded mansion was the highest form of achievement, the greatest thing he could ever aspire to, but his time with Arabella had taught him differently. Discovering what that fierce, haunted creature truly was, who she truly was—it was the best thing he'd ever done. He'd unlocked the strongbox of her heart and the riches there had dazzled him. Arabella had given him back something that had been stolen from him—a sense of possibility. She'd seen something in him, a flicker, a glimmer, a bright promise that he could be something more. Someone more. A man who didn't take, but gave. Or so he'd thought.

You really are nothing but a thief, Beauregard. A no-account boy from the slums. Your neck should've been broken by a noose years ago . . .

Espidra was right: He wasn't good enough for Arabella. If he were smart, he'd do his best to forget her and focus on getting to Matti as quickly as he could.

Beau walked on, mile after mile through the dense forest, shoulders hunched against the cold, wishing that the mix of feelings that had descended on him—melancholy, loss, and a strange, prickling uneasiness—would lift, but they only deepened.

His hands and feet were half-frozen by the time he saw the signpost: VILLE DES BOIS-PERDUS. A few minutes later, he was walking down the town's main street, looking for an inn or coffeehouse where he could buy a hot meal and warm himself by a fire. He'd left Camille's rolls in the snow by the moat.

His first glimpse of the town revealed a sad, dreary place with little promise. And then, with a startle of recognition, he realized he knew it—the bones of it, at least—even though he'd never set foot in it. He'd seen it changed, transformed, stitched in silver on the underside of a bedcover. But could this gray, lifeless place really be the foundation for Arabella's Paradisium?

Beau squinted, and the ugly square, with its rusted fountain, came to bright, beautiful life, planted with shady trees, dotted with benches, full of laughing children. The sooty village hall, its facade scrubbed, stood newly proud. And the school, its pediment crumbling, its windows boarded up, became the town's newly painted and polished centerpiece, the jewel in its crown.

He opened his eyes wide again and the vision faded. The broken-down little town was anything but a paradise, but Beau knew Arabella could have made it one. Like the greatest of architects, she saw with her heart, not her eyes. She saw not what was, but what could be.

A church bell rang, letting him know it was already noon, reminding him that he had things to do. He felt for the emerald ring. It was still safely tucked away in its hiding place. His thumb slid over it, back and forth, worrying at it. He knew he should be happy to have the ring, but he wasn't. It felt like an ugly scar, a reminder of something painful.

He started toward the blacksmith's, knowing that a large part of a smith's work was shoeing horses, and hoping this one might know of a sound animal for sale. As he crossed the square, he saw a group of thin children in threadbare coats and woolen mittens. Some were making snowmen. Two girls played a hand-clapping game as he passed them by, rhyming in unison:

> *Clockmaker, clockmaker, wind your clock.*
> *Watch the hands go tick, tick, tock.*
>
> *Round and round the dial they spin,*
> *Who will lose and who will win?*
>
> *Gray stone castle, murky moat,*
> *Where the living dead men float.*
>
> *Black rock, silver stream, split oak tree,*
> *Run like the devil if these you see.*

Beau stopped dead. A chill rattled through him. He turned around, hurried to the children, and crouched down by them.

"Hey, where did you hear that rhyme?" he asked them.

Startled, the children backed away from him. "Dunno," one said.

An older boy stepped forward protectively. "It's just singsong, mister. It don't mean nuthin'."

"But where did you hear it?" Beau pressed. "Who taught it to you?"

"Hey! You!" a voice bellowed. "What d'you want with those little 'uns?"

Beau's head turned. The words had been uttered by a large man standing in the doorway of a butcher shop. There was a menace in his voice and a cleaver in his hand.

Beau rose; he held his own hands up to show that he was no threat. "Just asking about the rhyme they were singing."

The man's scowl deepened. "You're too old to be playing kiddie games, son."

Giving the man a conciliatory nod, Beau continued on his way. He felt suspicious eyes upon him and upbraided himself. What was wrong with him? What was he thinking? Accosting little children like that? And yet, he couldn't let their strange rhyme go. The castle it described . . . it was just like Arabella's. The signposts it mentioned, the things that said *turn back*—the black rock, the silver stream, the split tree . . . hadn't he just passed all three of them?

Don't be ridiculous, every forest has streams and rocks and damaged trees in it, he told himself, *and there are plenty of castles along the borderlands.* And yet his nagging sense of unease deepened until he stopped again, gripped by a conviction that he should turn around now, right now, and go back.

Beau ignored the feeling and walked on, trying to reassure himself that the children's rhyme had nothing to do with Arabella or her castle, but just as he reached the blacksmith's, the children started clapping and singing again.

> *Gentleman, butler, gardener, groom,*
> *None of them can escape their doom.*
>
> *Maids and ladies, hear them cry.*
> *In a hundred years, they all will die!*

And there it was—the answer.

With a jarring dread, Beau realized he'd never heard the last lines of the clockmaker's spell. Because Arabella had hurled an inkwell at the mirror before he could. Images swirled through his head now—the cellar stuffed with enough provisions to feed the household for a century, the barrels of wine from a château that had burned down decades ago, the rotting finery guarded by a mirror-eyed monster. And Arabella herself, driving them to finish the bridge.

The curse ended in a hundred years, and the hundred years were up. "You stupid, stupid fool," he whispered.

He'd left her. Even though he loved her. He'd cut and run, just like he always did. Why? Because he believed the worst of her? Or because he believed the worst of himself?

Beau turned around and broke into a run. Out of the square, out of the town, back to the woods.

He ran faster than he had when the merchant's men were after him. Faster than the night he'd tried to escape from the beast.

Faster than he'd ever run in his life.

– EIGHTY-THREE –

The forest was Beau's enemy now.

Nothing looked familiar. It was as if every tree, every rock and stream, were conspiring against him. Trying to confuse him, turn him around, send him off in the wrong direction.

Snow was coming down now, driven by a merciless wind. In a few more hours, dusk would fall. Beau knew that if he didn't find his way soon, if he didn't get to the shelter of the castle by dusk, he'd be in deep trouble.

Eyes squinted against the vicious wind, he didn't see the ground slope away in front of him. He tumbled forward, landed on his hands and knees, skidded down a steep hill, and managed to stop just a few feet from a rushing stream. Groaning, he stood up and brushed the snow off his britches. He recognized the stream. He'd crossed it on his way to the town. He remembered clambering up the high bank. That cluster of rocks sticking up out of the water was what he used to cross the stream, wasn't it?

The rocks were snow-capped now. "Probably icy as well," he said grimly. He looked left and right, trying to see if there was a better way across—a downed tree, maybe—but there was not.

A brutal gust of wind came at him again, making him bow his head. "Why did you lie to me?" he shouted into it.

You know why, the voice inside him said. *To make you go. To save you.*

For most of his no-account life, no one had cared if he lived or died. But Arabella did. She cared so much, she'd built a bridge for him. And then she'd given her life to make sure he crossed it.

Beau knew the voice was right. Arabella hadn't told him the truth about the curse. After a hundred years, it ended.

And she ends with it.

Fear spurred him across the snowy stones. It was a bad idea. He was exhausted; his limbs were stiff and slow from the cold. His foot skidded across the top of one and he fell, bellowing with shock as his body hit the frigid water. Sputtering and shouting, he got to his feet, staggered through the water, and climbed up the opposite bank.

When he reached the top, he looked down at himself. His clothing was soaked. His mittens were gone. His britches were ripped, and his knee was bleeding. Mind and body numb, he lurched forward, but he hadn't taken five steps before his wounded leg buckled and he fell to his knees. Head bowed, he realized that he would die here. He was too far from help. And he didn't care. He'd never been so cold in his life.

"Beau! My darling boy!"

Beau's head lifted. His eyes widened when he saw who'd called his name. His mother was standing in front of a silver birch tree, reaching out to him through the snow, a look of heartbreak on her face. "Get going, Beau. Hurry!"

He nodded at her. He *would* go. Soon. Very soon.

"You're nothing but a useless boy! Go! Get out of here!"

Beau's head snapped around toward the new voice. His father was standing by a snow-laden pine, his red-rimmed eyes like burning coals in his bloated face, an empty whiskey bottle in his hand.

He felt another hand grip his shoulder. He turned slowly, too numb to be frightened, and saw Raphael bending down beside him. "Look at yourself, you hopeless idiot," he said. "You're going to freeze to death here. And for what? For a woman who couldn't care less about you. She'll laugh at you when you show up back at the castle, if she even lets you in. You're nothing but a thief, and that's all you'll ever be."

Nothing but a useless boy . . .

Nothing but a thief . . .

"N-n-no," he whispered through chattering teeth. Then louder. *"No."*

Beau squeezed his eyes shut. When he opened them again, his mother and father were gone. They were only an illusion, a deception manufactured by a brain that was shutting down.

And Raphael? His words? They were deceptions, too. In the howling storm, with the cold stealing life from him minute by minute, he saw that clearly.

Love had broken Beau. He had loved his mother with all his heart, and she had been taken from him. He had loved his father, and the man had walked away. He loved Matteo, and yet he'd had to leave him. And the pain of those losses had been unbearable.

But closing his heart was the easy way out. It was easy to build walls and hard to build bridges. Love wasn't for the weak. It took courage to love another human being. It took ferociousness. A baker had told him that. A woman who had lost everything but refused to lose hope. A woman who was ten times braver than he was. He hadn't heard her words then. He hadn't been ready to. But he was now.

With a yell that started deep down inside him and rumbled up from his heart to his throat, Beau got up. He pulled the collar of his coat

290

around his neck, pulled his cap over his ears, then put his head down and staggered through the storm.

He couldn't see much, only a few feet in front of him. Yet he saw everything. He saw the truth that he'd been running from his entire life.

The only way out of the darkness was to go deeper in.

– EIGHTY-FOUR –

Beau looked across from the cliff's edge to the castle, unable to believe what his eyes were telling him.

The bridge, the one he and Arabella had built together, was gone. The only evidence that it had ever existed was a few planks floating on the half-frozen surface of the moat.

He cupped his hands to his mouth and shouted. Once. Twice. But no one came. He stamped his feet, then hugged himself hard, trying to bring warmth back into his body. His clothing was frozen stiff. He couldn't feel his feet. After he'd fallen into the creek, he had trudged through the woods for hours. It had taken all his will, and every last bit of his strength, to keep putting one foot in front of the other. Mercifully, the snow had stopped, but the sun was going down. If he didn't get inside, and quickly, he would die.

"Valmont!" he bellowed. "Percival? Can anybody hear me?"

He saw movement inside the gatehouse and laughed out loud with relief. Someone was coming. Someone would help him. *Thank God.* But then a man walked out of the shadows and stopped at the edge of the threshold, and Beau's laughter died.

It was the clockmaker, in his black frock coat. He seemed impervious to the lethal cold and stood silently and solemnly, framed by the archway. He was joined by the ladies of the court. They made a gallery of the grotesque, with their grim, triumphant smiles and their garish finery.

Each one looked as if she'd dressed for a ball. Espidra stood at the clockmaker's right side, regal in gray silk. She held a lantern in one hand. The many diamonds she wore glittered in its light.

Beau hated the idea of being among them again, but he had no choice. "Get Valmont! Get Florian and Henri!"

He had no idea how to get across the moat, but he hoped they could figure something out. Maybe they could throw an old door into the water and shove it toward him with a pole and he could use it as a raft. Maybe they could somehow catapult a length of rope to him. Together, they would think of something.

"Go! Hurry!" he urged the courtiers.

But no one made any move to help him. And he soon saw that no one would.

"No," he said, stunned by disbelief. "You can't just leave me out here. You *can't*."

One by one, Arabella's court turned and disappeared back into the shadows. The clockmaker gazed at Beau a moment longer, and then he, too, left.

"No, wait . . . *wait*. Clockmaker, stop! You have no right! Who are you to doom Arabella? To leave me here to die? Who the hell *are* you?" Beau shouted at him.

There was a wrenching screech and then a window, high over the gatehouse, opened and a small head popped out. "Haven't you figured it out *yet*? He's DEATH, you blockhead!"

A child was hanging out the window. Beau squinted at her through the gloom.

"*Faith?*" he shouted.

Another head popped out next to hers.

"Where's Arabella? Get her! Hurry!" Beau shouted at the two sisters.

"Beau . . . Arabella is dying," Hope said.

292

A hole opened up in Beau's heart. He felt himself caving inward, falling through it.

"No!" he cried. He pounded the heels of his hands against his forehead, trying to think. There had to be a way to get to her. There *had* to be.

"We have to go," Hope shouted. "They're hunting us. We have to keep moving. Do something, Beau! Use the vines! The chain!"

And then they were gone. Had they been cornered by members of the court? The clockmaker? Beau had no way of knowing. All he knew was that if he was going to get into the castle, he was going to have to do it himself. But how?

The vines . . . the chain . . . Hope had shouted. His eyes scanned the wall above the moat. A length of chain was trailing down from an iron ring near the gatehouse arch. His eyes dropped to the thick, ugly vines growing out of the murky water and up the stone wall. He remembered tangling his feet in them when he'd climbed down the wall to rescue Arabella. They snaked off in all different directions; a few, twined together, stopped only feet away from the chain.

Beau knew what he had to do.

He took a deep breath.

And jumped.

- EIGHTY-FIVE -

Beau felt as if he'd been skinned alive.

The water in the moat was so cold, it flayed every nerve in his body. He'd hit feet-first, plunged deep down, then pushed himself back up and broke the surface screaming.

Swim, damn you, swim! his brain shouted, desperate to get his body out of the water.

Something else in the moat wanted to kill him, too. Beau heard them, bobbing up through the icy gray slurry, growling and gurgling.

The undead didn't mind the cold. They felt Beau's frantic thrashing movements and heaved themselves toward him. In no time, they'd surrounded him. He managed to push his way through the frothing scrum, but then one of them grabbed the back of his jacket and dragged him down. Heart hammering with terror, he swam harder, fighting to keep his head above water, but more of the creatures crowded in upon him. He got one last gulping lungful of air before the monster gripping him pulled him under.

Beau struggled to break its grip but couldn't. His lungs were bursting. Bright lights were exploding like fireworks behind his eyes. Pushed far past its limits, his body began to give out. His hands raked through the water, fingers scrabbling helplessly for the vines, but they were too far away. The fireworks started to dim. He couldn't hold his breath any longer. Any second now, his lungs would convulse, forcing him to inhale the turbid water.

He prayed to the saints to make his death a quick one, but the saints weren't listening. Or perhaps they were. Perhaps they had been all along. Because something hard hit him in the head. He jerked around and saw what it was—a board from the ruined bridge. He grabbed hold of it and, with the last of his strength, drove it into his attacker's face. There was a sickening crunch as the monster's skull gave way. Beau felt its grip slacken, saw it sink through the water. He kicked his legs hard and surfaced, gasping for air, turning in a circle, trying to locate the wall. More moat men lunged for him. He drove the board into the torso of the nearest one, shoving the creature out of his way, then whacked another so hard, his head flew off his neck. Bit by bit he made his way to the wall, jabbing and thrusting at the monsters, until at last the vines were in reach.

Just as Beau grasped one, though, another monster surfaced, only inches from his face. Its skull was covered in green slime. Gnarled black vines twined up through its gaping mouth and spread across its face in a web. Its bony fingers clutched at Beau, but he soon saw that it could do little more than claw his clothing, for more vines, snaking through its rib cage, tethered it to the wall.

"Excuse me, friend," he said as he started to pull himself out of the water.

One foot sunk itself into a V between two vines, another found a toehold in the crumbling stone. Inch by painful inch, Beau made his way up the castle wall, willing his numb fingers to hold on to the vines.

Finally, he reached the dangling chain. The frozen metal burned his hands as he grabbed it. Ignoring the pain, he planted his feet on the stone wall and leaned his weight into them, then pulled himself up the chain hand over hand. Halfway up, a fit of shivering seized his body. It was so violent, he thought it would peel him off the wall. He waited, eyes closed, until it was over. Then he made his way to the archway and grasped the iron ring.

Now came the hard part. The ring was several inches to the left of the threshold, and there was nothing inside the archway he could use to pull himself over it. If he wasn't careful, he would lose his balance and fall back into the moat. Steadying himself, he put his right foot on the threshold, and his right hand flat against the arch's inside wall. Then he started rocking his body left to right, faster and faster, until he'd built up momentum. With a guttural yell, he let go of the ring and pitched himself sideways. His right foot caught his weight and pivoted him into the gatehouse.

He stumbled but caught himself. Blood was seeping from the knee he'd gashed when he'd fallen into the stream, but he didn't even notice. He'd made it.

Night had descended, and as he staggered out of the gatehouse and across the courtyard, he saw fires burning in the torches at either side of the castle's doors, just as they had when he'd first come here. Terror tightened his ribs around his heart. He'd just made his way through a blinding snowstorm, had barely avoided freezing to death and then drowning, but these things were nothing compared to the fear he felt now—a fear that he was too late to save Arabella.

When Beau had first seen the clockmaker, he'd had the unshakable feeling that he'd met him before, but he didn't know when or where.

Now he did.

The first time the clockmaker had come to visit, he'd come dressed as an undertaker. He'd lifted Beau's mother's lifeless body from her death-bed, though Beau had begged him not to.

The second visit occurred a year later. The clockmaker had been one of the men who'd pulled his father's corpse from the river.

The third time happened when he was lying in a dirty alley with a knife sticking out of his chest. The clockmaker had knelt down by him, but Raphael had snatched Beau away. Now the clockmaker wanted Arabella.

Though Beau was half-dead himself, he made it to the castle doors.

The three times the clockmaker had come to call, Beau had been a boy.

This time, he was a man.

And this time, he would fight him.

- EIGHTY-SIX -

The castle was as dark as a tomb. Beau stumbled through the entry hall by memory.

"Arabella!" he shouted.

But he got no answer.

He turned in a frantic circle, and as he did, he spied a glow. It was coming from underneath the doors to the great hall. He pushed them open.

A gut-wrenching sight greeted him.

Arabella lay on the floor. Valmont sat by her, cradling her head in his lap. Her eyes were closed; her chest was rising and falling rapidly. Framing her in a semicircle were many of her servants. The ladies of her court stood behind them.

"Why are you all standing around?" Beau shouted at the servants. "Get her off the floor! Get her to her chambers!"

Valmont, his own breathing shallow, raised his head. "She will not be moved. She wishes to die here . . . with us, with her parents."

"No!" Beau cried. He knelt down by Arabella and took her from Valmont, pulling her into his arms. "It's me, Bells. It's Beau. Wake up . . . come on now, wake *up*."

"You're too late, I'm afraid," Espidra said, a smile cutting across her face like a scythe. "The curse ends at midnight."

Beau looked up at the towering golden clock. Midnight was only half an hour away. Time was winding down. Already, the servants had begun to fade. They looked as if they had aged a hundred years in a few hours. They were stooped. Their hair had grayed and their eyes had clouded. Some, like Percival and Phillipe, held hands, taking comfort from each other until the end. Others sat alone at the edges of the room, making their final peace.

Even Hope and Faith had dimmed. They stood in the far doorway, watching, their small faces wan, the light within them flickering.

Beau racked his brain, trying to figure out how to break the curse. There *had* to be a way; he just wasn't seeing it. He tried to remember the words of the clockmaker's poem. It said that Arabella had to love, and be loved in return. Well, she didn't love him; if she did, the third little sister would've shown up. If she did, the curse would've been broken. But he

297

loved her, and maybe his love would be enough. Maybe if he told her again, it would save her.

"I—I love you, Bells. You're my best friend. The only real friend I've ever had."

Arabella's eyes, unseeing, fluttered open. "Beau?"

Beau brought her hand to his lips and kissed it. "Yes, it's me. Can you hear me? I love you, Arabella. Please don't die . . . pleasepleaseplease don't die."

"I love you, too, Beau," Arabella rasped, trying for a smile.

Beau laughed out loud. He kissed her hand again. She *did* love him. They'd made a mistake, somehow. They'd done things out of order, maybe. It didn't matter. Because now things would be set right.

He turned to the clockmaker, grimly triumphant, eager to see him off. "Get out. Go. You're done here," he said.

But the clockmaker didn't move. He simply stood by his clock, his pale hands crossed on top of his walking stick, a half smile on his thin lips.

The first stirrings of a new fear twisted in Beau's guts. He looked around, expecting the castle to crumble to the ground. Or angels to appear. Or Espidra and her court to burst into flames. He listened for the rumble of ancient stone walls giving way, for the sound of celestial trumpets and the *whoosh* of hellfire, but all he heard was the ticking of the clock.

"Why is nothing happening?" he asked, turning to Valmont. "I told her I loved her. She said she loved me." He touched Arabella's hand; it was cold. Panic jabbered like a madman inside his head. "Maybe we said it wrong. Maybe we should have said it out loud. Right before we crossed the bridge. Or in the middle of the bridge or—"

Beau's heart dropped. *The bridge.*

"Valmont, what were the lines from the clockmaker's spell?" he asked. "The ones about the bridge?"

The old servant raised his head. His cheeks were wet with tears. *"Cross the bridge, unwind the years . . . Escape this prison of your fears . . ."* he replied. "The mistress was supposed to cross the bridge, but she couldn't. And now she never will. Because there is no bridge."

"But maybe we were wrong about the bridge," Beau said, grasping at straws. "Maybe she's not supposed to cross a real bridge. Maybe it's just a symbol—"

Valmont laughed bitterly, cutting him off. "We were wrong about everything."

But Beau refused to give up. He mustered a heartening smile and said, "Sit up, Bells, come on now. We're going to break this damn curse, we *will*, we'll figure it out, and when we do, you don't want to look like you're drunk, all sprawled out on the floor, do you? Come *on* . . . sit *up!*"

He tugged on her hands, but she was a deadweight. He slipped one of his arms behind her back and tried to raise her limp body, but she cried out in pain.

At the sound of her cry, Beau's forced resoluteness cracked; his smile fractured. "Somebody do something. Bring smelling salts! Bring her a glass of bloody brandy! You're bloody servants, aren't you?" he shouted.

Percival knelt down next to Beau. He bent over and gently pressed his ear to Arabella's chest. When he straightened again, his face was gray with sorrow. "I can barely hear a heartbeat."

"No," Beau said, his voice breaking, and his heart with it.

"The clockmaker's poem was a trick . . . a lie," said Valmont. "The curse can't be broken."

"Yes, it can," said a voice.

It came from the doorway to the kitchen.

Beau looked up. Fording her way through the crowd was a small, determined woman. In one hand she held a rolling pin, thrust out before

299

her like a sword. The other was resting protectively on the shoulder of a small boy.

"Be gone, baker, and take that filthy child with you," Espidra said. "There's nothing you can do."

Camille tightened her grip on the child. "Keep walking, Rem. It's time. Go to her," she said.

"Did you not hear me? Go back—" Espidra's words dropped away. The contempt on her face transformed into naked shock. "No," she whispered. "It *can't* be." She whirled around. "What are you waiting for, all of you?" she shouted at her court. "Seize them!"

Camille raised her weapon over her head, ready to protect Rémy.

Rega took a menacing step forward. The rest of the ladies followed her. "It's over for you, child," Rega growled. "One woman alone can't protect you."

But Camille wasn't alone.

Florian, Henri, Gustave and Lucile, Josephine, Claudette, Josette, Phillipe and Percival, Valmont . . . all the servants, marshaling what strength they had left, crowded around Camille and Rémy, pushing the courtiers back, clearing the way.

Surrounded by her friends, Camille continued on, shepherding her charge ahead of her. When they reached Arabella, she pulled Rémy's dirty cap off. Long, pale blond hair spilled out from under it.

The child stepped forward. She was small, like her sisters. Thin. Fragile. Grimy with ash and grease.

And shining like the dawn.

- EIGHTY-SEVEN -

Beau saw that the child was carrying a basket. When she reached Arabella, she put it down, then started to take things out of it and set

300

them around her. A stack of books, a compass and T square, quills and inks. Lastly, she pulled out a voluminous bundle of midnight silk. Beau recognized that, too. The child spread it over Arabella, and the silver city she'd stitched across it, so long ago, sparkled like stars in the night sky.

"You were here all along," Beau said, his voice hushed with wonder.

The little girl nodded.

"I hid her in plain sight," Camille explained. "I grabbed her right after Espidra cursed Arabella, dressed her in boy's clothing and said she was my nephew, visiting from the town and caught by the curse, just like the rest of us. I rubbed butter on her every day. Bacon fat. Cinnamon and nutmeg. All the things the court ladies hate." Camille smiled. "It worked beautifully, like garlic on a pack of vampires. They barely noticed her, and when they did, it was only to shout at her to go away. I only wish I'd been able to hide Hope and Faith, too, but Espidra got to them before I could."

"I can't believe it," Faith said. "You even fooled us. We never looked twice at the kitchen boy." She reached for Hope's hand. The light inside them strengthened.

"Help her. *Please*," Beau said to the child. "Why isn't the curse broken? *Why?*"

Love didn't answer him; instead, she walked over to one of the room's soaring windows, grabbed hold of the silk draperies, and ripped them down. Hushed gasps rose from everyone in the room as the silver thread caught the moon's rays, and the city of dreams that Arabella had stitched so long ago exploded into bright, brilliant life.

"Now do you understand?" Love asked him.

Beau nodded. He did. At long last, he did. He grabbed Valmont's lapels. "It's not about me, Valmont. Or any of Arabella's suitors. It never was," he said in a rush. "The clockmaker's spell . . . how does it go? *Despair's foul curse can't be unspoken, but there is one way it can be broken . . .*"

"*Mend what you have torn apart. Pick up the pieces of your heart,*" Valmont continued. "*Seek kindness, trust, a hand extended, till one you shunned is now befriended . . . That's how you will escape this curse, and undo this infernal verse . . .*"

"*And when to love you finally learn,*" Beau cut in. "*You will be loved in return.* That's what he said, right? The clockmaker? Those were his exact words?"

"Yes, yes," Valmont hastily replied. "But I don't see—"

Beau released him. His gaze was inward now. "*Till one you shunned is now befriended,*" he repeated. His eyes found Valmont's again. "He didn't mean for her to love a prince or duke or an earl or a blacksmith or a captain or a thief."

"Slow *down*, Beau," Valmont urged him. "You're not making sense."

"I can't. There's no time." Still on his knees, Beau grabbed Arabella's wrists and pulled her up off the floor. Her head lolled like a broken doll's. "Arabella!" he barked. "Open your eyes. Damn it, girl, wake *up!*"

Arabella groaned. Her head lifted a little. Her eyelids fluttered open, but her eyes were unseeing. The silver light inside them had dulled to a leaden gray.

Percival buried his face in his hands. Gustave and Lucile held each other. Other servants whispered prayers or wept. Beau didn't hear them. He didn't see them. He was looking at Arabella, deep into her sightless eyes, willing her to stay.

The *tick-tick-tick* of the golden clock was losing its rhythm. The long, sweeping arc of its gold pendulum was growing shorter.

It's too late, said a voice inside him.

And then he heard the steps—slow, measured, inexorable. Cradling Arabella in the crook of one arm, he lifted his head and faced the clockmaker. With a shaking hand, he drew his dagger from the sheath at his hip and pointed it at him.

"Stay back . . . I'm *warning* you," he said.

"Seriously, Beau?" Faith hissed. "You're threatening Death with death? Yeah, that'll work."

"Don't give up," Hope urged, her eyes on the clockmaker. "Find a way, Beau."

Love, at Beau's side now, took the knife from him and set it down. Beau turned his gaze from the clockmaker to her, to this beautiful shining child whom he had known once, long ago. She frightened him. Even more than the clockmaker did.

"You can do this," she said.

"Do *something*, Beau," Valmont begged. "Anything. Tell her you love her again."

"No, Valmont. It's no use. I'm not the one. There's someone else she needs to love."

Valmont got to his feet and looked around the room wildly, ready to grab the person. "Who is it? Where is he?"

"She," said Beau. "*She.*"

The clockmaker drew closer; his footsteps grew louder. He was only a few yards away now. Beau's eyes were on him, but his arms were around Arabella. He took a deep breath and started to talk. The words spilled out of him in a frantic tumble.

"Listen to me, Arabella, *listen*," he said fiercely. "Valmont loves you. So does Percival. And Phillipe and Gustave and Lucile and Josephine and Camille . . . and me. I love you. Because you're strong and bold and fierce and a total pain in the ass and you're *smart*. So damn smart. I love the furrow in your brow when you're drawing. I love the fire in your eyes when you're building. I love that you swear like a sailor when you think

303

no one's listening. I love how you fumble the steps when you dance. I even love the way you bite off a chipmunk's head. I love you, Arabella, flaws and quirks and faults and all. So please, please, *please* . . . can't you love you, too?"

The footsteps stopped. The clockmaker was only inches away. Beau felt his cold breath on his neck.

Beau squeezed his eyes shut. "No. *No*," he said, his arms tightening around Arabella. "Don't go. Stay here. We were wrong, all of us. All this time. It's you. It's been you all along. Oh, Bells, can't you see? *You* are the one you've been waiting for."

– EIGHTY-EIGHT –

Arabella was lost in the forest.

It was dark. She held her hands out in front of herself but could barely see them.

She knew the way back home, of course she did. She just couldn't seem to remember it. She needed to remember something in order to find the way again. Or was it someone? It was so hard to think. Her head ached. She was so tired.

Was it the way she'd felt when her mother told her that she should never say things like *sewer system* or *public baths* out loud, not if she wanted a husband? Was it the way she'd felt when her father said she must not talk about the *physics of keystones* or the *ideal height to girth ratio of load-bearing columns* because it made her sound absurd?

Was it the way other girls traded glances and giggled when she lingered by building sites instead of shops? Was it the way boys turned sullen when she knew things they didn't?

She started to take a few halting steps, and then a voice came out of the forest.

"That's not the way to your home, Arabella," it said. "It's the way to mine, though."

Arabella turned, startled. The clockmaker was standing a few yards behind her.

"These memories will only carry you further into the night. Look up, child," he said. "At the stars. At the night that cradles them."

So Arabella did. She tilted her face to the glittering heavens and remembered.

The way a shiny chunk of graphite felt pinched between her thumb and fingers. The way it slid over paper, making archways and loggias, porticos and pediments. Making the visions in her head real.

The way her heart swelled when she opened a book and found herself at the Temple of Dendur, the Parthenon, the cities of the Aztecs.

The way her head felt, so stuffed full of ideas she thought it would burst. Ideas for roadways and bridges, aqueducts and squares. Cathedrals and castles and palaces.

Tears stung behind her eyes at the unbearable beauty. Of the dark sky, the stars. Of her memories. Of the girl she used to be.

She looked at the clockmaker. "A hundred years," she said softly. "It took me a hundred years to come home."

"Some people never find their way back."

"Is it broken now? The curse Espidra placed on me?" Arabella asked, afraid to hope.

"Do you still not see?" the clockmaker asked. "You cursed yourself, my child, when you turned your back on your difficult emotions and succumbed to despair. Now you must make peace with them, and make a place in your heart for them. They belong there every bit as much as joy, pride, and compassion do."

"But I'm afraid of them. I let them out and a man died."

"The prince had a choice in how he behaved. The boy he was beating,

305

the defenseless animal he was savaging—they had none. You tried to help them." Death took Arabella's hand in his. "You tried to control your emotions, to keep them down, but they burst out and ended up controlling you. If you wish to break the curse, stop fighting them. Let them be. You need them."

Arabella nodded. She understood. "Without the darkness we would not appreciate the light," she said.

Death shook his head. "No, child, without the light we would not appreciate the darkness. There is good to be found in difficult feelings. How would injustice be stopped without anger? How would selfishness be curbed without guilt and shame? How would compassion grow without regret and remorse? Do this, Arabella, and despair will stay away. That is the one emotion you must guard against, for she is jealous of my power and wishes to do my job for me."

Death squeezed Arabella's hand, then released it. In his other hand, he held a tricorn hat. He brushed a bit of dust off it, then placed it on his head.

"You're leaving."

"For now."

"And me?"

"You may leave, too. But you must hurry. It's almost midnight."

"But you'll come back someday."

"I always do."

"When?"

The clockmaker gave her a rueful smile. "Wouldn't want to spoil the surprise."

Arabella nodded. And then she ran to him and threw her arms around his neck. "Thank you," she said. *"Thank you."*

And then she was gone, running out of the dark woods, running across the bridge from her past to her future, running for home.

EIGHTY-NINE

Beau knew that love had failed him.

He'd found the courage to hope again. To believe again.

And he'd lost again.

Arabella was gone. He lifted his head, steeling himself to look upon her lifeless face. But when he opened his eyes, he saw that her eyes were open, too. She was blinking them like a dreamer released from sleep.

"Beau, what time is it?" she asked, struggling to sit up.

"Don't move, Arabella, be still."

"Please, Beau . . . the time . . ."

Beau glanced up at the clock "Ten minutes to midnight."

"Help me up."

"Arabella, I don't think—"

"The curse isn't broken, not yet, and if I don't—"

"We all die," Beau said, scrabbling to his feet. He hooked his hands under her arms and lifted her off the floor.

Arabella clutched his arm, swaying woozily on unsteady legs, then said, "Where are they . . . the court?"

Beau looked around the great hall. "Over there," he said, pointing toward the windows.

The ladies had congregated under them. Some stood forlornly, their heads down, their fingers fretting at buttons and cuffs. Some were clamorous—shouting, stamping their feet, breaking things.

Arabella's fingers dug into Beau's forearm. "I'm afraid."

"Of what?"

"Of the beast. It feels like she's coming. Like I'll never escape her. Like she'll tear me apart."

"I'll help you, Arabella. Just tell me how. Tell me what to do."

"You can't help me. I have to do this alone."

Arabella touched his face then. She ran her fingers along his strong jaw, curled them behind his neck, and pulled him down to her and kissed him.

Beau kissed her back. And tried to hope. Tried to have faith. To believe that love would carry Arabella back to him.

"Be there for me. After," she said as she broke the kiss.

And then she ran. Across the great hall. Away from him. She quickly put distance between them, so he could not hear her when she said, "If there is an after."

- NINETY -

Arabella swallowed hard. She closed her eyes, marshaling her courage, then opened them again and stepped forward into the court of her emotions.

The ladies swirled around her like sharks. Iglut drew the first blood.

"Look at them, your poor servants, and those tormented figures in the clock . . . all suffering. For *decades*, Arabella. Because of *you*."

"I-I'm sorry. I'm so sorry," Arabella said, her voice small and tenuous.

"*Sorry?* You think anyone here cares that you're *sorry*? Do you think *sorry* fixes what you've done?"

"I—I didn't mean to do it . . . The prince was hurting Florian . . . He was hurting my horse . . ."

Hesma cut in, her words a greasy mumbling litany that made Arabella's heart fold in on itself.

"You're a girl with a very high opinion of herself, aren't you? Too good for the prince, too smart to keep quiet. You have your own ideas. You think you can build things. You think you can Change. The. *World*. You know what I think? I think you're pathetic. Have you heard what people say about you? Do you know how absurd you look, with your compass and ruler? Who do you think you are?" She burst into mocking laughter.

Their words felt like acid poured down Arabella's backbone, dissolving it. They were right. Of course they were. Who was she? Who was she to open her mouth? To speak up for herself? For others?

Lady Rafe, cringing, flinching, glancing around herself constantly, was next.

"Even if you break the curse, then what? One hundred years have passed. How do you pick up the pieces? The servants will never forgive you. The people in the clock are going to be so angry at you. And what will your mother say when she finds out the boy standing over there robs people for a living? He'll be out on his backside in a heartbeat. And then what? What, Arabella, *what*?"

Rafe's last words were delivered in a high, hysterical shriek. It set the others off. They crowded in at Arabella, demanding that she hear them. Arabella covered her ears with her hands, trying to block the voices out, trying to hang on to the last scraps of courage inside her.

And then another sound rose—the sinister ratchet of clock weights rising up their chains.

"The clock's waking up! It's nearly midnight! You're almost out of time!" Lady Elge squealed, clapping her hands.

"No!" Arabella cried. She pushed at her ladies, frantically trying to break free of them, but there were too many; they engulfed her.

"What are you going to do, Arabella? Banish us again?" Iglut taunted.

Inside the clock, wheels turned, gears clicked. The two sets of doors on either side of the arched track opened. From within the crush of her emotions, Arabella heard them. Soon the nightly pageant would begin. Soon the chimes would sound. Her eyes fell on the clockmaker. He was standing by his masterpiece. She heard his voice in her head. *If you wish to break the curse, stop fighting them . . .*

So Arabella did. She stopped pushing, stopped struggling, and stood very still. Then she reached out and took Iglut's hand, and Hesma's, and gripped them tightly. "I am not banishing you. I will never banish you again. I need you. All of you. Lady Iglut, when I've done something wrong, you make me see it. And Lady Hesma, you spur me to make amends."

Iglut stopped shouting. Her small eyes opened wide in wonder. She squeezed Arabella's hand, then gave her a tremulous smile. "Th-thank you, mistress," she whispered. "*Thank you.*" Hesma kissed Arabella's cheek, and then both ladies faded away like morning mist in the sun's rays.

Arabella turned to Lady Rafe next. "Thank you, good lady, for always protecting me. For turning me away from the unruly horse, the crumbling cliff, the too-thin ice. For keeping me from cracking my skull more times than I care to remember." She touched her hand to the back of Rafe's cheek and Rafe, too, faded.

Sadindi, LaJoyuse, Romeser . . . one after another, Arabella faced her difficult emotions, thanking them, embracing them, bringing them back into her heart.

She had just watched Lady Orrsow fade when something came hurling through the air and exploded at her feet. Arabella flinched at the broken vase. She knew who'd thrown it.

Lady Rega stood there, seething. Livid sores had erupted on her skin. She'd gnawed the heel of one hand bloody.

The golden clock's works ticked and spun, hammered and whirred, readying themselves. The long hand clicked ahead. It was now one minute to midnight.

Arabella dug her fingernails into her palms and took a small step forward. Rega saw her do it and roared like a bull, warning her off. She picked up a candlestick and brandished it, but Arabella kept walking, slowly, deliberately, until she reached the terrifying courtier. She faltered for a second, then swept Rega into an embrace, hanging on to her tightly as she struggled to break free.

"I've done you the greatest wrong, Lady Rega," Arabella whispered. "I should have listened to you. Instead, I turned my back on you. Closed my heart to you. I should have packed my books, pawned my jewels, and left this place for Rome, Paris, London . . . someplace where I could study and draw and build. Forgive me, Rega. Please, please, forgive me."

Rega tried to roar again, but the sound collapsed into a sob. She stopped struggling and touched her forehead to Arabella's, then she, too, faded. And then they were all gone, all but one.

The minute hand clicked home. *Midnight.* The clock's bell began to toll. The golden doors opened. The clock's court began its grotesque pageant. The figures, once so vibrant, were slowly disintegrating. Their clothing was fading. Jewels that had sparkled on fingers and at throats now looked like dull chunks of glass. Their porcelain faces were cracking; the painted smiles had contorted into agonized grimaces.

Arabella was almost out of time.

One, two . . .

She turned in a desperate circle, searching for her, for the proud head, the black hair, the ash-gray gown. "Where are you?" she whispered.

Three, four . . .

Finally, she spotted her; she was standing at the far side of the clock, staring up at its dial, hands clasped behind her back.

"Have you a hug for me as well?" Espidra asked as Arabella approached her.

Arabella stopped a few feet away from her. "I will not embrace you, Lady Espidra. I will guard against you the rest of my life and hope to never look upon your face again."

"But I will embrace you again, Arabella," Espidra said, walking toward her. "I will be there when those despicable children desert you."

Arabella shook her head. "I deserted them. And then I learned how hard it is to find hope in this world. To keep faith. To give love. I'll never let go of them again."

The clock bell tolled on, carrying them ever closer to midnight.

"Easier said than done. You cannot love another if you do not first love yourself," said Espidra. "Do you?"

She was close to Arabella now, close enough to touch her. She reached for her, but Hope stepped in front of her, blocking her. "We're going to work on that," she said.

Faith was with her. "Door's that way, Lady E," she said, hooking her thumb at an archway. "Don't let it hit you."

Espidra's eyes flashed dangerously, but she inclined her head. "Good luck, Arabella," she said.

"Goodbye, Lady Espidra."

The last chime sounded, hanging in the air. Espidra's eyes dulled to a milky white. Grooves appeared in her skin, like those in a burnt log. Her body kept its form for a second, perhaps two, then collapsed to the floor in a pile of ash.

"Look!" Camille cried.

Arabella followed her gaze. What she saw made her catch her breath. The clockwork figures—cracking and crumbling and slumping over only moments ago—were now straightening their backs and stretching their arms. They were drawing breath and looking around. Color bloomed in their cheeks; life brightened their eyes.

A kitchen girl was the first to step down. She moved forward slowly, stiffly, as if pulling her feet free of deep, sucking mud.

"Where's my brother?" she croaked in a rusty voice. "Florian? Are you there?" She staggered off the platform to the floor, her legs nearly buckling.

"Amélie? *Amélie!*" Florian shouted. He ran to her and caught her in his arms.

An elderly countess tottered down next, calling for a glass of brandy. She was followed by a bishop, a young page, a blacksmith, a guard. All in a rush now, the castle's inhabitants stumbled, shambled, tripped, and bumbled their way from the clock back into their lives. Cries, shouts, and laughter were heard as they found their family, their friends.

As Arabella continued to watch them, her heart swelling, she saw Camille move toward the platform, her eyes on a man, tall and strong, who was still standing there. At his feet sat a tiny girl. The look on Camille's face was full of yearning so raw and deep, that Arabella was afraid for her, afraid she wouldn't get what she'd fought so long for.

And then the tiny girl moved. She babbled and laughed. The man standing behind her bent down, scooped her up, and held her to his chest. He kissed the top of her head, then carried her down off the platform, to her mother.

Camille's hands came up to her mouth. As the man stepped off the platform, she cried out with a wild, ferocious joy and ran to her family. Her husband enfolded her in his arms, the baby girl between them.

All the clockwork figures had left the platform now, except for two. Arabella's parents, the duke and duchess, still stood on it. Proudly. Stiffly.

Arabella walked toward them, a mix of anger, sorrow, and love on her face. She reached the platform, then stopped, unsure what to do. The old Arabella would have waited coldly, imperiously, for them to come to her. Her parents would have waited, too—just as coldly, just as imperiously—for her to come to them.

But the old Arabella was gone. And the new one gathered her skirts in her hands and stepped up onto the platform. She bowed her head to her mother and father, then stood up. Taller, straighter, than she ever had before. Then she offered them her hands, and her simple act of kindness did what acts of kindness do—it melted resistance, dissolved anger, defanged cruelty.

The duchess's face crumpled. "Oh, my darling, darling child. I thought—" Her voice broke. "I thought I was doing what was best for you. Can you ever forgive me?"

"I already have, Mother," Arabella said. "With all my heart."

"We'll start over, Arabella. Things will be different," the duke said. "You'll have what you like—your books and tools. We'll find you a husband who makes room for his wife's interests."

Arabella's heart sank at her father's words, but when she spoke, her voice was gentle. "Papa, I'm leaving. I can't stay. You want me to fit into your world. I want to change it."

The duke looked stricken. "No," he said, shaking his head. "You *must* stay, Arabella. I can't lose you again, my daughter . . . my only child."

Arabella took his hand in hers. "*I* can't lose me again."

Tears came to the duke's eyes. He shook his head helplessly. "I am old, Arabella. This is hard."

"I know, Papa. I know."

The three stood together, close and yet so far apart. Trying to bridge the distances between them.

And Beau, who had been watching Arabella, turned away. He felt like an intruder. He looked at all the people in the ballroom, people hugging and kissing and crying. Separated for a hundred years and now together again. Gustave was embracing Lucile. Josette was weeping. Percival and Phillipe stood perfectly still, facing each other, palms pressed together, fingers entwined, tears rolling down their cheeks. Josephine limped over to them; they pulled her close. Their happiness was so huge, Beau could feel it. Yet sorrow was present, and he felt that, too. In all the years gone by. In all that these people had suffered. Time had stopped in the castle, but outside it, the world had moved on. There were so many things they had lost, so many people they had lost. It would hit them, eventually. Hard.

Standing outside of them, outside of their happiness and their grief, Beau was alone. Or so he thought.

A hand, small and warm, slipped into his. He looked down at the radiant child standing next to him. And Love looked back.

"She has a lot to deal with, after a century and all. But she'll kiss you again if that's what you're worried about. Pretty darn soon, I'd say, if that last kiss was anything to go by. I mean . . ." She shook her free hand as if she'd burned it. "Hot stuff!"

"Do you *mind*?" Beau said, highly uncomfortable.

"Friends?" she asked, squeezing his hand.

Beau gave her a rueful smile. "You're a hard person to be friends with."

"I know. But worth it. So . . . friends?"

Beau nodded. And squeezed back. "Yes, kid. Friends."

– NINETY-ONE –

The clockmaker looked up at his clockworks. Its hands had stopped, yet time ticked on for Arabella. For Beau. For all the people around them.

For now.

He would meet them all again one day. When the handful of hours and minutes that made up their human lives finally ran out. It was his task and their fate, and nothing could change it.

There were all different kinds of death, most of them hard and wrenching, yet the ones that hurt him most—for he had a heart, no matter what some might say—were the mortals who died long before he came for them. Those who had been taught more about fear and anger than love.

He walked across the clock's mechanical track now, where, until only moments ago, the figures had stood. Only the props were left. His fingers floated over a chessboard, a mirror, the back of a chair. He paused once, to look back at the thief, the brave baker, at the three little girls, and Arabella.

He hoped she would find a way back to life—a life she chose, not one chosen for her. And he hoped, very much, that before they met again, she would choose—every single second of every day left to her—to be passionately, unapologetically who she was: a builder of bridges, an architect of ideas, a woman who saw not what was but what could be.

The clockmaker smiled. He walked past the tall, golden columns of his masterpiece, through the clockworks doors, and was gone.

As the doors closed behind him, the enormous golden clock sighed and shuddered, like a living creature drawing its final breath. Its golden surface dulled. The hour and minute hands wound backward, then fell to the floor. A network of cracks opened along the dial and spread across the clock's surface. There was a rumbling, like the sound an avalanche makes. It grew to a roar. Then the golden clock crumbled. Numerals fell from the dial. The pillars toppled. Pieces of the facade hit the floor and shattered. As everyone in the great hall watched, the rubble of gears and wheels, of strike and chimes, collapsed into a fine shimmering dust.

A winter wind blew open a window. It rushed inside, swirled the dust up off the floor, and carried it away, into the dark, starry night.

NINETY-TWO

One year later

The beautiful carriage rumbled over the castle's new stone bridge.

Inside it sat three men. On top of it sat three children.

"This is dangerous, don't you think?" Faith asked.

"Not a bit!" Hope shouted.

"We'll be fine!" bellowed Love.

"We're all going to die," Faith sighed.

As the carriage picked up speed, Love lay flat on her belly and hung her head over the side, the better to see its passengers. She enjoyed their banter, their good-natured taunts, their friendship.

Percival was talking. "Why are *you* going into town this morning?" he asked Beau.

"To rob a bank," Beau teased.

"I wouldn't be surprised," said Percival. "I still can't believe the duke made you his chancellor of the exchequer. That's like putting the fox in charge of the henhouse."

"Yes, it is," Beau agreed. "The duke's a shrewd man. Think about it: Who knows how to get into the henhouse better than the fox? So who better to keep all the other foxes out than a reformed fox?"

"He has a point," said Valmont. "You can't deny it, old friend. Since he's taken over, he's made the treasury impenetrable, rooted out corruption, and found new ways to fund the realm's building expenses. Those are some remarkable achievements, if you ask me."

"Once a thief, always a thief, if you ask *me*," said Percival.

Beau shrugged. "One does have to keep the old fingers nimble." He held up Percival's gold pocket watch and let it swing like a pendulum.

Percival, scowling, snatched it back.

Love sat up and let her hands skim the wind like birds. The carriage trundled along through the forest toward the town. The men had business there: Percival with the duke's wine importer. Valmont with the duchess's jeweler. And Beau with the realm's new minister for capital improvements.

"On a day such as this, it seems even mortals cannot fill the world with problems," Love said, smiling up at the sun.

"Mortals can always fill the world with problems. It's their greatest talent," said Faith.

"Look!" Hope said, pointing ahead of them, at the town coming into view.

"Paradisium!" Love exclaimed as they passed under the town's newly painted sign.

A year ago, Ville des Bois-Perdus had been a gray place, its road pocked and potholed, its buildings falling to ruin. Now the roads were smooth. A new fountain burbled in its square. Trees had been planted all around it. The market hall had a new roof. Old people sat on benches talking to one another. Children ran and played in the sunshine. Soon they would attend a newly built school. The beautiful village that had been drawn in silver thread a century ago was coming to life.

The carriage stopped, first at a warehouse for Percival, next at a goldsmith's for Valmont, and then at a building site for Beau. The three sisters jumped down at the last stop and went on their way, disappearing down a winding street. Their work at the castle was done; they were needed elsewhere now. A hospital had just opened in the town, and the people who came there to be helped—their bodies injured or ravaged by disease, their heads filled with frights or sadness—had need of the children.

Beau was out of the carriage, a basket in his hand, before it even came to a halt. He stood by the building site for a moment, his eyes searching. Then they lit up, as they always did when he saw his wife.

Good architects build buildings, he thought. *Great ones build dreams.*

She was standing at a folding wooden table, going over plans for the new school with her head mason. Her hair was neatly coiled at the nape of her neck. Her clothing was practical: a brown twill skirt, a simple white shirt, a tan waistcoat, and black boots.

Matteo was by her side, fetching the right drawings for her, finding the right notebook. He was still too thin for Beau's liking, but there was color in his cheeks and he no longer coughed.

Arabella had wasted no time reuniting them. Only hours after the curse had been broken, as soon as it was light enough to see, they'd started to rebuild their bridge, with the help of servants released from the clock. A week later, they'd hurried across it and made their way to the town where Arabella had bought horses, saddles, and provisions, and then the two of them had set off for Barcelona. He hadn't wanted her to go, he'd argued with her, but she would not be dissuaded. They'd battled wolves and weather, and narrowly avoided bandits, but after a week of hard riding, they'd arrived at the convent.

Beau had been so afraid he'd be too late, he couldn't bring himself to knock on the door; Arabella had to do it. But then the door opened and Sister Maria-Theresa had greeted them, and moments later, he was sitting on his little brother's bed, holding him in his arms.

Arabella had sent for doctors, the best in the city. She had the finest foods brought to the convent, things the nuns could never have afforded, and enough of them to feed everyone. She'd had wagonloads of firewood delivered to warm the abbey. After three months, Matti had recovered enough to make the trip back to Arabella's castle, where the clear mountain air restored him completely.

Beau was deeply grateful for his new life, and yet one thing had continued to trouble him—the emerald ring still stitched into his old jacket. So one morning a few weeks after his wedding, he'd ridden off before dawn to the merchant's manor. No lights were on when he arrived; no servants were yet about. Quietly, he'd slid out of his saddle, crept to the front door, and placed a small box on the step. The ring was inside it, wrapped in a piece of paper with two words written on it: *Forgive me.*

As he'd turned to go, he'd cast a final glance at the manor, and at the place where he'd jumped on Amar, his horse, and galloped down the road to perdition.

There was a way back from that road. He knew that now. So did Arabella. On the hard days, and there were still many of them, she thought too much of time lost. She thought of relatives, of her servants' families and friends, all dead and buried. Of Percival and Phillipe's cottage in the woods, fallen to ruin. And then the tears would come. When they did, he would take her hand gently and lead her to the mirror. Sometimes it took ages before she could meet her own gaze and speak those same two words—*Forgive me*—to the girl in the glass, but it didn't matter. He stayed with her, arms enfolding her, for as long as she needed.

Arabella was rebuilding a town and, little by little, her life—as she and Beau built a life together.

As Beau walked across the building site, he saw Matteo roll up a drawing and hurry off to deliver it to a carpenter. And then, as if Arabella felt Beau's eyes on her, she turned around, and her lips, her face, her entire being broke into a smile. For him. Beau motioned to an old oak tree. She joined him there and helped him spread a blanket beneath the tree's sheltering branches. Beau placed his basket in the center of the blanket, and they both sat down. He leaned across the basket and kissed Arabella, and as he did, he tugged on the slender piece of graphite she'd threaded through her coiled hair to keep it in place, just to watch that hair fall down around her shoulders.

"Once a thief, always a thief," she said, laughing as she snatched it back.

"Percival said the very same thing."

"He's right."

"Maybe so. But you're a bigger thief, my darling Bells."

"Me? What did I steal?"

"My heart. And promise me one thing . . ."

Arabella arched an inquisitive eyebrow.

Beau kissed her again, then he whispered in her ear.

"That you'll never give it back."

EPILOGUE

Though this story is over, we won't talk of endings.
Endings are rarely happy. Just ask a gravedigger.
Instead, we'll talk of beginnings.
Messy, hard, painful beginnings.
Someone wrote you a bad start.
And now they want to write the rest.
They want to finish it, to finish you.
Don't let them.
Take the pen. Demand it. Grab it.
Break in and steal it if you have to.
But hold it in your own hand.
And then, from this day forward,
This never-again day,
With everything you've got,
Your guts, your brains, your bang-crashing heart,
Take a deep breath,
And write your own story.

ACKNOWLEDGMENTS

Once again, thank you to my talented editor, Mallory Kass, for making *Beastly Beauty* a better story and for making me a better writer. I appreciate you more than I can say. Thank you, too, to Peter Warwick, Iole Lucchese, Ellie Berger, David Levithan, Lori Benton, Erin Berger, Rachel Feld, Daisy Glasgow, Lizette Serrano, Emily Heddleson, Jalen Garcia-Hall, Melissa Schirmer, Jessica White, Seale Ballenger, Amanda Trautmann, Maeve Norton, Elizabeth Parisi, Paul Gagne, John Pels, the Scholastic Audio team, Elizabeth Whiting, and the rest of the Scholastic sales team.

A huge, heartfelt thank you to my agent, Steve Malk, whose enduring friendship and wise counsel mean the world to me, and to my foreign rights agents Cecilia de la Campa and Alessandra Birch for all the work you do on my behalf.

And lastly, thank you to my wonderful family—Doug, Daisy, and Wilfriede—for being my first readers. Your kindness, encouragement, generosity, and love keep me out of the castle.

ABOUT THE AUTHOR

Jennifer Donnelly is the author of *A Northern Light*, which was awarded a Carnegie Medal, the LA Times Book Prize, and a Michael L. Printz Honor, and was named to Time Magazine's 100 Best Young Adult Books list; *Revolution*, named a Best Book by Amazon, *Kirkus Reviews*, *School Library Journal*, and the Chicago Public Library, and nominated for a Carnegie Medal; *Stepsister*, an instant *New York Times* bestseller and named to the YALSA and Rise Best Young Adult Fiction lists and nominated for a Carnegie Medal; *Poisoned*, named a Bank Street Best Children's Book of the Year; *Lost in a Book*, a *New York Times* bestseller; the Waterfire Saga; and other books for young readers. Visit her online at jenniferdonnelly.com and on social media at @jenwritesbooks.